FLYBOY ACTION FIGURE COMES WITH GASMASK

FLYBOY ACTION FIGURE COMES WITH GASMASK

JIM MUNROE

HarperFlamingoCanada

 For information address: HarperCollins Publishers Ltd, Suite 2900, Hazelton Lanes, 55 Avenue Road, Toronto, Canada M5R 3L2.

This novel received the support of the Ontario Arts Council's Works-in-Progress Grant.

Canadian Cataloguing in Publication Data
Munroe, Jim, 1972–
Flyboy action figure comes with gasmask
ISBN 0-00-648091-8
I. Title.

PS8576.U5742F59 1999 C813'.54 C98-932754-1 PR9199.3.M86F59 1999

for the zinesters

Fighting evil by moonlight
Winning love by daylight
Never running from a real fight
She is the one named Sailor Moon!

chapter one

Before the time with Cass, I had only come close to doing it once since childhood. This all happened during my first year at the University of Toronto, characterized by predictable drunken stupidity. I was again unpleasantly soused, slumped in a chair in what looked to be a nice kitchen. It was hard to tell, because there was only a candle for light, so as to give the room the legislated party ambience. Specifically, it was a party full of people I didn't know.

Regardless, I *did* want to know the girl with the short black hair and wine glass. She was listening to this guy go on about his film project, nodding every so often and smiling in inappropriate places. I remember smiling back, half-hoping half-dreading she'd catch me. I wished he'd shut up so I could hear her talk.

The kitchen wasn't crowded, which was lucky considering what eventually happened. Just two or three pairs of conversationalists. Someone pulled up her plaid sleeve and presented her forearm to the candle flame. There was a wrench tattooed there, and when she flexed her muscle it wiggled.

"Bilbo the Dancing Monkeywrench," she said to her friend. Her friend laughed and raised her glass to Bilbo.

"This must be the party-trick segment of the evening," Film Guy said. He stepped back for effect, cracked his knuckles and bent his thumb all the way back.

It was funny he'd do that, because I often thought of my ability as a kind of extreme version of bending my thumb back — ugly, unnatural and ultimately useless.

"Oh bra*vo*," I muttered, but not quietly enough.

Black-haired girl looked at me. "Well," she said, "what can *you* do?"

I hauled myself to a standing position. "Me?" I asked her, watching the candlelight on her face. I noticed her mascara was fucked up, and liked her more for it. Everyone else was shadows, silent watchers.

And I was really going to do it. I really was. I took a breath and prepared to step out of myself.

Instead, I turned my head away and puked explosively onto the formica table I had been sitting at. The candle fell over and went out.

Dazed, I leaned over the table, looking at the mess I'd made. I dry-heaved, went to sit on the chair again and missed. Busted my lip wide open on the metal table leg on my way down.

"Projectile vomiting. That's really . . ."

"That's really *something.*"

"Yeah."

"Do you think he was aiming for the candle?"

There was a wave of laughter and my consciousness seemed to be borne out on it. I was grateful.

I had a crush on this waitress at the diner near my house. She was splashy generous with the coffee, so I found myself at Sok quite a bit during the winter.

"Haven't seen you in a while," Cass said, passing by with a breakfast plate.

At first I didn't think she was talking to me. Coffee and convenient location aside, Cass was the biggest attraction at Sok, and now she wasn't an exhibit any longer. Now I had to talk to her, an exciting and nerve-racking thing. Witty repartee only comes easily to me when I'm with friends. It wasn't coming now, naturally, because I was thinking of it as flirting.

"I like the patios in the summer," I said lamely as she passed. My coffee, the fourth, was mostly finished, and she filled it without asking.

"What was stopping you from taking a chair and sitting out front, like Frank?" she said, her eyebrows arching as she nodded towards an old Italian guy. Despite the unpleasant weather, he sat outside, a winter-steam tendril growing out of his head.

"Nuh-uh," I said. "You're a gawker if you do that. Too blatant."

"That's what those patios are," Cass retorted. "Gawk Central."

"Nuh-uh," I said. I had put some thought into it. "It's a different dynamic. If there's a crowd of people doing anything, then it's OK. Like dancing. All together, there's a mass delusion that swinging your limbs around like that is all right. But if someone's shakin' their booty in a bank line-up —"

"Nutbar," she said, grinning with one side of her mouth.

"Exactly. Not that I don't love dancing. I *looove* dancing. You?"

There was a pause. In that pause, I thought two-and-one-half things. *Because it'd be a crime against humanity if you don't, lookin' the way you do,* and *Oh, I think she thinks I'm leading up to asking her out to go dancing,* and *Oh dear, should I? how very stressful* —

"It's all right," she said, giving me a sideways look that I was utterly unable to decipher. She sauntered away in that way I so admired, getting some old guy his check.

Admission: up until that day, my admiration of her was based mostly on her body. She would wear these track pants and T-shirt combinations that *tried* to contain those heavy breasts, *tried* to hide her wonderful bum, but failed delightfully. I had always considered *voluptuous* a polite euphemism, but then I met Cass.

It was more than that. I won't pretend that it was a whole lot more, but she had a casualness that amplified her appeal immensely. No make-up, an Aunt Jemima handkerchief that barely kept her wiry, kinky mop of shoulder-length hair in check. And the clothes that looked like she might have slept in them. The sexiest of Sunday-morning-just-don't-give-a-damn looks.

But of course it wasn't just a *look.* For the two years I had been living in the area, she had been working here full time. When she took your order, fixing you with her dark eyes, you knew better than to mess with someone who'd been on her feet all day. Her breasts drooped slightly, but her slow and silent energy rolled like a thundercloud.

"So now you come back to us, now that their patios are cold."

I thought that was a poetic turn of phrase, but I didn't know if she intended it to be. So I just smiled and said, "Well, now I *appreciate* the blast of hot, greasy air when I come out of the cold."

She laughed, but I felt bad for calling it greasy, even when it was. So I babbled, "I totally love it. I'm thinking of getting a heater that pumps out Sok air."

She mimed turning a dial to different settings, "Hot and Greasy . . . Smells Like Eggs . . ." She did all this with her hand on one hip, a menu under her arm.

I laughed, surprised and happy to see a quick wit. It wasn't the only thing she would surprise me with — but it was the first.

I was doing a lab with Mary later that week.

"Did I tell you about her saying 'Now that their patios are cold'?" I had been going on about Cass all class.

Mary nodded, smiling. She adjusted the microscope focus with a deft finger and peered in. "I think I've got it. It's the second-section legs we're supposed to be examining, right?"

"I don't know." I hadn't been concentrating on anything but recounting my "conversation" with Cass.

Mary squinted at the blackboard. It always bothered me that she didn't wear glasses. She was such a sensible girl otherwise. She didn't get involved with jerks, she lived frugally, it just didn't make sense. She would look fine in glasses — I could clearly see her in a pair of no-nonsense wire frames. But then, being a twenty-two-year-old virgin, I perhaps wasn't the definitive authority on what was socially attractive.

Thinking this, I paused for a second, but then used my extra-powerful glasses to read the board.

"Isolate second . . . section of subject. Note the . . . differences in the second set of legs. Add to . . . cake mix."

Mary snorted, and crossed out *Add*.

"What the heck is that?!" I stared in amazement at the board, my voice rising slowly but surely. "Cake mix? What's *wrong* with this professor?" I enjoyed the minor attention I got from some worried-looking people nearby. In *this* class, I was the loudmouth.

"The entomology and cooking classes are being held together," Mary deadpanned, sketching in her notebook. "Part of the cost-cutting measures, I understand."

I chuckled. I opened my notebook and started copying the insect Mary was drawing. Mary was the only reason I believed I had a chance of passing this course. I had taken it for good reasons, but about a month past the drop-out date I realized that it wasn't something I wanted to study. My particular area of interest, specialized as it was, would be for someone with a PhD to take on — not a dabbler like me. My major was English, and at one point I was thinking of making it a biology/English double major. I thought again.

It was just my latest abandoned plan for solving the mystery of my kinship with the *Musca domestica.* None of the answers at the back of the textbook were the ones I needed.

"So other than the way she looks, and some witty lines, do you know anything about her?"

"Nope."

"I don't know anyone who waitresses full time. Judy does two shifts a week, and she's always complaining about how rude everyone is."

"I know she's been doing it for the last two years, at least. I wonder if she complains to her friends?"

"'There's this guy at work, this regular guy? He's such a creep! Always bothering me for refills . . .' Like that, you mean, right?"

"She doesn't sound like that at *all,*" I said, laughing. In my best girl-voice, soft and gushy: "'There's this incredibly interesting guy with these cool glasses? I'm just waiting for him to jump my bones.' More like that."

Mary laughed, shaking her long blonde hair, and made a correction to my drawing.

A couple of days later I was doing some laundry and trying to finish off a Balzac novel. Exams were coming up, and one or two of the books I'd skipped in each course turned out to be the ones that the prof suddenly realized were *utterly seminal* works. Luckily, I had gotten three-quarters of the way through Balzac before I was borne away by the biology avalanche two months ago, so I didn't mind the pressure to finish it.

I felt a kinship with Balzac. You gotta admire a guy who dies of a caffeine overdose. Shaking and babbling into the next world.

I was sitting there thinking that, then thinking about getting my next fix, then thinking about where I would get it, then thinking about Cass, when she passed by the window. She was walking along briskly, eyes on the snow, a crazy lumpy hat on her head and a grin on her face. It was magical, almost as if my thinking about her had brought her into being.

I walked to the door and opened it, thinking that I'd call out to her. She was already too far for anything but an outright yell to be audible, so I stopped. I could see her brown hat bobbing amidst the other side-walkers. I could see the plume of icy smoke from her, rising. I imagined it coming out from between her lips.

"I saw you today, passing the laundry on College," I said, immediately feeling creepy as I did so. *I saw you* is too too close to *I've been watching you.*

"You mean the one near Euclid?" Her face was suddenly grave. "I saw the weirdest thing there once. You want a coffee and a water, right?"

I nodded, waiting for the weirdest thing.

She left, her eyes distant in memory recall.

Sok was pretty empty — it was a weekday afternoon. The old guy that was usually fixed outside had slipped his leash. There was a family who looked like tourists to me, a teenage girl and a toddler and a mom and dad. Why they were touring in winter was beyond me.

Cass came back with my order, and was about to leave.

"What's so scary about Miracle Wash?" I asked, snapping a sugar packet.

"It's not scary. It's odd. I went by there one time, late night. It was dark inside, closed, but I guess some movement caught my eye. Then I noticed this guy sitting on a chair — "

"A chair *made of human bones*?!" I suggested, eyes wide.

Cass smirked and ignored me. "He was sitting there, reading a magazine in the little light that was coming in from the street. And he was barefoot."

"What?"

"Yeah, he was sitting with his feet curled up beside him, so I saw them clearly. Bare."

"He was the owner, probably. Asian guy, right?"

"Yeah, but don't you think that's weird? Bare feet in a laundromat? Those places are dirty — they're where people bring their dirt, for Christ's sake."

The look on her face appealed to me, asking me to confirm her uneasiness. I could not oblige. "But it's also where people go for cleanliness," I said. "It's an environment rife with paradox." She laughed and I was a happy boy.

She sat down at the table next to me, and rolled her feet in circles. "It's amazing what you see at night, walking around the city. Stuff you never would have seen if you had just gone to bed. It's like stolen time. I wish I could do it more often." Someone came in and she looked up, but he walked to the counter and said hi to the cook.

I was about to say *why don't you* when a parade of rape statistics marched merrily through my brain. "It's dangerous," I mumbled lamely.

She shook her head. "That's not it."

I waited for why.

"There's . . . another reason."

I kept my face impassive. She waited a second or two and then stood and walked around her tables. I was a little disappointed. Maybe if I had arched my eyebrow in playful curiosity, I would have gotten an answer. Maybe she wanted to tell me, but needed that extra prompt.

Then again, it might have been better to keep it casual. I didn't want to get involved in her life too quickly, after all.

Which, of course, was utter bullshit.

There's nothing worse than seeing a fly bang itself against a wall again and again. You just *know* that something's gone horribly wrong in its little fly brain, all ten cells of it. I always wonder what drove it crazy — a strangely shaped room, bad air, the longing for fly companions in a human-infested house. That last one I could have helped it with, I suppose. But who's to say that it was loneliness it suffered from?

I imagined that like a simple machine, the rubber band of its mind had snapped, but something kept spinning regardless.

I sat in my huge armchair and debated throwing the bug out the window (where it would surely freeze), or out the door (where it would annoy my roommates), or out of this astral plane (which would require vigorous and violent physical action).

I did nothing. I have a special rapport with bugs, even the crazy ones. I went back to my studying. I was reading about pheromones. They're easily some of my favourite things from the insect world. I was discovering that these smelly molecular messengers can communicate something as complex as "The queen bee is in the hive and all is well" — when there was a knock on the door.

"The queen bee is in the hive and all is well," I called out, and Phil came in. He had a little smile on his face and he walked over to the window and looked out.

"Mind if I read in here?" Phil asked after a moment of watching the snow, waving a book called *Games Zen Masters Play.*

"Go ahead, see if I care," I said cheerily. "Have a seat on the bed. Not as comfy as this chair here, no siree, but . . ."

"Shaddap," muttered Phil, flipping open his book. He had seen the chair sitting out in our neighbour's garbage too — he'd seen it first — but hadn't taken it because he thought it smelled of urine. But the smell must have been coming from something else, because once in my room it smelled of nothing. Phil claimed otherwise, naturally. He had been so desperate for a chair ever since, that he had been offering a lawn chair to guests.

"Mmmm-m!" I said, wiggling my bum.

Phil said nothing, his big-eyebrowed Korean face looking calm as he read his book.

"Smells in here," he grunted after a few minutes.

"Smells of nothing but happy-bum-sitting-pleasure," I burbled. I turned the page to reveal a cross-section of a bee, illustrated in unlikely colours.

Another few minutes passed. "Urine."

"Sorry, no vomit."

We were likely to spend the next few hours in this slow-motion argument. But my flying friend interceded.

"What the hell is wrong with that fly?!" said Phil, his teeth suddenly bared in frustration.

"Loony," I said.

"I'm gonna kill it."

"Don't kill it. It's a visitor."

Phil closed his book and started tracking the fly.

"Isn't there some zen game you can play? To make you clear your mind like the stream in a forest or something?"

"The only zen game I'm learning is how to shoot lasers from my eyes to fry stupid fly-loving white boys." Phil got up from the bed and held the book like a weapon. I leaped up from the chair and opened the door.

"Flee, fly, flee! The evil Asian's going to crush you!"

The fly, beyond hearing, bounced against the wall three more times and then *whack!* The book permanently united it with my wall.

"Aw, look at all that blood, Phil!"

There was a splotch almost an inch round on my white, non-glossy-paint wall. Phil looked at his book with amazement. He flicked the fly into my little garbage can. "There's a tremendous amount of blood. How could a fly have that much blood?"

"My wall . . . a testament to your barbarism." I was vaguely annoyed, but not enough to pretend I wasn't, which is what I did when I was *really* mad . . .

"It must have been drinking blood. That's why it was crazy . . . a poster will cover that up, hey? I'm sorry."

"You'd like that, wouldn't you. Another cover-up. No, people will know about this, Phil Lee. People will know about you."

He slunk out of the room. "Sorry."

I went back to my book.

I walked into Sok, stupidly. I usually go in only if Cass is there but I was walking in a daze, and once I was in, I was in. The cook had already nodded hello and as I considered leaving I had a daymare:

The cook, young but working towards being one of those classic diner cooks with the stubble and extra flesh, says, "Hey Cass, your boyfriend came in."

"Who?" she'd say, already annoyed.

"Your boyfriend with the glasses and the books. He comes in, looks around and sees you're not here, then turns around and leaves."

"Ah, probably forgot he had a class to go to," she'd say with a contemptuous curl to her lip, and they'd laugh together.

So to avoid that almost-tangible possibility, I took a seat at the counter. "Can I get some fries?"

The cook nodded. I had a novel in my bag, but I took out my agenda book instead. I looked over the stuff on tomorrow — I was going to a seminar on bug catching that the library was putting on for free, and I had also told Ken that I'd watch a movie with him. I was thinking I might be able to convince him to do the bug thing when my fries arrived.

"Well done, right?"

"Yeah, thanks!" I was always caught off guard when people recognized me. I figured I was pretty anonymous, bland even. Yet this was the second time in Toronto anyone at a public place had recognized me — maybe I was in Sok more than I thought. I was a "regular," I realized with pleasure — not a "fixture" like Frank, but a "regular." I ate my fried potatoes with a new relish, remembering all my past plates. I looked over at the bags of fries, covered in icy frosting, and gauged that I had probably bought two bags' worth in my combined visits. I was wondering how much coffee I had bought when Cass came in, complaining about the sleet.

The cook smiled to himself and flipped a burger like a coin, as if he was passing the time rather than working.

I went back to my agenda book, staring at it blankly in mid-chew. I had been prepared to be bored here for a while, then leave, and mark it up to penance for wanting Cass. But now she was here, lively and damp and cursing. I honestly felt my nerves tingling.

I tried to hide my happiness, only let a bit out on my face, but she grinned widely and smacked me on the shoulder and I felt my face burning. Luckily she went rooting for her apron behind the counter, and my blush had cooled by the time she popped her head up again.

"What's your name, anyway?" she said as she tied a bow behind her back.

"Ryan," I said, closing my agenda book. I wished I hadn't. I felt like that action said, *Let's have a conversation, now that you have disrupted me.* And that the book itself (University of Toronto emblazoned on the cover) singsonged, *Look, I'm a smarty-pants stu-dent!*

"Cassandra," she said, offering a hand that was chilled and damp. I mentally rewrote Cass as Cassandra in the blackboard of my brain.

"Ahh, your hand is so warm," she said. "So, Ryan, have you lived in this frozen wasteland all your life?"

I thought she meant Canada. "Um, yes. What about you?"

"Vancouver, until about two years ago." I could tell that she was going to regale me about the beauty of Lotusland, where it never snows and pot grows between cracks in the sidewalk. I steeled myself, waiting for the Cliché Train to pulp me.

"Only on the nastiest of days do I miss the weather there. Van winters are hell. It's dark and wet for four months, and it's like this mass experiment in light deprivation. People wilt."

She looked around the diner. Except for me, it was empty. "'Course, mean-ass days have their plusses."

"Why'd you come to Toronto?" I said. She sat down and spun around on a counter stool two away from me.

"Well, my band broke up here, mid-tour. Plus I wanted to live for a while in a place other than Vancouver, and Toronto seemed as good a place as any."

"What band?"

"Fuck You, Mr. Man."

I stared at her.

"Never heard of it, eh?"

"Oh! That's the name! I thought I was being too nosy."

She laughed. "It's funny we didn't get that reaction more often, but we were well known in the hardcore scene."

"Like hardcore punk rock?"

She nodded.

"What happened on tour?" I asked, thrilled to have her ear for so long. I had the uncanny sensation of being the shy guy in the movie, who, because of a disaster or an alien invasion or some other happy circumstance, is trapped with a beautiful girl in a diner or an abandoned cinema. They pass the time by telling each other stories, dancing to old jukebox tunes, and necking.

Then Frank shuffled in and ruined it all. He pulled his Maple Leafs toque off his pink head and despite my mental command of *counter, counter, counter,* he took a table. Coot.

The stool squeaked when she stood. My plate glinted greasily under the lights, as a good diner plate should, and I tilted my head slightly to see if the refraction would reveal small things about the future.

chapter two

The man held up a jar with a label reading "Bug Cemetery." It even had a little gravestone on it.

Ken laughed and whispered, "This guy is great. He's so *deep* about the whole thing."

I nodded and smiled, but I was a bit annoyed. It was definitely catering to children, and I had called ahead to make sure it wasn't going to be a kiddie thing. But Ken and I were the only attendees whose feet weren't dangling, and the territory he was going over was very familiar to me.

"They have a tiny kingdom of their own, these little critters, so don't think you own them. They might bring back an army of their friends and attack you some day!" The man's face was pouchy but quite lively, and his little talk was better than average. It was funny (well, eight-year-old funny) and taught that the insect world was to be marvelled at, not just observed.

Ken was watching the kids in the audience, mostly. Making faces at one of them. I was glad he wasn't bored silly, because it wasn't possible to leave that small room without feeling like a jerk.

But it was almost over, and the man was taking questions. One boy, his face engulfed in glasses, asked if it was OK to play with bugs, does it hurt them? Ken, looking at the kid, said *aw, what a cutie* to me.

"I don't know for sure, but I don't think so. I'll tell you what my granddaughter does. When she digs in the garden, she finds these June bugs sleeping just under the surface — they go there when it's cold, you see, 'cause it's warmer there. She picks them up and puts them in her pockets," he mimed putting something in his cardigan pocket, and patting it very gently, "and then she goes inside and takes them out and plays with them. They're sleepy, but then they warm up and frisk around, and when she gets tired of playing with them she goes and tucks them into their dirt beds." The children brayed with delight at this last image and the kid with the question looked happy.

"Do bugs eat people?" was the next question. It came from a big kid who knew better. The old man's answer was pretty honest, although he made parasites sound like pets.

A few more questions and then it was over. At forums like these I would usually chat with the speaker, get a feel for how adventurous and open-minded he was. Every so often I'd run into a rogue scientist this way, willing to entertain even the most absurd of questions, and I'd offer my lab assistance. I'd usually find out, through gradual prods and such, that their open-mindedness only extended so far — so I couldn't trust them, ultimately. Not with the questions I had.

But this guy seemed small-fry. I had heard that he was involved with some pretty groundbreaking stuff concerning insect myths, and I knew I had heard his name before, but it looked like he was more into the children angle. Still, I didn't like to think of this as a total waste of time, so I scribbled up a note with my number on it. His fans, a tall girl with a grave face and the little boy with the glasses, had books for him to sign. I passed the note to him over their heads and left. I glanced back through the window and saw the little boy making tiny adultlike gestures with his hand as his mother beamed on with pride.

"So you're a real bug scenester," Ken said. "I knew you were into them, but you're like a mover and shaker."

"A little bit," I said. We had gone to a restaurant to get out of the cold and to fill Ken's belly. He was a vegetarian, so he was eating some noodley stuff. I hadn't been here before but could read by the backwards name in the window that it was called Kensington Bakery.

"I've been interested in the Little Kingdom since I was a kid. I know most of the people in the city who are involved with the subject, met them over the years. There aren't really all that many. That Crawford guy just moved to the city, so I wanted to check him out."

Ken was deep into his noodles, so as he nodded they bobbed up and down. He was one of the few people who didn't look at my interest in insects as an extended childhoodism or an odd fetish. He had a mind that was free of the dust and grime that most people accumulate over twenty years, quick to dream and laugh and slow to judge. He had old-man hair, white-blond, with crinkly, wide, youngster-eyes.

"I like buggies. They're nice. I think I'd like some to eat right now," he said, gnashing at his noodles.

"Would you eat bugs?" I asked, thinking about the vegetarian thing.

"If they were baked in a nice cake, I would."

I batted a salt shaker back and forth. I had already gotten my caffeine fix, and couldn't really afford to be buying stuff all the time. Luckily, batting a salt shaker back and forth was free in most places.

A guy with a tuft of blue hair passed by the window and waved at Ken, not stopping but smiling. "That crazy Mark . . . he'll catch his death of cold," said Ken. "Oh . . . you met Mark . . . didn't you?"

"Don't think so."

"At Maxwell's party. Last . . . oh, maybe you weren't there. He goes around with my other friend Valerie."

I remembered meeting Valerie. It was hard to imagine her beside the guy who had just passed the window. Then again, Cassandra and I were hardly twins separated at birth, so that line of thought ended up giving me a hypo of hope.

"She does a poetry zine, too." He mentioned the name.

"Never heard of it," I said.

"That's 'cause you're a jerky boy. She's published some of my pictures in it."

"Everyone's published your pictures."

"Yep, there's a lot of dopes out there," Ken said with a laugh. "I told you about the Random House deally, right?"

I shook my head.

"Oh! Well, they want to publish the *Definitive Baby Sneaky 5000*," he said, making loopy quote marks with his fingers.

"You're kidding! That's incredible, man!" I was amazed, jealous and amazed again. Ken had been publishing a comic for about a million years that he gave out for free, a mystic photocopy sandwich containing flashes of political fierceness and genuine oddity.

"Boy, was I surprised. I don't even have them all. I try to keep one of each but sometimes I give them all away by accident," he said, spearing his side order of raw vegetables. "Wow, this pepper is so fresh," he mumbled, his eyes widening.

I was a bit baffled. "So have you signed . . . contracts and stuff? How did they find out about you?" I couldn't imagine how they saw Ken's black-and-white drawings as a marketable commodity.

"No, it's still being worked out. They'll probably pull out," he said without apparent concern. "They're just trying to get deals with artists that are doing similar stuff to Palaver."

"Who?"

"The guy who does all the anvil things. You remember, I showed you some of his stuff . . . it's in this crazy colour spattering. I know I showed you."

I was watching the girl behind the counter sell someone some seed cake. She was attractive, her Cantonese-accented voice was really loud, and her nail polish was sparkly. "If you say so." I looked back at Ken. "Do you see her nail polish?"

He looked back and we admired it in tandem. It was silver.

He turned again towards me. "So I'm reading this book by this guy, Genet — it's wicked. It's got these thieves . . ."

We talked for a few hours after that, about wicked thieves and other things.

When I arrived at the London bus terminal, I looked for the Scary Bus Lady, who was the person at the counter who always seemed to be staring at you. A quick survey among regular bus users had revealed that I wasn't the only one to look up and find her dull gaze locked on my eyeballs. Except, however, when you were buying a ticket — then it was nearly impossible to catch her eye. As I walked through the station she came out of the back and it actually took four seconds (I counted) for her to start staring. I added this information to my mental file marked Bus Lady, Scary.

Dad was standing beside the car in the parking lot, facing away. He stuck up above the cars like a pin marking a location on a map. Usually, he had the newspaper spread out on the roof — but today he was just looking out onto the road.

"What's up, Sid?" I said loudly, making him jerk. "The paperboy blacklist you again?"

He mumbled something I didn't hear and got into the car.

I opened the door and saw today's *London Free Times* on the seat. I picked it up and got in, thinking as I did that it was odd he had brought it but hadn't read it. I reached around and buckled in, glancing over at Dad when I did so.

He was holding the steering wheel tightly and staring straight ahead. His eyes were squinched up, like the light was too bright or he was bracing for a punch. He said, "Your mom has breast cancer."

I looked down at the paper in my lap. On it, there was a man beside an oversized cheque giving the camera a thumbs-up. I heard the click of the belt buckle and the car starting. "Are they . . . sure?" I asked.

Dad nodded. "Pretty sure." He put his hand on the parking brake and then took it away. "Are you ready?" he asked me, his hand just lying there. "I mean . . . we can . . ."

"No, I'm ready," I said.

His hand moved back, and I watched it go about its work for a while until it came to rest on the steering wheel. I didn't want to look out the window at the wash of movement, for obscure reasons, and looked down at the man on the newspaper instead. He was a lottery winner, the caption said, and I could see why Dad wouldn't want to read about something like that at a time like this.

Dad made a sound like he was clearing his throat, but it might have been half a cough. I waited, but he didn't say anything. I asked, "How long have you known?"

"She found out this morning. Your mom called you, but you weren't in."

I was glad I hadn't known before. The bus ride would have been hell. Instead of looking forward to a nice meal and maybe a bath, I would have been picturing my mother's funeral.

We rolled up to the house. I looked at it, bright and normal, and couldn't think of anything. I got out before he parked in the garage and stood there twisting the paper into a thick roll. He emerged from the garage and we went in together.

Lisa sat there, flipping through a fashion magazine, her black hair lank and listless. "Hi," she said, fairly normally. I could see she had been crying, though.

I should have tried harder. I should have made *her stop smoking.*

"You should be helping your mother," Dad said, starting to get a little mad.

"She said she was fine."

I realized that Mom was cooking. I was horrified. I went into the kitchen. She was pulling a roast out of the oven.

"Hello, Rye, supper'll be on in five minutes. You're just in time."

She looked normal, which was more than I could say about Dad or Lisa. "Mom, you shouldn't be exerting yourself. I mean, Dad said . . ." My voice hitched and I knew that it would crack if I pushed it on.

Mom looked at me with a sad smile, as if I was the one suffering, and held my hand. I thought again about all the times we tried together to get her to stop smoking and started to cry.

"Oh," she said, hugging me. "Don't."

Lisa burst out crying and hugged the two of us. Dad stood nearby, a stubby glass in one hand.

When Mom spoke again, her voice was thick. "I feel fine. You don't think I want to eat your father's cooking, do you?"

Lisa laughed at this, a little hysterical. "Like . . . remember the charcoal burgers?" We all laughed a little at that infamous moment in Slint family history, and even Dad's grim face cracked a little.

Mom gave us one last squeeze and said, "Let me finish dinner. Can you get those veggies sliced, Lisa?"

Lisa feigned reluctance, her face puffy with tears, then opened up the knife drawer.

Dad and I moved out into the living room. I wanted to ask him about the tumour but I knew Mom would hear, and I should really ask her. It was hers, after all.

"How'd your midterms go?" said Dad, sitting on one side of the couch.

I took the other side. "Not bad. Haven't got the results back yet, but the only one I'm worried about is bio."

"The bug course . . . yep, one of the things you learn is," Dad paused to turn towards me and make sure I was listening. I already knew what he was gonna say. ". . . that some subjects are very interesting, but you don't want to actually study them." I had expressed this sentiment a few months ago, worded slightly differently, and now it was being laid before me as a new-found pearl of wisdom. I simply smiled and nodded, because if I said anything, he'd say: *No! Huh, maybe you're right — you knew what you were talking about! Got your noggin from yer dad.* I reminded myself how rare it was to have a father that actually *listened.*

"And work?" I returned.

"Not bad, pretty good . . ." School — check, work — check. It was a ritual that could have been hollow, but it had the creamy filling of genuine caring. "They said there shouldn't be a problem getting some time off to be with your mom."

It was amazing how her sickness could even change the school/work conversation, the most routine of routines. I realized that every discussion we'd have from now on would contain this knowledge just below the surface.

How long? I thought. *How long would it take? How long did she have?*

My thoughts must have been on my face, because Dad put a hand on my shoulder. I caught a whiff of whisky as he leaned towards me, and his squeeze was a bit too hard. He sighed, then stood up and went into the kitchen.

I was alone in the room, looking around at the things that Mom had chosen years ago. It occurred to me that coffee table was appallingly '70s, and I realized that I had never considered the furniture on any level except *our home's furniture.* My sister came in and caught me staring at the coffee table. Instead of bugging me about it, she just sat down.

"So the Scary Bus Lady wasn't looking at me," I said suddenly, grateful for the unbidden topic but not really able to summon a lot of enthusiasm for it.

"Were you buying a ticket?"

"No, this was today. She just came out of the back, though. It took her four entire seconds to lock on."

"I think she just stares at everyone who comes in."

"Yeah." I shifted uncomfortably. My back was still sore from the ride up. I wondered if I had time for a bath before dinner, but then Mom came out. Mom, who despite having a cancer growing inside her and probably wanting a cigarette very badly was still making dinner for her lousy son, a selfish brute whose primary concern was his own minor back pain.

"Suppertime."

My mom's cancer changed my television viewing patterns profoundly. I was in the habit of flicking on the tube and surfing while eating dinner: a little bit of the news, a little bit of a fashion show, a little bit of the *Simpsons* rerun and then I was usually done. I figured it was better to sample small bits of crap rather than to eat a whole meal from one pile.

The first day I was back from London I hunkered down in front of the tube with my macaroni and cheese and flicked it on. I was going back and forth, trying to find something interesting and artsy on the brainer channels, and passed the operation channel twice.

On the first pass I caught the words *diagnosed with breast cancer.* My heartbeat speeded up as I flicked past ten channels on automatic before stopping on a music video.

I wonder why someone dying of a terminal disease agrees to be ogled by gawkers? How much do they get? Are operations that expensive in the States?

I ate my macaroni. I thought about all the good food my mom made for me, and how I was wasting all her efforts by eating this lazy processed crap. I flicked away from the video where a man with a bubble guitar was soloing, sped past the operation channel and landed on a cartoon. But the bright sugarworld couldn't erase the glimpse I got of scalpel cutting into breast.

As I watched *Sailor Moon* for the first time, this is what I was thinking: *How will my mother, who can't bear being seen in public without her make-up, deal with a missing breast? Why should she have to endure something that she'll find so disgraceful? Where is the justice in that?*

I remembered Mom holding me up and turning on the water in a hospital bathroom. I was crying from the need to pee, a thirteen-year-old man-child with his tonsils newly removed and swaying from the anaesthetic. Mom smoothed down my hair and called me Ryan O'Brian like she did when I was a kid and it made me feel less ashamed because it's OK if your mom sees your thing when you're a kid, it's OK if you cry, and Mom feeds you sherbet when you're a kid.

"I am Sailor Moon, champion of justice and fighter of evil — and that means you, Negaverse slime! Prepare to be punished!"

I liked this tough-talking little manga girl. I put my clicker down.

We stopped by Sok after class. Cassandra was working in another section. Mary got mint tea — she followed some routine, a seven-herbal-brew cycle. I didn't know how she kept track.

"Don't you worry that you're using some valuable part of your brain for that? That you're using synaptic energy for something that is essentially useless?" I was jealous, of course.

"It's not useless," she said, her eyebrows crimping. "It keeps my palate fresh. Everything loses its magic, even Chamomile." She breathed the word like it was a lover's name. "But Chamomile is three teas away . . . there's still Raspberry, Licorice, and Peppermint."

"No, I understand that . . . but you could keep it on some scrap of paper instead of filling up brain cells."

"I remember things without trying. Like your phone number, 535-6222. I've called you at home — what? Once or twice?" She shrugged.

This disturbed me. I was completely reliant on my phone book and wanted other people to be similarly dependent.

"It doesn't take any energy," she said.

"Ah," I said, pointing at her with my spoon, "no *detectable* energy. Your brain, however, must have finite resources, don't you think?"

"I *think* she is wildly attractive," Mary said quietly, nodding at Cassandra. "I must tip my hat, sir. I expected some bimbo."

"Really?" I said, flattered *and* hurt.

"You'd be surprised at how many of my male friends tout some beer commercial babe as Aphrodite rising." She scrutinized Cassandra, who was across the restaurant. "Think she's a dyke?"

"No," I said too quickly, a chill hand fondling my stomach.

"She kinda dresses like one, all sloppylike. Well, you'll find out. And report back to me. Right?"

I nodded, numbly. Was she interested for me? Or for herself? Was she hinting at something? Should I ask, or what? It didn't matter to me, either way. I had never known any homosexuals in London, so I didn't know what they dressed like or really anything about them except for movie stereotypes.

"91887542," she said, and took a sip of her tea.

Was that some kind of code? My mouth opened and closed.

"Your student number. Remember that time you were inquiring about dropping bio, and they asked for your number?" She tapped her head and smiled. "Now you don't think I memorized that on purpose, did you?"

"How much did you study for the bio midterm?" I said, thinking of the all-nighters I'd pulled over the years.

"I learned long ago never to disclose that information," she said airily, "lest I be lynched."

Frank came in and unwound the huge scarf that held his golf hat in place. He apparently had a new hat for each day. An old couple waved to him and he smiled weakly as he shuffled to his counter seat.

"How's an oldster like that walk around on a day like today?" Mary asked. "His bones must be thin little icicles."

"Frank makes it out most days. This is where he gets his Ovaltine. Been drinking it for the past sixty years."

"There's no palate variation *there*," Mary said disapprovingly.

"Nope."

"I have to tell you something, Ryan," Mary said, all of a sudden.

I raised my eyebrows. *Is this where she tells me that she's* —

"I'm going to smoke a cigarette."

I took a sip of coffee. I couldn't believe it. "My mom's got breast cancer."

She got up. "Now I really need a smoke."

I sat there while she went to the counter and bought a box of low-tar death. I watched as she sat down and opened it up. I waited till she inhaled, then began. "I went back to London last month. She had just had her physical, and they found a tumour on her breast that . . . wasn't benign." For some reason I couldn't bring myself to say *malignant*.

Mary carefully blew the smoke away from me, watching me with round sympathy eyes.

"Anyways, she's in a good mood. She made an amazing trifle for dessert." *What the hell did that matter?*

"How's your sister handling it?"

"Fluctuating between hysteria and ignoring it."

"Sounds like the normal routine," she said, managing to inject sympathy into the cold fact. "You feel guilty, right?"

I nodded.

"My brother was the guilty one in our family. He had tried to help Dad to quit every Father's Day." Mary's dad had died last Christmas, and she had borne it with hard-headed sadness. I didn't know her as well then, but I remembered being in awe of her humour and strength.

"I keep saying to myself, 'One more time might have done it. One more time.'"

"Stop it!" Mary gave me an anguished, annoyed look and waved her cigarette. "You know how stupid that is. You can't control the actions of others. You were there for her, but she made her choices. Now let it go, you self-obsessed fuck." She stabbed out her cigarette.

She was right, of course. It had very little to do with Mom, or even the idea that she was dying — I hadn't even begun to deal with that. It was about Me, about my frustration at not being able to control my loved ones.

"Plus — it's not even necessarily from smoking. It's not lung cancer."

Mary looked sombrely at the shape of her cigarette. "I appreciated your support when I tried to quit, but it can't come from outside. I've been buying a pack a week for the last month."

"Which is better than a pack a day," I said to hide my shock.

"Yeah, but it looks like it'll work back to that. A few more a day . . . you know."

The guy who was waiting on us swung by on refill duty. I poured a packet of sugar into my coffee, then put it on the pile of empties.

"Holy, talk about addictions," Mary said, counting them. "They're like scalps, or animal skins . . . sugar skins." She lit up another smoke.

"Yeah, I'm up to about four cups a day. Six sometimes. But I'm starting to worry about my bladder."

"Ulcers?"

"You can get ulcers in your bladder?" I said, horrified.

She shrugged.

"It's just that I drink water with coffee, to counteract the dehydration effects. But I take a dozen pisses in a day. Sometimes twice in an hour. I'm just worried I'll wear out my equipment, you know."

"I have to —"

"Me first," I said, leaping up and heading for the washroom.

I returned to our table and relieved Mary. The diner was getting a little busy as dinnertime approached. Mary's fries arrived, and I debated whether it would be stealing when I knew they would be freely offered to me. The debate lasted until I finished salting them.

"Your friend left," Mary said as she sat down. She took a fry. "Winked at me and walked out the door."

"Sure she wasn't winking at the place where I was last seen?" I said flippantly, but felt disappointed. My plan had been to ask her out today, and find out if she was interested once and for all, damn it. I was going to follow Mary out, lag a little behind, then casually pop the question. I figured having Mary there was a plus — she would see that I had friends, at least. I almost always came in there alone, and I was worried that I seemed like a loser.

"I was gonna ask her out," I said, pronouncing *ask* like *axe* to show how casual I was.

"Too bad you didn't let me go first," she said vindictively. "She walked right by the table on the way to the door. Then I wouldn't have had that little accident on my way to the Little Girls' Room. Watch your step on the stairs next time you use the facilities" — she looked at her watch — "which should be like, five minutes from now, eh?"

"Do bladders-the-size-of-walnuts run in the family?" I pondered.

"What the hell is that on your finger?" Mary asked, ignoring me.

"It's a Sailor Moon ring. I got it for a buck." As if the cheapness of it excused anything.

Mary looked disgusted.

"Look, have you ever even seen the show?" I appealed, hiding my hand under the table. "It's about Girl Power. She's a bit whiny, sure, but who wants another grim hero?"

"We should go." Mary looked at her watch.

"They almost always beat the monsters without any help from Tuxedo Mask, the boy — they're *scary* monsters, too. They have to overcome their fears and anxieties . . ."

Mary got up and put on her jacket. "The sexy little kilts are key in stopping the monsters, I suppose."

"All school girls look like that in Japan!"

She smiled and said sweetly, "I prefer girl heroes based on the Amazonian model — women who would cut off a breast so they could draw a bow faster."

"Ahh!" I said. Nothing else came to mind. We paid and left. Mary pointed at the streetcar coming to a halt. I nodded and she ran off.

"Bring me the head of Sailor Moon!" she called out, and disappeared into the streetcar.

chapter three

I was walking to the grocery store when I saw her coming towards me, her eyes floaty.

"Hey Cassandra," I said, a little too loudly.

She looked around and settled on my face. "Hello." Her smile was slow to come, but steady, and I stopped. She stopped too, and we half turned to face each other.

"On your way to work?" I inquired, unable to pull anything meaningful from the brain-hive.

She nodded, still smiling. She smoothed some of her curly hair behind an ear.

"Huh," I said. Pause. "You working this weekend?"

"Nope. I get every third weekend off."

"You feel like going dancing?" I wanted to dance a little, as a sample, but my body was locked.

"Um . . . OK." Her eyes watched mine with a disconcerting calmness.

I broke our eye contact, looking for the off-camera cue cards that would feed me my next line. "Friday?" I eventually improvised.

She started to walk away. "OK. Meet me at work. I get off at nine."

I nodded, realized she couldn't see me, and called out "Sure." She had turned her head in the pause between nodding and speaking, and then turned it back.

Something in that movement, beyond the way it sprayed her curls, was beautiful. Otherwise I might have interpreted her few words and abrupt departure as indifference. A song I had heard earlier that day rose in mental volume, its wonderful cheesy stupidity.

I bought my vegetables with vigour that day.

What the hell was I thinking? I thought as I held the spaceship door open for Cassandra. I entered behind her, with as much enthusiasm as I would have if there had been an anal probe waiting for me.

The creative minds behind the Mothership club hadn't gone *that* far to recreate the ET experience, however. I caught a glimpse of whipping lights beyond the silvery-walled foyer we were in. I checked my coat and Cassandra did the same, and I got to see for the first time what she wore outside of work. From the top: hair corralled in a scrunch, scant make-up, a T-shirt that said "Fuckf*ce" and sweat pants of undesignated brandage. And her everyday flat sneakers, which pleased me. I considered high heels a small step away from Chinese foot bondage.

"Shall we?" Cassandra said, nodding at the door. My brain, right then beating itself for not asking her to a movie instead, was suddenly anaesthetized by her cool, and I followed her into the club.

People had heard the call of the alien, apparently. The place was octagon-shaped, with a huge saucer as the roof. In the centre of it was the distended control booth from which the DJ presided. Along the sides were the bar and large, pill-shaped capsules.

"I suddenly remember that the guy who recommended this place is a huge *X-Files* fan," I yelled to Cassandra over the bass. She laughed, and we moved deeper.

Moving through a dance floor thick with people requires a certain finesse. A dance-walk is required, since a normal-walk breaks the collective behaviour, and this is rude. It helps if a girl leads, because she can blaze a trail without sparking aggression.

When she reached a certain density of dancers, we gently asserted our space and started to get funky. It was a fuzzy techno beat, and it had a few grooves to choose from. I picked the one in the middle and jumped in.

I looked around. She had led us to a good spot — like being surrounded by trees in a forest, it was nice to be surrounded by dancers. When you couldn't see the bored sideliners, taking petulant pulls at their beers, you could almost believe the whole place — nay, the whole world — was kickin' up its heels.

I admit to a love of dancing. It is one of the few communal activities I indulge in. Despite the grim looks of many of my fellow dancers, I usually smile, and was smiling when I looked over at Cassandra.

Luckily she was a smiler too.

I had thought she would be. I remembered the smile she wore when she walked alone. I tried not to stare at her, and not stare anywhere else in particular. Even if I was staring at a spot that she couldn't see, she might think I was checking someone else out. It was a complicated business.

The guy next to me felt he needed a little more room than he was getting, his stubbly head bopping angrily. Since I had space to one side, I let him have it, though it irked me to do so. A little while later, my hostility danced away, Cassandra pointed to one of the pill booths. I nodded, and we dance-walked off.

In one, two guys were tentatively kissing as two girls watched and giggled. In the next, four guys were yelling at each other, but stopped to stare at Cassandra's chest. At another, we slipped in as two people slipped out.

It was warm and silvery inside the booth and smelled of metal.

"Why do people wear those alien shirts to this place?" she asked, nodding to the half dozen or so within sight. "It's like wearing a Dracula shirt to a goth bar. It's just overstating the obvious."

"I agree. But I don't really know why it's annoying."

"By being so obvious about it, they make the whole thing seem like a fan club. Then everybody here, by association, is a fanboy-or-girl." She paused. "And of course, all of them in their Kindergarten Ts."

"Is that what they're called? I never knew." I had, of course, noticed the phenomenon. It was as if every gal's favourite T-shirt had shrunk in the wash, but they wore them anyway.

"Uh huh. I have a friend who loves it, though. 'I have breasts! I have breasts! And the world finally knows it!' I, on the other hand, always wanted them to be detachable."

I smiled politely and didn't move my eyes from her face. "Did you know that the Amazon women cut off a breast so that they could draw their bows more easily?" I said, thinking that moving from her specific breasts to breasts-through-the-ages would make me less anxious.

She winced. "That's a little too mutilatey. Maybe not detach, then — deflate."

I had an image of myself blowing into her nipple and saw "blow-up dolls" looming on the conversational horizon. Not the ideal get-to-know-you discussion.

"So why did you stop touring with Fuck You, Mr. Man?" I said.

"Because breast-feeding on tour is a bitch."

I considered possible meanings for this. Childish band members needing constant support, perhaps?

"I wasn't prepared to truck around the southern states in the summer with a baby."

My mind scrambled for a nonplussed response, and came up empty.

"And I had had it with most of the band, anyway. Linda — the singer — had treated me as a gender traitor ever since I decided to have the kid. Erin was cool, though. The drummer. I made her the godmother. Maude ignored the whole thing and got drunk a lot."

"So you just decided to stay here? Did you even know anyone in Toronto?" Some guy lifted the sound-dampening curtain as I said it and I had to repeat myself.

"Nope. Which was how I liked it. Not that I was ashamed of having Jess," she said, looking at me sharply. "It was — well, I was having problems."

She wasn't looking at me now. She was looking out at the crowd, or rather at the shapes through the plasti-window. Then her brow furrowed, and her jaw set, and she told me. "I thought I was going crazy, and I was planning to check into a mental institution."

"Really?"

"Yeah. But I settled down once they got a new bass player and left for Montreal. I crashed in this punk house for a few days and then found the Sok job. I lucked out with a really cool landlord, too. I gotta get a drink, my throat's getting sore. Want a beer or a cola or something?"

"A beer, a beer would be nice."

"It'll give you time to process all that," she said, slipping out of the silver pill.

Yikes, a part of my brain said, *I've got a crush on a crazy punk rock girl with a kid. Wow,* another part said, *the stories she must have!*

The place had gotten even busier in the meantime, and my empty opposite seat got me plenty of nasty looks from pill-seekers. I wished Cassandra had left a bag or a coat to prove that I wasn't a total hog. While waiting, I thought about what she had told me, and remembered something I'd heard that rang true: a person who takes you into her confidence expects an equal confidence in return. Not as an exchange, really, more like a smile prompting a smile.

I had only one secret, and it was a whopper.

In fact, I rationalized, it was much more extreme than what Cassandra had told me. I had no real justification for telling her. I felt relief and disappointment in equal amounts, and my heart slowed to its regular speed.

"Here ya go. Hope this is OK." She had a tumbler of clear bubbly stuff, and put the bottle in my hand.

"Sure is," I said as I handed her some money. She reseated herself and played with the lemon on her cup rim. I took a cold slug of beer. "I hope that's not tonic water."

"Nope. Ginger ale."

"As long as it's not tonic water."

A little silence, offering her the chance to choose some other line of chat. She sat there, a small smile on her lips, bouncing her head to the muted spaceship throb.

"So why'd you think you were nuts?" I said.

"It's a real step for me, you know," she said, somewhat to herself, "to be able to discuss that period. To *integrate* it into my life's history." I wanted to smile encouragingly but I was afraid to. Then she seemed to remember my question. "Why did I think I was nuts . . . well. I remember the moment of conception, the moment that led to me having Jess. I was impregnated by something inhuman. Something not from Earth."

I did not excuse myself and run for the hills, I am proud to say.

"I know how it sounds. Believe me, I *know*. It sounds like a joke. Knocked up by an alien. Getting it on with the missing link. *Really* Close Encounters." Her eyes showed a sign of weariness. "I didn't see the humour of it back then. I was barely keeping it together when we got to Toronto — I was visibly preggers and people kept asking who the father was. Fuck, people were fucking obsessed with it! All these radical feminists asking the same question that had been asked for *centuries*. Who cares who the father was?"

I nodded. I could see her point.

"And every time I would trot out a lie about some guy after a show, some stranger, and people were a bit disturbed by this. But fuck it, I did sleep around quite a lot on tour, it helped keep the edge off the boredom. And it could have been one of them, but the thing was, it wasn't. It was this luminous *creature*, this — anyway, every time someone asked me about the father I came closer to cracking."

The pauses between swallows of my beer were getting shorter and shorter.

"And it seemed like every city had a friend or two who felt they had a right to know all about it. So Toronto was the last straw. I knew that

Linda had a Toronto friend of hers in mind to replace me, so I just played the show on autopilot, said goodbye to Erin and scrammed."

She stopped, shook the ice cubes in her glass and smiled at me. "Probably a bit more than you expected, eh?"

I shook my head. "I just feel like such a kid."

"How old are you?"

"Twenty-two."

"So am I."

"Really."

"Yep."

"So after that, it was OK?"

"Nope, that's when the trouble started."

I waited.

"I had been keeping numb on movement and people, as well as the usual drugs, while on tour. When I stayed at Jason's, he was usually at work, so my paranoid fantasies had full control as soon as morning sickness had finished with me. Jason's roommate was this total prick, too. He wasn't really a friend of Jason's, just a guy who had answered an ad."

Unlike everyone else in the city I didn't have any bad roommate stories, so I waited for her to get back to the main story.

"I was sure that the father was going to come back for his kid. Or it was going to kill me on the way out, that it was going to be a green lizard type of thing. You seen V?" She crunched an ice cube up and swallowed. "But nope. Nothing happened. And then I had to take care of Jess, which was the best distraction that I could ask for."

"Any . . . alien characteristics?" I probed.

Cassandra looked at me hard, searching my face for an indication of mockery. I actually froze as she did this, feeling like a single move could trip her emotion detector.

"She's an odd kid, but then again, I raised her."

I nodded. "Did it — he — look like that?" I tapped the table, which had a pattern of white alien heads on it. A friend of mine — the *X-Files* friend, in fact — maintained that the similarity in the alien head description proved that they existed. I couldn't have cared less, but that was then.

She shrugged. "A little. Like a really crude stick-person drawing looks human." She smiled, and I relaxed a little. "The eyes were less buggy."

Her choice of words reminded me of my conversational obligation. She had told me something significant about herself — it might not have been *verifiable*, but still gave me a privileged view into her life. I had to return the favour.

I drained the final dribble from the bottle and set it aside. I told her what I had never told another living soul. Something I had only uttered aloud locked up in the bathroom, and even then with the worry that the forbidden words would rend the air.

How to say it? Transform? Transmogrify? They all sounded like words from a science fiction story.

"I can turn into a fly."

"Ready? You don't have to go if you're not into it."

Jack was standing at my door, his eyebrows high.

I closed the book I was reading and pulled myself off my bed. "But I *am* into it, Jack-o." I started putting on my shoes.

"What's with this?" he said, pointing to my shrine. On the wall, above the bloody smear left by the insect's passing, was a sign that read *Phil Lee: Bugkilla.* Below it was taped a piece of a photo that caught Phil in a rare moment of hilarity. I had cut it from a picture of our housewarming party.

"Mr. Zen was reading in here," I said, "when he took it upon himself to send one of the wingèd folk to the next plane." I pulled on my jacket.

"A single fly made this splatter?"

"Yep." I stood at the door, motioning him out.

He went. "We have to go to Who's Emma's first, all right?"

"Where?" I said, locking the door.

"The punk store. Where the reading's being held." We headed downstairs, pausing at Phil's room. In the hushed tones of the bomb defuser, Jack said, "Phil, don't look now but there's a *fly* on your wall."

Without looking up from his book Phil's hand shot out and smacked the wall and the imaginary fly. Jack gave him a thumbs-up and we left the house.

"I'm glad to finally see the vicious side of Phil," Jack said.

I skipped down the steps with small hops. I always liked how the frosted wood squeaked, and waited, with a perverse anticipation, for the day it'd crack under my weight. Jack checked the mailbox, looking through some white, bill-like envelopes and putting them back. "No one loves us."

We started walking through the bright sun and slush. "I have to get new shoes," I told Jack. "Shit. They're soaked already," I said cheerfully.

I was in an impenetrably good mood, and it was because of the brisk air and the night before with Cassandra and marching along with Jack-o.

Jack took a small and crunchy apple out of his pocket and handed it to me, removing another for himself.

"Oooo. Thankee."

We turned onto College St. and decided to walk it rather than hop the streetcar. We passed by this middle-aged Italian guy, who stood on the sidewalk and contemplated a sign marking the end of the bike route.

When we were out of earshot, Jack said, "Did you see that guy? I want to be that guy. Just standing around in my lounge suit, thinking about stuff. Taking a whole morning to walk around the block." Jack shot a look back.

"I've seen that guy before, too," I said. "When I was waiting for a streetcar, I saw him trying to use his toe to pop a juice cap up in the air. He was at it for about ten minutes. I assumed he was going to get on with the rest of us, but he just stood there, juice cap in hand, other hand in his pocket. It was a Wednesday afternoon, and all I could think was 'Why isn't this guy at his job?' What do you figure he does?"

Jack shrugged. "It isn't rare that someone is off work, really. What's weird is that he can get into that mindstate at all. Standing there, alone but in public, totally self-absorbed while everyone else is rushing around him, even people that don't need to. People like me rushing to socialize, or return a book to the library."

Jack was on Unemployment Insurance, and was using it as a kind of Alternative Arts Grant to further the state of Canadian poetry.

"How is your writing going?"

"I got a few good hours in this morning. I think I may have a decent handful by the summer."

"Huh!" I said. I didn't understand Jack's dedication, but I admired it as I admired people who made things from scratch, be it swords or cakes.

"I wanna write poems that pop juice caps up in the air, poems that confuse people like me and you," Jack said. "Here it is." He pointed towards a small storefront with a wooden sign that asked blankly, "Who's Emma." The sign also had two silhouettes of dancing women in long flowing gowns, which looked a little like an ink blot test. There were a few smokers sitting outside at a picnic table. One of these, wearing an overcoat that made him look like a Russian revolutionary, greeted Jack.

Jack waved back and we went in. The place was postage-stamp-sized, with shelves everywhere. There were a couple of student-looking kids flipping through the CDs, and someone sitting on a stool reading a book. I tried to get a look at the title but he sort of angled it away when he saw me staring.

Jack pointed out a guy with a blue tuft of hair who was working behind the counter. It was Ken's friend, the guy we saw after the bug talk. "That's Mark, but he looks pretty busy now . . ." he said, loud enough for Mark to hear. He nodded briefly, his tuft bobbing, and went back to writing a receipt.

"So the thing is that this store has no bosses or paid employees — it's totally volunteer run and organized," Jack informed me. I nodded and started flipping through the seven-inches, amazed at how much punk rock still came out on the small vinyl format.

"I was at the last meeting, and all the decisions get made by consensus. Everyone has to agree." Jack was stressing the point and I glanced at him to fake that I was listening. I went back to the stacks and found what I was looking for: a Fuck You, Mr. Man record.

The cover was a cartoon drawing of a highly pierced punk girl swigging from a Molotov cocktail and levelling a shotgun at a cop. The back had the song titles and the credits listed (Bass = Cass).

"Hey Jack, got 'em right here," Mark said, his customer walking towards the door. He pulled out a stack of lime-green posters and showed one to Jack.

"This looks really good," Jack said, a small smile spreading on his face. I looked over his shoulder and shook my head.

"This won't do." I looked Mark in the eye. "I'm Jack's agent. You'll have to increase the size of my client's name approximately 300 per cent. We're also pushing for a name change — something like 'Jack's Night.'" I nodded and looked at Mark, who was also nodding.

"How about: 'You Don't Know Jack,'" he suggested.

I smiled. "Riiiight. That's the stuff."

"All right, why don't you wait downstairs in our Negotiation Room. I'll send my Negotiation Experts down with their Negotiation Implements and we'll see if we can't smooth out the small bumps in this agreement."

"Sounds *great*," I said, my face plastered with a shit-eating grin.

"Jesus," Jack said, wheezing. "Too much sarcasm in the air. Not enough real oxygen."

Mark smiled and handed him a chunk of flyers. "Think you can handle this many?" Jack nodded, and Mark pulled a bucket from behind the counter and a can of condensed milk, which he opened and poured into the bucket.

As it emptied, Jack asked, "Did you do this at work?"

"Yep." He pointed to a tagline at the bottom of the flyer that read *Unintentionally Sponsored by Pinko's Copies.*

The music, pop punk with boyish vocals, became comprehensible:

> I am just a humble man
> who you could do much better than
> still I ask respectfully
> will you waste your life with me?

I imagined saying that to Cassandra, and my heart adrenaline-pumped.

Jack picked up the milk bucket and turned to me. "Hold on a sec, let me get this first," I said, laying out some cash for the record.

"An oldie but a goodie," said Mark, calculating the price. "You know that the bass player lives around here, now?"

"Yeah, Cassandra," I said.

"She comes out to our monthly meetings now and then, just to leave us star-struck," Mark said. "You guys are very welcome too, even if you're not stars. Our next one is February second, the potluck starts at six."

We nodded and I grabbed the stack of flyers, Jack a staplegun and staples.

"Godspeed," Mark said as we pushed through the door.

" . . . a huge cop came up to me and said, 'I *saw* you down at the Stock Exchange, and I'm keeping an *eye* on you,'" the guy in the overcoat was saying as we passed the picnic table. A short black girl and a guy with hippie hair listened, amused.

We stopped at a pole and staplegunned a flyer to it, the third and fourth corner needing multiple staples before it took. "Mark's a nice guy," said Jack. "He's going out with Val."

"Yeah, I think I saw him once before. With Ken. I would have introduced myself, but he didn't seem that interested."

Jack shook his head and smiled quietly.

"And Val does a poetry zine?" I said.

"Yeah," he said, carefully brushing some milk on a cement pole. I positioned it and smoothed it down. We stood back and looked at it. A corner drooped and Jack slapped some more milk on it until it stuck.

"The Val you like?" I prodded, pretty sure of the answer.

"Yeah," he said, brushing the next pole with less energy.

We passed a market stall with all kinds of nuts in partitioned boxes. "I'd live right here if I was a bird," I said, nodding at an open-air display that resembled a smooth multicoloured patchwork. "Free food." A sign depicted a big-bottomed female peanut sassing an admiring pistachio with a Jamaican accent.

"How did it go with you and that waitress?" Jack said.

Four quick snaps and the flyer was up, covering up a show flyer for last weekend. "Really good. We went to that alien club, the Mothership, the one that used to be Fat City on Queen West?"

Jack smiled and shook his head no. "You forget how uncool I am." He milked the side of a *Toronto Sun* box and I flyered it.

"Anyway, I was really worried I had done the wrong thing, bringing her there. But then we danced and it was fun . . . she was a great dancer, she smiled and moved —"

Jack nodded and glowed pleasure. "Ah."

"Then we sat down and talked in this little booth thing, it was like a pod from some seventies British sci-fi show — I kept expecting it to blip into a time corridor or shoot out into the stratosphere. And she told me a secret and I told her one and, *wow*, it was great." I had been waiting all morning to tell someone, to make it more real by speaking it.

"You've got a secret?" said Jack. We were out of the market and on a main thoroughfare; a streetcar clanged as if to celebrate that fact.

"Yeah. It's a pretty good one, actually. But as you know, it's part of the courting ritual to take one another into each other's confidence."

"And you find it *helps* the courting process to reveal your impotence?" Jack said, pausing to milk up a section of a bank's wall.

I laughed, too hard. "What? *That's* not my secret," I said. After a beat: "*Everyone* knows about that!" A bank employee passed by as I was placing the poster, and didn't even look us over. "Is this legal?"

Jack shrugged. "They all get torn down over a day or two. Overzealous city employees."

"A *day* or two?" I said, discouraged. "I thought it was more like a week or two."

"Don't think about it. At least we didn't have to pay for the copies. A pile like this, coloured, would cost $20 at a cheap place. Luckily Mark works for the Man."

We switched implements, and I hooked the bucket on my wrist. I took a good look at the flyer. There was a nicely reproduced picture of a girl with glasses saying something irate to a crowd — a previous reading, I presumed:

> FUCK LOVE
> February 14
> Come out for the harshest of bitter love poetry, featuring Valerie, Jack, Ken and YOU! Bring in your hate-filled screeds and join us in kicking cupid into a bloody, unrecognizable pulp.
> @ Who's Emma, an anti-love community space.

I had to smile, thinking that this Valentine's Day might, for the first time ever, come something close to its hype. For me, anyway. I brushed the next pole, using way too much milk in my excitement. "Flyer me," I said.

"Sure," Jack said, and paused. "But first, tell me what your secret is."

"Nope."

"Then I'm afraid I won't be able to help you out with your flyer problem. No secret-telling, no flyer-pasting."

"They're your damn flyers," I said mildly.

chapter four

I sat down at the counter and watched her small-talk with a college, footballylike guy. She gave him change and he gave her a dazzling smile.

She walked back to the counter and noticed me in a double-take fashion, a smile growing. "Hey ya, Flyboy," she said with a happy rather than a teasing smile.

"Hey, Alien Girl," I said, even if it didn't make sense. She was like an alien in my world, an advanced species with lore and science to bestow.

"Be back in a flash," she said, tossing her apron under the counter and walking to the back. It was so strange to be here to meet Cassandra instead of just to pathetically admire her.

I looked around the place. It was pretty busy, but the other waitress seemed to have it under control. She walked from one table to the other as if they were lifeboats, tending to their needs in a brusque but comprehensive way.

When I looked back I noticed the stare of the cook, who dropped the basket of icy fries into the oil with an ominous *tssshh.* I gave him a tight-lipped smile and a nod and tapped my hands on the counter to fake a jaunty unconcern.

I wondered what was behind those eyes. I wondered if he had feelings for Cassandra. I experienced a moment of empathic vertigo as I imagined myself as the Boyfriend — that sinister, alpha male archetype I had pitted myself against in a dozen futile battles. The cook stepped away from the grill and wiped his hands but said nothing.

Cassandra walked out in her plainclothes and waved to the cook, who said goodbye in a neutral way. We passed through a cluster of people who were reading the menu beside the door and headed for the gallery.

"So she said that there's gonna be food there," Cassandra mentioned as we walked. The street was crowded, and it might have been just another late rush hour in Toronto but for the lighting. The sunset and precipitate caused an orange cast that was joyously apocalyptic. Times like this I felt that watching the world end might be fun.

I noticed a lime-green flyer for the reading, and realized we were in the area that Jack and I had postered. I was about to mention it but she spoke first, and then I forgot about it entirely.

"I love this crazy light. I get off most nights at six, so I can tell when the seasons are changing by the amount of light I have on the way home," Cassandra said. "I like it when the sun's setting now, because it feels right to have it mark the end of my working day. When there's too much light, it makes me feel like I should do something — when it's pitch black it makes me feel like I've been working my life away."

"It looks like this every night at this time?" I said, shocked. Where had I been?

"Well, not this weird. But check out this corner," she said, stopping me. "The sun's dropped behind the buildings, but you can still see it in the reflection of that building." She pointed, and I winced. After the burn in my eyes faded, I looked around. Everyone was walking around in this unearthly light like they didn't even notice it. I wondered if it was like this in Alaska, with the twenty-four-hour days.

"Reminds me of the Northwest Territories," said Cassandra.

"I was just thinking about that!" I said. "Have you been there?"

"Yeah, we moved there from Winnipeg when I was six. Don't remember too much about it. We were only there two years before we moved to Vancouver."

I had made one move, from London to Toronto. I decided not to mention that, and asked her about the Territories.

"We lived in a city, so it was pretty much the same. The weather was different, and there were more Native people . . . there it is," pointing to a storefront. There was a sign that read "The Sparrow Collective presents *Nests.*" The window display was empty except for a tiny nest with an egg inside. As I watched, it jerked, and jerked again. I pointed it out to Cassandra.

We went into the gallery. "First priority: find the food," Cassandra said without moving her lips. "Southwest corner, forty feet from present position."

"Move, move, move."

The room was uncrowded, and it looked like we were going to make it.

"Cassandra," came from behind us — the whistle of an incoming shell.

"Go on without me," Cassandra muttered. "I'll try to meet you there. When it's safe." She turned around, and I continued my tense saunter towards the food. But I figured I was OK — I didn't know anyone in the art world. So I stopped to look at one of the pieces, a feather nest with a brambly, woody robin as its occupant. It was a cocky move, and I relished it, stroking my chin as I surveyed it from a few different angles. I could clearly see pastries, *puff* pastries on the table, and different varieties of natural juices.

I turned to make the last few steps.

"Ryan!" At first I thought it was my imagination, and I kept moving. But a hand was quickly approaching, and there was no escape. "Ryan, how you doing?" the bearded, crazy-eyed man asked me as his beefy hand pumped mine.

"Just fine!" I said, wondering if enthusing over my fineness would convince this stranger I had a clue as to who he was. Out of focus, and out of reach, was the table, a veritable groaning board of unattainable delights.

"I had heard you had made the move, and I kept expecting to run into you."

I adjusted my glasses, once again wishing they had a minicomputer built in. *SUBJECT IDENTIFIED: Brian Wong*, would run across my field of vision in glowing green, perhaps supplemented with a variety of other data (marital status, job, weapon of choice, favourite cocktail) that I could weave into conversation.

"It's a pretty big city," I mumbled.

"You know, I don't think I've seen you since my last show. The one on bomb shelters, you remember that?"

Suddenly, miraculously, I did — this was a friend of mine from London, a high-school buddy. Steve. And his bomb shelter show *was* quite memorable.

"How could I forget! The pounding explosions, the fury of the art teacher . . . the sausage rolls shaped like A-bombs . . ." I said, looking lingeringly over at the table.

"Yeah, those were angry days," Steve said. "And Katie outdid herself with the food this time — wait till you try the scotch eggs." I had a one-second window to jump on that offer, and missed it. "But I'd like to get your feedback. I still remember your critique of the last show, and it really helped me."

He led me away from the table and towards his piece. My dismay was lessened by the compliment. "You seem to be focused on habitats, in one form or another," I started, warming to the subject.

I saw Cassandra arrive at the table, having managed to avoid engagement with anyone. She shot me a smile, and I was happy one of us made it, at least.

I had the television on mute. Sailor Mercury blasted bubbles at the plant thing soundlessly but effectively.

I was on the phone to my sister. "So she's really cool. She used to be in a punk band, and she's waitressing now," I said, leaving the alien baby part out. Lisa's a little excitable.

"So when do we get to meet her?" she said, in a goofy voice.

I forked some lettuce into my mouth. "Right after hell freezes over," I said calmly. "But maybe not that soon." I took a second to appreciate the hundreds of kilometres that separated me from my family.

"Well, it's a good thing you met someone," she said. "We were beginning to wonder about those Toronto women."

I hadn't had any relationship news to relate since I had moved out here. A coffee date or two, but nothing to call home about. My sister usually took up the slack by talking about the guys in her life, who traditionally started off as paragons of humanity and quickly devolved to sleaze. No one measured up to Dad.

An ugly thought ambled through my mind: *If Mom died, would Dad start dating?* It suddenly started a slideshow of Dad at the beach with a bimbo, Dad dancing in a shiny hipster shirt, Dad running through the snow and laughing with some other woman.

"Is Dad drinking?" I said in an effort to derail the horrible train of thought that would end with Dad doing the nasty.

It must have sounded sudden, because Lisa paused before she answered. "Well, he was, at the beginning. But he's slowed down now. Still a lot, more than before, but not super-serious."

"Huh." I didn't want to ask how Mom was, and nothing else was important, so there was a pause. Sailor Moon was eating some cake in exaggerated cartoon fashion and her talking cat, Luna, looked on disapprovingly.

"Huh," Lisa said back. "Well, I'll tell them you called."

There was a knock on the door. "Come," I said, in my best Picard voice. "Yeah, get them to give me a call when they have a chance." Phil came in, and sat down in front of the TV.

"OK, give Cassandra a kiss for me."

"Yeah, whatever," I said, a grin crawling over my face, enjoying and mortified by my sister's lameness. "Later."

"Byye."

I hung up and Phil looked back at me with his dark eyes. "Turn it up, turn it up." I unmuted it. Phil looked back. "Did you know that one of the biggest audiences for this show in Japan are males aged eighteen to twenty-four?"

"Really?" I said through a mouthful of raw cauliflower. That was disappointing — I had relished the idea that I was evading my demographic destiny. The ads for toys between cartoons were amusingly ineffective, although I must admit I had bought more than one Nerf product in the last two months.

"They cut out all the ass shots for the North American audience, of course, and the gay subtexts. That's why the shows are short enough for the 'Sailor Says' do-goodie bit at the end, which also satisfies the educational content laws."

"Why do you think I have to eat, watch TV and talk on the phone at the same time?" I suddenly mused. "Why do I require three different simultaneous stimuli?"

"Your vacuous western culture has necessitated the endless chatter of the monkey mind. All white folk are thrall to it," Phil said conversationally. He wiped a bit of dust off the screen.

"As you are in thrall to Sailor Moon, it seems."

"But as you see, I am focused on this single stimulus, getting as close as I can without suffering radiation burns." And it was true. His big head was entirely blocking the screen.

"While carrying on a conversation with me."

"True," he conceded. "As well as wearing a cock ring."

"Can you never, never, *never* say that again," I said, carrot in hand.

Phil shrugged and smiled. "Okily-dokily."

I chewed on my carrot and asked, "Is it the one you bought at that vending machine? Promising *Pure Animal Pleasure?"*

"Nope. I lost that in Melissa's car." Phil and Melissa went out. "Packaging and all."

"What?"

"Then she gave the car to her dad . . . he cleaned it out before it was sold."

Melissa's dad didn't approve of Phil. It was hard to imagine what he would do when faced with this nefarious toy. I would have made a joke — it was a topic with veritable joke landmines — but my empathic response to the drama and the horror left me utterly speechless.

Sailor Moon was done. Phil started flipping through channels. "I don't know for sure. I may have lost it in my room at my mom's place, but that's almost as bad."

It couldn't be as bad as the scene that was forming in my mind — a fat, tired, mostly faceless old Italian man dustbusting the upholstery on his hands and knees and coming across the poorly printed but utterly explicit pink packaging. Picking it up in his sausage fingers, squinting at it, flinging it out of the car with a squeak. Trying to continue cleaning the car, but with haunted eyes, looking up and beseeching his god once in a while. For me, this scene was real.

"Who knew the chaos you were unleashing with the turn of a vending machine knob?" I said. "It was as if it was attached to some huge machinery of fate."

Phil snorted.

"Why did you —" *buy it anyway* died on my lips as I remembered why.

"Some *idiot* kept saying I should buy it. That since it was made in Korea it was my national duty. 'People in the marital aids industry have to eat,' the idiot said."

"Shouldn't listen to those idiots," I mumbled.

Phil looked back at me with silent eyes. He looked back at the TV. "Nothing happened, anyway. It was a few weeks ago."

I didn't know whether to be relieved or disappointed.

I was passing by Miracle Wash one day and looked in to see if it was dirtier than it was clean. Someone with Cassandra's hair was doing her laundry. I chastized myself for turning everyone into Cass, but then she turned around and waved.

"Hey, cutes," she said, opening the dryer door. "I'm sorry I had to leave the gallery so suddenly."

I sat down on the bench. "Well, you had already eaten your fill, so why not?" I attempted an unhappy look that probably failed to conceal my pleasure at (a) being called *cutes* and (b) the beauty of the chance encounter. Miracle Wash, indeed.

"Tell me you got one of the huge pastries." She flopped the laundry on the counter and used her hand to show me just how big they were. "With the raspberry filling?" Her eyes were rapture.

"I got one cracker," I said. "One *dry* cracker. No juice or beer was left by the time I got there."

She sat down beside me, waving a fly away from her clothes. "I never kill them after what you told me. When are you going to prove it to me, anyway?"

I shrugged nonchalantly, but my heart speeded up. "Whenever you like."

"I mean, I'd prove what I told you, but I can't. But you can actually do it in front of me, right?"

"More or less," I said. "What are you doing tonight?"

She was caught off guard. "Tonight? Well, actually, me and Jess — my kid — hang out on Sunday nights. Watch TV." She scratched her head. "Unless you'd . . . like to meet her."

"Well, if I wouldn't be intruding . . ." I said.

"Nope. We just watch a couple of hours of *Sailor Moon* episodes. She likes to watch them with me. Do you know the show?"

I showed her my Sailor Scout ring, wordlessly. She smiled and shook her head, and went back to folding her laundry.

In my mind, I continued the conversation:

"What do you watch kids' shows for?" she might say, sometime.

"It's not any more stupid than any other TV. I like the idea of girls watching this and imagining they're various characters. Getting inspired. Reminds me of watching G-Force *when I was a kid."*

Weak. I tried something else.

"Sailor Moon is such a whiny little brat," Cassandra could say.

"She is, but don't you think that's better than having a stoic heroine whose only difference from a clichéd, stereotypical male hero is her gender?"

Jesus, that sounded stilted and pedantic.

"Isn't it interesting how their little outfits so perfectly display tits and ass?"

"But there's ribbons and stuff to conceal the contours, except during the transformation scenes!" I'd say desperately to Imaginary Cassandra, who had taken on the tone and virulence of Mary. *She wouldn't let her kid*

watch it if she hated it that much, I told myself, trying not to let my nervousness show on my face.

Cassandra held up a tiny T-shirt. It had a faded print of the blonde schoolgirl in question, hands on hips. "She loves this thing."

She went on to untangle some unmentionables, so I had to focus. "Yeah, it looks like it's been through a few battles."

"Yeah. Her cousin gave it to her. As well as all the tapes of the show. Man, kids go off things fast," she said, shaking her head. She started packing her laundry into a well-worn backpack. "And it's so intense — one second they're watching it three times a day and the next they could care less."

"It was on three times a day?" I said. "Jesus, I'd never get anything done."

Cassandra laughed. "At its height. Now only oddbods and deprived children without cable will watch it."

"Oh, *I'm* the oddbod, eh?"

"Yeah," she said hitching up her backpack and giving the dryer one last look. "I'm just being a good mother."

We left. Her cheeks glowed as she breathed. Suddenly, she burst out with: "I can't wait to see you turn into a fly!" Cassandra skipped ahead a little and looked back, eyes ablaze. I experienced a cold dropping in my stomach, similar to a roller-coaster feeling. I watched the ground as I walked over her snowprints.

"It's not all that dramatic," I said.

"It'll be dramatic for me," she said.

We passed a café, and Cassandra pressed her face up against the glass and waved energetically. I couldn't see anything inside, what with the glare, but I had an annoying urge to see if it was a man or a woman she was waving at.

It started to snow, the heavy white flakes that coated early February. "Do we want munchies?" Cassandra asked, pointing to a dollar store. I thought she meant for my show, but then I realized she meant for the video.

We paused for a moment outside Dollar $aver$, the excess of the store spilled higgledy-piggledy onto the sidewalk as if there had been a retail avalanche earlier that day. Cassandra went in and I followed.

A Chinese woman with heavy make-up was alerted to our presence by a tinny electronic chime. Cassandra went searching for snacks, and I hung around the counter, where the store manager didn't have to worry about me slipping a package of smelly markers into my jacket. I noticed a few boxes of Sailor Moon merchandise all but crowded off the shelf by the kurrent kid kraze.

I wanted to buy a ring for Cassandra. But I couldn't. It was too dramatic, too symbolic, too sappy. I really wanted to, but I was utterly paralyzed. Then I thought — Jess.

Cassandra tossed a Salt + Vinegar chip bag on the counter.

"Does Jess wear barrettes?" I asked.

"Nope," she said, "but she likes shiny stickers." I put a package of them on the counter.

"I want a ring like yours," said Cassandra, a half-ashamed smile on her face.

"You should get one," I said. "They've got all of the Scouts right here."

"Do they have Sailor Mars?" she said. Sailor Mars was the tough one who argued with Sailor Moon a lot, but they were friends when it came to the crunch. I located it and put it with the other purchases, which I paid for. I picked it up and she wiggled her finger into it.

"Very nice," the old Chinese woman said, as Cassandra displayed it for her with a glamorous flourish. So I got to buy her a ring, and we had worked together to make it a tolerably undramatic and still significant moment. Cassandra pulled her mittens over her hands — she had these great red mittens that made her hands look like sleds — and we went outside.

We took all these side streets and short cuts through tiny parks and large parking lots, and I was watching her face as she talked so I really had no idea where she lived. I always took advantage of when Cassandra spoke to really look at her — it's not staring then. Of course I was listening to her as well. She was talking about the differences in the neighbourhood where she lived in Vancouver and the one she lived in now.

We had to walk down a back road to get to the place, and I asked, "Does it get scary here at night?"

"Not for me," Cassandra said, smiling mysteriously. She unlocked the gate and let me into the small yard, locking it behind her. There was a set of stairs, and at the top, Cassandra stopped.

"This is a really nice place to sit in the summer," she said. I looked over the jumble of roofs, a willow tree in the distance, the beginning sunset. "Too fuckin' cold today, though."

We moved inside and walked by a woman bent over a pot in the kitchen. "Hi, Olive," Cassandra said, and got a raised hand from the lady, who didn't turn away from her work.

"We share that bathroom," she said as we walked by it to the stairs. There was a little girl standing still and quiet, who watched us.

"Hi Jessy," said Cassandra in an unfamiliar soft voice. "Go on up," she said, lightly patting the child's bottom to push her on her way. The kid's small legs made every step a stretch, and I walked up slowly. I could see from the back of her head that Cassandra was smiling.

At the top of the stairs introductions were made. "Jess, this is Ryan. He's a friend of mine." Jess had most of her hand in her mouth, so a handshake was out — I gave her a friendly wave. She returned it, watching me with big grey eyes a little too arresting to call cute.

Cassandra put the chips down on the counter and took off her jacket. "Well, what do we want to do next?" she said, looking at me.

"thailor oon," said Jess, talking around the hand.

We both looked at her. She took her hand out of her mouth with a *sssllp*. "Sailor Moon," she repeated, her eyes entreating us.

I dreaded having to wait any longer. "I can do it first, and then we can put on the video," I said. She smiled and nodded quickly.

"OK, Jess — can Jess watch?" she said, almost as an afterthought. I nodded. It didn't matter what kids saw as long as they weren't traumatized. They couldn't convince anyone of something like this.

"OK, Jess, my friend is going to try to turn into a fly."

"Fly?" she asked, wobbling her hand through the air.

"That's right," I said.

They both sat down on the couch. I stood before them, feeling like a magician, a fraud. Downplaying the showmanship, I said, "I'm gonna change into a fly, buzz around in a circle, and change back. But my clothes are gonna fall off, and so if you don't see me right away it's probably because I'm covered in my clothes, so just shake them gently so I can get out."

I looked out of the room. There was another room down the hall, and the door was ajar. "I can't transform back here, because I'll be buck naked."

"What a show!" Cassandra said, wiggling her eyebrows.

"And no one wants that," I rushed on, pleased by her enthusiasm. "After I fly around, I'll buzz into that room and wait for you to dump my clothes in there and close the door."

"I think we should be able to watch the *whole* thing, so as to make sure you're not faking it somehow."

I couldn't think of a clever and flirty answer so I just turned into a fly.

I willed myself up through my head, and I saw the huge structure of my empty clothes crumble and flop silently. Cassandra had one hand on the couch as if she was ready to stand, but didn't. In the dozens of reflections of my multi-eyes, her face was blooming wonder as she scanned the room.

"Holy shit," she said.

Jess sat there, watching me, her eyes tracking me as I buzzed in slow, lazy, glorious circles. God, it was good to fly again! I hovered, dove and stretched my minute limbs. My proboscis smelled some good stuff in the garbage can, but I refrained. Not in front of an audience.

Cassandra had found me and said, "That's incredible, Ryan. That's . . ."

She got up and gathered up my clothes, and my ring fell. She laughed and picked it up, then deposited the pile in the other room.

I landed sideways on the huge expanse of white, the proverbial fly on the wall, waiting for her to return. Now that I had stopped flying, Jess was looking at the TV longingly. Cassandra returned, careful to leave the door wide open, and went to sit down.

I flew through the hall and snapped back, landing on my feet. My hair felt a little thick, but my skin wasn't slimy — I had been worried about the residue, even though I was in fly form for less than a minute. I pulled on my pants and undies in one convenient move, then my ring, then my shirt, and then I headed back to the stage.

They clapped when I entered the room. I bowed as I wiggled into my shoes. "Let's see Sailor Moon top that," I said, sitting down.

chapter five

Someone knows. Another person knows. A human besides myself knows. Cassandra knows I can turn into a fly. I was trying to concentrate on the professor, but the thought returned with machinelike regularity.

My brain had been repeatedly telling me this ever since it happened. At first jubilantly, then just as a news update, this new reality assailed my psyche — and I feared for its stability. It was as if my brain was rebuilding itself.

The prof was writing some crap on the board. I scribbled it down, not reading it, leaving comprehension till after. She knew, she knew, *she knew.*

Why was it such a big deal? I thought. *Because now you could do this!* my brain said, showing me a clip: camera pulls back, I suddenly stand up. Clip-Me yells "Look at me, I'm really a fly!" And I turn into a fly, sending the class into screaming chaos. Clip ends.

I started to shudder. There were a million variants of this clip, all bad. I wondered about my choice of declaration: *Look at me, I'm really a fly!* What did it mean? More specifically, what did telling one trusted person have to do with telling the whole world?

I hadn't really predicted how dramatic the aftereffects would be. After showing Cassandra, I sat through two entire episodes of *Sailor Moon* that I had already seen, just so my adrenaline would wear off. I had imagined different things, different feelings to accompany taking this step, but this speed anxiety was not one of them. It completely overshadowed my excitement for Cassandra, and when she had asked for my number as I got ready to leave, my mind blanked.

I stood there, feeling like a moron, but also a little scared. Up until then, I had pretended like the whole thing wasn't affecting me, cheering on the Sailor Scouts and eating chips with my regular gusto.

"I just want to talk to you about a couple of things, why this is so exciting for me," Cassandra had said, flushing a little, indicating Jess as her reason for not discussing them now.

I was completely dumb, unable to even speak.

"Well . . . maybe I'll just see you at Sok sometime," she said. Her hurt look was like a kick to the old braincase.

"Five three five six two two two," I said, looking around for a pen.

"You don't have to —"

"No, please, I'd love you to call me, I'm just a total space case today."

She had taken the number down.

A few days after my unveiling, I'd calmed down a bit. I had kept away from my normal dose of coffee and that had helped.

"You have . . . two new messages," the recorded voice said.

"Hi Ryan," said Ken. "Nice message, you've got a point about those clowns. They must be stopped. I'm just calling to chat, so . . . call me back."

I deleted the message and waited for the next one.

"Hi Ryan. This is Cassandra. Give me a call. 599-3507."

I listened to that message two more times. There might have been a faint nervousness about it, but nothing more. I debated over whether to keep it or erase it and decided to erase it. There was no point in using up space in Bell Laboratory's message bank when it was probably overtaxed anyway.

Sometimes, when using the invisible answering machine service, I would have this irrational image of a huge reel-to-reel anachronism with flashing lights starting and stopping. It was among thousands of unmarked machines just like it in some subterranean vault, and if I was there in person looking for the one my messages were recorded on, it would be as futile as trying to find a particular grain of sand on the shores of the Dead Sea.

I recorded Cassandra's number in my phone book (under C, since I didn't know her last name) with no real excitement. I felt bland about it, this cherished event. I was unable to disassociate her from the tremendous stress of having my secret no longer a secret.

I also hadn't listened to the record of hers I had bought at Who's Emma, and I had been determined to before I talked to her again. I didn't have a player — it was at home (London, that is), and I hadn't been in a frame of mind to remember it last time I was there.

Already, I was recalling the whole terrible visit as a movie-of-the-week.

None of it seemed real, none of it except for my sister's lank hair and my father's whisky breath.

I grabbed the record and a blank tape from the top of my dresser and went downstairs. Jack's door was closed, and I knocked. He opened it ridiculously quickly.

". . ." I said.

"I was just on my way to the washroom," said Jack, explaining his pre-emptive strike.

"Oh. Can I use your record player?"

"Yeah — oh, you're playing that? Wait till I get back." He left and I placed it on the ancient machine, upon which an ear trumpet would have been appropriate.

Jack's room had changed little since I had last seen it. His bookshelves were his wallpaper. Jack collected books, a habit as expensive as any addiction. I kept *my* books at the public library and drank away the occasional pang of jealousy.

I sat on his futon, a bed he compulsively folded up into a couch. I had never seen it folded out, actually. I looked through the tome of poetry he had set to one side, putting it down before he got back. I didn't want to start him up on some British aesthete.

"Why do you fold this sucker up all the time?" I asked.

"Because I don't have anywhere for visitors to sit. And I feel weird having them sit on my bed," he said, his face wrinkling. "Feels like I'm coming on to them. Next thing I'll be snuggling up and dragging the blanket over us."

I blinked. "Huh. Can I tape this?" I said, waving the blank I'd brought.

"Nope," Jack said.

I went over to verify, and indeed there was no record button. It looked strange, like a four-fingered hand. "Fuck."

"Sorry."

"Don't 'sorry' me. I'll expect you to get up to speed pretty damn quick, Jack. Your consumption levels are significantly lower this quarter, anyway. You don't want a Poor Buyer rating on your citizenship card, do you?"

He didn't answer, having snatched the seven-inch from my hand and removed the lyric sheet.

I leaned over and gave him the hairy eyeball. "*Do* you?"

"I guess I don't," he said. "But let's see what Fuck You, Mr. Man has to say about it."

We played the record. It was sarcastic, short and punk rock. It was better than most hardcore I had heard, and the lyrics were pretty good too. There was a song about birth control, a song about gardens, one about the Mothers of the Disappeared in Latin America. The last one was sung and written by Cassandra, "Fuckdoll Comment Sheet":

> Was I a distracting enough distraction?
> Did I provide complete satisfaction?
> Did I convincingly conceal revulsion and/or rage?
> Write further suggestions on the back of the page

I sat there for a second trying to reconcile this voice with the careful one that had been on my answering machine.

"That's the woman you went out with?" asked Jack.

I nodded.

"Lucky bastard." His eyes started to traverse his legacy of titles, as they eventually always did whenever I ventured into his *sanctum sanctorum.* "Have you read *The Female Eunuch*? It's a classic feminist work."

"The only remotely feminist thing I've read is Paglia. For that po-mo course."

Jack grimaced. "Bleh. Apologist for male dumbness. This one's much better. Germaine Greer." He pulled out the book and handed it to me. The dated, seventies look of the book appealed to me, and I had always been a little ashamed of my sketchy knowledge of women's issues, so I accepted. I felt a little silly, though — what, was I studying for a test?

"Thanks."

He nodded.

"This will enable me to stalk and trap my female prey more efficiently."

We laughed the Evil Men laugh, slapped each other on the back, and would have lit up cigars had we had them.

I removed the record and headed back to my room. I passed Phil on his way out, wearing a loosely knit toque. He took the book from my hand and looked at it, handed it back without comment, and walked out.

Back in my room, I shut the door behind me and locked it too, by habit. Then unlocked it — people didn't barge in around here, so why be so anal? I guessed it was left over from living with my family, when Lisa was liable to treat an unlocked door as an invitation to come in, sprawl on my bed, and waste time that I was planning to waste alone. It was annoying then, but I supposed in time I'd come to miss it. I know I already missed every irritating trait of my mom, the cancer having changed them into quirky virtues. The way she'd constantly brush my hair, producing a comb from thin air, just the memory of that made my nostrils flare and eyes burn.

I lay on my bed, trying to formulate what I could say about Cassandra's song. "Witty"? "Angry"? True, but calling someone's work "angry" seemed dismissive. "Vitriolic" and "raw" seemed better. I picked up the phone and dialled her digits.

I checked the time. She should be home if she came straight home from — "Hello?"

"Hi Cassandra. It's Ryan."

"Oh hi! How are you?"

I decided to answer this stock question honestly. "Pretty crazy. I've really been sorta — unbalanced by the whole thing. Showing you and all."

"Really."

"Yeah. I never expected that. My brain didn't seem to mind my telling you, but *showing* you was another matter. But it's getting better now. I go without thinking about it for hours on end."

"You seemed so calm after it happened."

"Yeah, I'm a pretty good pretender. But it echoed around my brain for a couple of days. Did it affect you at all?"

"Yeah," she said. "In a good way. My experience with Jess's father . . . is something I know to be true. Unless I question my eyes and memory, which I have no reason to. But I have no proof. And everything else in the world, in my life, is so completely normal. But now —"

"I'm proof. I'm your proof."

"Yes. But more has happened since that. Like now that that problem is solved — well, not that it's solved, but I no longer am questioning my sanity — I've remembered something else."

I thought of a joke, but kept my mouth shut. Thank god.

"When I was six, my uncle tried to rape me."

"Oh, fuck."

"I said *tried.*" There was silence, and I heard her take a breath. "The family story has always been that Uncle Chuck had gambling debts and so made himself permanently scarce. But something weirder happened."

"What?"

"I don't know what. Not involving aliens, don't worry. I think I did it. I think I made him disappear."

"Disappear? Like leave the city?"

"No, like leaving everything. Like into thin air."

I managed to stutter a single-syllable word: "How?"

"How do you turn into a fly?" I could hear her challenging smile.

"Uhhh . . ."

"Exactly. But anyways, what are you doing on Saturday?"

I glanced up at the calendar. "Valentine's Day? Nothing. Oh, there's this thing at Who's Emma . . ."

"That's what I was going to ask you to."

"Great! Yeah, I'd like that." A synapse fired. "Are you going to read something? I heard your song on the *Fried, not Baked* seven-inch."

"Oh?" Her voice was surprised, but surpleased or surpissed I could not gauge on a single word.

I hurtled on. "I got it at Emma's. It was vitriolic and" — *raw* seemed too much of a rock critic word — "nasty. I liked it."

She laughed. "Actually, Val and Mark wanted me to read 'Fuckdoll,' but it doesn't feel right, somehow."

"Huh," I neutralled.

"Yeah," she said, adding nothing.

"Why's that?" I prodded, finally.

"Well . . . it's just not entirely honest. It's a good song, I like it, but it doesn't give a . . . complete picture, I guess. It presents one perspective really . . . strongly, but I think it's too simple. 'Cause I was feeling more than that, it was a lot more complex, and that song is only one of the voices in my head. But it was the least compromising voice."

"Compromising . . . to who?"

"To the idea of being a strong woman, I guess. But since then, I've revised what I think a strong woman is. All the conflicting ideas and desires, paradoxical even, have to be a part of the equation."

"So it's not really a mellowing-with-age thing . . ."

"What have you got there?" Cass asked.

I didn't know what I had. "Got where?"

"It's a fork. Be careful," Cass said.

I couldn't decide if the conversation had taken a turn for the surreal or if I had missed something. A fork in the theoretical argument?

"Can you say fork, Jessy?"

"Fork," I said. "I can. Fork fork, fork fork fork."

"Sorry," Cass said. "No. No mellowing. My feminist ideals are more firmly integrated with my day-to-day life now than then. I've just got away from the wartime mentality, the girls versus boys stuff."

Her vocabulary and intelligence were giving me a buzz. I curled up on my bed. I managed to say, "You just said the F-word. I'm supposed to be alarmed by that. It says so in the Boys' Manual."

She laughed. "You're fucked anyway. I'm sure it forbids revealing your superpowers to feminists."

"Oh, shit. I'm in the soup now."

"'In the soup.' Great phrase."

"Yeah," I said glumly, "but all the great phrases in the world won't help me in front of the Boys' High Tribunal, as I'm arraigned for my indiscretions."

"Not even 'The feminazi used alien mind-control tricks'? 'Cause I did, you know."

"Well, maybe that."

By the time Jess's bedtime rolled around and she had to go, I was feeling like this was the best conversation I had ever had. I put the phone in its cradle, content to never have it ring again.

On V-Day, Phil was sitting out on the stoop, watching the cars. I removed his toque and dropped it in his lap, then sat beside him.

"Stop it," he said with an absurdly exaggerated petulance.

"Waitin' fer Melissa?"

He nodded.

"Have a nice night planned?" I said, sarcasming the words past saturation point.

He nodded. "Yep."

Jack came out. "Oh, waiting for your chariot, *boy*friend?"

"Yep. Where you guys headed?"

"Not that it concerns the likes of you," I said, "Mr. Well Adjusted, Mr. Unavailable, Mr. Sexually Satisfied —"

"Mr. Boyfriend," spat Jack.

"— but we're headed to the FUCK LOVE Bitter Hearts Reading at Who's Emma."

Phil nodded. "*That* thing. The Punk Singles Night, you mean?"

I laughed, but Jack glowered.

"What are you bitter about, anyway?" Phil said to me. "I thought you had something with the Sok waitress."

"She asked me to this thing," I said, beaming foolishly. "I'm just bitter by habit. I don't want to break Jack's mood. He's gotta get psyched up. Otherwise I'd mention that this is the first time I've ever had a date on Valentine's Day."

They looked at me. Jack said, "I think it's better that way, sometimes, not to know what you're missing —"

"Bull*shit.* Every movie, every story, every goddamned *commercial* has some element affirming the importance of capital-L-love. My ignorance doesn't save me," I said, "any more than it saves the Cuban from dreaming about capitalist riches."

"That's the spirit, Ryan," said Jack, slapping me on the shoulder.

"What a convoluted analogy," said Phil.

"Well, you'll have a lot of time to untangle it," I said, going down the stairs. "As you sit here alone all night. Melissa's not coming."

Jack walked after me.

When we hit the sidewalk I turned around and looked at Phil's hunched form. He waved. I shook my head, and Jack pushed me ahead.

"Don't waste your time with him," he said. "So did you get her a valentine?"

"I'm not telling you."

"That's the same as saying yes."

"If I say yes you'll want to see it, and if you criticize it, it'll make me incredibly nervous. I'm very susceptible to criticism."

"You're also susceptible to wussyism, it seems." Jack was in one of his rare bantering moods, perhaps to distract himself.

"OK, Mr. Ironman, show me the poems you're going to read."

"Point made," he said, suddenly frozen.

A pause. I tried to think of something soothing to say, but all that came into my mind was *So is Val gonna be there?* and that would just key him up tighter.

"Oh!" I remembered the cock ring story, and debated telling it. Would it be too gossipy? I hated gossip. But I figured that it didn't really reflect badly on anyone.

Jack was looking at me. "Oh what?"

"So we were at this cheesy bar, right, Phil and I? And there's this vending machine . . ." and I told the story in its unedited glory — complete with the father's anguished bellowing at the sky.

By the time it was finished, we had arrived.

The smokers were clustered around the picnic table, looking cold but more cheerful than before, as if they sensed the end of winter. Ken was among them.

"Hey dudes," Ken said to us, doing a robotic dance move and laughing at our immobility. He had a steaming mug in one hand and a wispy cig in the other.

"Hi, Mr. Pants. How are your pants selling?" I inquired.

"Totally badly," Ken said. "I keep wearing them out. How you doing, Jacky? Haven't seen your ugly mug around for a while."

Jack pulled his hat down to his eyebrows and gave Ken a dockworker's glare. Ken said *Blaaah!* and recoiled.

"Let's go in let's go in," I said, doing the cold dance. We entered the store and there were people of varied acquaintanceship — met-onces, seen-arounds and utter-strangers. No Cassandras, though. I smiled and nodded to the met-onces, specifically Val and Mark, and side-glanced at Jack to see him take off his pulled-down hat and greet Val with an almost smile. Val motioned us downstairs, so we obediently squeezed by the number of people chatting and flipping through records and headed down the stairs.

The basement was tiny, but carpeted and warm. A number of people looked at us as we descended, none of them Cassandra. I checked my watch.

I found some space and hunkered down. Jack sat, very close to the neighbouring people. "You've got some room over there," hissed Jack.

"'S'for Cassandra," I whispered too, though I didn't know why. The people had all decided to face one wall, the one that had a FUCK LOVE banner.

"*Sure* it is."

"Fuck off. Shouldn't you be rehearsing or something?"

Jack pulled a sheaf out of his jacket. He unfolded it and pointed one typed line out to me: *for Val.*

"Uh oh," I said.

"Yep," he said gravely. "Uh oh is right."

No wonder he was all nerves. "Couldn't you . . . do it less publicly? Do something less . . . insane? Like get a tattoo or something?" I was starting to get contact hysteria.

He shook his head.

"Why?" I said.

"I'm not going to read the dedication. But there's details in it that will tip her off, and probably Mark too."

That lessened it a bit. "But you're not going to stare at her or anything, are you?"

The look he gave me was scornful.

I almost repeated my appeal, but my initial shock had lessened and had been replaced by a clinical interest.

"She asked for bitter love poetry," Jack said. "I get home one day and Phil told me she's called. I was so happy. So I call her and it's about this — she wants me to read some bitter love poetry. And I realized, she has *no — fuckin' — idea* . . ." Jack shook the look of amazement off his face. "So I decided to do it."

A foot tapped my hip. "Make room, Flyboy." It was Cassandra — she must have made her way across to us while I was boggling about Jack's kamikaze poetics. I bumped Jack over, and the people next to him gave up some inches.

Cassandra wedged into the space. "Were you saving a space for someone without hips?" she asked.

"It was just a token space I was saving, not meant for human use," I said. "It was representational."

She smiled as she unwound her scarf. Her red cheeks made her look exceedingly healthy, and her lips were tough and desirable. *You look so beautiful,* I didn't say.

"I like your hat," I said. It was a jaunty little red beret. "It sets off your cheeks," I added, with a little more panache.

"Yeah, that was the plan. I took the weather into account when I threw together this ensemble," she said, with maybe a trace of pleased embarrassment. She removed the rest of her things, the hat last.

They were fiddling with stuff at the front, microphones and the like. *Now or never,* I thought, and pulled out the small envelope and gave it to her, not looking. When she was occupied with opening and looking at it, I dared a glance: she was grinning.

It was one of those elementary school Valentine's Day cards, with a boy and a girl holding hands on it. I didn't write anything on it. I was scared. "Had one left over from Grade four," I said gruffly.

I felt a hand on my chest and I looked down. She was pressing a small heart to my chest. She hit me with it again and I took it. It was a collage of alien images, from the Martian-style to ones from *Dr. Who* to the "modern" image. I flipped it over and there were all sorts of fly images, illustrations from textbooks and photos and cartoons.

"This is . . ." *so much better than mine,* I thought, " . . . amazing."

"Put it away," she said out the side of her mouth. "Remember where we are."

"Right," I said, and tucked it into a pocket. "Oh! This is my roommate Jack," I said, and introduced them. "Jack's about to do something stupid but brave," I said.

Val took the stage. Jack's nostrils visibly flared.

Damned holiday, I thought, telling the divine-throated cherubim stowaways in my head to keep it down.

chapter six

The kettle squealed and Cassandra got up and lifted it with one hand, flipped a cassette tape with the other. She pulled down some mugs and teabagged them, then filled them. She didn't ask me what I wanted.

"I've only got raspberry, hope that's all right."

Her kitchen, which she had suggested instead of a café, was warm and painted with earthy brown-reds. As I looked around, the music started — a lazy guitar and a lazier singer that I didn't recognize.

"Pavement," she said, nodding to the tape player. "I didn't think much of this until maybe the fifth listen, then it just made me smile and smile. The lyrics are fairly unfathomable."

"Lyrics are pretty big for me. If it's got good lyrics, it almost doesn't matter what it sounds like. But I'm not a musician." I said it with a flourish that added, *like you are.*

"Neither am I. I just play music."

"Yeah, but you can appreciate chord changies and stuff."

"Changies?"

I laughed. "Yeah, everything's with a 'y' after I hang out with Ken. Wasn't he awesome?" He had read out, panel-by-panel, some of his love-themed comics.

"He was great — he has this incredible physical craziness. He's such a natural performer." Cassandra's eyes sparkled over the rim of her mug. "Oh! And did you see the older couple I was talking to?"

I nodded. A robust man and a woman with a lacy hat.

"Well, I'd seen them at stuff before, and I noticed Ken left his bag with them. So I asked them how they knew Ken. And they said, 'We made him.'"

"His parents?"

"Yeah! What an amazing thing to say. 'We made him.' I think I saw them at another reading that Val put on. Hers was good, eh? You could really tell she'd read before."

"Yeah. I wonder if it was about Mark? Or some other guy?" I had problems imagining Mark inspiring tender emotions, somehow.

Cassandra shrugged her shoulders, a smile playing about her lips.

"What?" I finally asked.

"Just that you assume it would be a guy," she said, looking amused.

"Huh," I said, not knowing whether to apologize or what. I wondered if there was a chapter on it in *The Female Eunuch*, which sat unopened beside my bed.

"It's true," I said. "I'm pretty stupid when it comes to those things. I don't have any openly gay friends. One of my friends I suspect is a lesbian, but she's only made these broad hints . . ."

"A *suspected* dyke, eh?" she said, smiling, seemingly enjoying watching me squirm. "It wouldn't be that blonde you were with at Sok, would it?"

"Yeah!" I blurted, stunned at her perceptiveness and then at my indiscretion.

"She gave me a few looks. She seemed a little queer. But it doesn't mean she's a lesbian. She could be bi. Bi like me." She watched me calmly as she said this, and I didn't know if it was to gauge my reaction or to show she wasn't timid about it.

"Bi Like Me," I repeated. "Sounds like it has potential to be a book *and* a major motion picture."

She chuckled, and looked into her empty mug. She got up and refilled it from the kettle and offered some water to me. I declined.

I felt a need to talk about my orientation, but whether it was to match confidences or differentiate myself I wasn't sure. "It's never been an issue for me. I can't even tell a good-looking guy from an ugly one."

Cassandra just looked at me.

"I know it's weird for a woman, because women can always tell which women are good-looking, but I just can't tell. Does this sound like denial to you?"

Cassandra shook her head. "It's kind of like a colour-blind person trying to convince a cop that the red and the green light look the same."

I nodded. "That's a really good way to put it."

"While I, on the other hand, explain that they both look green to me."

Something occurred to me, and put a twisted smile on my mug. I almost didn't say it, but then I did. "But with the alien encounter, wouldn't your orientation be 'tri'?"

She smiled broadly and slumped to be able to give me a kick in the shins. "Have you had sex as a fly?"

"Fuck no!" I said. "Bleaah! No way!"

"Why not?"

"'Cause I try to spend as little time as possible as a bug. I don't even eat, because garbage and rotting meat is what looks good to me as a fly. A fresh apple tastes like plastic."

"So you haven't experimented at all? Like to find out if you eat a lot as a fly if you're full when you switch back to human, stuff like that?"

I shook my head, hoping that she wouldn't ask me to. I imagined her horrified look as I re-humaned in front of her, naked but for disgusting globs of fly goop.

"*I've* been experimenting," she said.

I raised my eyebrows.

She picked up a spoon on the table and tossed it my way. "Hold that under the table." I did. "See, like it is, I can't make it disappear.'Cause I can't see it."

I nodded, hoping my face was calm. *God, I hope she can do it. I don't want this wonderful girl to be delusional. Although it would account for her interest in me*, a nasty part of me poked.

"Now hold it just a little above the table, so I can just see a bit." I did, and held onto the rest with a fist. "OK," she said, looking at it with half-lidded eyes. "Ready?"

I nodded, and the silver spoon disappeared. I held up my fist to look at it, and she gave a small laugh. "Weird, huh?" I opened my hand to see if there was any residue, and there wasn't. I almost looked at the floor but then thought that was silly.

"Check this out . . ." She reached over and grabbed my arm and pushed my sleeve up. Her hands were smooth and warm. "Now this is a trick that I wish I knew when I was a self-conscious teenager. It would have saved me a lot of pain."

I looked down at my bushy arm and suddenly a circle the size of a dime appeared in the hair. I touched it — it was smooth and sensitive, but I could feel tiny stubble.

"It didn't go beyond the surface," I said. "You can feel that it didn't take it down to the root," I said, and Cassandra touched it. I kept my arm as still as my rabbit-heart would allow, and with all my mental power willed her to keep her skin on mine.

She traced the perimeter of the circle, slowly. "And around the edge the hair is only half gone, so the circle comes out right." She looked up quickly and caught my half-drugged look.

She seemed amused. "What, is your forearm an erogenous zone?"

Wherever you touch me is an erogenous zone. "I don't know," I said, quickly pulling down my sleeve and looking down at the table. I wished I had jacked off last night. My head felt like it was packed, ear to ear, with stupid horny sperm, all attacking my tiny brain as if mistaking it for an ovum.

Cassandra picked up our mugs and carried them to the sink. I waited for the *Well, I should be getting to sleep* dismissal.

"Let's go to the living room," was what she said, and I felt excitement and anxiety at the same time.

Her living room was well named — it was exceptionally livable. Her couch was the epitome of comfy, a huge soft overstuffed patchwork beast. I made a beeline for it, tucking myself into a corner. She sat in the middle, turning herself towards me.

"OK, so the two of us have these incredible abilities, right?" She held her hands palms-upward as she said this.

"Right."

"We have to face facts. We're superheroes."

I shrugged. "Or freaks."

"No, if we had, like, a third eye that let us see into the future, we'd be freaks. As it is, we're completely normal when we want to be." Her face was very convincing.

I had always felt more freak than hero, but it was hard to explain. It was just an emotional thing.

"So why don't the two of us go out there and fight evil?" She said it with a smirk but her sincerity was plain. Other than the "two of us" part — which I liked — the suggestion induced the mental equivalent of watching a wall of a hundred TV sets, all tuned to different channels. Too much, too much. Too much to process.

Another part of me acknowledged that she was right. But I had many issues of my own to deal with — my mom being the biggest one. "It's just . . . with my mom and everything . . ." I had told her about that on our way here. And it sort of felt like an excuse, mentioning it so soon.

Cass nodded. "But there's nothing you can do about that."

Of course not, I thought. I was almost angry she had pointed it out, but that was stupid too."I've been conscious of my fly-thing" (I wasn't gonna call it *superpower*) "for my whole life. It's been enough for me to keep it a secret and try to research possible causes of it. I just want to keep out of trouble and the tabloids, Cassandra."

She laughed. "MAN CAN TURN INTO FLY: Wants quiet life, tells reporters."

"They'd have a field day with you, too, Alien Consort."

She was silent for a moment. "Why do you wear that?" She pointed to my Sailor Moon ring.

"It's to show my resistance to market trends, by ironically enjoying programming entirely outside my predicted demographic," I fluidly lied.

She rolled her eyes. "Bullshit."

"I'm a pedophile?"

She shook her head.

The extreme answers considered beforehand, the pure and the greasy one, were not true. Now I thought of something middling, yet somehow even more embarrassing. "Because I identify with Sailor Moon?!"

"Exactly. A bumbling little girl with all the wrong priorities becomes a hero. Admit that that appeals to you."

"Never," I said glumly.

Cassandra twist-pinched my arm.

"Ow ow ow OK! A little." She let go and I rubbed my arm.

"So are we a dynamic duo?" She looked at me with a bright-eyed grin and I realized that I did, indeed, want to be involved with this person, whatever she did.

I shrugged my shoulders and grinned back. "All right."

She sat back, relaxing her huckster pose. "So," she said, folding her arms and then unfolding them. "How do we seal this pact?"

I looked at her serious eyes.

I moved my head forward, infinitesimally. *Would removing my glasses be presumptuous?* was the thing I thought just before she kissed me. I managed to come to life halfway through, and it was over, her dragging away with a slight tugging on my lip.

"There," she said, and I moved forward and kissed her before her mouth could close over the word, Indiana Jones rolling under the stone door at the last second. I took off my glasses then, lifted my hand to touch her chin and kissed her smile, sliding my hand back past her jawbone to the back of her neck, stopping there and stroking that secret place.

She bent over and kissed my neck. Jesus. I jerked involuntarily — I'm ticklish. She pulled away, and my lips wouldn't form the words, *No, god I like that, keep doing that,* but I could look at her and kiss her there, under the ear, pull at her earlobe with my lips. "I can't believe you like me back," I said to her in a groggy, quiet voice.

It was then that I felt that this had been my whole life, an unspoken quest to find someone who *liked me back.* I hugged her and hugged her and that was it and that was enough.

But the way she rubbed her leg up between my legs was pretty nice too.

The next day was a bit of a write-off. I was cleaning the bathroom since it was my turn and because I was too happy to do school work. Pulling hair from the drain, on the other hand, was perfectly OK for my mood.

Phil opened the door.

"Lucky I wasn't cleaning the floor," I said. "Don't you usually knock on closed bathroom doors?"

Phil put the lid down on the toilet and sat on it. "Jack told me you were finally cleaning the bathroom."

"He said that? 'Finally'?" Jack was really good with cleaning up and I felt like I was a dodger in comparison. He *was* home all the time, mind you.

"Well, no, but he should have."

I was pulling out a tremendous rope of hair, soapy and multicoloured. It's quite a challenge to get as much of it out as possible, and I prided myself on my patient but firm pulling technique.

"I always think that if you pull it all out, you'll find a shrunken head at the bottom," Phil said.

"Ahh," I said, lifting a good half-footer out of the tub. I put it in the garbage rather than the toilet. I used to flush it, but then I imagined that it would cause huge problems for the city works guys — I had an image of four sturdy, grossed-out lads pulling a gigantic hair rope out of a sewer drain, trying not to slip in the greasy water dripping from it.

"So . . ." Phil said. "How did your thing go?"

"Well," I powdered the pink bathtub with Old Dutch as I pondered how to tell this story, this archetypal story that had been told so many times.

"We . . . kissed and stuff." I started to scrub.

"Really?" Phil said.

"Yep. My first kiss. We're not all experienced lovers like you, you know."

Phil chuckled. "So did you do it right?" he asked.

"She's supposed to laugh uncontrollably and then kick me out immediately afterward, right?"

"According to the Lee School of Good Lovin', she is."

"Then it was a textbook case, perfessor."

I turned on the hot water to rinse the tub. I said, "Look, I've just spent the last twelve hours in a romantic delirium. You can't expect me to say anything sensible. Less than usual, even. All I know is that we agreed to fight evil together, and then kissed to seal the deal."

"I knew you hadn't . . . you know, that stuff . . . Thank god . . . but didn't you play Spin the Bottle? Was it really your first kiss?"

"Yeah. The end of an era." I sat on the edge of the tub and stared out into space. "Well, I told you about my acne-and-chub-plagued teenage life. I wasn't unpopular, really . . . just undesirable. And unaggressive. And picky."

"How was it? Everything you expected?" Phil asked.

"More or less." I thought about it. "It wasn't the act itself, it was just amazing to me that it was actually happening. I had begun to doubt that it would. It was like this reaffirmation of faith," I said, throwing up my arms to the heavens.

Phil laughed. "Well, how was the reading?"

"Did you know that Jack read his love poetry about a person in the audience?" I hadn't talked to Jack. "Actually," I said, struggling off my knees, "let's get it from the horse's mouth." I tossed my little scrubber into the tub and walked out. Phil followed.

"I thought it went fine, though. But let's see how Jack perceived the event," I said over my shoulder, and the way we were walking down the narrow hall felt like the bits in *Dave Letterman* when he makes the camera follow him down the halls of NBC studios.

Enjoying the drama, I paused before opening the door, my hand on the knob. "What if we open the door and he's just swinging there? Gone and hanged himself?"

Phil said nothing.

"You have to clean up. People usually shit their pants, don't they? I'm not that close to Jack."

"I get his room then," Phil said.

"OK." I opened the door. Jack was sitting at his desk, back straight, tapping his pencil on his open notebook.

"Damn," Phil muttered.

"So Jack," I said, walking into the room and biting the bullet. "What happened after I left?" I asked, almost sitting on the bed-not-folded-up-in-a-couch but then remembering. So I stood there and wiped my damp hand on my pant leg.

"She said how much she liked them and I said they were about her and she said 'oh' and I ran away." He demonstrated the last, two leg-fingers dashing off across the desk.

"'Oh'?"

"Yeah, she seemed shocked and looked away."

"Well, you won't have to always be wondering, at least," said Phil.

Jack nodded, his face placid. "I was surprised she was so flustered, though. I expected her to deal with it cool-headedly, tell me she was flattered but not interested. But she didn't say that."

"Well, you ran away. Which was probably a smart thing." I turned to Phil. "Boyfriend's a big punk rocker, with blue hair and boulders for fists."

"Gravel for brains," added Jack.

"Now, now," I said.

"Doesn't write. How can he appreciate her? Why would she go out with someone like that?" he said, anguish peeking through.

"Maybe she likes having her own territory," Phil said. That was a good point. I was glad Phil was here, saying reasonable things, because my brain was orbiting Venus.

We stood there. I watched him tap his pencil on the book cover, wondering if it was possible to remind him *hey, it works sometimes, yesterday I was all lip-locked with this incredible person* without it sounding like I was rubbing it in.

"Ryan's got some good news," Phil said tentatively.

"I'll read the damn newspaper if I want the news. Get out. Shut the door." He turned back to his desk. "Let me get back to my oh-so-important writing." This was all delivered with good humour, so we left him.

Phil was ahead of me and he entered the washroom and shut me out. I stood there, not really thinking it was worth going to my room. I heard a fart and I pounded on the door. "Pig!" I bellowed. Phil tee-heed. He flushed and left, wiggling his eyebrows. I went in and kneeled down to resume scrubbing the tub.

Mary was trying on suit jacket after suit jacket. The one she had on was a thickly woven plaid.

"Well?" she said. I shook my head and looked back at the overcoats.

"Only if you can take the used car saleswoman jokes," I said. I took down an overcoat and draped it down my front. Too short. I wanted it to go well past my knees.

Mary had gotten into the leather jackets. "Whaddya think?" she said, popping the collar up.

"Very butch," I said, watching her reaction in a wall mirror. She smiled and tried the zipper.

I looked over at the counter woman, an attractive member of the gothic subcultcha, as were most members of the hip-used-clothing-retail-biz. She had two lip rings, one in each corner, and didn't seem to notice us.

I pulled an overcoat off a hanger and tried it on. It was heavy, but that was good since I wouldn't be wearing anything underneath. "Do I look like a World War One flying ace?"

"Is that what you're going as?" Mary asked. I had told her I needed a costume for a party. "Yeah, pretty much. You'll need whadda-ya-call-ems, though," she inarticulated, making gestures towards her face. I stared at her. "Goggles. The cute little goggle-things," she finally said.

"Yeah!" I said. I hadn't thought about that, but they would be cool, and hide my face too. I looked around, and asked the counter woman. She shook her head no, staring at me. I wondered what the intensity was for.

I went over to the mirror and took another look at myself in the overcoat. It was dramatic, and fairly cheap. I wiggled my shoulders around.

"It figures you're a closet soldier-boy," said Mary.

I decided against a closet joke. "It's a theme party. Heroes."

"And god knows there's nothing more heroic than being duped by propaganda and butchering civilians," sniped Mary.

I thought I looked pretty damn suave. I noticed it had a maple leaf patch on the sleeve, and that sold me. I went to the counter and watched as the woman used a huge pair of scissors to sever the tiny string and price tag. I gave her a pocketful of cash and avoided her gaze when she returned the change. Did I know her or something?

Mary and I left. "Why was that woman staring at me?" I said as we turned onto the water-ice sidewalk.

"She stared at me, too. It might be a weird eye thing. It reminded me of a condition my friend's friend had. He was always like this, up in your face." Mary got up in my face, popping her eyeballs. "He was this odd guy, so it was more disturbing than a pretty goth girl."

"Tell you the truth, I thought she was hitting on me," I said. "But, me being the married man I am . . ." I threw up my hand. "What could I do?"

"Married," Mary sluffed. "You may have been a one-date fling, just a convenient fella to kiss. Ever think of that?"

"She called me the other day," I said, skipping around a bit as we walked down the street, "Cassandra Cassandra Cassandra called called called." That was when we had talked about getting costumes. We had made plans to meet on Friday night. She had been very mysterious about her own costume.

"Ugh!" Mary gasped, pointing to the headline displayed in the *Toronto Sun* box: NATIVE PEACE WILL COST ANOTHER 40B. "The bias those bastards have is so bloody obvious."

I slowed my skipping.

Mary shook her head. "It's just such a loaded way to put it — oh, this place might have goggles."

We were in front of an army surplus place. There were khaki clothes in the storefront window, with a row of empty boots lined up beneath. It was as if the soldiers had been disappeared. As I looked at the plateglass, the reflection of a cigarette billboard caught my eye.

I turned and glared at it. Mary looked at what I was looking at, then looked away. "Yeah," she said.

"Maybe this place'll have rocket launchers," I growled.

We walked in. There was a guy behind the counter with your typical moustache and biceps, but the guy who greeted us was a hip club kid with baggy namebrand clothes.

He gave us a lackadaisical smile. I wondered why he was working here rather than a Club Monaco. I wondered why the displacement bothered me.

"Do you have those flying-goggle things?" said Mary, who probably despaired of my ever speaking.

He nodded and sauntered off. We went past displays of patchy backpacks, canteens and paperweight grenades. Eventually we came to a shelf with a bunch of the goggles. I picked a pair up. They were oily and heavy.

"All of these have seen action," said the kid distractedly, crossing his arms and looking in some other direction.

"It's for a costume," Mary said, probably wanting to make it clear that we weren't gun freaks.

He shrugged and played with change in his pocket.

I pulled it on. It was a good fit, and I could see all right. "How's it look? Is there a mirror here?" I looked around and Mary smiled.

I was led to a mirror. It was kind of geeky looking. As I was trying out my field of vision, I noticed a shelf of gasmasks. Off came the goggles.

Now *this* was more like it.

"Very heroic," Mary said.

The gasmask covered my whole face. It was heavier, but it would also disguise my voice. I pulled the price tag around so I could see it through the lenses. It wasn't cheap, but I could handle it. I removed them, and the club kid looked at me funny.

"Hey, you were at the Mothership a while back," he said.

I nodded, then asked, "Why are you working here?" I wondered if my tenuous connection was enough to make that question seem normal.

He shrugged, indicating the counter man with a point of the chin. "My friend's uncle. I'm filling in for him."

"Ah."

"So that girl you were with," he said. "Is she your woman, or what?"

I suppose I had started the snowball of confidences. I didn't know what to say, and I felt Mary's gaze even though I couldn't see her. I stuck with the facts. "Well, we were kissing the other day."

He smiled, and he had crooked teeth. I couldn't tell if it was a jealous smile or a smirk at my naivety in contrast to his depraved, club-kid sexcapades. He didn't elaborate, just offered to ring up the gasmask.

"Like he's doing us a favour," Mary muttered. He heard and glanced back, expressionless, looking at Mary for the first time.

I didn't wear the gasmask home, but I kept the overcoat on.

There was no one home when I got there — I was disappointed, because I wanted to flaunt my costume. But then I figured it was probably smart to keep it from Phil and Jack. It wasn't that I didn't trust them, but their knowing just statistically heightened the probability of discovery. Then I began to worry about Mary knowing what the costume looked like, but decided I trusted her — she knew the value of keeping a secret.

I hung up the overcoat and the gasmask in my closet, since I didn't have any special glass vacuum-sealed superdisplaycase to put them in. They looked kind of silly there, alongside my camping equipment, and I decided to keep my eye out for a discarded wardrobe in the trash. I couldn't remember if I'd ever seen one, but people throw out everything, eventually.

I checked my messages.

"Hi Ryan, this is Joe Crawford calling. It was serendipitous you came by the children's talk I gave because you had been recommended by a colleague of mine and I was about to look you up. I wanted to find out if you'd be interested in helping out with my work. What I'm involved with is the cataloguing of insect stories, from mythic references to anecdotes to urban legends, and I'm looking for an assistant to help with . . . well, a variety of things. Get back to me if you're interested." I took down the number, wondering if it paid.

The next one was my mom. She sounded tired, but since it was before ten, I called her back. I listened to the rings, wondering why I was hoping to get the answering machine, when she answered.

chapter seven

I took my gasmask out of the bag, pulled it on, and pushed the buzzer. I was a little early — I misjudged how long it would take to walk to Cassandra's place.

There was some condensation on my lenses. I rubbed them clean with a bit of overcoat sleeve just as I heard the door rattling and snapping.

The old lady from the first floor looked at me strangely so I removed the gasmask. "Cassandra's expecting me?" I said, less than assertively.

She let me in and past, muttering something that sounded Slavic or Hungarian as she locked the door. I left the gasmask off so as to negotiate the stairs easier.

I got to the landing and heard them in the kitchen, the sound of a sewing machine running. I pulled the gasmask down into place, and when I looked again, I saw Jess regarding me gravely. I started to take it off again, but she went into the kitchen, so I put my hands into my pockets.

There was a quiet exchange between the two, then Cass came out. "Well hel-lo there!" Cassandra said, some fabric in her hand. The look on her face was amazed and amused. "Wow!"

"Well, you called me Flyboy," I said. "And it's something I can be . . . and I don't need to wear a lot underneath."

"But you're wearing clothes now, right?" she said with a sly smile.

I nodded mutely. I had considered showing up "in full costume" as it were, but I thought it would be a bit creepy.

"I think the lady downstairs would have seen my bare ankles and called the cops."

"She woulda taken care of you herself," Cassandra said, heading back into the kitchen. "Have a seat. I'm nearly ready. Just doing some final alterations."

I sat down on the overstuffed couch and felt the fabric,

remembering with a pleasant jolt that we had made out here. I looked around trying to cement this memory. A small TV, a huge painting of an elongated man talking to (or eating) a squirrel, and some squat, rounded figures on a shelf.

Jess came and sat down beside me. She looked up at me, a normal kid thing to do except there was a slight tilt to her head that gave her gaze an analytical cast. She held out her closed fist, and when I lifted a hand she dropped a spool of black thread into it.

Cassandra appeared in the doorway, her eyes distracted and searching. She saw the thread in my still-open hand and snatched it back with a scowl, left the room.

I looked at Jess, her head still cocked. "You trying to get me in trouble?" I asked her.

She giggled and bit her lip and seemed distinctly unalien. I wondered why I even questioned Cassandra's story when, after all, we were meeting tonight to launch our equally insane superpowered adventures. It would make sense that our talents were not the only impossible things on earth — it *didn't* make sense that there were no other impossible things, in fact. Would I only accept things I was *forced* to, by the evidence of my eyes and experiences? Couldn't I just abandon my rationalism and float through life?

The sewing machine hadn't thundered for a while, so I expected Cassandra's entrance at any moment. Jess had slipped off the couch and was playing with the carpet, so I stretched out my arms, feeling the fabric of the couch. I suddenly had a vivid fantasy of fucking Cassandra right on that couch, and felt a little dizzy as the blood rushed away from my head.

"A new face in the fight against evil — Misplace!"

Cassandra faced me, hands on hips, looking like a total fucking superhero. She had this stretchy one piece, red and black, that went from her ankles to her neck. She even had a strip of it to cover her eyes.

"Incredible," I said. The pre-teen crushes I had on Rogue and other comic book characters came back to me in full force. No wonder I had been willing to go along with this idea. "And I like the name, too — Miss Place."

"That's Ms. Place," she said, waggling her finger. "It's no one's business whether I have a superhubby or not." She looked at Jess. "How do you like my outfit, kid?"

"Sailor Moon," she responded.

"You got the idea. OK, it's time for you to go visit Mrs. Grachie."

Jess nodded and ran to her room. She came out with a blanket and headed downstairs. "Bye-bye," she said to me, and I waved.

I almost had an urge to say *she doesn't have to go* — I think out of a sense of polite house manners, but as I looked at Cassandra I realized that I wasn't feeling polite tonight.

"Also," Cassandra continued, "I have this." She turned around (much to my delight) and showed me a small loop that had been sewn in at the back, about hip level. In the loop was a black dildo. She pulled it out and turned towards me.

"When I want to disappear something, I point this at it. So people will think it's the wand doing it. The magic wand acts as a decoy in case I get caught."

"The magic wand also looks like a magic dildo," I said.

Cassandra looked down at it. "Oh my god, you're right. It's not," she said, handing it to me. "It's wood. I painted and sanded it. I wonder why I . . . It's funny the way the unconscious, works isn't it?" she said brightly, without a trace of embarrassment. Her expression was more intrigued, as if by a scientific find. "But it does look exactly like a dildo. Not like mine, but like other ones I've seen."

Up until now, all of my knowledge had been derived from books. My experience in the field, as it were, was nonexistent. But despite this — maybe because of it — I can be as cool as the best of them when talking about sex. I kept going. "It would have a pointed symbolic effect. The dildo, I feel, is a perfect symbol for personal sexual liberation for women. Not that it's gonna smash patriarchy . . ."

" . . . but it may sodomize it," finished Cassandra with an evil glint in her eye.

"Ahhh!" I said reflexively. I was way out of my conversational league.

"I don't really think so . . . I mean, I agree with you, about it being a symbol of power, but I don't think it's appropriate. If I was able to make people spontaneously have an orgasm —" she paused, then clarified, "I mean, if that was my superpower, then yeah, the wand looking like a dildo would be appropriate."

"You could get one that really looked like a magic wand," I suggested. I thought the decoy idea was a good one.

"I was considering going with the whole witch thing, like all in black, since it's appropriate to a person who makes things disappear." She undulated her fingers at me. "But I'm really more a bang-and-crash superhero than a sneaky witch."

I hadn't thought about whether my costume really suited my personality — I had only been concerned with whether it was functional and cool looking.

Cassandra looked herself up and down in the full-length mirror on her bedroom door. "Do you think it's too sexy, though? I mean, it's no worse than a bathing suit."

"You'll have difficulty avoiding that particular problem." I murmured. "Perhaps if you were wearing well-padded sackcloth — no, you'd still have problems."

She grinned. "Well, at least I don't have a Barbie figure. The world weeps when another of those images are xeroxed. When I was young I used to think it was so unfair that I had breasts to be teased for but not be pretty enough for the boys to fall in love with."

"That's just crazy," I said, failing to come up with anything flattering that didn't sound patronizing.

"People *are* fucking crazy," she said. "That's just the way it is. Halfway through my high-school years I figured out that my shape was close enough to industry standards to afford me a certain type of clout. I figure my tits won me my place on the student council. All I had to do was ignore infuriating comments every so often, and be cheerful regardless of how I felt. If I got angry, it was dismissed as PMS anyway."

I nodded, feeling a twinge of guilt recalling the times I had accused my sister of the same thing.

"After that I sort of reacted against that fakey-fake lifestyle, and took great pains to camouflage my shape. But now when I do that I feel like I'm some upper-class type slumming because it makes her feel less like a rich bitch. But the bank roll's still there, you know? Anytime she wants, she's got an escape hatch. She'd be better off putting that guilt or energy or whatever into convincing her rich friends to donate money or whatever . . . using that power instead of denying it's there."

"Do you . . . think that applies to your disappearing power as well?"

"Yeah . . . yeah, I think that applies to that as well." She stopped adjusting her costume and turned her thoughtful eyes on me. "I feel like I'm going through a life change. I feel more inclined to *do* things . . . rather than *not do* things."

She walked towards me and slid her hand around to cradle the back of my neck, then slid her tongue into my mouth. After the kiss she looked at me and said, "I just wanted to do that. It didn't have much to do with what I was talking about."

"Haven't you always done things?" I said, my hands enjoying the smooth material covering her shoulders.

"Back when I quit the band I was sick of yelling all the time, and I deliberately took myself out of that kind of scene. It also had to do with taking care of Jess, but it was more than that. I was starting to see myself as a cliché, and that really wore me down."

"From what I heard, you weren't cliché. I don't think I've ever heard anything like that song. It must have . . . affected a lot of women."

She went and sat down on the couch. "Yeah. In retrospect I don't think we were, or I was, stereotypical . . . and we did a lot to inspire the women who came to our shows and listened to our stuff. But it's about how *you* feel, and I felt really constrained by the image of the band. So I started reacting against that, in a bunch of ways. Sometimes I even feel like not getting an abortion was a part of that."

"Really?"

"I don't know. I can't really second-guess myself." She paused. "Do you want a beer? I've got beer and juice. No coffee, though."

"It's all right. I'm tanked up anyway. A beer would be nice, though."

She got up and thumbed at the wall unit on the way out. I thought she meant the TV and had a strange flash of unhappiness — watching TV would be so boring compared to talking with her. But from the kitchen she called, "Put on some music, will you?"

I looked through the music and found a CD with a person holding a snow shovel on the cover and put it on. Punk rock with hard-edged female vocals issued forth from the speakers. I was relieved — I realized I couldn't bear a schmaltzy romantic soundtrack to everything we said.

"You know how you were saying that you felt constrained by the image of the band?" I called out to the kitchen. "Once upon a time I couldn't read in cafés or diners because it was so horrible to me that people might think I was one of those pretentious assholes."

She came out and passed me a bottle, listening. "But then you found out about free refills . . ."

"Yeah . . . I said, fuck it, I'm going to do it anyway and live the life. And here I am today."

She stroked the hair above my ear and I leaned reflexively into her hand. I was amazed at how natural it felt, this new language of touching. "So at some point the revulsion of being something you hated became less than the attraction of doing something you wanted to do. That's exactly what I'm talking about."

I was tempted to say, *yeah, we're so exactly alike* and enter into an impassioned smooch, but something held me back. "But *you* went and stirred the hearts and minds of a generation of punks, while *I* went to get a coffee." That plainly put, I even depressed myself. I took a long swig of beer.

Cassandra seemed a little annoyed. "Look. Different people use their energies in different ways. I never faced up to the fact that I had a superpower until now — I suppressed my memory of it. You lived with the fact of your difference for your whole life. That's a kind of strength."

Her reference to strength made me think of my mom — would having the wrong kind of strength kill her? She had the kind of strength that would let her forgive her ungrateful brats for anything, but kicking a habit she hated was something she couldn't do. Cassandra sat facing me, her red-clad legs folded under her, her brow knit. Why did I have to be so grim right now?

Then something occurred to me that made me suddenly and completely happy. "Cassandra," I said. "Can our first mission be to kill cigarette billboards?"

I gave her a second to absorb my suddenly jaunty mood and finished off my beer. I leaned back to set the empty on the crate she used as a table. It was stencilled BANANAS. I remember this so clearly because the moment I leaned back — *Did you find that crate in an alley somewhere?* popped into my mind — Cassandra lifted my T-shirt and started to kiss my belly and chest. I fell back on my hand, the ticklish sensation robbing me of enough strength to get upright. *Did it smell like bananas when you brought it home?* Eventually I was able to grab her shoulders and pull myself up and onto her body, kissing her face with a half-dozen hit-and-run-style pecks.

My mind, bizarrely, kept coming up with these dull, conversational remarks. I couldn't keep the next one from spewing out. "Did you know that the ancient Hawaiians had a taboo against women touching bananas?" I babbled. She couldn't have had any idea where the subject of bananas came from, it having evolved entirely in the closed bubble of my mind.

"*Real*ly," she said, jamming her hand down the front of my pants and violating ancient Hawaiian tradition. My jeans button popped open as she shifted her grip. "What was the penalty?"

It *was* death, but now wasn't the time to be a stickler for historical accuracy. "I believe they were forbidden to take part in the village chores," I said, "and banished to the beach huts until the next full moon."

And so inspired, I let my hands be as bold as hers, pressing up against her breasts, up and down. I pulled the springy material of her costume away from her tits, slid it back and forth against her pebble nipples.

"And what was the penalty for *ravishing* a banana?" She squeezed my cock and my cleverness disappeared, the squeeze causing it to spray out of the back of my head in a fine mist.

"Uuuhhh," I said. I was deep within the sugary-sweet sex fog, and I aimed to make her equally stupid, to strip her of her wit. I traced the seam of her costume down to where it bisected her crotch, and cupped it, rubbed it. Cassandra kneeled up from her position on the couch, pulling slightly at my penis to do so. It was painful, but better than being let go. She ground against my hand, and I worked my fingers, the base of my palm, the side of my hand into her pubic hair.

I had never done it before, never touched a pussy, but score one for instinct. She gave me a fast distracted smile, pushing hard enough for me to feel ridges through the material. She gasped and said *uh fuck* and then yanked down my pants. I had worn a pair of relatively new white underwear, but still worried for a moment about piss stains before she said, "Lie back, bananahead. I'm about to outrage Hawaiians."

I couldn't tell for sure that I was in her mouth, there was just a warmth. Then she increased the suction power, and there was a sensation that felt as fucking great as it sounded. (I don't know why I got off on the sound — more proof, maybe, that the ubiquitous-depraved act was happening.) She looked up, probably to confirm that I looked as stupid as I sounded, grinned and went back down.

I sat up so I could see her. I caught glimpses of her face, alternately amused and focused, as her waves of hair allowed. I felt the Y of her crotch just below my knee, and pressed up a bit.

"Uhng," she said mid-suck, and I *felt* the word that meant she was aroused and god it was good. I worked my left leg slyly and firmly into her crosshatch.

Her strokes became irregular and interspersed with little laughs. The idea of turning her on made me incredibly turned on. I realized that I was really close, and said, "uh, I'm . . . uh . . ." and she nodded. She stroked my balls, as if encouraging my sperm to come on out, and then they did.

Wow.

I saw white, then red, and gradually my body unspasmed, muscle by muscle in a pleasant roll call. "Oh, my, god, Cassandra, thank, you, that, was, oh, my, god."

She spat my come onto my pubic hair. "OK, now clean up," she said conversationally, wiping her lips with the back of her hand. "Then get your ass back here."

I lay there for a few more seconds staring at her, a smile invulnerable on my lips. She smiled and planted a closed-mouth kiss on them.

Then many thoughts occurred in lightning succession: Does she think an open-mouthed one would gross me out? What does spitting it out mean? It was the obvious thing to do, but it was still disconcerting when all I had as a learning model was the world of pornography, where people seemed to use it as a milk substitute. Was it a sign of assertion? Disgust? Practicality?

Fast as these thoughts came, Cassandra looked impatient, and I started to get up, putting a hand under my spermy friends and half hitched up my pants.

"Actually . . ." she said and looked at the jism, and it was gone. I felt where it had been, and there wasn't even any residue.

"That was a little close for comfort," I said. She unzipped her costume, pulled it off quickly and kicked it to one side. I stood there, staring, and she said, "What, did you expect a striptease? Let's get down to business."

She sat back in the couch, naked all over. She was imperfect, she was perfect.

I started to pull down my pants, slowly and still staring at her. I gave her a saucy look and spun around, wagging my ass and gyrating to every other beat of the punk rock playing in the background. Pants off, one sock, two socks.

She picked up her bottle of beer and let her eyes wander over me. When they (finally) got to my face, she blurted out, "You're blushing! You're blushing like a bandit!" I stopped my "dance" and, legs dramatically placed, removed my last piece of clothing. Slowly, I pulled my T-shirt over my belly, chest and head, gave it the traditional whip around and loosed it in Cassandra's direction. It missed her but she hooted out loud anyway and made as if she had a dollar to put in my G-string.

"For my finale," I said, and turned into a fly.

She looked around, and by the time she realized what was happening, I was on her tit and running for the nipple. She squealed and reflexively swatted, but in that incredible slow-motion way people have when I'm a fly. So I took off, and landed directly on the left nipple, then as she jerked, took off and headed to the right, then back again, and forth again, until she wised up and covered her breasts with her hands.

I dove down to her mostly exposed vagina and just buzzed around there for a few seconds before her legs started to crash closed. My take-off was a bit sticky so I was just able to drop between them and fly clear, last-minute X-Wing-outta-the Death-Star style.

Then I changed back and rushed to her side. "What's wrong? It wasn't that *fly* in here, was it? Making you all — itchy?" I started scratching her breasts and kissing her neck.

She smiled and leaned back, and I slipped two fingers into her pussy.

It was a new thing for me, but it was pretty obvious what to do. It was incredibly slick and warm and smooth in there, and I just kept pushing against that small hard clit in different ways, until I found a couple that Cassandra seemed to really like. And she was quite obvious about what she liked — the sharp intake of breath coupled with hair-pulling meant to *keep doing that*, a direction I (or any horse) could learn to follow.

I leaned into my work, using my free hand to squeeze and frisk her breasts, wondering about them. The nipples were obviously sensitive, but was the rest of the breast sensitive itself or was it just because it was so close to the nipple? I idly licked her brown nipple and it sent a shock through Cassandra. So, keeping my fingers pumping away like little oil rigs, I set myself to sucking first one nipple, then the other.

She hugged my face to her breasts with considerable force. I sucked away, gratified and amused by her sudden desperation. When she let me up to switch to the other breast, I craftily stole down south and gave my cramping fingers a rest.

I was expecting an incredible odour to assail me, but like most things about sex, it had been overemphasized. I remember grinding my rough tongue relentlessly over what reminded me of bedsheet folds, the trembly pressure of her legs straining against my jaw muscles, the feeling of pride I had when she came.

We lay there for a long time, while our wet spots dried.

I got home at ten the next morning — Cassandra had to work. We had breakfast with Jess, who didn't seem to be alarmed by the presence of another person at the table. She was more concerned with the absence of Cheerios.

I walked into my house, my gasmask in a bag, and sat down to unlace my shoes. Phil walked down the stairs and started putting on his shoes, tutting and hissing at me for using the shoe-chair.

"You're just getting in *now*?" he said.

I placed my shoes against the wall with a certain smugness.

"Eeeeewwwwww," he moaned. "Excuse me," he said, removing a pencil from his pocket and spoke into the eraser. "He's found another of his kind to mate with. The situation is now classified Red. Repeat, Code Red."

I walked away, a grin on my face.

"Come and tell me," said Phil.

I took the stairs two at a time. He didn't beg any more. Which was a good thing, because I wanted to tell him. I got to my room and closed the door, locked it by reflex.

I had realized on my walk home that there was no way to talk about last night without feeling like a bragging jerk. More than wanting to become a certain type of person, I had worked all my life to avoid becoming someone I hated — the bragging jerk, for instance.

All the same, I was glad he had seen me come in. Actually, it was perfect. I didn't have to compromise my nice guy persona and the word still got out. I lay on my bed and congratulated myself, hugging my pillow and imagining it was Cassandra. But unlike many such pathetic scenes in the past, the person whom I imagined hugging actually wanted to and did hug me in real life. There was a swell of joy at that thought and it swirled up from my spine-base.

I wondered what would be different in my life now, now that things had gone this way with Cassandra. I wondered what it would be like to hang out with someone all the time. I wondered what it would be like to have someone to lie beside at night who would hear my whispers, my farts and my sleeptalking. I wondered if she'd want me to move in. I wondered if I would love Jess. I wondered if I loved Cassandra.

The superhero thing was an afterthought. It was just something exciting we could do together. I had a pleasant fantasy of us fucking on top of some pebble-roofed building. I thought about how nice it was to have someone to go dancing with.

I checked my phone messages.The first one was from a cop.

"This message is for Ryan Slint. Mr. Slint, I know what you're up to."

My hands clenched the pillow. How had we gotten caught when we hadn't even done anything yet? I imagined Cassandra's face, stricken with anxiety.

The voice continued, and I realized it was the bug guy. "You're waiting for me to offer you a wage before you call me back. Well, so many people have spoken so highly of your skills and dedication that I'm prepared to offer you $15 an hour. I would have liked to offer it to you at the beginning, but the foundation grant was just recently approved. Please contact me as soon as your busy schedule allows." There was a touch of droll humour in that last comment, but it was truer than he knew — between school and building a secret identity (and, now, all the supersex), I hadn't had time to get back to him.

A girlfriend and a fifteen-dollar-an-hour job — all in one week! I checked the second message, presuming it would tell me I had won a vacation in Amsterdam.

"Hi Ryan, it's your mom. Call me back."

I hung up, I noticed, with unusual speed. When I also noticed how I had to relax my knitted brow, I knew there was something really wrong. A call from my mom, despite the fact that it brings back an unhappy reality, shouldn't *annoy* me. What was I angry at?

I thought about it for a while, came up blank. I dragged my ass over to my desk to get some work done.

chapter eight

"It's possible that this treatment will get it all out," Dad was saying. I had trouble telling if there was hope in his voice or not. He never took his eyes off the traffic, in any circumstances.

We were headed back to the bus station. There was just enough twilight to see that the trees that lined the streets of London were starting to sprout. Time passing, with my mother's illness, seemed dreadful.

As we crossed through the centre of town, a small cigarette billboard caught my eye and dragged a hiss out of me. "I hate those things. They're everywhere in Toronto. Cigarette billboards," I clarified, realizing that it wouldn't have crossed Dad's field of vision.

"Well, you can't have freedom of speech only for things you like," Dad said. "It's censorship. I'd say I agree with the Supreme Court decision."

When the decision was made to allow cigarette companies to advertise, after a several-year ban — or rather that the ban was an unfair violation of the corporation's Canadian Charter rights — I hadn't taken much notice. The companies had claimed that they would only be doing certain types of ads and for many months there were none. Then, within weeks of finding out about Mom, the huge billboards appeared.

We arrived at the station. Dad automatically got out with me, and we walked towards the squat grey building. "Well, I've heard there are some people who are exercising their freedom as well," I said carefully. "There's this billboard that says 'The Target is Satisfaction' and they've changed 'Satisfaction' to 'Children.'"

Dad laughed and I felt proud, 'cause it was my idea. "Clever. But vandalism is vandalism."

I tried to steer him away from that. "But don't you feel that they're in incredibly bad taste, Dad? Reminding everyone who's known someone who's died from it, always in people's face about how satisfying and cool it is."

I finished my sentence and turned to the counter. The old guy insisted on seeing my student ID before he'd give me the rate. It was annoying, because I was using it as a bookmark in one of my texts. I'd never been asked before — if my appearance screamed anything, it was STUDENT, to the extent where sometimes I worried people wouldn't take me seriously.

"I don't believe that people are controlled by advertising, Ryan," Dad said. "I don't think your mom was . . . tricked into smoking." He had finally broached the relevant subject, but I could see from his face that it drained him.

I didn't want to drain him, I realized. I didn't want to argue with him, to win. How would it help to show him that the world he worked for and believed in contributed to his wife's sickness, even if I could? I didn't say anything.

"It was nice that you were able to spend a couple of days with us," he said.

"I would have liked to stay longer, but school . . ."

He nodded.

We waited in line together. I could smell the smoke from an old guy a few people ahead of us in line. I looked at the ground, the concrete soaked with oil, and thought that there are few more powerful grime magnets than a bus depot.

Just to refute that, our shiny bus pulled up and Dad gave me a tight smile. "All right, Sid," he said with a handshake. (Calling each other "Sid" was one of our more absurdist family traditions.) "Stay out of trouble," he added with an extra pump.

I wondered, startled, if he had figured out that the billboard story was about our plans. I was barely able to mumble my response, "Take care, Sid," before I got on the bus.

I squeezed through the aisle and into a window seat. I looked out and, of course, he was there, and would be until the bus pulled away.

It used to annoy me that he wouldn't just drop me at the station, and this final watch was the icing on the cake. Did he think I was going to climb out of the sunroof or something, and catch a bus to Africa? All through my teenaged life, I refused to acknowledge the final watch and he would just stand there, sometimes the only one on the platform. Pretending he couldn't see in the dark windows, like he was only watching the bus.

As the bus pulled away this time I waved, suddenly, just to see. Shock registered on his face and he lifted a slow arm in response, and that was all I saw before the bus rounded the corner.

She pushed me against the kitchen counter and kissed me loud, playing with my ears.

"There's *people* out there," I whispered, lifting her hand in mine and kissing it, sucking at her knuckles.

Ken and Jess were laughing in the living room.

She watched my eyes, and I sucked her fingers. There was a whisper from Ken, a pause, and Jess appeared in the doorway.

"Water," she said.

I instinctively, guiltily, pulled away from Cassandra, but her hand closed on mine. She said, "Don't. It's OK."

Jess repeated. "We need water. Ken said."

"A cupful or so," he called.

"A cupful," Jess repeated.

Cassandra stood and watched her child silently. Mystified by the scene, I started to look around for a cup.

"Pleese," Jess said, and Cassandra went into action, filling a tumblerful of water and handing it to her. Jess ran off. Cassandra looked disappointed.

"What? She didn't say 'thank-you'?" I said.

She nodded.

"I'm surprised you care about stuff like that," I said.

She shrugged. "I think it's good to be appreciative of things people give you. I was always glad my mom taught me that." I nodded. "It's not all crap, the normal parenting stuff, but you have to sort it through for yourself. My first inclination was to do the opposite."

"Beat her mercilessly, feed her crack, dress her in blue —"

"Exactly." She threw open the cupboards. "See? No cute kiddie stuff, either. That was tough. There was this one set with Peter Rabbit that almost broke me. It looked like the one I had."

"Why didn't you get it?"

"Half a week's pay for that fucking thing. And it's not really for the kid, the kids don't care about stuff like that. It's for the parents, so they can talk about how cute it is and so they feel like good parents. It's a fucking con."

I noticed how she used the plural of *parent.*

"My parents used to send all this expensive crap, child-sized phones and stuff like that. I got them to just send money. I told them that every fifty bucks sponsors a day of me staying home. So I get a few days a month that I get to stay home and play with Jess, which is more important than having cute little Nike shoes or whatever."

It sounded great. My parents were not into giving money, however — they liked to see me opening the gift and my eyes lighting up and that crap. "And your parents are into that?"

She nodded. "Yeah, they even put 'Cassandra/Jess Bonding Sponsorship' on the little line for description on the cheque."

I laughed at that.

"My parents are really open-minded. Ex-hippies. A little hard to live with, though. They've always got some drama going on." She rolled her eyes and I smiled, imagining what kind of shenanigans two reefer-smokin' oldsters could get into. "Not stable, but supportive. Mostly."

"Mine are straight as straight can be," I said. "I wouldn't mind a little drama . . . although what we've got now is pretty dramatic, I guess."

Cassandra's eyes dimmed a little. "Yeah . . . how is your mom, anyway?"

"It's weird. I mean . . . she's really kept her spirits up. But I find myself so mad about the whole thing." I looked over at her. She seemed to be half listening to Jess and Ken, but I kept on. "A little bit mad at my mom, for being so unchanged and brave and fatalistic. At myself for . . . I don't know, not suffering enough? The most important person in my life is going to die and I can only find the time to visit on weekends?"

"It can go on for years, Ryan. Years where she's constantly stressed out for putting everyone's life on pause."

"It's not, like, rational, I know, I just get all angry thinking about it. If I was really depressed, that would make sense."

"Well, this thing about killing the billboards."

"Yeah, but even that." I lifted my hand and dropped it. "It's not *pure.* I hate the companies for . . . squeezing profit out of misery, but my mom's choice to smoke comes into it, too. And we don't even know for sure that smoking's the cause."

"There's always a good reason for inaction," Cass said. "Always some perspective that shows that it's more complex than you thought at first. But —"

"Help!" came from the living room, and my thoughts broke and ran for the pastures.

"That's the call to action, Flyboy," said Ms. Place, and we burst out into the living room. Ken was innocently painting the canvas and Jess seemed fine — fine, that is, except for a blue streak on her chin.

"Did someone call for help here?" Cassandra said.

"Nope," said Ken, whistling out of tune.

"Yes," said Jess. "Me." She pointed to her chin. "He painted me!"

Ken made a face. "Meeeee?"

Jess broke out in frighteningly loud laughter, her little body convulsing. Ken had really worked her up.

"So how's it going?" I asked, taking a look at the canvas. The blue and white depiction of a smoking teenager in rifle crosshairs was almost finished.

"Have you been bothering Mr. Ken, demon seed?" she asked her child, smearing the paint into a pentacle design.

"Aw, that's a cute pet name," I said.

"She kept telling me to paint her, so I did," said Ken.

"Not like that!" said Jess.

I looked at my watch. I didn't want to keep Ken for too long — I had called him on short notice and now it was almost midnight. We decided to take him into our confidence — about doing the billboard, but not about the rest — and he was into the idea, as I thought he would be.

"I didn't know if you could draw real people," I said.

Ken snorted. "This is the easy stuff. Especially with a source," he said, nodding to the magazine scrap Cassandra had found. "Well, it's pretty much done."

Cassandra stepped around and looked at it. "Wow, that'll be perfect. Eh?" She looked at me. I nodded. The depiction was striking and the blue paint gave it some style.

"Any other stuff?" he said. "Maybe I'll just finish off little demon seedy here." Ken moved towards Jess in a monster-style, and she held up the paint brush she was clutching as if to ward him off. Ken fell to the ground, covering his eyes.

Did Jess do something to him? was my instant and panicked thought. I looked at Cassandra (frozen shock) and to Jess (who yawned hugely) and back at Ken (back on his feet and smiling at me).

"Whoa, that's one powerful entity you've spawned, Cassandra," Ken said, rubbing his eyes.

Jess yawned again, and sat down.

"One pooped entity," she said. "I'm gonna put her to bed."

She picked Jess up. I made a mental note to ask her if she was thinking what I was thinking when Ken collapsed.

The man himself was oblivious, putting on his shoes. "So does she have a pet name for you yet?" he whispered. "Funny monkey?"

I shook my head, folded my arms, smirked.

He had a hand on the doorknob. "So let me know how it turns out." I gave him a thumbs-up.

After he left I had time to get myself some orange juice, stretch out on the couch and think with a shock about how comfortable I felt at Cassandra's place before Cassandra herself reappeared.

She went to look at the canvas again. "I was thinking that I could get some red paint and redo the crosshair parts like that. We could use it for the word part, too. I was going to ask him for his help with that, too, but I figured we could do it ourselves."

"Smarrrt thinkin', lady," I said, winking. "He'd probably do it but I don't want to waste his time with something we can do ourselves."

She was curled up on my body, and it was uncomfortable but there was also something really nice about it. "Do you think it'll be OK? Maybe we should go with the paint idea . . ." she mulled, looking over at the canvas.

I had originally pictured doing it that way, but then Cass had found these pictures of billboard refacements in a magazine called *Adbusters*. Some "culture jammers" in Sydney, Australia, had subverted a car ad with canvas overlays. "No," I said, trying to sound more sure than I felt, "I'll be the one up there and I don't want to be fiddling with stencils and cans and stuff."

"That was a weird moment with Jess and Ken, eh?" she said, evidently done with the planning for the evening.

"You mean with him clutching at his eyes? Yeah."

"Sometimes I wonder about her having . . ."

I nodded. "Well, with her heritage. Not that my parents can do anything cool . . ."

"She really enjoys drawing pictures."

"Yeah." I had seen the kid's work on display at the Fridge Gallery, under magnets. "But they're crappy."

She whacked me in the chest with a full-out fist. "Fuck you! She's not bad for three."

I laughed. "I know one-year-olds who could smoke her ass."

She reached up and tried to grab my nose, but I wouldn't let her. She tried jumping up and down on me but I started moaning ecstatically. Almost spilled my juice, though.

"Actually," she said, mid-jump. "*Actually*, there was one time when I was looking all over for my hair scrunch thing and Jess comes up and hands me this drawing. I'm in this huge hurry so I smile, you know, and go to put it up on the fridge so I won't scar her for life. When I put it up there I notice it's a toilet, which was strange, but even stranger is that Jessie doesn't want me to put it on the fridge. I go on looking for the scrunch and eventually have to leave. A week later I find it, *guess where?*" She jabbed me in the chest. "Guess!"

"In the toilet?" I said.

"No, behind it." She looked at me, annoyed. "I would have noticed it sooner if it was in the —" she broke off, leaving me for the lost cause I am.

"Huh. St. Anthony, look out!"

"Don't spout your religious propaganda at me!"

"He's the guy you pray to when you've lost something," I said in a singsong know-it-all voice.

"They have a saint for that? How petty."

"That's just what a heathen like you would say."

Jab.

Sitting at my desk I wrote on the line provided for *Subject*: FLY TRANSFORMATION NOTES. I opened the school book up and put the date in the corner.

I've done this before, I realized with a disorienting wash of déjà vu. Grade two, science experiment. *Wow, I had completely forgotten.*

I was so enthusiastic about the project — the teacher's explanation of the scientific method that promised to unravel even the most puzzling of conundrums, from gravity to ballpoint pens. If it could explain why a piece of metal moved things as if by magic, explaining my strange condition would be child's play . . . or so my child's mind reasoned.

The next week we had to talk about our ideas for a project. Ms. Blanchard, who always scared me a little even though I always did my homework, went row-by-row. Someone wanted to change paper into money. Ms. Blanchard told him that that was impossible, and no one could do the impossible, could they, class? *Nooooo,* said the class, and I felt butterflies cocooning in my tummy.

Someone else wanted to see how long they could survive underwater. I thought that sounded great, and looked down at my book — "How To Turn Into A Fly" — and had a happy moment thinking about how useful this knowledge would be, almost as life-enriching as knowing how to read.

Then Ms. Blanchard's high-strung voice cut through the air and slashed open the cocoon in my stomach, releasing the butterflies. "What would happen if Kelly drow — got hurt while doing that?" Several kids shouted out, *drowned, dead, killed,* and although this didn't answer her question she went on. "Right, class — so no experiments on yourself, or other people . . . or pets."

I looked sadly at my proposal and scribbled it out, with two different colours of pens so no one would know. With seconds to spare, spurred on by the bawling out she gave one unproductive kid, I came up with a less exciting alternative.

I spent the next few weekends sullenly threading Styrofoam balls to demonstrate the question "How Big Is Our Solar System?" My mom asked me what was wrong, but I couldn't tell her — she had showed me that flies were dirty, that the fly swatter (filthy as it was) was an instrument of justice. My only hope had been to figure out why I was this way and then show her it wasn't my fault that I was also a dirty insect.

My next serious fly memory was watching the Hulk. The poor dumb guy was constantly hunted by the legitimate authorities, which was terrifying for me — the *army* was after him, not just some freak-killing mob. I realized that if anyone found out about me I would be experimented on, have my wings pulled off, tempted with delicious sewage to test my endurance . . . Luckily, I had an edge over Bruce Banner — I had no equivalent to "hulking out," and didn't spontaneously transform except when I thought "I'd like to be a fly." So the rest of my life, until meeting Cassandra, had been governed by caution.

There had been plenty of temptations in my early life — my teenage hormones had wanted very badly to see the girl's change room through multi-eyes. Then I had discovered (in chronological order) pornography, masturbation and a way to keep said impulses in check.

There were many reasons why I didn't do the change often.

1. Being naked after the change made for logistical problems.

2. If the changes were of any duration, parts of my body became

coated by a green, jellylike goo that made me nervous and just grossed me out.

3. My main motivation for turning into a fly was mostly to watch girls undress, and I felt that this was immoral. I was quite religious during my teenage years, when I wasn't stealing pornography and getting drunk.

4. There was always the chance that I could be swatted or attacked by a cat or something. I was quite sure death meant death, and I didn't relish the idea of my mother having to deal with a crushed and naked son, despite it having some melodramatic appeal in my depressive moments.

These reasons were good ones — some founded in rational thought, some more emotional, but good reasons overall. But over the last few years they had lost their power. I don't know why — they just had. So I had mostly been staying in my old, untransformative self out of habit more than anything else, until Cassandra came along.

I sat before my new booklet, smoothing out the fold, and started to let out the curiosity about myself from the Pandora's box where it had always been. I started with Cassandra's question:

If I ate/defecated/mated while in fly form, would it carry over to my human form? (Looking at it, I changed "human form" to "natural state.")

What is the green goo? (I changed "goo" to "substance" and added "caused by prolonged transformations?") Is it biological or chemical in form?

On my desk sat a specimen jar, opened, with two rotting rinds from fruit that I had eaten the previous week. The apple and banana were stinking, by human standards, but I ignored my revulsion as I prepared to transform. I checked the door one last time, placed my glasses on my desk, and *bugged out.*

The most blatant change is my visual scope. It zooms back and instead of the porthole of human vision, I've suddenly got *fly-o-vision,* with hundreds of images giving me a sharper and more comprehensive view of my surroundings. My wings vibrate, giving off this low-level buzz, and I can move in all directions with a thought. My movements feel spastic, and for the first little while it seems like I'm inside this tiny ship, controlling it with mental commands.

After buzzing around for a while, looping and feeling the air roar and rush against me, I become more connected with my fly body. I'm ready to land on something.

The tremendous speed at which the fly moves makes this more

challenging than it sounds — the surface of my desk approaches far too fast for comfort, and for a long time I couldn't land because I couldn't will myself into hitting something that fast any more than I could stop myself from blinking when someone fakes a punch. It feels like falling from a building, or rather how I imagine that would feel. So I have to become very conscious of the sped-up world of the fly, and imagine that I'm inhabiting a fast-forwarding movie. When I do hit the ground, my hair-thin legs absorb the shock like springs. The mass of the fly makes the shock almost nothing, anyway. It kinda feels like jumping on a trampoline.

Walking on something integrates me completely with my fly body. From the moment I transform, my brain knows I'm a fly — but there's a delay before I *feel* fly-ish. Fly-walking is different enough (sticky, multi-legged) to make it completely click home that I ain't human no more.

Anyway: walking on my desk, I became conscious of a delectable odour. I pointed my proboscis north and walked towards the apple core and banana peel.

Halfway there, I nearly walked into the lens of my glasses, but realized in time to circle around, gawking at the intricacy of the hinge, the fine detailing that I was never able to see because — duh — I couldn't be wearing them and looking at them at the same time.

The core looked like a glorious Grecian pillar, the irregularities smoothed out by the mist that covered it, like a swath of gauze. It even formed a little pool around the base, and I stopped there, poking out with my proboscis. I looked up and realized, *Now if I was a normal fly I would have flown rather than walked.* I lifted off and landed on the side of the core, happy there were no other flies around to see my mannish behaviour.

I had barely landed on the brown, spongy, divine-smelling surface when I started to vomit bile on it. I originally thought it was drool, because it didn't have the gut wrenching that human vomiting did, but when it started to hiss and bubble I realized what it was. I saw with distaste that some of it slid down the core to dirty the desk, where Man-Ryan often ate. The bile had turned a small portion of the core into a pudding softness, so I (mentally) took a big breath and poked my nose into the mess.

It was like drinking a milkshake through a straw, but a dizzyingly delicious milkshake laced with opium. *More, more* was all I could think, and when I finished the part I had dissolved, my body ejected more bile, but this time I could barely wait for it to do its work. I tried to focus enough to note the sensations — it was sweet, so very sweet, and filling, but not flavoured any particular way, apple-y or otherwise.

I lifted off from the core and landed drunkenly on the peel. I went to a soft part and spewed. This time I couldn't finish it all, but I had enough to discern that it had no particular flavour either, and was a little less sweet. It still tapped immediately into my pleasure/euphoria centres, however.

I was totally bloated and had trouble taking off. When I got to the middle of the room I willed myself back to human form, and my vision snapped back to single-view. No more bloating. No feeling of having eaten — in fact I was a little peckish. I stumbled to my bathroom, my feet feeling unnaturally unsticky, and took a look in the mirror. I had green goo all over my face. I looked down to see my body coated with the stuff. I scraped some off of my cheek and put it on the side of the sink, for later transferral to the sample jar.

Looks like fuckin' larval eggs, I thought as I stepped into the shower stall. *Lucky I didn't decide to experiment with mating.* This conjured up an image of tiny insect eggs along the lining of my stomach that made me ill.

The same feeling of disorientation I got after becoming a fly happened when I reverted to human form. This numbness, this physical-mental incompleteness, accounts for why it wasn't until that moment that I realized that the green goo coated my lips, my tongue, the inside of my mouth, as far back as feeling went in my throat — the Vaseline-consistency residue going, perhaps, all the way down into my stomach.

After the first painful, gut-wrenching vomiting into the stall, I was able to make my way over to the toilet bowl and continue ejecting bile for an undetermined amount of time. I swear I could have smelled apple, but it was just as easily a delirium-induced odour. My scientific objectivity was only good for so much.

Hot water washed off the green substance with no trouble, as usual. I went to the kitchen, ate some dry bread (to get rid of the bile/goo taste) and then hit my bed. Just before I switched off, I realized that Ms. Blanchard had damn good reason to forbid self-experimentation.

"Fuck it's cold," Cassandra said. "You must be fucking freezing."

We had parked a few blocks away and I had immediately begun shivering when I had left the car. I had expected to — I was naked but for my boots and my overcoat — and the excitement of the moment distracted me. I shrugged.

"All right, tough guy," she said, and looked up at the billboard. At least it was the same one. Cass had had a last-minute panic attack that they would change the campaign and make our preparation useless.

I looked at Cassandra and caught her smiling at me. "You look funny without your glasses," she said.

I had left them at home since they inevitably got smeared and dropped when I bugged out. "Better?" I asked.

"Different," she said. "Like I'm committing crimes with someone I don't even know."

I wondered if she was serious. I would consider wearing contacts if it would make me more attractive. I know that makes me sound flakey, but I would. Some people have told me they like me in glasses, though, so it's hard to get a definitive reading.

Thinking about the contacts-glasses debate got me thinking about something other than my goo-anxiety. My experimentation, instead of relaxing me, had made me more fearful of bugging out than ever. And instead of talking it through with Cass, I had decided to play Mr. Ready-For-Anything. It was not a role I was particularly suited for.

We were at the base of the billboard, which was aimed at the oncoming highway traffic. We hoped it would turn a few heads in morning rush hour at least, because we had heard that the more visible alterations were covered up pronto by the sign company, to prevent negative attention directed at their clients and copycat crimes.

Cassandra took a look around. She was going to handle lookout, and so hadn't dressed in costume. The area around us was dead, however, a vacant lot — we had to slip through a crack in the fence, but it was pretty easy to get to. "OK," she said. "Be as quick as you can." She removed her backpack and hefted it.

She hurled it in a fantastic arc. It hit the billboard a third of the way up and fell to the ledge. We had a tense second waiting to see if it would fall farther, but it didn't. "Give us a kiss," she said, and I did, and (before the kiss-energy wore off) turned into a fly.

It was hard going, because it was windy, but I got up to the ledge. A strong gust of wind almost bashed me against the billboard — so I switched back.

I was standing on the ledge, in the glare of the lights, pale and stark naked. I stepped gingerly over to the bag and pulled the canvases out. I could hear laughter from below, and *heh-hehed* myself, but I just wanted to get the job done.

We had prepared the back of the sheet with double-sided carpet tape around the edges and had found a long, collapsible metal pointer. I extended that and checked to see that it reached above where we needed it to go. It did.

The first one was a breeze. The target symbol on the original was on the lower middle part of the billboard, so I was able to place and smooth out the picture of a kid smoking by hand, only using the pole for the top corners.

The second one, the word "Children," which was to subvert the slogan "The Target Is Satisfaction," needed to be placed a lot higher. I shakily lifted it with the pole and slapped it over the word. Damn! It was a little off. And Christ, my balls were freezing — unsurprisingly — I mean, my little buddies weren't used to the light of day, never mind sub-zero temperatures.

But the corner was secure, and by sliding the pole along the word I got the rest of it, tracing where I thought the tape was. I took the pole away and squinted at it — without my glasses it looked fine, but I wasn't sure. I heard a muted round of catcalls and applause from below and decided that the job was done. I dismantled the pole, put it in the bag, and leapt off the ledge as if diving into a pool.

I kept my eyes shut, chicken that I am, but had a real good stretch in freefall.

I wasn't sure about distance so I bugged out early. I watched the bag land a few feet from Cassandra and I buzzed down in a quick series of spirals.

Zap! I threw my human body on Cassandra, who crumbled with quiet screams. "I knew you were gonna do that, you bastard!"

Ecstatic in my goo-less human skin, I frantically rubbed my naked body over her wool and cloth, muttering "So warm . . . oh so warm. Feel my balls. Just feel them. They're ice, I tell you."

She struggled up and grabbed my overcoat, throwing it at me. "I'm not falling for that one, buddy. Let's scram."

I jammed my arms into my overcoat and pulled my boots on over raw cold feet. She wore the backpack. We walked away, sauntering as casually as can be expected, and when we got to the fence I looked back at the billboard. It wasn't as good as the ones in the magazines — we had fucked up the size a little — but it was legible, and it was done. I imagined my tiny white body skittering to and fro on that faraway ledge, my pale white bum displayed for the 4 a.m. highway drivers, and I looked with awe at the dark outlined girl striding ahead of me.

Before I met her, the closest thing to a cause I had was evading my demographic destiny. Now I'm a streaking culture jammin' revolutionary.

chapter nine

We had breakfast at about four in the afternoon. I was cooking eggs.

"I used to be vegan," Cassandra was telling Phil. "But when I was pregnant, I got nervous. I've always been iron deficient. So I started eating milk and eggs."

"Otherwise you would have died," I said, just then getting some cheese from the fridge. It made me nervous to have them talking about vegetarianism (she was and I wasn't, and we hadn't talked about it) and when I got nervous I got flippant.

"No, I doubt it would have made a difference, really. It was just the idea that if I miscarried or gave Jess a birth defect, I'd always regret it."

I watched to see how Phil would react to this unidle chit-chat. He sat, as usual, quiet and expressionless. Then he said, "A lot of the Korean diet is vegetarian, but western influence has made steak and such very popular. The heart attack rate, naturally, has risen dramatically."

"Yes!" I gloated, and then wondered how Cassandra would take this style of abuse-repartee. I didn't look away from the pan because I was worried about burning the omelette, and prove myself a walking, talking, Stereotypical Man.

"Just another case of cultural genocide by the white man," said Phil, a little louder.

"Well, you've got some blood on your hands yourself, if that sign in Ryan's room is true," I heard Cassandra reply. I had flipped the omelette like three times, but I flipped it once more just to be safe. It was ready, and I hadn't burnt it!

"It was just a damn fly," said Phil, pretend-frustration and anger on his face. I realized that I had never seen Phil genuinely frustrated or angry. Facially, anyway. With casual panache, I slid a plate under Cassandra's nose and she smiled at me.

I went back for my own and Phil followed me. He

looked in the empty frying pan and gave me a sad look. I popped the toast up and brought it over to Cassandra.

"'Scuse my fingees," I said and sat down.

"This is perfect," she said after a bite, and I gave an aw-shucks shrug.

"Any left for a poor hungry boy?" said Phil, looming over us, hand on belly.

"No room at this table for fly-haters," I said.

Cassandra broke a tiny flake off of her crust and put it on the table. "Here. Now don't you wish you were a fly, Phil? If you were a fly that would be a tremendous meal."

I laughed but had to fight back a small wave of nausea as I remembered my fly-feeding. I felt a little ashamed of that whole episode, really, for some odd reason — like a bad drunken night. I hadn't told Cassandra about it, and the secrecy made it worse.

Phil went over to the fridge and got an apple.

"So how do you know this guy?" Cassandra asked me, nodding to Phil.

The first real friend I made in Toronto. But I have trouble with sentimentality before breakfast, so when I said it I put *friend* in scare-quotes. She asked where we met.

"Don't tell her," I said. "No one can know about —"

"Same mental hospital," Phil said. "Of course, I was the doctor."

"*I* was the doctor," I insisted. "Unless doctors wear straitjackets, Mr. Longsleeves."

"I'd ask where you met him," Phil said to Cassandra, "but we already know *far* too much about you."

"Bastard," I said, sure that I was red as a beet.

"Cassandra blah blah is so, so blah blah . . ." Phil rattled on.

Cassandra smiled and looked into her omelette. "Shut up or I'll have to smooch him in front of you."

"You know I've never seen Phil and Melissa kiss?" I distracted.

Phil shrugged and filled a cheek with apple, obviously so he wouldn't have to speak.

"There's no proof of intimacy," I said. "For all we know they could be cousins — and not even kissing cousins."

Phil laughed. "Yeah, from the Italian side of my family."

Cassandra finished her omelette and looked at my plate. I moved the last bite of toast and she slipped the plate from under it. "We in a hurry?"

"A little bit. I told Mrs. Grachie we'd be back to pick up Jess in the afternoon." She clattered the plates together and moved over to the sink in a way that recalled the first times I had seen her, a fluid but calm waitress.

I looked at Phil and he looked as if he saw it too. I was inclined to say something about it, but it felt wrong . . . but then it felt wrong that it felt wrong. If there was really nothing wrong with waitressing, why wouldn't I tease her about it?

"We should get back in time for the six o'clock news at my place." She scrubbed the plates and put them away. I stood up and got ready to go.

"Seeya," Phil said as we swept out.

"Make sure you put that in the garbage," I said, pointing to the apple core. "Don't want to attract —"

"Yeah, yeah."

We weren't in the papers — neither the suburban *Star* nor the redneck tabloid *Sun* — and we weren't on the news. The billboard refacing had gone totally unnoticed by the public at large. Cassandra was mad. When I came into Sok a few days later, she had been to see the billboard.

"They took it down — it's like it was never there." She was really crushed. I'd never seen her so down.

"Well, I mean, it's been two days."

Her hope, when it wasn't covered the day after, had been that it just hadn't been discovered. I hadn't expected much, so I wasn't nearly as disappointed.

She called me a day later. "So can you meet me tomorrow at noon?"

My first instinct was to say, *yes, anywhere, anytime*, but I went the less pathetic route. "Uhhhh . . . it's Friday, right? I don't have a class until 2:30."

"Good. My friend Pat has agreed to give us a primer in media outreach. Do you know where the school paper is?"

I didn't know what she was talking about, but she sounded revved up, and this was a good thing. "I'll find it."

The next day I found myself at the information desk in a school I had attended for three years, feeling froshy. "I'm a-lookin' for the *Varsity.*" I used the silly pronunciation to mask how stupid I felt.

The woman at the desk showed me a map in the student council–produced agenda book, and pointed at the right building. She let me have the book, too. "There's some good coupons in there," she said, and I nodded.

It was in a totally different sector of campus, a large renovated house that reminded me of my grandma's place. I approached by the side door — the front was locked — and just walked in. It felt funny, just walking into someone's house.

There were two people in the room, one working on a computer and the other pinning sheets of the paper to the wall. The headline read "Another Valentine's Day Massacre," and the photo was of one of the poetry readers at the FUCK LOVE performance.

"Hey, I was there," I said to the person who had pinned it up.

He, a short black guy with glasses rather like mine, nodded. "Our arts editor wrote it. So don't blame me. I just lay it out. I don't even read it." He seemed to switch gears. "You new here?"

"Yeah. I'm supposed to meet Pat —" I looked at my watch — "ten minutes ago."

"We're in here," came from an adjacent room. It wasn't Cassandra's voice.

The guy I was talking to went back to his work, turning away so I was unable to give him a goodbye nod. It bothered me, not being able to achieve polite closure. I told myself I'd wish him well on the way out.

In the next room were a bunch of desks and cubbyholes, and behind one of the screens were Cassandra and, I presumed, Pat. I had assumed that Pat would be a guy, but Pat was not. I felt a moment of shame at my predictable sexism.

"Sneaking in the side way, eh?" Pat said, eyeing me and tapping a pencil on her fingers.

"The front's blocked." I nodded to the door that led out onto the street, which was mostly covered by boxes.

"The front's over there," Cassandra said, pointing the opposite way from where I came. "Haven't you ever been here?"

I admitted *no* and Pat burst into action. She got up and walked into the front room, which was bustling with people. "*This* is the Front End." The phone started ringing. "All these good people are *Varsity* staffers." Many of them waved at Cassandra and me. "They're doing various important things but I'm *sure* one of them will eventually answer the phone." It rang once more before a harried Asian girl answered it. "We have staff meetings in this room, too." She pointed back the way we came and we obeyed.

As we were leaving, the Asian girl called, "Pat, for you on line one."

Pat waved around the room. It was less chaotic, and looked like serious work could get done in the cubicles although there was none getting done today. "This is Central Control. All the editors have desks here, but most of them aren't here today since we went to press last night. That's the Production Room. Lemme take this call."

Cassandra walked into the other room and was immediately chatted up by the guys in there. I stood at the doorway, not wanting to crowd them, and listened to both conversations.

Pat: Well what would be the point? Why would I have said that?

Cassandra: We would have to wax them up and paste each page together.

Guy: Yeah, it used to happen like that. Before my time. What paper did you work on?

Pat: (Laughing) Bullshit. Such bullshit. Whered'ya learn to lie like that, man? It's a gift.

Cassandra: *Martlet.* The University of Victoria newspaper.

Pat: OK. And let me know about Saturday.

She hung up. Her face was delicate and expressive, but she usually assumed a placidity that made her inscrutable. The ability to invoke calm, or at least the appearance of it, must have been valuable for her in the newsroom setting. I was thinking about this when I realized that she was waiting for Cassandra, and had nothing to say to me. Cass returned, and I was relieved that I didn't have to make conversation.

Someone came in and asked Pat about the next staff meeting, and she rattled the date and time off as she sorted through two piles of papers. Then she gave one pile to each of us.

"Just some stuff I've come across about media activism. Let me give you a bit of background," she started, launching into her talk without a formal beginning. "I've been in the student press for four years in total. I was attracted to it as a valuable way to extend my activism, and now it's extended to the point where it's the most significant expression of my activism. I don't really give too much credence to the idea of journalistic ethics — it seems to me to be founded on a false premise, that of objectivity, and geared towards reinforcing the liberal status quo. So my personal ethics are more important to me than maintaining journalistic distance, which is why I'm talking to you."

She looked around. "Do you guys want a coffee? I want a coffee." We shook our heads. I looked around for a chair as Pat strode off in search of da bean juice. Cassandra already had a seat, and gave me a raised eyebrow look as she flipped through the small pile of materials we had been given.

Pat came back, calling "With a sponge, maybe," over her shoulder. She slipped back into her chair and set her huge mug of coffee on the desk. "Now. If I was a normal straight newshound with an eye towards getting a cushy *Toronto Star* job, then I wouldn't be telling you the ways to get media coverage. But give me an example of what you're trying to get coverage for." She looked at Cassandra when she said this, so I stayed quiet.

"Well, two hypothetical people go out and alter a cigarette billboard."

Pat took a sip of coffee. "Do they document it?"

"You mean, with photographs? No."

"Do they contact any news sources? Show that it was politically motivated rather than senseless vandalism?"

"No. They just assume that this very public act will naturally attract news attention."

"Not too many things automatically attract attention," Pat said. "Especially if they don't have the key ingredient: conflict. Which brings me to my key lesson in perpetrating media activism — always provide an angle that involves conflict. The media can't do much without it, but when it's there they can hardly resist it."

"Conflict?" I asked. I envisioned a huge city-wide battle involving me, Cassandra, Godzilla and the Riddler. Pat looked at me as if trying to read me, and her attractive eyebrows were phenomenally expressive. They said *you can speak?* to me.

She turned back to Cassandra. "Say you've taken interest in the Shell boycott. Ken Saro-Wiwa was murdered while he was educating his people about the negative effects of Shell's oil fields in their country. It may not have been an assassination ordered by Shell, but they certainly benefited from the silencing of this activist — you decide it's important that the public be made aware of this connection. How would you go about it?"

I opened my eyes wider and Pat laughed. I didn't know why. Cassandra gave her a look. "Dunno, Pat. Why don't you tell us."

"Well, you could put out a press release about this international issue, addressing it to all the dailies."

I opened up my backpack and fetched a pen and paper. I scribbled "1. Press release to media outlets."

"On what kind of letterhead?" Cassandra asked, focused.

"Whatever letterhead you want it received on," said Pat. "Sometimes that's the organization you're paid by. Sometimes it's 'Students for a New

World.' Sometimes it's 'Stopping the Deadly Shell Games.'"

I liked the last one, and grinned. Pat was tossing this info mostly off the top of her head, and I couldn't help noticing what a fetching head it was.

"The press release was coupled with a well-organized poster campaign, a flyposter that had Ken's face and tragic story. There was a call for people to boycott on their own, or join the rallies for the cause."

This was new to me. "There was a rally? What was the turnout like?"

"Well, it was pretty weak, but a rally is a standard of left-wing organizing — I'm pretty used to them," she said, her face a little tired. "But generally, the old guard handles that part of it, and the younger people get the interesting things going."

"Like?" said Cassandra, sounding a bit impatient. At the time, I wondered why.

"Well, in the Saro-Wiwa action, we had a great way to present the blood on the hands of the Shell corporation." Her voice dropped. "A couple of people made up these red paint balls from light bulbs and went to a bunch of gas stations at night. They hit the signs so that the yellow signs were just dripping with red paint." Pat's face was beaming and her hands came to life.

"So the press release, in addition to hyping the rally, made mention of how there was a renegade group doing these actions, and while they were unconnected they were still supported. The bloody signs made for a great visual, too. We also provided numbers for interviews, via phone of course. But a lot of groups do that — have a legitimate, 'front' organization and a direct-action, guerrilla wing to carry out the less-than-legal activities."

I was impressed. This was a clever setup, and my mind worked to see how we could make it work for . . .

Obviously, this was what Cassandra was thinking. I looked over at her and she had a small smile.

"I've got something planned for a women's issues event, Pat," Cassandra said carefully, "and you've got the best activist experience for the job. Would you be able to help us?"

"I can't take on anything else," Pat said immediately, looking at me. "I can't afford the time. But I will be able to be a consultant to whatever projects you've planned, and I have a pretty big network."

"In your network," said Cassandra. "Are there any media-savvy women who would help me with an unorthodox project with a feminist angle? Who'd be able to handle press releases, video, computer communications?"

This was the first I'd heard of any of this. I tried to look filled in and watched Cassandra get to business. Her face was intense and her lips were tight, in contrast with Pat, whose casual manner seemed a little too casual.

"You know the little maxim about being judged by the company you keep . . ." Pat said, looking everywhere but at me.

I stopped taking notes.

Cassandra stood. Cassandra walked out.

At first I thought she was going into another room for something, but then I saw her actually leave the building.

Pat gave me a shrug. "Nothing personal."

I started to ask her what she meant but she lifted the phone. I shoved my stuff into my bag and left.

"I can't believe that bitch," Cassandra said when I joined her outside. "Can you believe her?"

I had never hear her refer to anyone as *bitch*. "That was weird."

"I'm sorry I put you through that," Cassandra said.

I shrugged, a little unsure as to what I had been put through.

"Let's get some pizza."

"You think you can just throw pizza at the problem?" I said, adjusting our route so that it aimed towards Cora Pizza. "And what about these secret plans? I thought we were a team, Ms. Place. Or maybe you figure me more for the loyal sidekick . . ."

"I was just planning on the go," she said, a little guiltily, perhaps. "Brainstorming. I've had this idea for the Take Back the Night rally, and she would have been a good person to help co-ordinate it. But she's not really trustworthy." She looked at me. "Do *you* know any high-powered PR dykes?"

"Um, no. Do they have to be dykes?" I asked, the slur sounding odd off my tongue.

"I guess not. But she's got to be a she. I'd feel weird if it was a guy handling the press for a women's event."

"I know one friend who'd be interested," I said, thinking of Mary, "but I don't know how hip she is to press releases and such. She's in my bio class . . . oh, you know her — Mary."

She thought a second and then nodded. "Right. Haven't met her yet."

I smiled, satisfied. We both had a mental sketchbook full of partially completed drawings of each other's friends.

There was a bunch of people outside the parlour, mowing down on quarters of pizza. Most of them were U of T students — I could tell from the school jackets and age brackets. The tree branches bounced gently with the arrival and departure of tiny birds, their ball-bearing eyes on the bits of crust below.

Cassandra ordered a veggie slice and I followed suit. We got our crusted items and went to sit outside. Without fanfare, Cassandra said: "So Pat and I fucked for a while, back when I was working for the paper. Before she was editor-in-chief, she was the women's issues co-ordinator, and we worked on this article together for the annual queer issue. It was an article about different brands of vibrators." She chewed and swallowed. I waited, entranced.

She looked at me quickly. "Well, Pat convinced me that her journalistic integrity would be violated if we didn't do rigorous testing."

"No choice, really," I said, leering around a bite of pizza.

"Yeah, so I don't know how you feel about that." She watched me, waiting for an answer.

I didn't feel jealous about it, for whatever reason. "It doesn't arouse feelings of jealousy, if that's what you mean. It arouses . . . well, it just arouses. But it would have been better if I had known about it in advance. 'Cause now the way she was acting towards me makes sense."

Cassandra nodded. "There's more to it, more than just our relationship. She's not exactly male-inclusive when it comes to feminism. She's actually pretty separatist."

The whole scene became a lot clearer. "On one level," I said, "it makes perfect sense. If she's gay, what use does she have for men? Actually, it's kinda weird that gay men and women get along at all, because they have nothing to unite them."

"Except a common political cause," Cassandra pointed out.

"That's true." I thought about something else that bothered me. "You know, if Pat was a guy, and he had been involved with you, and then he dissed me like that, I'd really be pissed off. But I just don't find Pat . . . threatening."

Cass looked as if she had eaten something sour. "Well, you're pretty fucking stupid, then. She'd fuck you up without half trying," said Cassandra without malice, and I believed her, but I didn't feel any more fear. "I guess you're a little homophobic, and a little sexist."

"Yeah," I said, surprised and dismayed.

"Better that you know it and admit it," Cassandra said, then frowned, catching herself. "But I *would* say that. I really want you to be special, Ryan, not just some average jerk."

I nodded. I felt a little safer and a little less fraudulent.

"They were some of the first people who welcomed me to the city," Cassandra said. "The queer community, I mean. I've always had my problems with the separatist thing. But it was pretty open from the beginning. I was pregnant, after all, so everyone knew I was bi."

I thought about the alien element. "They didn't know you were interspecially pregnant, I assume."

She looked at me funny. "Is that a word?" I shrugged. "Nope, I didn't tell them about that. I may have gotten more social points for being with an alien rather than a boy, however." She mulled it over.

"Was it a boy alien?" I enquired.

She nodded. "Yes." She was down to the crust. "I was really drunk at the time, so the first thing I remember thinking was *what a darling little skinhead boy.* The purple light let me know that something weird was happening, but it was kind of soothing. There was this overwhelming smell of lilacs, which was an improvement from the foot smell that usually stank up the van. He climbed on, and put it in, and started to move pretty much the way humans move, but smoother."

She finished her pizza. I wasn't halfway done, but I couldn't pay attention to my food. "Smoother," I said.

"Yeah. After a few minutes, I came, he came, and then I fell asleep."

"So you came. With the alien." It didn't sound like what I had imagined. "Didn't his spectral, bug-eyed face put you off at all?"

"I couldn't even see his face. They're really small, Ryan," she said, motioning chest-high.

"Except where it counts, apparently," I said dryly.

"It was this uncanny feeling of floating on a purple sea," she said.

"Huh," I said around the jealousy in my mouth, thinking how the green-headed monster was impossible to predict.

chapter ten

I walked up the stairs to our porch. Jack was sitting there, reading a book with a shiny rocketship on the cover.

"Hello, friend," he said, with a small smile.

It was just warm enough to be outside comfortably. I sat down beside him, on the wooden chair; the cushioned chair looked better but I knew from experience that it would be slightly damp until late May.

"What's that about?" I asked. I kinda knew from the cover, but I asked anyway.

"It's a Ray Bradbury collection," he responded. "An old favourite of mine. They're short stories about the sad and difficult times Earthmen had when they tried to settle on Mars."

"You've read it before?"

Jack nodded, looking at the book as if he expected it to attest to this. "Yep. This time I started seeing all sorts of odd political undertones that I never noticed before. 'The sentimentality about Earth bespeaks the xenophobia so prevalent in the mid-fifties'—" he started, in his Irritating Prof voice, then stopped. "But I got swept up in the melancholy of it, the red dust and the ancient dead."

Jack looked in a bad way. I didn't know whether to try to joke with him or to just let him continue along this weary path until he could see his sun cresting the ridge. The porch suited the latter approach, and silence prevailed.

He didn't go back to his book, though, just fluttered the pages. "I suppose it was — I know it was — the only thing I could do about Val. The poetry reading, I mean," he said, realizing that I wasn't with him in the last half-dozen synaptic links that had occurred in his mind. But I didn't really have to be, and I nodded to let him know that I had been following in my own mind.

"I guess I had to let her know. It was eating at my gut. It's like a what-if universe that poisons this one. You know, like those comic books — 'What If . . . The Hulk Could Think?' 'What If . . . The Fantastic Four Had Different Powers?' What If . . . Val Had Feelings For Jack?"

He smacked the side of the book into his palm. "Do you want a beer?"

I nodded.

He got up and grabbed a pair of empty bottles from the other side of the chair. I was automatically alarmed, and when he went in I stood briefly to count the remaining store of empties. Five. I sat down, feeling nosy. It was a little worrisome, though — I'd never known Jack to drink alone.

Well, he wasn't alone now, another voice in my head said brusquely.

And when he came back with the beer bottles he was grinning. *Company cheers the soul, and a drinking partner doubly so*, I thought.

"I don't regret doing it," Jack said, twisting the cap off with a *psst*. "I do wonder if the *way* I did it was the best advised."

I shrugged. "It was a dramatic choice," I said. "I think it was a gutsy move. If she was interested, I think that she would have been swept off her feet."

"But she's not interested," Jack said, glumly. "And there's the rub. So the performance was really just an opportunity for me to get up in front of friends and make a frickin' fool of myself."

He sounded upbeat, but he wasn't. This was my cue. "I didn't see any fool up there," I said, with a mixture of disinterested criticism, just-the-facts and quiet assurance. "I saw a guy reading some damn good poetry."

I let that hang in the air for a few seconds.

Jack snorted and took a slug of beer. "Yeah?" he said, and took another.

"Uh huh," I said.

"Well, you're not to be entirely trusted," he said. "What with a good-lookin' gal by your side. You were probably less attentive than your average bitter audience member."

I smirked. It felt like we were out of the forest and daylight was just over the next hill. I relaxed and took a swig of beer, remaining silent. I, of course, had a million things to say about Cassandra, but it was customary for the Single Guy to have to twist it out of the Lucky Bastard. I was patient.

"Do you love her?"

Jack was speaking in a casual way, but I knew that this was not something he would ask casually. I had expected, scripted, practised for *What's she like* — the usual first volley. But Jack wasn't in a tennis-playing mood.

And the thing was, I didn't really know. We had been so busy having fun that I hadn't considered if our hearts were as one and all that. I had been concerned with other things: how to be around her as much as possible without boring her, for instance, concerned me more than whether our passion was infinite.

"Um . . ." I said. I had always been somewhat dismissive of my crushes, my infatuation with girls that had always been a one-way thing. *It's not love if it's not mutual,* I had cautioned myself. But now I was in a situation where she might actually feel the same tugging. My mind immediately began playing out the potential scene, where I ask her if she loves me. She started calmly explaining that I was just a — and I yelled "Cut!" to freeze the scene and realized I was quite terrified of what Cassandra felt (or didn't feel) for me.

"I am very happy that she puts up with my hanging around," I said. "I realize that sounds pretty lame, but I don't really know."

Jack shifted in his chair, propped his shoes up on the railing. "Well — here's some hypothetical situations. A litmus test *pour amour*," he said, lifting one finger. "She has to go away — like to war or something unavoidable. Response?"

"Sinking feeling."

"Not bad, considering this is only hypothetical. Second: She starts avoiding you, for reasons you never understand."

I had a momentary feeling that these were culled from Jack's bumpy romantic history. But I concentrated, and imagined, and created a scene that was pretty anguish-filled.

"Anguishy."

"She starts going out with someone else."

I had been wondering about this one. I knew jealousy would come into it. I felt abstracted from the situation. I had been prepared to go with Jack's cue for male or female, but he had nixed that option with the ambiguous "someone else" — not "another guy." So I imagined Cassandra going out with Pat, keeping it to chaste images so as not to get turned on and all mixed up — them at the soda fountain, them looking into each other's eyes with a Christmas tree in the background, riding a bicycle built for two. Nothing. No response.

Then I imagined her in the same situation with an alien — snuggling up at the soda fountain, riding a specially adjusted bicycle built for two — it was more entertaining than anything else.

I tried to conjure up a guy, a faceless guy, hand in hand with Cassandra. But she wouldn't hang around some faceless hunk, so it fell apart.

I moved to a guy I hated — a guy from my high school, who had bullied and terrorized me. It was possible to imagine — he was a charming, handsome guy. I got an evil, sick feeling. But was this caused by hate of the bully or love for Cassandra?

I made a frustrated sound. And quickly, so he wouldn't assume that that was my total answer, I elaborated: "I've no damn idea. It's so convoluted that I can't even follow my own train of thought."

"Huh," said Jack from the darkness. He leaned over and placed the empty bottle on the ground with a *tink*.

I finished mine, and went in to get more.

The class had come to a merciful end. I had felt the weight of the pointlessness of school quite keenly lately — I was sitting in my seat, languishing, waiting for the professor to finish his seemingly interminable lecture.

The huge hall was half full, and I wished I was with the absent half. I had actually skipped the last four or five bio lectures, because what was the point? There was some kind of interest-draining field in these halls, some subsonic hum that prevented the absorption of knowledge.

I looked over guiltily at Mary, taking her complete notes in her oh-so-readable handwriting. She was the deciding reason why I was so slack, since she was willing to let me copy her notes. I would later read her notes, hear her voice in my head and think, *this is pretty interesting stuff,* although in class it seemed as interesting as the phone book.

But now, of course, came the price.

Mary was packing her books into her leather bookbag. I closed up my blank, token notebook and slipped it into my backpack.

"So, uh," I said, as if this minor piece of grovelling was new in my mouth. She didn't look at me but her face became expectant. "So, can I get a copy of those notes?" I was unspecific, avoiding "today's notes," because I actually wanted the last few classes' notes. Unless I was up front with that, she would balk, demanding more begging.

"It's not so bad when I think, 'Oh, he missed the class due to deathly illness,'" Mary said, "but when I'm sitting right beside you as you stare out into space, dreaming about what's-her-face." She threw a hand up into the air.

It was dramatic, and I figured it was mostly bluster. I gave her a mournful look. "I know, but you're doing it anyway. Why should both of us suffer?" She rolled her eyes and I went in for the kill. "And your notes are so —"

She cut me off with a raised hand. The look on her face was exactly the look when her tea was too strong, like with cheap herbal mixes. Considering I was trying to sweeten her up with honey-laden words, her expression was perfectly appropriate.

"All right. I just feel like your fucking secretary," she said, and I saw there was some realness beyond the drama, and felt like a bastard-fuck.

"Look, let me do something for you. I'll write an essay for you," I said recklessly, immediately regretting it.

She shook her head. "No. I'll think of something, though, Slint. You *wish* you can get away with a little essay. I'm gonna make you pay tru da nose."

I liked the threat in her voice. It made me feel less guilty for some reason. I got down to business: "OK, let's hit the library and we can get the copies done before we meet up with Cassandra." We moved out of the lecture hall, moving quickly because we had dilly-dallied long enough for the place to clear out. Because I was used to moving out of the hall sluggishly, brains and bodies thick molasses, moving at a regular rate in the space made me feel super-speedy. In the dizzy fast-forward clip, I had all the hope in the world that we could do the copying before meeting with Cassandra.

Mary checked her watch. "You've got it all planned out, you weasel."

I nodded with a smile, careful to stop it from curving into a smirk. "I would have just met you at the library, but I thought I would seem less like a mooch if I came to the lecture."

Mary shook her head. "Nope. Mooch. Brain mooch. Brain leech."

"I know it didn't work. But I try, you know."

We merged into the steady stream of students outside the lecture hall and something occurred to me.

"Oh! Um, Cassandra's going to ask you for help with something. I don't know what it is, but it's probably really exciting," I said, meaning it. "I'm just warning you in case you feel really used and abused."

"As long as it isn't you asking me for stuff," she said. "What is it?"

"I have next-to-no idea. Something to do with Take Back the Night. And superheroes." I skipped a little when I said this, and looked back to see her looking at me with a smile. I was glad, because I was feeling goofy and I wanted our decision to tell Mary to be the right one.

"Really exciting, eh?" she said, as we passed out of the building and crossed the street. U of T isn't one of those enclosed campuses, so we had to avoid a couple of taxis which seemed determined to soak and/or kill us.

"More exciting than crossing the street, even," I said as we arrived on the other side. The hot dog vendor a few feet away tempted me with savoury wafting and low low prices, but I resisted — we'd probably get something to eat with Cassandra. Now, it was the library or bust. I checked the time and tried not to do the math too exactly, because it was almost a quarter after and I was determined to get it done.

It was a conflict I often had — the knowledge (rational) that I couldn't fit two things in a thin timeslot, defeated by the desire (emotional) to do so anyway. It ended in disaster or delirious joyful success, an artificially created do-or-die situation. Doing a million things before I had to catch a bus or plane was a favourite. It was silly but fun.

We arrived at the library at the optimum time. I don't really know what it is — it's a phenomenon I've noticed but never cared to study — but there's a time (a magical time) between the hourly classes when the photocopiers are free and the lines for checkout are fast-as-hell. One day I would make a graph, the curve being the same for most hours but spiking at the lunch hours.

I had the card ready, and slipped it in, praying that I hadn't been optimistic in remembering the available credit — $3.20 came up and I smiled, smiled big, and looked over at Mary and hoped that my robo-efficiency had infected her.

It had. Once in, Mary was all the way in. She had the binder open and flipped through the pages, and didn't even scowl as she handed them over. I started the work, automatically dividing them into In and Out piles, leaving the lid open as it copied. The green glow made me feel like a mad scientist.

"That stuff gives you . . . radiation poisoning," Mary said. "The lid is lined with protective lead."

I realized that the pause was due to not wanting to say *cancer*, and I admired her ability to conversationally swerve with the reflexes of a race car driver. "All for the cause, Mary," I said, flipping and pressing. I glanced at the copies — they were coming out fine, with the black borders caused by the open-lid technique. It wasted some toner, but hell, for ten cents a copy I figured that toner was rightfully mine.

Time check: still within the realm of vague possibility. The card readout said $1.20. Just a few more . . . I gave Mary the thumbs-up signal and wondered giddily if superheroes got to feel this rush on a macro level. Would my nervous system be able to take the strain?

"Done and done," I said, handing a perfect pile back to Mary, who was distracted by a gaggle of girls. "Heads up, soldier, this is a precision manoeuvre." I said this as I made the copies disappear into my backpack and headed for the exit. I slowed, realizing my obnoxiousness just in time, and said thanks.

" . . . And I was like, 'What the *fuck*,'" one of the girls said. "'What the *fuck* do you think you're *doin'?*!'" The other two burst into laughter.

I held the door open for Mary and she passed, dropping my forgotten copy card into my shirt pocket. "Lucky you said thanks, precision-boy."

"Heh," I said eloquently. One day Mary won't be able to make an ass of me, and the other signs of the apocalypse will follow forthwith.

We sped across to the pub where we were supposed to meet Cassandra, speed-walking most of the way — giggling as we passed each other.

"That's running!"

"No 'tisn't!" In my best Monty Python dead-parrot accent.

We got there in perfect time, just as Cassandra and Jess were entering. We grabbed a table in the mostly empty pub.

"Hi Jess! Remember me?" I said.

She was sucking on her hand, and nodded. She looked very young in the bar, I think because she was so timid. In the house she marched around like a little adult.

Cassandra gave her hand a gentle tug, and Jessica voluntarily slurped it out just as the waitress came up.

"Well, you've already got something to eat," the waitress quipped to Jess, "but what about the rest of ya?"

We all chuckled and Jess smiled to see us laugh. I was momentarily locked in by her huge grey eyes, thinking again about her daddy, when Cassandra said, "I had to take her to the dentist today. This is my daughter Jessica," she said to Mary. "And you're Mary, right?"

"Sorry — Mary Cassandra Cassandra Mary," I speed-introed, embarrassed.

I was still gazing at the menu uncomprehendingly when the waitress came to me.

"Uh, I'll have what she's having," I said idiotically. Mary snorted, but very quietly, since she didn't know Cassandra well enough to let her veneer of polite charm drop to reveal the caustic charm underneath.

"I thought you hated fish," said Cassandra, looking at me with mild curiosity.

Instead of letting the concrete life preserver go, I clung to it all the more. "Today is the day," bloop, bloop, "Today is the day I give fish another chance." I could already taste the vile memory and smiled to hide my nausea.

The waitress went off and I focused on the conversation. "Well," Cassandra said, as if sensing my rejoining the conversation, "how interested are you in feminist politics?"

Mary gave a small smile. "Not tremendously interested. But I find myself . . . drawn to certain elements in that community."

Coy coy coy, I thought to myself.

Cassandra didn't even pause. "Are you queer?"

I held my breath. I had no idea how Mary would respond to this, I was even a little scared as I watched her frozen slack face. "I don't know if —" I started softly.

Jessica pointed suddenly out the window. "Mom. Birds." Cassandra looked at the spot on the patio where the many-coloured pigeons had landed, and nodded and smiled to Jess. Then she looked at me and Mary. "I know it's an obnoxious question, but we're going to be putting ourselves on the line with bigger secrets than who you find cute."

I realized that she was right. I was about to tell Mary about my fly-thing and I was still balking at prying.

"I'm bi," Cassandra said, "and I want to stage a stunt that will confuse, baffle and scare the big men of this city."

Mary looked her in the eye then. "Yeah, I'm . . . queer." Then she glanced at me. "Big secret, huh?" she said with an attempt at a grin. It was woeful, a little.

"That's it, Mary, you're out of the will," I said, and it fell flat but it was better than nothing.

"Good," said Cassandra, looking at Mary. "I like it when people have a personal reason to fuck shit up. It's the abstract theorists that I don't trust."

"I didn't know when I woke up this morning today would be the day," said Mary. "The coming-out day . . ." She looked a little shellshocked.

"Ah, quit yer navel-gazing," said Cassandra gruffly. "If Flyboy here figured it out, you must have been hinting pretty broadly." I winced a little, but Mary just smiled.

"Flyboy? What kind of pet name is that?"

"It's not a *pet name*," I said. "It's my superhero name. On account of my being able to turn into a fly."

The food arrived and everyone tucked in. Jessica seemed unaffected by her foodlessness, although she asked Cass for her toothbrush. I put my hands around my fishburger and hoped Mary would question me so I could delay eating this horrible-smelling thing, but she had taken my comment as a joke. I looked at Cassandra.

"Well, that's a little hard to prove right here, but he *can* turn into a fly. I've seen him do it. I also have a superpower," said Cassandra.

I admired her. She was playing it as straight as can be, and it sounded so terrifically absurd that I realized that Mary had not even begun to begin to take us seriously. "The ability to tell superhuman lies?" Mary said, not looking up from her plate.

Cassandra looked at me. Jess, white-and-blue toothbrush sticking out of her mouth, looked too.

"Well, make something disappear," I suggested. "Cassandra can make stuff disappear," I explained, feeling silly.

"And where does it go?" Mary said in a patronizing voice.

"We don't know," we both said at the same time, and I realized with horror that this just heightened the looniness of the whole conversation. Mary burst out laughing.

I suddenly had a great, two-birds-with-one-stone idea. "Make my burger disappear," I said. Cassandra looked at me, astonished. "We have to prove it to her," I appealed, trying to sound practical but the desperation kind of creeping into my voice.

"Are you stoned?" she said. "You'll still have to pay for it."

I opened up the burger. "Well then, just the fish. She can be very exact and just make parts of things disappear," I mentioned to Mary.

"No way. I'll have them wrap it up and eat it tomorrow if you don't want it, you lunatic. Waste food like that —" She shook her head. She picked up a salt shaker. "Now, they'll never miss *this*," she said.

"Oh come on!" I said. "A salt shaker? That makes it seem like a cheap parlour trick. Do you have a pack of cards or a rabbit?" I said sarcastically.

"OK," Cassandra said to Mary, "you decide."

Mary looked around. "I hate the bartender here —"

"No people," we chimed, and I put my hand over my face.

"You two are the fuckin' Bobbsey Twins," Mary said, then put her hand over her mouth at the swear word and looked at Jess.

Cassandra waved. "Forget it. Choose something."

"How about that . . . dang poster over there by the bar," she said, nodding at some Bud beer-babe poster.

"A little visible, but a well-chosen target." Cassandra glanced around. "Now you see it . . . and now you don't."

It, of course, disappeared, and revealed a patch of blank wall underneath. It was a bit stark, and the bartender slowly walked over to the wall. He touched it, and I looked at Cassandra a bit anxiously, but she was just calmly eating. I followed suit and before I realized it, I had given fish another try.

"Oh," I said around a mouthful. I had automatically taken a big bite, 'cause I was so hungry, so I was barely able to let my disgusted moans escape.

"Does he whine this much when he goes down on you?" said Mary.

"'ey!" I said, scandalized.

"No," Cassandra said smirking. "Lucky for him."

I finally swallowed, ready to defend myself, but they had finished. I looked at Mary. "Well?"

She looked at me. "I don't know how you guys did that."

"I didn't do it. She did it."

Cassandra waved her hand slightly. "It doesn't really matter *how* I did it. When we do this thing, this action or whatever, we're going to do it as superheroes, costumes and all — anyway, this is the plan."

She told us the plan, stopping halfway through to get Jess to come out from under the table. I listened, pretending I knew it already.

The bartender had returned to his roost behind the bar, no doubt trying to forget the oddity that had scratched his otherwise banal day. I know how he felt. Often, I think the brain struggles to erase the memory of strange events, because they're out of line with the worldview that allows you to function on a day-to-day level. It's like a burr of metal on a piston, an aberration that eventually gets worn off. But when the strangeness is a part of you, it's almost as if the piston is misaligned, or warped, and I don't really know what that does to your brain-machine. I guessed I'd find out.

"That fucko is a date rapist," Mary said, glaring at the bartender. "My friend . . ." she started, and then thought better of it. "I wouldn't mind seeing him . . . get disappeared? Disappear him? How do you say it?"

"Disappear him," Cassandra said absently. She was looking at the bartender and I had to stop myself from saying *don't*, because that would make it all the more possible if I had to ask her not to. It had to be *impossible*.

"That's what happens in Central America," Mary said, placing her cutlery neatly on her plate. "Enemies of the government are 'disappeared.' A bit sinister, that connotation."

I was glad she pointed that out, and I realized from the casual look on Mary's face that she didn't really believe that Cassandra could have disappeared that guy just as easy as pie. Or if she believed, she wasn't emotionally conscious of the reality of the situation.

I looked at Jess, who was looking at her mother. "Any cavities, Jess?" I asked. Jess looked at me and shook her head. Then she offered me her toothbrush, complete with saliva.

"Brush your teeth," she said. When I didn't take it, she gave it to Cass, who wrapped it in a bit of tissue and put it away.

"Let's get the check," Cass said. Then, "So are you in?"

"Sure," Mary said. "Until you find someone more qualified to be a superhero media agent —"

Cassandra made a noise with her mouth. "Qualified, schmallified. Make up for it with attitude. You'll learn as you go."

"Like us!" I said with a grand gesture.

"So you can turn into a fly, huh? How come you never told me?"

"I never told anyone," I said, smirking. "Sound familiar?"

She ha-haed.

"That's why I'm doing that stupid bug biology class."

"To give you greater insight into your buggy self? You'd think that if you had a personal reason to pay attention you wouldn't need to rely on *my* notes."

"You're a Note Copier?" Cassandra said with distaste.

Mary looked at me, waiting in vain for an excuse to roll out of my goofy mouth. "Aw, he's all right," she said.

chapter eleven

"It would be impossible not to love her."

We were on the subway, on our way back from my parents' place. The subject of our conversation, Jessica, was nodding off, her little legs sticking out off the seat like toothpicks in pants. Cassandra was looking tuckered, too, but she smiled.

"If your parents were determined to disapprove, they would have found a way," she said. "And your dad sure didn't have to show *that* much enthusiasm," she said. "Moms are obligated to *ooh* and *aah* a bit, but dads are exempt."

"He just went nuts!" I said. "Did you see him before dinner, fooling around with the salt and pepper shakers?"

Cassandra laughed. "Yeah. Lisa must have been spoiled rotten." She shook Jessica as the subway reached Bloor and we got off. It was late on Sunday night so the place wasn't the Tokyo hive it usually was. On the escalator I turned around. "Dad's love of kids isn't limited to girls, though. It wasn't until high school that he stopped love-bombing me — he was sorta awkward in the teen years, with both of us."

The subway light appeared in the tunnel, and the train trundled in its cartoonish way into the station.

"That's funny," Cassandra said. "My parents were just dying for us to grow up. I think I was one of the few kids who learned about sex from their folks instead of their friends." Cassandra shook her head, pausing in deference to the familiar roar of the subway. "They were just *dying* to tell me. I didn't even know what they were talking about at first," she said as we entered.

I smiled. I had a story about this topic that I had never got to tell anyone. I savoured the moment, sitting back and starting. "When my cornball dad came in and sat down on the bed — cornily — and said he was going to tell me about the Birds and the Bees, I thought, *Finally, the mystery's going to be solved.* Then he started talking about all of this stuff that had nothing to do with bees, and at the end of it I looked at him and said, 'What about the flies, Dad? Where do the flies fit in?'"

Cassandra paid me in copious laughter, so much so that Jessica came fully awake and looked around. She started squirming, getting up on her knees and pulling Cass's hair out of her scrunch.

"Ow! No, Jess." She fixed her hair. "What did he say?"

"I don't remember. If I was him, I would have been plenty disturbed."

The last stop had been Spadina, so the next one was my stop — if I was going to go to my place instead of hers. I had already decided that if she asked me to come over, I would; despite spending the whole weekend together, I wasn't antsy, or claustro, or bored. I picked up the strap of my backpack and leaned forward in a ready-to-go posture.

"99 KENNEDY 99 KENNEDY 99 KENNEDY," the subway loudspeaker blared, then proceeded to give an earsplitting litany of static subway babel that was seriously cramping my timing. I was beginning to panic that I wasn't going to be able to deliver my independent-yet-open-to-debate farewell line. Then it stopped.

"Well, I guess I'll head off to my hovel. Give you some Ryan-free time."

"You don't have to," Cassandra said. She was leaning back with her arms and legs akimbo, as if she was on the couch at home. "I mean, you're welcome to stay over. I have to work, but you can let yourself out."

"OK," I said, and we kept looking at each other.

"Your mom was really cool about the vegetarian thing," she said. Mom had made a bunch of dishes, most of which Cass could eat. "She was asking me questions about it. She showed me this file where she had all these veggie recipes she had clipped out of the paper. She said that she made them because she was worried about your dad's cholesterol, but he never ate much of them, so she and Lisa ended up eating them."

"Yeah, Sid's a meat fanatic. Took me out for steaks on my twenty-first." I had gotten more comfortable about the whole vegetarian thing when I saw how unjudgmental Cass was about it. Still wasn't exactly French-kissing her after a hot dog, though.

"'Heart-attack bound' is how she put it. I could tell how worried she was, her eyes went all spacey." Cass frowned. "I felt sad that she was more worried about him than about herself."

"She's still off the cigs," I said.

"Yeah," she said. "Hey, is there an ashtray shaped like a lung underneath your sink? I thought I saw that when I was throwing something in the garbage."

I nodded. Dad had brought it back from the States.

"OK, I just wanted to make sure I wasn't seeing things. I kept thinking people were talking about your mom . . . being sick, and they weren't. I was a little preoccupied with it."

I nodded. Now that I thought about it, that lung-tray was a little morbid. We used to think it was funny. "A lot of Dad's friends smoke," I said. Then it struck me that Mom shouldn't have to see that tray every time she opened the cupboard door to throw something out. But maybe she didn't even see it — maybe it was so familiar it was invisible.

"Here we is," Cassandra said. She stood up and put Jess's hand in mine. In the few seconds between breaking into the light of the station and stopping, Cassandra removed a magic marker as thick as my arm and wrote "NO MORE DEATH ADS" on a cigarette ad.

Jess laughed. "Good drawing, Mom!" she said tugging on my hand and pointing.

As if I could miss it. I felt my blood explode into my brain. The other subway patrons offered no proof they were even conscious. The subway stopped with a jerk — the movement made me burst into a light sweat — and we walked out.

Cassandra had tucked the marker away as casually as if she had used it to sign a cheque. We walked together, silently, until we had reached the escalator and the subway was long gone. Jessica's hand squirmed a little and I loosened up my nervous grip.

Cassandra leaned against the black rubber railing. "That was for your mom."

"Aren't you nervous at all?" I said, anxious and mad and proud all at the same time.

"Yeah, but I keep telling myself that they can't do anything to me." Cassandra spun around as she stepped off the escalator. "No jail can hold Ms. Place." She said it with a flair that almost masked the tremor in her voice.

I slapped down the three of swords and Phil winced. "Shee-it," he said. "I thought you already played that."

I smiled as I claimed the cards and surveyed my hand. "Senility strikes again."

We were at 50 Plus Donuts, an orange-and-grease-coloured place with a few old farts and a too-young counter girl. For some reason Phil and Melissa met here. I didn't really know why and it was time to find out.

"What is the appeal to this place, bucko?" I said. "Doesn't Melissa get leered at?"

"These guys are past leering," Phil said, nodding to one rubber-tire-lipped oldster. "Plus, I get here first." He tossed an ace of feathers down and won the round.

"Pull that feather outta your ass?" I inquired.

"That's nothin'. Pulling a sword outta my ass, now that's something to watch for."

We were playing Brisk, which is played with an Italian deck of cards with cups, swords, feathers (well, feathery clubs but we called them feathers) and suns as suits. I had a deck in my junk drawer, left over from my high-school days, and Phil had been intrigued by it. Amazingly, though I have trouble with my fucking postal code, I had retained the rules of this obscure card game.

So we would Brisk-it-up every so often, but hadn't had the guts to venture into the Italian coffee bars with our deck. I couldn't shake the fear that it would be confiscated by the owners in the name of Cultural Reappropriation.

"Hey, do you think if we brought Melissa with us we could play Brisk in the bars on College? With the old guys?"

"The Italian ones?"

I nodded.

"No way. What if you've taught me wrong? I would be mortified . . . Melissa would lose her citizenship . . ."

He won the next hand. I wasn't paying enough attention, more concerned with yelling and slamming the cards down than with actually strategizing. I had tried to impart this key bit of Brisk playing but Phil didn't get it.

Every so often my brain would murmur, *Tomorrow's the big day.* After the stuff that was going to go down tomorrow, who knows what would happen? We might have to go on the run. We might be captured by scientists somehow. We might get on *Late Night with Conan O'Brien.* I hadn't asked Cassandra what she thought about the show, but if Ani DiFranco played on it, how could she refuse?

I tossed my cards on the table and went up for another coffee. I brought up my cup and gave it to the dark-faced young girl. As she went about getting my double-double (being so exacting about the amounts you'd think it was a chem experiment), I looked at what she was writing. It was written in a different colour ink for each paragraph, so it wasn't for school, but there was a textbook — *One World, Our World* — underneath it.

She gave me the coffee and I paid. "Shouldn't you be working on your geography homework?" I said with a waggling finger. I was rewarded by a surprised and guilty smile and left feeling like my homey Holmes.

When I turned around, Melissa was taking off her jacket and sitting down. Noting with amusement the octogenarian attention locusing on her, I joined them.

"Come to play Briskola?" I said. The stray thought passed through my head that this might be the last time that I could kick back and relax with my two friends; then, it was gone.

She looked down at the cards for the first time and laughed. "You guys were playing?"

"Yep. Phil insisted I teach him. 'Maybe then,' he said, 'Maybe then Melissa's father will welcome me into his home.'" One of the only details I knew about their relationship was Melissa's disapproving father, and I jumped on it like a bed you know you're not supposed to, you're going to pay for it, but it's just *so much fun.*

"So how's it going?" Melissa asked, then focused her probe. "Oh! Phil tells me about some woman?"

"Cassandra," I said. "We went to visit the folks this weekend."

"*She* went with you?" asked Phil. I hadn't told him, as my retaliation for him never offering any information about *his* relationship. It was a low-level hostility, neutral even, but it was a hollow gesture: I knew we were meeting up with Melissa and he would find out when I told her.

"Yeah. Jessica too. Dad was nutty about that kid."

"They didn't react badly to her having a child?" Melissa asked, her eyes wide.

"No . . . I told them in advance, though, so it's not like it was a big surprise. It was good. The whole weekend was good. We didn't get sick of each other. I thought we would, but then I even stayed at her place on Sunday night."

"Oh ho ho," Phil said, shuffling the Brisk cards and wiggling his husky eyebrows. "You know what *that* means . . . it means I watched *The Simpsons* all alone!"

"We got home too late for it, anyway." I asked casually, "Didja tape it?"

Phil shrugged and became engrossed in the faded-out close-up photo of donuts that dominated the far wall. It was supposed to inspire purchases, but actually inspired fear.

"Well, that's a good sign," Melissa said. "That you didn't get sick of each other, I mean."

"Yep. I even had to bring her house keys to work, after I got up. I felt very grown up. I was swinging them on my finger all the way to Sok." Melissa looked a little confused. "That's where she works."

"Strip club," offered Phil helpfully.

"Diner. I had to sort of hand them to her on the sly, because I don't really know what past relationship she has with the cook. That is, I don't know how he feels about her. If I was that guy and some young punk sauntered in with the girl of my dreams's house keys, I'd spatchelize his ass."

Phil started to say something when a guy with a long brambly beard stopped at our table.

"I, uh, wanted to know if you had change," he said. I shook my head and said sorry. So did they. He gave a pull at the bill of his baseball hat — WordPerfect, the faded lettering advertised — and shambled to the next table. I wondered where his bag was, where he kept his stuff. When I noticed he was wearing a Batman jacket, I had the ungenerous thought that he was not exactly what the promotions department had in mind.

"Do you know he likes her?" asked Melissa.

"No. Maybe he's married. He's not hideously ugly. He's got pretty big arms."

"Well, if he can cook and he's built, he's probably got a couple of women on the line."

I shrugged. "He's got this De Niro thing going on, too. That's good, right?" I verified with Melissa. Sometimes I imagined guys were handsome and they weren't, and vice versa.

She shrugged. "Yeah."

"Yeah, he's got the mohawk and the gun that keeps popping out of his sleeve when he's trying to cook."

They both sat there in silence.

I floundered on. "Yeah, and every time I try to talk to Cass he thinks I'm talking to him. 'You talkin' to me?,' he keeps saying."

Still no response. Phil started to grin at my discomfort.

"You haven't seen *Taxi Driver*?"

They shook their heads.

"I recognize that line from an *SCTV* skit, though," said Phil. "Second-generation reference."

"Seen anything recently? That's good?" asked Melissa.

We took a while discussing the various cinematic fare. I had opinions on everything I'd seen, and a few I hadn't, and delivered them with the endearingly annoying gusto that is my trademark among friends. At times, I even forgot the events to come.

When the *Sun* box started to smoke, I knew we were in pretty deep. A minute earlier, a young girl had put change in the slot, but instead of taking a paper out she had put something in. Then she'd run away, her long hair swishing, and was welcomed back into the crowd.

By the cheers from the marchers, it appeared that the hatred of the right-wing tabloid was pretty universal. I kept looking back at the smoking box.

"They just started a fire in a *Sun* box!" I told Ms. Place, who was walking beside me, her eyes scanning the sidelines.

"Keep watching your side, Flyboy," she said. "And don't talk." I followed her orders. I didn't want to screw it up.

It was a beautiful day for an insurrection. It smelled like spring, which is a hopeful time to be marching. Cassandra, in costume for the first time since my first time, looked outlandish enough to stand out even in this crowd of diesel dykes, punk girls and odd-looking women.

With my gasmask and shapeless overcoat, I was presumed to be one of these odd-looking women. This was a women-only event, which made me a little tense and a little exhilarated. Every so often, this big woman with blonde hair would glance over at me and look suspicious.

Three young high-school girls about ten feet ahead burst out singing, in perfect synch:

No sleep till
that man is found
no sleep till
that man is out of town

Looking at them, I recognized one from that day I'd been at Who's Emma. Cassandra smiled at their energy, and I was relieved. I hadn't seen that since we had started marching. Superheroics should be fun, after all.

"There's supposed to be twenty of them," she said.

"They're probably hanging around together somewhere, since it's been a pretty ruly crowd."

Smashing glass and the roar of the crowd erupted from behind us.

I smiled. "*Somewhat* ruly."

"I'm just paranoid they've been tipped off, somehow."

"Well, the only person who knows other than us is Mary, and —" I broke off, holding my hand to my head. "I *told* you that she's the daughter of the chief of police, right?"

Cassandra put her hand up and squinched her eyes closed. "Don't."

"Wha-a-t? I told you about that, right?"

"I wish your mask had an elastic so I could pull it and let it snap back in your face."

I looked around again. It was a lot better than I thought it might be. The women were cheerful and only got angry looks on when they shouted. But there were kids and grandmas and a pretty good mix of races, too, all having fun and Taking Back the Night to boot.

"Shoulda brought the little superhero. Alien Girl."

Cassandra nodded. "I usually do but —"

"First target at two o'clock. See him?"

Cassandra tip-toed and said, "I can see his head. I'm going to have to make my way to the side. You stay on this side and make sure we don't miss any there."

I nodded and watched anxiously as Cassandra made her way through the crowd. I could see the cop, I could see that his arms were folded and his mind was closed. He had the archetypal cop face, layered cement with deep-set, dull eyes. His body language spoke his animosity, his crossed arms as symbolic as crossed swords on an ancient house's crest. I was *glad* we were fucking with them.

Ms. Place reappeared back at my side, her face flushed. The cop hadn't even noticed. I scanned again.

"Nine o'clock, three of them." She took off again without speaking. I kept looking, taking a second to look at the crowd around me. They were oblivious to what was going on, and the big blonde woman who had been watching me earlier was nowhere in sight. That was good, because I really had no answer to give her if she said something like:

"Couldn't let your girlfriend out alone for one day, could you?"

I had been trying to formulate a retort, or a defuser, but I was coming up blank. I presumed Cassandra would know better how to deal with it, anyway.

She returned, flushed. "Oh, it's so tempting to disappear their sandwiches . . . their hats . . . their moustaches."

"You didn't —"

"I said it's *tempting*, Flyboy. Did I miss any on this side?"

"Nope. Did they notice anything?"

"Not yet." Cassandra looked back at the three she had just hit.

It was a little like leaving behind time-bombs of mystery, randomly programmed. At any moment, they'd realize: *My gun is gone!* What would they do? How would they explain it to their superiors?

Ms. Place went ahead a little to hit the half dozen or so that lounged against the barrier. It was there to direct the crowd down the side street. She stepped out, within a few feet of the barrier, and pointed at each one in turn. One of them — just one of them, mind you — leered and winked from his spot lounging against the barrier. If I had the power, that barrier would have been sent off to Nowhereville. But Cassandra had more restraint, and slipped back into the crowd and met up with me.

"What did the fucker say?" I asked.

"Same ol' lame shit," she said. "But they saw me. The others might have missed me but for sure *they* saw me." She took my hand and held it, rubbed it on the fabric stretched over her belly. "We're on our way to notoriety."

I laughed. "I thought you were gonna say, 'We're on our way to jail.'"

"That too."

An hour after the incident (I imagined the police report saying), the perpetrator and her accomplice detached themselves from the crowd and entered an unmarked sedan. Witnesses say that the licence plate was obscured by mud.

"Hey, nice touch with the mud," I said to Mary, who white-knuckled the steering wheel through downtown traffic. Somehow I had ended up in the backseat. "Smart. And this is the perfect getaway car. Nondescript . . . I feel like I'm in a *Starsky and Hutch* episode."

Cassandra and Mary watched the road ahead, leaving me to continue yammering. "You know what we should have got? A police radio. So we could listen in when they find out."

Cassandra looked back with a faint smile. "Next time."

"Are you OK, Ms. Place?"

"Yeah. I'm just kind of worried about Jess. I'm usually home by now, if I was working."

I sat back a bit.

"She's with Mrs. Grachie, in the apartment below mine. I don't suppose there's any time to —" She appealed to Mary, then stopped herself. "No, never mind. It's just that she gets upset sometimes."

"My uncle's place closes at ten. It's gonna be a tight squeeze as it is, to get the fax written and sent before then . . . we could drop you off, maybe . . ." Mary looked at her with a fair amount of sympathy, considering how rigidly she was driving.

Cassandra shook her head. "No. I want to be there. She can live without me for a few more hours."

I leaned forward again. "You're doing a great job driving, Mary. You've been practising since our trip to Scarborough Campus." We had had to pick up a book in one of the outlying suburban libraries during a snowstorm, and it was so tense that I stopped talking — I actually went chatter-free for a full thirty-minute period. I had closed my eyes, feigning sleep, because the silence was so heavy, but I didn't close them fully because I wanted to keep an eye on the road.

"That was with my grampa's bald-tired boat during a snowstorm," she clarified to Cassandra.

We came to a stoplight and a squeegee kid came up and washed our windshield. She had black eye shadow and short blue hair. Mary handed her a loonie and the kid's tired expression brightened, and I noticed a stud in her lip, a silver mole in the middle of her face. For some reason, it all seemed very Oliver Twisty. She ran back to the corner and the lights changed.

"Someone's gotta keep her in make-up and falafels," Cassandra said, watching them at the corner as we took off.

"Yeah, yeah — I know," Mary said. "I only give to the girls. The cute ones."

Cassandra looked at her. "It's just that I've seen these kids turn around and buy CDs with eighteen dollars in change. Not that music and culture isn't a necessity . . ." she said, quite seriously. "It's just that they make it so easy for the media to ignore serious issues like shrinking welfare cheques in favour of a visually dynamic piece on 'Squeegee Kids: Scary or Sad? A little freakshow for our home viewers.' But that's the media's fault, really. It's just frustrating to see how much attention they get and how little actually gets said."

Something occurred to me. "Aren't *we* in danger of exactly that? I mean, being turned into a freakshow?"

Mary laughed. "Yeah . . . when you guys were walking towards the car it was like something out of a movie. They're great costumes. Good contrast between the two of you, too."

"This is why getting the fax out is so important," responded Cassandra. "We're going to be able to put our spin on it in a way that should be irresistible to the media outlets. I hope. Unlike the squeegee kids, we're going to have a spokesperson, and unlike them, we're going to have a clear political agenda. But you're right, there is the danger that they'll turn us into cartoons."

Mary nodded. "I was thinking that it might be a good idea to put together a whole package on you two, with photographs and histories and the whole bit."

"Can I sign my photos — *Flyboy*?"

Cassandra laughed. "Seriously, though. What about a video release? Not like a music video, but like revolutionaries? Like the Black Panthers or something?" She looked back at me, her eyes sparking. "Would that not be the *best*?"

I smiled and shrugged. "Sure. Yeah." It sounded crazy in one way, and fun in another. "As long as we could find someone trustworthy to help out."

Mary turned into an alley and parked in a reserved parking spot. "My uncle's," she said.

Cassandra was pulling on a sweater and some jeans over her costume. I just had to change jackets, and we went into the copy shop, a small downstairs place. It was fairly empty, except for one guy in a leather hat and a sallow face who was haggling with the guy behind the counter — Mary's uncle, I presumed.

"Four cents is too much," the customer was saying. "I can go down the street and get two and three cents. What about three-and-a-half?"

The uncle, a short toupeed man, was pecking at a calculator. "Three point seven five is the best. No less." I marvelled at the situation of haggling for a fraction of a cent. It added up, of course, but it must be wearing to constantly be arguing about a piece of a penny.

The guy nodded. "OK," he said, and he gave him a band flyer. The uncle told him fifteen minutes and he left.

The uncle turned to us, beaming. Mary spoke first. "These are the friends I was talking about, Dawn and Michael." I shook hands with him, told him to call me Mike. His name was Francis. Uncle Francis kissed Cassandra's hand and Mary hit him on the shoulder.

"Sorry, but I see a beautiful woman . . . ?" He threw his hands up. "Can't help myself." He led us over to the computer. "So do what you do, but don't ask me. I know nothing." He flattened his hands and indicated *nothing*.

We sat down. "My cousin set this up for him," said Mary. I suddenly wondered if any of us knew how to work this funny little machine, because I knew about as much as Francis. Then Mary took a disk out of her bag and I felt relieved. She popped it in the disk drive authoritatively and I felt downright relaxed.

"Now what is it I do here? Make dumb jokes and watch other people do the work?"

They looked at me darkly.

"I'm a fast typist, you know," I said with a little finger flourish.

Mary made room for me in front of the keyboard, and we got to work. She had written a draft of it already, based on what we figured would happen:

"The police force was symbolically castrated today during the feminist rally, Take Back the Night. A dynamic duo going under the moniker Superheroes for Social Justice has claimed credit for the bizarre action — the disappearance of eleven police guns from the officers attending the rally.

"One of the two, 'Ms. Place,' has explained why. 'The group who organized the rally had requested, politely and in writing, that female officers be assigned to the march. They failed to respond, and subsequent phone calls revealed that they had no intention of respecting the organizer's reasonable request. Flyboy and I decided that it was time to offer our unique services.'

"The two claim to have abilities beyond even their own understanding. Ms. Place is allegedly capable of making things disappear while Flyboy can change into a fly at will.

"Flyboy, who didn't use his powers during the rally, stated that he felt that the force's action was inexcusable. 'I was disappointed that they seemed to miss the point of the rally. It's about specific feminist issues, yes, but it's also about creating a climate where women feel safe — and many of the participants find hulking, heavily armed macho men less than soothing, regardless of their oath to Serve and Protect.'"

We had it finished a little before closing. Francis hadn't paid us the least attention, he was bent over a ledger and didn't even look up to watch Cassandra. "I love being able to edit my quotes into an intelligible statement," she said.

We printed it out and moved over to the fax machine. Mary set it up so that it wouldn't show the name of the copy shop. She amazed me with her level of preparedness.

"I would have totally forgotten about that," I said. "You sure you don't have any superorganization powers?"

She smiled and pointed to the letterhead, which had an e-mail address. "My friend Jeff is a hacker guy, and he was able to set us up with this totally untraceable contact address for interviews and stuff."

We both made impressed noises. She started punching in numbers from a sheet she had with newspapers, TV stations, all written in her familiar neat handwriting. It wasn't just neat — her handwriting was *innocent* looking, I realized.

What the hell was I doing — corrupting my friend? Or was it the other way around?

chapter twelve

We got home in time to put Jess to sleep. She was calm, but curious. "Where?"

"I was out fighting the Negaverse, honey."

Jess seemed happy with that. "I get first shower," said Cassandra on our way out of the room. I didn't argue, despite my ponginess — it must have been hot in that costume. "Why don't you see if there's something to eat?"

I called to check my messages. "You have no new messages," the recorded voice said smugly. "I am a loser," I said to Jess. She blinked and went to the kitchen.

I looked through the fridge thinking that I didn't want food, I wanted to get out of my grimy clothes. I heard the shower hiss to life just then, and I remembered how *roomy* Cassandra's bathtub was. Jess had stationed herself at the kitchen table and was crayoning with tongue-biting concentration.

Paying no attention to me. I bugged out and flew through the hall and down the stairs, buzzing a melody I call "Insect Mischief." I got to the bathroom door and walked under it with plenty to spare.

I buzzed to the middle of the bathroom, feeling the steam condense on my wings, and switched back. My bare feet appeared slightly above the pile of clothes Cassandra had quickly ditched.

"Is there room for two in there?" I baritoned casually. Her shadow froze, then she pulled back the curtain. Her face was cross.

"You're lucky I didn't disappear you, bozo. Don't sneak around a girl with superpowers!"

My cheesy smile melted faster than mozzarella in a microwave.

"Oh, stop," she said, opening the curtain wide. My cheesy smile reconstituted and I whistled my tune as I stepped into the tub. Cassandra was blocking all the water, so I picked up the soap and started soaping up her back.

"I'm such a softy," said Cassandra.

"Why?" I said, soaping around to her belly.

"I can't leave Jess for one day without worrying about it. *She's* not worried about it."

I kissed her on the side of the neck, tickled her as I washed the hair under her arms. "That's normal. Isn't it?"

"Exactly. *Too* normal. Smothering. I'm trying to live a life of my own again, and my conscience keeps hammering at me. I've got an incredible naked guy in the shower with me and I'm just complaining."

I hugged her, smelling her wet hair. For some reason, her saying that made me tear up — I figure it was the tension of the day. I took the bar of soap and used it on her breasts.

She leaned back against me then, smiling and silent. I felt her nipples harden as I slicked back and forth over them. I pressed my cock against her, sandwiching it between my belly and her ass, felt her pressing back. With my hands I pressed down on her breasts, pinching her nipples with the sides of my fingers, causing a quick intake of breath and a lingering kiss for my hand. *All this wondrous squishing,* I thought lightheadedly.

"Time . . . it's time for you to fuck me," said Cassandra, turning off the water. I hadn't washed my hair, but she was right.

"Race you to the condoms — loser gets the wall side," I said, stepping out, towelling off and flying under the door — not even stopping to land and walk under. I was getting better at flying. Pretty soon I'd be ready to take on the Death Star and end Darth Vader's evil empire once and for all.

Before I had even rounded the corner to the stairs, the door had burst open and towelled Cassandra ran out. I jacked up the speed — her hurtling figure was pretty frightening, and I was scared she might run into me.

I was up the stairs and in the room before she had even got to the top of the stairs. I transformed slightly above the bed and dropped onto it. She burst in and ran towards the bed, dropping her towel — and suddenly making for the bedside drawer.

"The race was for the condoms, not the bed, Wall Side. Go on, move your pretty ass over."

Damn. I moved over, taking the side that would mean I had to crawl over her to go to the washroom or whatever. "OK, but you saw how much coffee I drank today, Cassandra — I figure tonight's a six tripper."

"What's that green stuff?" she asked, settling in beside me.

I looked down and saw a thin layer of residue on me. I had registered it with some part of my brain but assumed it was a layer of sweat. "Oh geez. That happens when I stay a fly for a long time. I guess it was because I was really pushing my flying speed. I don't know what it is. It's kinda gross, huh?"

Cassandra took some in her fingers and smelled it, rubbed it for consistency. "It's like lubricant," she said, grabbing Mr. Willie with her residue-smeared hand and sliding it up and down.

A shocked "Whu-hey" emerged from my mouth, and Cassandra started rubbing herself all over me, a wicked look on her face. I didn't know if this stuff was hygienic, I didn't know if it was radioactive.

But *damn* if it weren't funky.

It was later that night that I found myself staring into space, unable to sleep. After sexing our already-tired bodies to exhaustion, Toronto's two favourite superheroes fell asleep. But an hour or two later I got up to go to the washroom (pulling on some clothes because it was all the way downstairs) and, unusually for me, was unable to instantly resume sleeping.

And this was the thought that kept running through my mind on a demonic tapeloop: *We're going to get caught.* I imagined the cops kicking down our door and incapacitating us with needles, long and sharp. They would have to, because Cassandra wouldn't go with them voluntarily. She might even disappear one of them.

If she did, we'd be doomed. Utterly. Because I wouldn't know whose side I was on. I felt we were a danger to society already, just having the power we did. I felt like we should be locked up. If they could lock us up together somehow, I might even consider it.

But they wouldn't just lock us up. We'd be pulled apart, nerve by nerve, until our bodies were senseless slabs of meat. *The gold is there somewhere,* they would tell each other, but I knew that, whether it was there or not, they would kill us in the digging.

I would co-operate. Cassandra would resist. Cassandra would die and I would live to mourn her and to loathe my own lack of resolve. I presumed the authorities would be utterly ruthless in their analysis — if they weren't, then once the word got out they would be replaced by a hungrier agency, who wanted our secrets more. It was this understanding that had kept me from approaching the authorities all of my life — what I had was so valuable that it would turn men rabid. I had often wished I could be a spy, to know what I was doing was right and be backed up by a nation's moral certainty.

Instead, I was trying to carve my own way through fields of ethical dilemmas, and when the light was dim it was hard to see what was ahead. My joyful anger came from her, my weak flame fed by her proximity. It was only because I loved her that —

I realized that I loved her then. What a tragic and horrible thing that was. I was paralyzed, my tapeloop chewed to a stop. Soon after, I drifted into sleep.

The next day I woke up without an ounce of horror or tragedy in my veins. It's funny how it works sometimes, how anxiety consumes itself. I had an early class and left the house just as Cassandra's alarm went off.

The classroom was half empty as usual — mostly because it was a small class, but the 8:30 start time didn't help matters. I didn't know anyone in this class, except to nod to. The thin little professor walked in, looked around at our low numbers with a scowl, and set his coffee down with a tap. He paused for the murmurs to die their slow deaths, and started a lecture on our latest text. As usual, his style was deceptively casual, and by the end there was such a confluence of ideas and commentary that I couldn't decide whether they had substance or were just sleight-of-hand.

The class ended and I left, passing from the campus to the city streets, my feet eating up the sidewalk slabs until the diner's neon sign buzzed above my head.

Inside, it was really busy. Cassandra moved quickly between the tables, too quickly — something was wrong. I stood at the door for a second before the other waitress noticed me and tapped Cassandra on the shoulder. Cassandra looked at me, said something to the waitress which was not well received. Cassandra signalled five minutes with a pleading look unfamiliar to me, and the waitress gave grudging assent.

Cassandra pulled me out the door, me saying, "I've never seen you beg for anything before. You must really want a smooch."

We stopped at a *Toronto Sun* box and she disappeared the glass front, reaching in and pulling out a copy. I looked around quickly to see if anyone had noticed what she did, but it looked OK. "What?" I said, looking at the cover.

"Turn the page," she said, leaning against the brick building. I did. The Sunshine Girl page, which featured a new, scantily clad woman every day, today had a picture of Cassandra.

"Oh, man," I said, looking over at Cassandra. She was crying a little, quickly brushing the tears away.

"I want to fucking kill the fuckers," she said. "I'm so mad. I'm so fucking mad."

I looked down at it again. It wasn't actually a photograph, it was an artist's rendition of her — an artist heavily influenced by the *Heavy Metal* style of drawing, with a lot of lip gloss and airbrush and visible nipples. It actually kind of nauseated me, that they could change her like that. The box beside the picture was even worse.

This sexy vigilante claimed to make policemen's pistols disappear at a protest yesterday. Miss Place is one superbabe we'll be keeping our eye on!

I didn't know what to say. She took the paper from me and jammed it back into the box. "The *Star* gave us about two inches of column space, buried in the back," she said.

"Well, that's pretty good, isn't it?" I said, remembering that I had picked up the U of T paper. I pulled it out of my bag and handed it to her. The headline was "TAKE BACK THE NIGHT GETS ENERGIZED" and the article discussed how the younger generation was making it a more rambunctious, spirited event, citing the *Sun* box burning and a broken bank window as proofs. Alongside that was a sidebar on "Ms. Place: Superfeminist!"

It read a little like a gossip column, but it was largely complimentary and ended with: "Whether or not she has superpowers is irrelevant — with her flashy fashion and kick-ass politics she's bound to make a media splash. Keep watching this space as your intrepid reporter attempts to get an exclusive interview with this mysterious figure."

It was signed "Chris Westhead." Cassandra read it, a smile growing. "That's the pseudonym Pat uses when she wants it to seem like there's a legion of reporters at the *Varsity*. Well, that's good. I didn't know what she'd do. I can't tell if she knows it's me or not. I'd just as soon she didn't."

Cassandra seemed back to herself as she scoured the page once again.

"Don't think I don't notice that Flyboy is conspicuously absent from any reports," I said.

She snorted. "Maybe next time they'll humiliate you, too."

"But wait!" I said, and grabbed the mangled *Sun* from the box. I flipped through, frantically, to the back. A blond, barechested man named Leonardo grinned back at me. "Damn. I hoped I might have made Sunshine Boy," I said, disappointed.

"I have to get back to work," she said, holding up the *Varsity.* "Can I keep this?"

I nodded. She gave me a kiss and I hugged her, crinkling up the paper. When she went in, she was smiling.

"My job here is done," I said to the closed door and the deaf passers-by.

The party had finally reached a tolerable saturatio where it no longer felt like a bunch of people sitting around. Like thin soup or weak coffee, an under-attended party is a mockery of the real thing.

Cassandra was on the couch talking to Matthew, someone from Vancouver who evidently knew everyone she did. I leaned against the wall, pulling at my Sailor Moon ring, wondering if I was obligated to listen to their conversation. I was pretty new at this couple thing.

A couple of bright-haired young kids passed by. One of them noticed my ring. "Whered'ya get that?" she said, plucking at her eyebrow piercing.

"I rolled some kid outside the playground. Got his cookies, too."

She looked at my face and ran off to rejoin her friends.

Stupid, I thought. *God forbid you ever give a straight, unthreatening answer, Ryan.* I wondered briefly where Ken was. It was his party, so I suppose I had to let him alone to do his hostly duties.

An incredibly bad smell suddenly appeared. I wondered where it was coming from, and then I heard this odd, pinch-faced guy talking. "So he gave me a bottle of it for Christmas, but I was too drunk to drink it on New Year's. He makes it himself, it's crazy cheap." He was holding a murky glass, which I decided was the odour culprit. I made a mental note to leave the winemaking to the professionals.

I looked over at Matthew and Cassandra, whose conversation seemed unaffected by the fetid fermentation. They seemed to be having a whale of a time, actually, Matthew's face cycling through surprise, anger, hilarity, in a ten-second period. I decided to find some snacks rather than be found sneaking looks. I wasn't jealous, really, just at loose ends: the place where I ended up at most parties.

The kitchen was pretty busy, filled with people attracted to kitchens in parties — those who cared more about keeping an eye on their beer and a hand in any new snacks than the comfort of the living room couches. I was able to snag a piece of pita without disrupting anyone's lounging position.

"This stuff any good?" I asked the kitcheners at large, poised with my pita above a bowl of yellow dip.

"It's hummus," said the nearest guy, then showed me his back. *Damn,* I thought. I had a friend who could discuss the party snacks at length, and it was a thing to behold. He'd rate them for people who approached the table, often with helpful tips like "too damn hot," and "leaves a cheesy ring around your lips." I, however, left the kitchen with the ice unbroken.

I walked straight through the room where Matthew and Cassandra chatted with the impressive gait of someone determined to get to the other side of a party. I admit it — I didn't want Cass to see me floundering and awkward.

I passed a tableau: " . . .Well, he's not here, so it's not an issue, is it?" The speaker was a girl — Val, Jack's obsession, talking to Mark. Mark was leaning close to her, his blue tuft of hair hanging over a pronounced scowl.

I kept walking, pretending not to recognize them and escaped around the stairs. As I ascended to the second floor I wondered what the hell I should do with this tantalizing fragment. Should I tell Jack? Was it even about Jack? I nearly ran into Jo at the top of the stairs, so flurried were my thoughts.

"Ryan Slint!"

There was a funny kind of lighting in that stairwell, and it suited her very well. I found myself smiling, stupefied for a moment. I almost told her, then and there, that she looked like a movie star. Then she said something.

"Where's the fire, Ryan?"

"I — always run upstairs. Downstairs, too. I don't know why. Ever since I was a kid."

We talked for a while about that, and I internally wondered why I hadn't said the movie star thing. I'm sure she would have just accepted it as a compliment and felt good about herself. But what if it was flirting? I hated flirting, especially by accident.

"Jump off any patios lately?" she asked.

Jo had been there for my infamous Patio Dive, which happened during my first year at the pub we went to Friday after Friday. The same period of time that I had exhibited my pukin' party trick, although it had been more mortifying since there were far more friends at my Dive.

"I guess Liz isn't in any of your classes this year. She says her film class is pretty dull without you there."

Both versions of *The Fly* had been on the syllabus last year. I had had a few (thousand) things to say. Same thing had happened this year, when Kafka's *The Metamorphosis* had been under the microscope. It was less interesting though, since I knew more than the TA, and hadn't wanted to show him up too badly.

"So what else are you up to, Ryan?"

Trying to break into the superhero game was all I could think to say. It's funny how something can loom so large it obscures everything else. But then it made me think of a connected piece of news. "I'm seeing this fantastic woman. Cassandra. Maybe you'll meet her later." *And, if God is merciful, you will not mention some embarassing first-year drunk-story.*

"How's your love life?" I said boldly, now that I had established myself as a disinterested third party.

She made a disgusted sound. "I live through my friends. It's pathetic."

"I know what that's like," I commiserated. There was a pause while I left Jo to mull over how pathetic her life was, and I tried to think of a new subject but every folder in my brain was marked "Superheroes": "Superheroes; costumes of," "Superheroes; worries of," "Superheroes; sex between."

A woman with a pair of square glasses showed up, talking a mile a minute to Jo. I gave a smile and excused myself, walking past a few populated rooms and finding Ken outside one of them.

"Ryan . . . my good friend," Ken greeted me with a Czech accent. He was sitting on a narrow stairwell and holding a thin spliff in his fingers. "I don't want to take this out to the porch, because there's too many people and this little guy is teeny-weenie," he said, meaning the joint. "But I don't want to smoke it by my lonesome."

"You have reached an impasse, it seems?" I said, with the same Eastern European flavour. "I . . . would be willing to help you out with that."

"Did Cass and Jess come? I've been running around saying hello and didn't see them." Someone squeezed past Ken, patting him on the head on his way up.

"Jess is at the sitter's, Cassandra's here. Should I invite the crazy woman up?"

He nodded assent and I went downstairs, where Mark and Matthew were talking with Cass. I waved to a now-jolly Mark as if it were the first time I'd seen him and whispered in a delicate shell ear that Ken was going up on the rooftop to soak up some foliage, and did she care to partake?

We snaked with speed through the darkened hallways — in one particularly quiet enclave Cassandra copped a feel. I tee-heed and covered my ass with my hands.

"So now you grab my ass, now that their asses are cold?" I referenced. She asked if I felt ignored and I said no in a deliberately unconvincing fashion.

"Ready to ascend?" Ken asked, after hellos. We were.

The top floor had a bedroom with the light on. Val was in there, showing her zine to a skinny guy with gold-rimmed glasses. They didn't see us, and we went into a tiny closet with a ladder.

Ken went first, pushing the hatch at the top open with a crunchy sound.

I motioned that Cassandra should go first, then copped my revenge, squeezing and poking relentlessly until she was out of range. Then I went up. Cassandra, at the top, was closing the hatch, looming over me. I could hear Ken's laughter and him saying, "That's it, kill him! Keeel him!"

But I wasn't to be stopped. I threw open the hatch and levered myself out. "I wish I had a knife to clench between my teeth," I said.

"Arrr," pirated Cassandra. "This is some great rooftop, Kenny-Kenster."

It was a flat roof, with slanty stuff happening near the edges and a garden taking up about half of it. A patio with huge, rough-hewn furniture took up the rest.

"Have you been up here before, Ryan?" he asked, moseying over to the patio.

"Yep. The housewarming party. Last summer." Practically the whole party had been up here then, it was so bloody hot. Now, however, the current of warmth in the spring breeze was wonderful to feel.

Cassandra was looking at the garden, still covered with winter plastic. "You into gardening, Ken?"

"No. Marieke's really into it, though. So that's all the house duties she has."

"So she hasn't been doing anything all winter? She might just leave," I said, settling myself in a patio chair. "You might want to think about that."

"Strange . . ." Cassandra said. "I noticed a woman packing a suitcase . . . and she was wearing a nametag."

"Re-a-lly," I straightmanned. "What did it say?"

"An odd name . . . began with an *M*," she said, looking over at Ken with her eyebrows arched.

He chuckled and took the toke from behind his ear. I looked out at the stars, relaxed but feeling anticipation at the same time. It had been a while since I had smoked up. Ken took the fire into the joint and made it stick.

"Wow, you can see the CN Tower from your place," Cassandra said, taking the joint and sucking some smoke into her lungs. The top of the tower was visible through a jumble of buildings. "Ya pay extra for that, I bet," she said, after she released the smoke.

"So how's it going, Ken?" I asked, determined to get this conversation on an interesting track before I got stoned. "How's the book deal going?" I said as Cassandra handed me the joint.

"Oh, it's not," he said with a chuckle. I was mid-toke when he said this and started choking a bit. The smoke burned my nostrils and my eyes watered, much to the others' amusement.

"Don't take it so hard, keed," he said to me. I got up and handed him the joint, wiping my eyes. "I had told you it was probably gonna flake out." He turned to Cassandra. "There were these publishing guys sniffing around, wanting to do a compilation of all my cartoons and drawings."

Cassandra nodded. "Ryan told me about it."

"Yeah," Ken said with a smile. "Ryan was more hyped about it than I was."

"Well, a book deal . . ." I said with a shrug. "Finally, Baby Sneaky 5000 would get the respect he deserves!"

"Respect would ruin Baby . . . he'd be rolling around on new wheels every week, smoking garbage bags full of opium . . ."

"Eating rich foods and sampling wines of all types — especially the *cheap* brands," said Cassandra.

"Avoiding his duties as the spiritual leader of the Annex . . ." I continued, then shifted back onto the serious track. "Such a drag, though." I wasn't just saying that — I was inexplicably affected by this. I guess I had seen it as a way for Ken to get money for doing something fun and worthwhile. I guess —

"I never thought it would go through," Ken said, breaking off my endless wondering. "I kind of hoped it wouldn't, so I wouldn't have to decide. I saw Palaver's collection in the bookstore . . . it was horrible."

"Really?"

"No, I mean, it had these great full-colour plates of his stuff and that was really nice. But it was this huge unwieldy format, and the cover was so bad. It was this collage of his work, superimposed over photos of Greek statues. I mean, he obviously takes from that as an inspiration, but to make it so blatant." Ken frowned. "Bleagh! Horrible."

"I haven't seen it," I said. "Have you?"

Cassandra had been silent for a while. She licked her lips, slowly, and said, "No, but I imagine he had to give up his control of presentation — for marketing and such — in order to reach a larger audience."

Ken's face screwed up. "But if I was him, I would look at that book and just feel my energy drain away. I wouldn't want to draw for a long while. What does it matter if you make a couple of thousand if you lose your drive? Every time I saw it, it'd be like a punch in the gut."

"I know exactly what you mean," said Cassandra, becoming animated. "You think, 'People think this is me, the whole me. But it's only the most obvious part.'"

"Did you find that with your band?" asked Ken.

"Yeah, people were real quick to label us as Angry Young Women, Riot Grrrl, but it's not as bad because you have a band name to hide behind."

"And what a name it was," I said.

"Yeah, it was a good choice, although we didn't plan it that way — it was pretty hard to paint us in any colour than Militant Maroon with a name like that. They could slag us in their reviews and stuff, but they couldn't really demean us without seeming really jerky. They couldn't call us babes or vixens or whatever, is what I mean."

"That's good," said Ken. He flicked the ashes from the roach and put it away.

"It's OK. It worked. It didn't tell the whole story, though. I did a song about a guy I had a crush on and it never got recorded. When I wore something less butch the singer would mock me. So there were boundaries, you know?"

"Boundaries," repeated Ken, standing up. "There was a guy from one of the publishing houses and he took me out to lunch, and he was totally excited about me. He'd never seen stuff like it before and he was genuinely into it. I was like, 'Hey, take it easy, dude, they're just comics.' But he had gone to the vice-president and begged for the assignment, or whatever. I was trying to get him to publish them as mini-comics, in the same size and everything, and package them in some interesting way. He was all anxious and like, 'There are boundaries within which we work.'" Ken made the hand sign for *boundaries:* two flat hands spaced a precise distance apart. "Poor guy," he finished.

"Poor guy? He sounds like a bit of a . . ." I said.

"No way! Steve's a great guy. I invited him, tonight. He's the guy with the gold-rimmed glasses . . ."

"That skinny guy with Val?" I asked, wondering if Val was angling. Shmoozing.

"No, he's not skinny. He was in the kitchen."

Cassandra put us back on track. "Why do you feel sorry for him?"

"He's got this awful job, being so close to all of these boring boring books and having to deal with these money people all the time. He was desperate to get me a book, but not really so I got money, or so his company made money, but so his job would have meaning to him again. He's a young guy, and his job's already so dull to him that he was totally depressed when he called me up. 'We've decided not to go ahead with the project,' and I was like, 'Oh, OK. I'm having a party this weekend. You should come.'"

Cassandra smiled at me, the lingering wide smile of the marijuana fiend. I smiled back. The pot hadn't had much of an effect, although my field of vision kind of bunched up occasionally, like a rumpled carpet. I felt good, though, seeing how happy she was. Her eyes were clear and sharp, and I noticed by contrast how tired she had looked until now. Now she looked ready to save the world again.

chapter thirteen

Cassandra leaned over and yelled in my ear, "I want to totally fuck over those bastards."

I looked around the dance floor for the unfortunates she was talking about. I couldn't see any easily identifiable bastards — a few idiots, maybe — so I shot her a puzzled look.

She smiled for a moment, tapping her ear as the DJ spun the first few bars of the upcoming song into the dying grooves of the last. I couldn't pin down what it was, but a lot of people were getting excited.

The female vocalist was loungy and I dug dancing to her voice and the whole kitschy sound — I even forgave the chorus for having the word "love" in it. Cassandra was all smiles, wearing this slinky blue dress that she had found in a Goodwill five-dollar bin.

I had been with her when she found it, a few days before Take Back the Night. She had been almost as excited as I was for her to try it on — it needed a few alterations, but it was a classic sequinned wonder and wore its decades well.

But it hadn't appeared. At first I thought it was because she hadn't had time to do the alterations. I think it had more to do with that Sunshine Girl shit, though. Today she was in a great mood — when I showed up at Sok today she practically dragged me across the road to this place. I hadn't asked her why, I was almost afraid to jinx it.

The song ended, and we left the floor to white boys stomping around with their hands out, mouthing the roughneck hip hop lyrics. Two people left a booth and we moved to it like sharks on blood.

Once in it, Cassandra swept up my peasant's hands into hers and gazed into my eyes. Her hair was up, to suit the outfit — she had made a transformation in the diner washroom in two minutes flat. Not fussing with make-up gave her the speed advantage over most chicks.

Her fond look was making me nervous. "What're you so happy for?"

"I've been feeling *fine* ever since the party. I like Ken a lot. He put me back on track. What he was saying gave me a better way of thinking about things. I was so caught up in an intellectualized, feminist analysis of my position that I wasn't giving any thought to my emotional reaction."

A waitress came by and Cassandra ordered a plate of nachos. "I love your dress," the waitress said, and Cassandra demurely accepted the compliment, holding up a hand to indicate the price. The waitress was suitably impressed.

"My mom says that you should never admit to a really good deal," I said.

"Bollocks," said Cassandra. "I want everyone to know that it's possible to dress like this on the cheap. It makes people feel better to know that. So," she continued in a rush, "the thing with the Sunshine Girl crap is that I always knew it was a risk to dress in that costume — that the possibility that they'd whore me to sell papers was there. I even, abstractly, thought that it would backfire on them, because they'd be giving publicity to a figure that pretty much directly attacked their conservative bullshit."

I squinched my eyes as I nodded to show that I was *mostly* following, but still a few cars behind.

"But while I understood that risk intellectually, I still had problems coping with it emotionally. Because I always worry that I'm not feminist enough, that —"

"Here you go," the waitress said, setting down the plate of nachos while holding a tray of beer aloft. "$4.95."

Cassandra gave her a five and a loonie.

I waited for her to continue but she just launched into her nachos. Eventually she looked at me frozen in pause, the model listener. I took a token nacho when she motioned me to.

"Well, anyway. I was pretty stymied for a while, because I didn't know how to respond in a way that was balanced and politically pointed, because I guess I felt complicit — I was convinced that if I hadn't dressed up like that, they wouldn't have been able to exploit me. But that's that same mentality that says: she was wearing slutty clothes so she deserved to be raped. Blame-the-victim shit."

I nodded. This explained her depression. It was more complicated than the boys-in-the-schoolyard-pointing-at-her-tits embarrassment that

I had unconsciously assumed it was. I had simply felt bad because she felt bad — I hadn't really thought about the reasons.

"Go on, I'm not going to be able to finish these on my own." I took a good handful of nachos and wondered why I was still being polite at this stage of the relationship. *If she's sharing bodily fluids with me, nachos are a given,* I thought.

"So," she said, pointing a nacho at me for emphasis, "I've discovered that when something hurts me, or affects me in a bad way, I get all of this anger, this energy that rolls around inside me. If I don't disperse it somehow, it keeps spinning around in my gut, making me depressed and anxious. But I've found, in the past, what works well for me is to fire it back at the source of the hurt — or as close as I can figure."

"Harnessing it, kind of," I said. I squeezed my nose. The smoke was irritating it, drying it out.

"Yeah! So when something bugs me, I don't let it accumulate and then explode at some innocent person, like you or Jess or whatever. I focus it and wreck a billboard. Like the leering macho bullshit I take from men on a daily basis makes me work at feminist stuff harder."

She leaned forward. "And the times when I've been at my most miserable — and the last couple of days have been nothing compared to it — were times when I felt like I could do *nothing* to kick back."

"Like when?"

"Well, we had encouraged the *Sun* to cover us with the press release, and they did. I asked for it, in a sense." She shook her head. "But talking to Ken reminded me of how money-inspired media distorts everything. And then I started to realize how ludicrous it was to think I was powerless. I'm probably the most powerful person on Earth!" she finished, with a big grin.

I was amazed. She had dug herself out of a hole and scaled a mountain with nothing except a pick of hard-headed rationality. I felt pretty useless. I was there to listen, nod and soak up smoke. And the way she accepted, even revelled in her superpowers! I had spent my lifetime trying to grow into them, like a kid given drafting tools that fascinate but baffle him. Sure you can draw with them, but they can obviously do much more.

"Our rings are pretty accurate," I said, holding forth my Sailor Moon ring. "While I fumble around, complain and wish I was just a normal girl, you prepare for battle."

Cassandra laughed and her eyes liquefied. "No, look, it's not that simple. I spent my life unconscious of my powers. So I was able to deal with other issues, like sharpening my political claws. You've more or less lived your life as a mental fugitive, conscious of it all the time and the danger you're in, and so obviously you're not going to be on the attack."

"Wow," I said, impressed. "Is that what you tell your friends?"

"It's what I tell myself," she said.

"Well frankly, I was up most of the night after we took back the night. I was sure cops were going to kick the door down." . . . *and take you away from me*, I thought, but didn't say.

"I honestly feel like you have a stronger grip on the reality of it," said Cassandra. "I think it's more a part of your brain. I think that if you weren't around, I could forget about it again. Fucking weird, huh?"

"I don't know what kind of grip I have on it," I said. I had a nacho I'd been holding for the last minute in one hand. "I wasn't worried about jail, like I should have been. I was worried about . . . well, I was thinking that if we could share a cell, it would be fine, I'd go quietly."

She looked touched by this absurd confession. "But you know that they'd . . ."

"Yeah, I know." This was ground I had been over and over. "They'd dissect us. And you probably wouldn't go quietly in any circumstances."

"Not to jail, I wouldn't," she said, almost sadly. "I'd break you out, of course."

We laughed at this movie cliché.

"So back to the business at hand . . ." Cassandra said.

"Which is . . . ?" Hoping she meant dancing.

"Vengeance," she said, her eyes aflame.

I waited for her to continue. She did, and I was amused and intrigued. It was cruder, had less of a political agenda, but didn't directly involve cops. This was good.

"This is an excellent song," said Cassandra afterwards.

"Is it from the seventies or does it just sound like it?" I asked.

"It's a new song, I forget the artist."

"It's the wa-wa pedal. It sounds like a porno," I said. I don't think I had ever said that word in front of her.

She laughed. "You're right! Wow, if it wasn't for the vocals it would be a total porno soundtrack. People would be out on the dance floor pulling off their clothes . . . having generic sex . . ."

I thought for a moment. "I wonder if this band's doing it deliberately.

They must be. It's brilliant, really, because the guys that are listening to it will subconsciously register it."

"And what, get turned on by it?" Cassandra finished the nachos, finally. It was a monster serving.

"No, not just that. Guilt, anxiety, fear, as well. Still, it's a potent emotional —" I searched for the right word, my hand in the air — "*mélange.*"

Cassandra snickered. "Ah, porn and pretentious French words go together like, like —"

"Chips anna dollar store," I finished. Then I gave the proof. "*Ménage à trois,* French ticklers . . ."

"Let's not forget the now-demure French kiss," Cassandra offered.

"There's never any *other* types of kissin' going on in those pornos."

"Let's dance to it," she said. "Oh, and I can get a beer now."

"You couldn't before?"

"Well, I didn't know if I was going to have to drive the car or not. I don't just *assume* you're willing to do any crazy-ass thing I think of," she said.

"You should," I said. A shy smile, one of the rarest of my troupe, appeared on my face. "If it's with you, and doesn't involve first-degree murder, you *should* just assume."

Her face softens sometimes, and it makes me relax just to look at it. It did now, and she kissed the back of my hand and set it back on the table. I inclined my head towards the dance floor with a questioning look, and soon we were jacking our bodies to the finest tunes.

I think it was something truly old school (as opposed to the pseudo stuff that had sounded like porno muzak) like James Brown's "Sex Machine." I always liked dancing to old school — it's inherently funny to be dancing to something way out of cultural context, I don't know why. And it's almost required that you try out your most audacious, most outrageous — your bad, baby, *super*bad — dance moves.

I was swimming, first the front crawl and then the butterfly, when I noticed Mary, in a big puffy coat, looking around. I swam over to her. "Hey hey! Dint you see me onna dance floor?"

"Oh, I saw you all right," said Mary. "I just didn't want to admit knowing you." She looked distinctly out of place, and the look on her face was a little anxious so I forgave her. "I was hoping Cassandra was sitting on the sidelines somewhere."

"Not bloody loikely," I guffawed. "How can you miss her? The vision in blue dancing beside me?"

Cassandra, unalarmed by my absence, waved at us.

"Oh my god," said Mary, waving back. "She's so femme."

"Femme-inine? Yep! Geez, when are you going to get glasses?"

She ignored me. "Do you have a table here?" Mary asked, bumped by two short girls that she spared a glance for.

I ignored her. "The coat check's over there. Then you can report for dance duty, Ms. Sachs!"

She shook her head adamantly.

I specialized in luring friends into dancelike situations. I would have hustled her onto the floor right away but dancing in a coat could be fatal. People were known to sweat to death, unable to stop once the beats started sinking in.

"Come on, dancin's fun!" The standard opening gambit.

"Oh, I know," she said casually, or as casually as you can while shouting over music. "I've been dancing all night. At a better joint than this, I might add."

"Where?" I asked, noticing that there was someone in a Kangol hat paying Cassandra too much attention. He was a guy we had commented on earlier, who seemed to like to move to the middle of the dance floor and remain stock still except for the songs that he deigned worthy of his participation.

"Place called Buddies." She, too, was watching Cassandra, who seemed oblivious to Kangol's attentions. She saw us looking at her and moved over to where we were standing. Kangol made like he didn't care.

"Buddies?"

"Ask your friend. Maybe she won't remember, though," Mary said with a smirk.

"Won't remember what?" Cassandra yelled, putting a hand on Mary's shoulder.

I told her. She swatted Mary.

"Buddies in Bad Times is a queer bar," Cassandra said.

"Oh!" I said. "Was it fun?"

"I'll tell you outside. I'm double-parked."

We got our jackets, Cassandra chatting briefly with the coat-check woman. She had a strip of masked tape over her bosom that read NO I HAVEN'T GOT A PEN. We left as a really good song was coming on. Never fails.

"So . . ." I said on our way down the stairs. "Was it what you expected?"

I didn't know what *I* would expect. I had a bizarre image of a dance hall with Maryish women sitting on chairs against the walls, with empty dance cards. I didn't want to seem like a complete ignoramus so I kept my mouth shut.

"It was pretty great. All of these cute girls returning my stare," Mary said with a grin. "And Alex was hilarious," she said to Cassandra.

"Later, Jorge," Cassandra said to the bouncer.

"Do you know everyone in this damn city?" I sputtered, amazed.

"Gimme a break, I work across the street," she said, unable to suppress a grin. To Mary, "Yeah, Alex is crazy."

Cassandra slipped her arm into mine, turning me into a gentleman. I was speechless momentarily with the niceness of it. My poise spontaneously improved.

"She is, at that. She's pretty serious about that leather girl, though, eh?" Mary probed.

"Damn serious," Cassandra confirmed. She glanced up at my baffled face and took pity. "When I called Mary tonight, I set her up to go dancing with some girlfriends of mine."

Mary had been leading the way, her puffy white coat glowing even under the streetlights. She glanced back at us and smiled. "Thanks for that, by the way. I never could have gone by myself. God, with that catwalk it's nerve-racking to go even with people. All those butch women leaning against the railing, staring at you . . . Horrible!" But there was a big smile on her face.

We got to the car, not double-parked in any way, shape or form. "Liar," I said to Mary, and she slapped the keys into my hand.

"Anything to stop you flailing around," she said, slamming the door.

"Fuck you, Ryan's the best fuckin' dancer in the world," Cassandra said, waving her fist.

I shot her a steamy look. "Thanks, doll." We kissed until spoilsport poked the horn. We disengaged and I breathed in her beery breath like it was nitrous oxide. Then she crawled into the backseat.

The cursive "Oldsmobile" on the dash started me up as I rolled that sucker out of there. "My 98 Oldsmobile is superfly . . ." I couldn't remember many more lyrics to the old Public Enemy song. "Take this ticket go to hell and stick it . . ."

"OK," Cassandra said. She had shucked her jacket and was lounging sideways, her blue dress asparkle, her eyes a little sleepy. "Let's get the key points down."

Mary flipped open her notebook, and I realized the reason why I was driving. *Man, people are organized around here,* I thought self-consciously. I glanced at the supine Cassandra in the rear view and had a crazy, happy thought: *She is totally exactly like Catwoman.*

I suppose I'm supposed to make this into the incredibly exciting scene where the cops catch on to our daring scheme and start chasing us.

I whipped around the corner, knocking over these jam-packed garbage cans and squealing down a one-way street. There was an eighteen-wheeler that must have had something to prove,'cause it blared its horn and bore down on us.

I sped up. No white-trash trucker was gonna bust my cajones.

"Jesus Christ," Cass screamed. "What the fuck are you doing?"

Out of the corner of my smirk, I said, "What I do best, baby, what I do best." I ground the accelerator into the floorboards like a cigarette butt.

Right when I was able to read the fine print on his out-of-province decals, I made another hairpin turn into an alley tight enough to throw sparks — but not to stop us. Then some freakin' motorbike cop with an Evel Knievel complex wheelies into the alley behind us, and starts gaining. He's already got his piece out, so before he can give us the leaden hello I ask Cassandra to take care of the guy.

She glances back and he's minus one tire. On a bike, that's a 50 percent reduction. The guy feels it. For a merciful few seconds.

No, nothing *nearly* like that happened. Which is good, because the problem I always had with being a superhero — the reason why I didn't wanna be one without Cassandra — was that I didn't like being the tough-guy hero. Which is not to say that I didn't like *talking* like one, but it just wasn't me to *be* one.

What we did that night was methodical. Systematic. Not spectacular, but also not suicidal.

We drove Mary to her uncle's place, sitting outside in the car for a little while as she got down our quotes and stuff for the press release. She also gave us a sheaf of papers, e-mail that had arrived in response to the last action. Most of it was stuff that Mary had responded to herself, questions about the organization and people wanting to get involved, but one of them was an effusive letter asking for a personal interview.

"This is from Pat, someone we know," Cassandra told Mary. "You can trust her — like, she's not a cop. But we can't meet her, obviously. I don't want her to know," she said, chewing on a nail. "Why don't you offer to meet her? Tell her we'll do telephone interviews."

That arranged, we waited for her to get inside — she had keys but was worried they wouldn't work, that her uncle had given her the wrong ones — but then she disappeared into the dark interior of the shop.

We started on that street, Cassandra tracing our route on a photocopy of a map with a blue highlighter. When I saw a *Sun* newspaper box I would say, Right! or Left! We were rolling along at about forty clicks an hour.

Cassandra disappeared the first one with a finger gun, but because we were going at a decent speed, and there were so many, Cassandra eventually just glanced up from her map and disappeared them with little fanfare. It being well into the wee hours, there were few witnesses. The chain that held it to the pole simply became slack and dropped, the motion and the tinkling attracting a curious glance at most.

Even at one corner with a large crowd waiting for the streetcar, the disappearance caused little detectable response. I watched the spot where it had been and saw a small kid walk around the area and wave his hand through where it used to be.

"Was that a midget?" said Cassandra.

"No, it was a kid."

"What the hell is a kid doing out at" — she checked her watch — "3:14 a.m.?"

I shrugged. I spotted a box. "Left!"

We rolled around, stopping for gas once and coffee once. The driving was fine — the streets were deserted, so I was able to keep an eye out for our targets without getting us killed. Kept to the speed limit, although even if we were stopped it would be hard to imagine a cop finding a highlighted map suspicious.

We were quiet for a lot of the time, and I found it OK. Cassandra had brought a couple of tapes, mellow stuff like Billy Bragg and Cowboy Junkies that softened the air rather than charging it. Eventually, on the last few streets, she curled up against me.

"It's getting bright," she mumbled.

"Yeah . . . but there's no actual sun. How is that? Where is it coming from? Is it convexing around the planet to us? Because — Right!"

Cassandra didn't move from my shoulder, I guess she didn't open her eyes fully, because she got the wrong box.

"That was a mailbox!" They were the same colour.

She jerked up and looked out the back window. "Got it."

How much mail was in that box? I wondered.

"Fuck!" said Cassandra. "I hope there weren't any personal letters in there."

We were pretty glum for a little while. We weren't superheroes, we were superjerks. *At least it wasn't someone in a red snowsuit,* I consoled myself. I didn't say it to Cassandra because it'd just remind her that that kind of mistake could be made, as long as she was using her power with the safety off.

"Stop here," she said, pointing at a mini-mall. She got out, taking her map with her, and made a phone call.

"I got Mary to put it in the press release. The mailbox thing," she said in staccato as she got in and buckled up. There was a stoic look on her face.

"Makes us look pretty dumb," I said.

"I know. Me more than you. But I had to do it."

I could see why, but my ethics were a little more elastic when it came to maintaining self-image. But she had more invested in this than I had, and it was obviously not an easy decision that she made — it just seemed like it because she made it quickly.

"So Mary's still working on it?"

"Yeah, she's almost finished it. She wanted to read it out to me, but I told her that I'm sure it's great."

"Wow! You actually refused control?"

"Yep. I'm not the boss. She puts the work in, she gets the final say on it."

"Left, right," I signalled.

The sun was starting to stab little shards into my retinas. "So how many more streets?" I asked. "How much longa maaaaam."

"This is it."

"This is the last one?" She nodded. "Fantastic," I said, and shielded my eyes from the sun.

"Do me a favour and disappear that big fireball in the sky, willya babe?" I thought about that for a second and then asked her seriously, "Could you do that? Could you disappear the sun?"

Cassandra sighed, and I glanced at her. Her brow was furrowed and worried. "Probably. I mean, I can see it . . ."

Something occurred to me. "But it would be eight minutes before we'd know about it. Because the light we see takes a while to get to us."

Cassandra shrugged, biting a nail to clean it.

I was still spiralling in my *Ask Mr. Science* world, attributing Cassandra's quiet to the late hour and exhaustion. "Can you disappear light? Have you ever tried?"

She looked at me. "I don't wanna think about it, Ryan. Especially after the mailbox. If I can fuck up like that, what's stopping me from destroying the whole world? By accident?"

"Oh, come on — one mailbox! I mean, real superheroes destroy whole buildings in, like, their fights in mid-air." I mimed the punch and the flying through the air and the smashing buildings.

This pulled a smile out of her.

On a roll, I continued. "Plus, if that happens we can always send out a press release — 'Citizens of Earth will have eight minutes to prepare to live without the sun. 'It was an accident,' explains superheroine Ms. Place. 'I was trying to disappear the clouds so that the picnic would be a success and — whoops!'"

Cassandra's smile faded. "What's even worse than doing something by accident is the possibility that I could do it on purpose." Before I could say anything she continued. "And I have been angry enough to destroy the world, believe you me. There have been times, Ryan . . ."

I believed her. I had never *felt* it myself — I'd known that I, and everyone else, was capable of tremendous evil, but only at an intellectual level. It reminded me of a line in *Chinatown* where a character says something like, "Most people never have to face up to the fact that given the right place, and the right time, they're capable of *anything.*" I had felt a chill down my spine listening to that, as if the cold truth of it had entered my body and stayed there, but I also thought to myself: *I am one of those "Most people."*

But evidently, Cassandra was not.

"But not recently. Recently life has been sweetness and light, and it's partially thanks to you. We're done."

"What?" I said, trying to understand the two contradictory statements, trying to take in air while my heart speeded up exponentially.

"We've finished the city. We can go pick up Mary now. Make a left here," she said as she capped her highlighter.

"Oh . . . fuck . . . thank god," I sputtered. "I thought you meant *we* were done." I gave her a look. "You did that on purpose," I accused.

She leaned over and smooched my neck. "No."

When we got to the copy shop, a delivery truck with the *Toronto Sun* logo on the side rolled by.

"He's not gonna have a lot of work to do today," I said, and we went in to get Mary.

chapter fourteen

The next day I woke up after only six hours of sleep and couldn't drop off again. I didn't want to wake Cassandra — it was pretty rare that she got to sleep in, as opposed to my slothful student schedule. I knew from experience that rustling around, putting on clothes, or even just getting up would wake her. Once up, she'd want to check on the papers, to see what kind of coverage we got. I just wanted to putter around a bit.

So I bugged out, hovering anxiously as Cassandra's arm, no longer supported by my chest, fell a few inches to the mattress. She slumbered on. I flew around the room, a pile of orange peels from last night smelling awfully good. I hadn't had breakfast yet, I realized. I considered walking across them with my tastebud-laden feet (just a lick, so to speak), but feeding was less of a voluntary thing for a fly. If it tasted good, I would automatically spew forth the acids to prepare it for eating.

I swooped under the door and into the hall. It was empty. I reconnoitred Phil's and Jack's rooms, but they were open-doored and empty, which meant that they were somewhere else in the house. I flew into the kitchen and quickly found a low shadowed part of the wall to land on.

" . . . pretty late," Phil was saying. He was rooting around the fridge in his boxers, shirt and nightcap. I gave him that nightcap last Christmas, figuring correctly that its purple stripiness would contrast hilariously with the supremely sombre mould of his face. He had taken to wearing it constantly, and it gradually was drained of humour as we got used to it. As soon as an uninitiated viewer saw it, it was magically recharged.

"Not as late as Ryan and company," said Jack, spooning some oatmeal into his mouth.

"Oh, Cassandra's here?" Phil said, pulling his face out of

the fridge. "Better put something less sexy on." He started out of the kitchen, then backtracked to load up the toaster.

"Take off that damn hat," Jack called after him. I watched Jack for a minute, scanning the paper. I was tempted to do a flyby to see what he was reading, but multifaceted eyes aren't great for reading. I figured I'd have to land on his head to read, and there was no point in tempting fate to satisfy idle curiosity.

Phil strolled in, now with jogging pants over his boxers, and still wearing the nightcap. "There we go. Chastity belt locked up tight. Can't be too careful with that woman around."

I hoped they weren't going to launch into Cassandra-slagging. Luckily, Jack was more concerned with the hat issue. "Will you take that silly thing off?"

Phil shrugged and made motions like he was trying to pry off his cranium. "It's stuck," he whined. The toast popped up and he set about tending to it.

"It's practically noon," Jack pointed out.

"It's 11:55 in the a.m. I'm allowed to wear it all morning. Ryan said."

I, of course, had said nothing of the sort. The lies had begun.

Jack was clinking the bowl as he got the last atoms of oatmeal from it. "I don't care what that sex-havin' bastard said. Do you realize that they could be having sex right now? While you cling to your hat-wearing." Jack looked at him with scorn. "It's a token gesture, to make us both forget that there's s-e-x going on right underneath our noses."

Phil raised his eyebrows. "*Right* underneath our noses? Like the bacteria multiplying in our mouths?" He smacked his lips and smiled a strawberry-eating smile.

"And who knows what they were doing last night? Out to the wee hours of the morning, coming in smelling of *sex*."

"Eeww." Phil grimaced over a bite of toast.

"Well, I don't really know about the smell, for sure," Jack said, pouring himself a half glass of orange juice. "I just assume."

They ate and moved around silently for a while. I considered leaving. Phil consulted his watch and removed the hat. Jack didn't notice, but when his watch bleeped he whipped around to Phil, opened his mouth — noticed the bare head — closed his mouth, and turned back to the newspaper. Phil had been looking out the window, and either missed or ignored the aborted action.

At this point I started to question my motives for eavesdropping. Watching my friends go through the usual goofy banter was fun, but I realized I had also hoped that I'd hear something that they wouldn't say in my presence.

I used to have a moral objection to spying like this. I hated gossip for gossip's sake. Why was I so casual about it now? I had crossed a line that I had held to for my whole life, not even thinking about it!

It was this whole superhero business, I realized. I had gotten so used to switching back and forth that I'd become blasé about the whole thing. But there were reasons I didn't spy — there are some things it's better not to know. Even about your friends.

"So whad'ya think of her?" Jack asked Phil. I tensely waited for the reply, almost flying out of there, but for some reason staying still.

"They seem to be 'happy,'" Phil said, making the quotation marks with his fingers. He had evaded the question but Jack didn't press him. Instead, he said *yeah* in a genuine tone.

"Got no one in this place to be bitter with any more," Jack grumbled.

I was in an office lined with books, stuffed with books, stinking of books. Smoke and books. I wondered if the prof had a library at home. I wondered if he missed them when he was on leave, or whether they had become part of the job he was on vacation from — a kind of suit jacket he wore for decorum's sake, but was glad to leave behind.

Basically, I was doing everything but what I should have been doing, which was reading the book in front of me. It was a version of the Vietnamese fly myth, which was really more about the boy than the fly.

A landlord, appropriately greedy and unlikable, comes by to collect. When asked, the boy says that his mom's out "selling the wind to buy the moon." The oblique answer annoys the landlord, who demands clarification. The boy refuses. The landlord offers to waive the debt in exchange for the info. The kid, canny as can be, says OK — but there needs to be a living witness. This is where the fly comes in.

The landlord points to a pole, on which rests said insect. The boy, satisfied, tells him the answer to the poser — that his mom was selling fans (wind) to make some cash for some lamp oil (moon). The landlord, his mental itch scratched, goes away — but comes back later, naturally, having "forgotten" ever having met our precocious protagonist.

To court it goes. The mandarin in charge asks for a witness and the kid names names. "There was a fly there," he pipes up, "sitting on his nose."

The landlord, jubilant at catching the little brat in a lie, scoffs: "It was not! It was on a post!" And thus admits that there was a meeting after all.

Beyond wishing that this kid was present at the O.J. case, what was there to learn from this? I jotted a few notes down about the differences in this version from the two previous ones I had read. Joe was working on a book that collected insect mythology from all over the world, and he was paying me good money to do the preliminary cross-referencing and collection. He had some kind of grant, as well as some pull at the university, so was able to pay me and provide this temporary office.

I had only been doing it for a week, but Joe was an excellent boss — he was appreciative of my skills and didn't seem to be in any rush. "Be thorough. The world's been waiting a long time for a definitive collection of this kind, and it can wait a little longer for a work of quality." He spoke in complete, well-crafted sentences that contrasted strongly with the way he had talked to the kids during that library lecture. It was kinda spooky. I didn't know which voice was the natural one.

I checked my watch. It was nearly time for lunch, so I grabbed the phone and called Cassandra at the diner. She picked up.

"Hi, I was wondering how much you charge for a plateful of good lovin'?"

"Hey Flyboy. It is so dead here, you wouldn't believe how dead. We been playing cards it's so dead."

"Frank isn't there?"

"Come on. I didn't say we'd been hit by a tornado, did I? Of course Frank's here. Say hi, Frank," she called. All I heard was clinking dishes. "Frank raised his hand. Frank thinks we're in the age of vid-phones."

"Frank just has some dignity," I said, amused at her patter. She had been charged ever since the *Star* had given us front-page coverage. "Any more about us in the funny papers?"

"The *Sun* has this ridiculous piece, vigilante this and terrorist that . . ." she said quietly, but still exuberantly. "They've had to leave piles of papers out with an 'honour system' cashbox to one side. I've already seen two of them ripped off and one broken open. So I'm happy. Avenged. How go the bug myths?"

"Not bad . . . there's this one that kinda bothered me . . . do you got a sec?" She did, so I told her the Vietnamese fly one. "It's called 'The Fly' but the fly is this totally passive thing. It's not even a character. I mean, it could be a mouse for all it matters — it's the boy's cleverness that is significant."

"What do you want, though?" Cassandra said. "For the fly to change into a human and approach the bench, naked and dripping with green stuff?"

I smiled, but Cassandra couldn't hear that. I slowly said, "Maaybe . . . I don't want the fly to be such an insignificant element. But you might be right, it could be that it's a reflection of my own passivity, that it bugs me so much —"

"Ah! You said it." Cassandra crowed.

"What?" My mind was a little numb with concentration, with watching itself work.

"That it 'bugged' you. I wasn't going to say it, but you said it."

"What have you been dosing your coffee with, sister?"

"Come by after, and I'll *dos-à-dos* you."

I paused. "The green stuff grosses you out, doesn't it," I said, more of a statement than a question to make it easier for her to admit.

"Wha —? Nothing that comes out of you grosses me out. No, Ryan," she chided. "It's like hair gel or something."

"There's an idea," I said, "Flyboy Hair Gel."

"Don't quit your day job," Cassandra said. "It's an acquired taste. Gotta go."

"Yep."

I figured I was due for another coffee break. On my way back from the kitchenette, I passed by Joe's office and he waved, on the phone. He had scheduled the last few weeks for work on the book, but would be starting his lecture tour of elementary schools in a week or so.

He had given me the task of working my way through the stories he had chosen, just familiarizing myself at first — he wanted my suggestions for possible thematic sections or other ways of organizing them. So I had access to all these great collections of myths, and I found myself moving beyond the insect theme now and again. The ones about the shapeshifters had obvious appeal. The ones I read treated it a few different ways. One was born a frog but had grown up in a human family. He wanted to marry someone, and even his foster parents were freaked out: "You aren't even human," they said.

That really resonated with me. Sometimes I worried about getting stuck as a fly. Sometimes — not often but sometimes — I worried that I was really a fly who could turn into a human rather than the other way around.

But this guy had a happy ending, shucked his skin after the marriage and emerged a handsome prince. No glasses and nerdy looks for this shapeshifter. But the shedding of skin had a biological flavour to it, a scientific angle. No abracadabra and *poof.*

I preferred this to the purely magical one, like the shapeshifter who learned it from ancient books. I guess because my own transformation left a green residue, I took it to mean that there was some energy expenditure, some chemical reaction, that accompanied the change.

I thought, not for the first time, that an analysis of the green substance could answer a lot of questions. I thought back to the small bottle that still rested in my bathroom cabinet, and then to my decision to wait until I had more private access to equipment before I looked at it. In hindsight, it looked like a flimsy rationale. I wasn't really scared of exposure through the analysis, and I wasn't really afraid of what I would discover. Be it a scientific-seeming or a mysterious substance, I wouldn't really act any differently.

It didn't really matter to me any more.

I didn't care how it worked. I had found a certain kind of peace with it. In the past I had poured all of my adolescent anxieties and fears into it, using my nervous energy to research and obsess about my oddity. Like a kid of another age might study masturbation — how long will the hair on my palms grow, and how often can I do it without going insane — my preoccupation with it had lessened. Mercifully.

I flipped through the myths, now, with a less driven curiosity. The groping for answers that had characterized my earlier studies, the almost lustful desire to unravel the mystery of my life, had dissipated. All it had taken was a girlfriend with a mission.

"Ryan, can you pop in when you're finished whatever you're doing?" asked Joe, leaning in with a distracted smile on his face.

I tidied things up a little, just so he didn't think I leaped at the sound of his voice, and went on over to the office across the hall. It was a cleaner office with a really nice, comfy-looking chair. No smoke smell, either, and a good view. The office I was in used to have a view, but the window was blocked by more shelves and bricked up with books.

Joe smiled as I entered, finished what he was writing and looked at me. "Well," he said. "How are things in the bibliophile's lair? Making some progress?"

His watery eyes fixed on me, and I nodded to jog them. "I just finished going through the three versions of that Vietnamese fly myth," I put some Enthusiasm™ in my voice — Bosses Love It!

"Grand — oh, that reminds me. What do you think of this?"

Joe opened up a window on his computer, an internet browser. He went to the Favorites menu, where he could access his most regular web sites. Most of them had the word *insect* in them, and one was named *my little ones*, and he selected one named *fly*.

The graphic that was coalescing on the screen was large, so it took a while to load. I looked at the screen, wondering about *my little ones* — someone's insect collection, perhaps? — and suddenly, I realized what I was looking at.

It was a really grainy overhead shot, but I could tell from the banners it was the Take Back the Night rally. In a terrifyingly red circle were pinpointed myself and Cassandra.

I looked, slowly, up at Joe. The fucker stared back at me, resting his chin on his hammy fist, an eyebrow raised. I was staring at him, wondering how he had found us out.

"Do you recognize the two circled figures?"

I slowly looked at them.

Joe was too excited to wait for my dull-witted responses, and barrelled on. "The figure with the mask goes by the pseudonym 'Flyguy' and claims to be able to *turn into a fly*."

The realization hit me like ice water: *he doesn't know*. I smiled then, wider than was warranted, and said, "Oooh yeah, I heard about these two. Calling themselves superheroes?"

Joe nodded, excited.

"I think his name is Flyboy." I said. Flyguy made me sound like a McDonald's mascot.

"That's right . . . and do you notice how the mask, the gasmask he's wearing," Joe said, poking at the screen, "has an extended mouthpiece and exaggerated eyes — much like the proboscis and eyes of the fly?" Joe tapped his head. "He's put some thought into it."

I could barely stifle a snicker. "Yeah, well, from the quotes I've seen they seem to be quite —"

"But you know what this means, don't you?"

I shrugged.

"The fly mythology continues its cultural metamorphosis. I hope we can get some good headshots of this character," Joe said. "I'd like to include him in the book. This is current, hot stuff. Happening here, too. We're tremendously lucky."

"I'll keep an eye out," I said, nodding.

"Anyway," Joe said, putting his hands behind his head and leaning back. "Sorry to disrupt you. You know my schedule next week?"

I got up, my head spinning. I turned to leave and asked casually "Where did you get a hold of that picture, anyway? I've seen artist's renditions of them, but nothing photographic."

"A friend of mine's on the force," Joe said, leafing through a wad of papers.

"Huh," I said, an anvil dropping and stopping my spinning head rather handily. "Well, just call if you need me," I said with fake cheeriness and left the room.

I went back to the office and made a show of working. Really, I couldn't focus at all, so I flipped through the book and stopped here and there. I read a tale called "The Finn Messenger" that told about a guy who could transport himself across the world by lying down in a magic chalk circle. He'd get paler and paler, start shaking, and suddenly stop. He wouldn't disappear, but he could produce an object that would prove that he'd been to that other place, like a spoon

As soon as we left the diner, I told Cassandra about the picture.

"The cops routinely take pictures at protests," she said. "It was probably taken from a videotape. Was it sharp?"

"No, it was pretty blurry."

"That's good. If it was a picture with a camera, I might think we were being singled out."

We turned left when we should have turned right. I looked at her, but she was deep in thought, so I didn't ask her where we were going — it was a nice, tree-lined street and I imagined I could smell the blooms. Other than the constant, low-level fear of being busted, it was a perfect little jaunt.

"So Paul is totally messed up about Catherine," Cassandra said. She had long ago defused my worry that the cook had a thing about her, though his recent break-up with the other waitress had put me on the alert again. "I've never seen anyone so consistently down. All the time he's down. I've never seen someone so single-minded about it. I'm too easily distracted to keep that up."

A clutching part of me thought that I would like her to be a bit less sympathetic, but I nodded anyway. We cut diagonally across a park and came to a school.

"Oh! I'm sorry," Cassandra said. "Do you mind if we go to the library?"

"Nope," I said with my hands in my pockets and a crooked smile.

"I hate when I do that, I just assume — "

"Forget it, foxy. I would have asked if I was worried."

There was a thin-cheeked woman smoking by the door, puffing away guiltily. It was weird to see guilt on a teacher's face, and weirder still to see her try to cover it up with a weak smile. Cassandra said hi and I thought about Mom for a minute. *I should call her tonight.*

It was a regular school, but there was a sub-basement with the official Toronto Public Library sign on the wall. I was pretty astounded. In fact, I was speechless. I looked down the hall for an explanation, but all I saw was a colourful sign that requested that all visitors report to the office, please.

"Shit," grumbled Cassandra. "It doesn't open for fifteen minutes."

"Let's wait," I suggested, my interest piqued by this little library. "We can go out to the playground."

We crunched over the gravel and sat on the monkey-bar dome. Cassandra got inside and I sat on the bar, gazing over curiously at the doors we had just come through.

I mean, this was a library a couple of blocks from my place that I had never even *heard* of. It wasn't on any of the branch maps — I had methodically visited each one, checking them off in my first few flat-broke and lonely months in Toronto.

Maybe this was a secret library, only for the devotees and those who satisfied certain criteria: never incurring any late fees, a spiritual understanding of the Dewey Decimal System and heightened alphabetizing skills. They would have library cards with holographic arcana and raised type.

I looked over at Cassandra and wondered aloud whether she had library-centred fantasies. She snorted and said something about it being too small for fantasies. "It's not the size of the library, it's what you do with it . . ." I said, putting on an anxious face. She covered her face with an arm.

Maybe parallel dimensions were involved. Libraries, being storehouses for alternative universes, were likely to overlap in this fashion. We might find, upon leaving, that the world was changed. That there were no regular-sized libraries, just twice as many mini-libraries, all nestled away in the basements of government buildings, laundromats, even the occasional bistro. But they'd be called libes, instead of libraries, and you could borrow clothes as well.

Cassandra sat up. "I thought Jessica might go to this school," she said, somewhat wistfully.

"Why are you speaking in the past tense?"

She paused, then shrugged. "I figure that things might be changing soon."

I looked at her, waiting for more. She looked back, silent. "Why?" I asked.

"'Cause of the superhero stuff."

"How?"

"I don't know. But it doesn't feel right to plan too far ahead."

"That's so mysterious, Cassandra. Very unlike you."

"I know. But it's just this vague feeling. I shouldn't even have bothered — well, you asked me, really." She pulled her knees up to her chin. "I usually keep things in my head until they've resolved themselves. Like baking bread."

"Cassandra's Easy-Bake Head?" I said.

Someone came out of the school and did something to the door. We got up.

I held the door open for Cassandra and entered the small library behind her, alert with anticipation.

It sucked. Well, I'm being mean, but really the only interesting thing about it was the librarian. Cassandra made her way to the videos and I chatted the old lady up.

She was wearing a red kimono (silk, it looked like) and a Blue Jays cap. "Well, the mini-libraries aren't listed because they're really only for the people who live within a few blocks. There's a few dozen in the Toronto area."

She seemed pretty normal, despite her clothes — I guessed she had picked up the kimono used or something. "What do you think of book-mobiles?" I asked, following my intuition. I had always been fascinated by the long truck of reading pleasure.

"I drove one for fifteen years. It was hard to get around corners, but I liked it because people would come in who were intimidated by the libraries. I would recommend books and talk to them, and get a feel for what their life was like. I was able to issue library cards there, and I figure I did two or three a week, which is more than lots of still libraries."

It took me a second to realize what she meant by still libraries, but then I did. I imagined her rocking around in a bookmobile, and then thought she might have an eccentric (rather than unconscious) taste in clothes. Cassandra checked out a bunch of kids' books and a calypso CD.

I nodded goodbye and as we left I said, "That's a lovely kimono," and she just kept smiling and nodding.

When we got outside I said *damn.*

"What?" asked Cassandra.

"I couldn't tell if she knew it was a kimono or not. How does she usually dress?"

Cassandra shrugged.

"I couldn't tell if she just thought that kimono was an interesting type of blouse or whether she liked the contrast with the hat."

"What does it matter?" Cassandra said with a snort.

"I dunno. Oh, hey, did I tell you about this really great Norwegian folk tale? The hero, called the Ash Boy, kills the troll."

"Poor troll."

"Yeah, yeah. Anyway, he takes the gold and silver the troll's got in his lair, and with this he's able to pay back *some of his family's debt.*"

"And?"

"Well, I mean," I sputtered, "no happily ever after for this kid — he's just keeping his head above water at the end."

Cassandra laughed. "Norway's a cold place."

chapter fifteen

"What? What did you say?" I screamed at Mark.

The feedback ended, finally, and we applauded.

"I hate those interminable noisy, screechy endings," Mark said. "It's like finishing a sweater with straggly bits of wool."

"What did you say about Ken?"

Mark took a slug of beer. "He was busted. He's in jail."

I opened and closed my mouth. I watched the opening band wind up their instruments, and they appeared to be doing it almost grievously. Then one laughed and kicked me back to consciousness.

Cassandra came up and ruffled Mark's blue tuft. He seemed to like it.

"What would they arrest Ken for?" I said, almost too quietly.

"Ken was arrested?" Cassandra exclaimed.

"He was walking around at night. They thought he was suspicious looking so they searched him, and he had a joint on him."

"They arrested him for one joint?!" Cassandra looked as shocked as I felt, but I could see anger rising in her while nausea slowly sank into my pores. "That's really fucked up."

"Let's go sit down," Mark suggested.

We were all here to see Valerie's band, Unpleasant Gents. Mark introduced us to a woman he worked with, Bethany, who aimed her eyes at us for a second and nodded as Mark filled out the connections and details beyond our first names.

"Does Valerie know you're here, Cassandra?" Mark asked. "She'd be totally nervous if she knew. Same instrument and all."

"I met her at Sok and she had just made up the flyers."

"Oh, that flyer was total shit," Mark said.

I had seen it — it wasn't shit, it was a nicely designed

poster with an image of a swank, devil-horned millionaire type on it. I guess my consternation showed on my face, because Mark was grinning. "Oh, ho," I said. "*You* designed it. Well, you can fish for compliments all day, bucko, you ain't gonna catch anything in this pool."

Everyone laughed, and I leaned back and basked in it. I had bypassed my normal new-person shyness by being almost fooled by Mark. I decided I liked the guy — at first I had disliked him, maybe because I was a little intimidated, but also because he was Jack's rival. But he wasn't so scary when he was talking and smiling, and I found his admiration of Cassandra really appealing — she got so little, that I could see, and she deserved so much.

At the diner, she had to deal with a lot of crap. There were these two girls who kind of idolized her, but other than that I had seen a lot of idiots treat her badly. Not that she didn't throw it back at them, and more besides, but it was really amazing that she had the energy and poise she did. She was untouchable, she was unbreakable, she was a fucking *titan.*

All of this I thought in a rush, the smoke stinging my eyes as I stared at her, while Mark urged her to get back into a band. "I'd start one, just to get you making music again," he finished.

Cassandra smiled and shook her head. She patted his hand. "You're sweet."

"I'm not sweet, I'm selfish. I just want more like the *Amazon Allegiance* LP," he said, flailing his hands as if he could pull convincing words out of the air. "Do you know that you're mixing it up with genius here?!"

I shrugged. "She hasn't even let me listen to the LP yet," I said.

"It's so *old*," said Cassandra.

Mark put his head in his hands.

There was quiet, as quiet as it gets in a bar, and I filled it. "So tell us more about Ken. How'd you hear about it?"

Mark propped up his head and, reminded again, his eyes were sad. It's amazing how some people — most people, even — have a limited tolerance for sadness. If they're being honest, it comes to them like waves rather than soaking and submerging them utterly.

"Are you sure he's in jail?"

"Yeah. I heard from Gillian and then I called his parents' place, because he would have called them for bail. But supposedly they don't do it on the weekend, so he'll be in the Don until Monday."

"They don't let people out on bail? So he's in there right now?" I said, imagining the poor guy sitting on a cold toilet, watched by the other prisoners. That was what I always dreaded — the exposure, the indignity.

"He's in the Don Jail?" Cassandra said. "The Don is the toughest penitentiary in Toronto. What the fuck is a guy who smokes the wrong kind of cigarettes doing there?"

Mark nodded to all of our questions. Then he got up and left for the bar. He had a while to wait, because they were understaffed and overcrowded, but Mark had no problems getting noticed.

As I watched him approach the bar, I noticed Jack coming in, messy hair and straw-coloured satchel on his hip. I waved him over.

"You got my note?" I assumed, and he nodded, looking around and sitting beside Bethany in Mark's seat.

"Am I in time?" he asked. His eyes searched the stage. I tried to decide by just looking at him whether he was here out of curiosity or obsession. I had never told him about the snatch of party conversation I had heard between Val and Mark.

"The Unpleasant Gents are up next," I said. "Then a band named Slowgun."

"What's with these names?" said Jack. Then, as he often does, he answered his own question. "I guess it's a bit weird, expecting people to come up with a name that'll reflect their work, now and forever. Imagine if a writer had to choose their name?"

I was in the middle of imagining that — only able to come up with bad examples, like Sad McSad and LuciFire — when I was distracted by seeing Mark coming back with a whole armful of beer bottles. I imagined instead what would happen if Mark saw Jack's taking his seat as symbolic of trying to replace him in Val's eyes. A flurry of bursting brown glass and beer mixed with blood?

Mark calmly distributed beers that were, he explained, courtesy of Val's inability to use her drink tickets. Jack got the first one, with a smile from Mark. It might have been a bit tight, but it was well on this side of civil. Then he took the seat beside me.

I watched as the Bethany-Cassandra chat opened up to absorb Jack, and turned to Mark who was silently watching the empty stage. "You ever do any of this rock 'n' roll stuff?" I asked.

He shook his head and said, "Naw. I'm not an artist, or a poet, or a creative guy at all, really. I'm an en*thu*siast." He pronounced it like some people would pronounce *artiste*, with a little bit of self-consciousness but unbitter.

I said, "I dunno. You've done a good job with the flyers I've seen. That takes a certain kind of eye."

"Well, thanks." He bit at a nail with a delicacy that contrasted with his size. "I see myself as a promoter, kind of. A patron." We talked about his plans to set up a zine and music distro, Cassandra offering a few comments.

I noticed that Jack and Bethany had their heads bent together, the features on their faces jerking with animation and amusement. I was about to quietly point it out to Cassandra when the stage lights came on.

Val adjusted the mike down to her level, squinting at the lights. "Hi, we're Unpleasant Gents. Prepare to squirm."

They moved into a rocky number with moog synth accompaniment. The guy tickling the plastic ivory was wearing a Spiderman costume, sans head. Val sounded good, from what I could hear of her.

There were a few young kids moving back and forth at the perimeter, the unashamedly geeky giving their thin limbs a shaking. Mark got up and I thought he was going to join them, and considered doing so myself, leaning forward in my seat. But he made a quick U-turn towards the soundboard.

I leaned back, on to Cassandra. I made like I didn't know what I was leaning on and looked around. She started with the tickling so I pulled away, but not before she sucked a big kiss on my neck.

Valerie's voice became clearly audible then, and it happened so close in time to the kiss, I thought Cassandra had sucked some obstruction out of my spine. When Mark came and sat down, however, I realized he had fixed the sound levels.

> Striping the walls again
> Because they got rubbed off
> It's not a cage it's a candy sweetness
> Bon-bon jail

Val had a sure voice and a renegade smile. I hadn't read her poetry and I wondered how like the songs it was — I figured pretty similar.

Cassandra leaned on my shoulder and breathed through my shirt.

"Why did you quit playing bass?" I asked her. I had to yell.

She moved away from me, an inch maybe. "I didn't, exactly. I pawned it. The day before I got the Sok job."

"That must have been hard."

Cass just shrugged. I looked at her, and then beyond to Jack who was looking at Bethany looking at the stage. She smoothed her reddish hair away from her eye and saw Jack watching her. I looked away before she saw me, too.

The song finished.

"Thanks for coming out, everyone. Slowgun, Toronto's best jury-duty dodgers, will be delighting you soon. But our next song is about the new superheroes in town."

Cassandra's head lifted off my shoulder.

Val continued, "You've all heard about them, right? As you can see, we're dressed up as other — inferior — superheroes. I've got the Wonder Woman bullet-deflector bracelets," she said, holding up her arms, deflecting a sunful of light with her gold wrists. "And we've got Spidey on the synth and git-are, and — show 'em your cape, Nick!"

Nick, an Asian guy behind the drum set, lifted his red cape and pointed to his gel-solid-parted Superman hairstyle.

"Finally we have someone to protect us from the cops!" she said, and launched into a song that intertwined the music from the Spiderman and Batman themes with the chorus:

Flyboy and Ms. Place
Getting on the Man's case
They be always in his face
They came from outer space

Then there was a few ribald guitar licks and superhero poses. Cassandra squeezed my hand under the table. Her eyes were bright, spotlit.

"Outer space?" I asked Mark.

He shrugged. "It's a necessity with these indie-rock bands to mention outer space at least once per set. Otherwise they're drummed outta the clique."

It was obvious that Mark wasn't part of that clique, which protected itself with layers of thrift store clothing rather than colourful razor haircuts. I wondered how much he liked the music and how much of it was boyfriendial obligation.

There were a few more songs after the superhero song and they got a generous helping of applause. Cassandra went up (dragging me by the hand) as they were putting their stuff away and hugged Val. I said a few complimentary words amid Cassandra's torrent. Val smiled hugely and tried to clean her glasses while Cassandra pushed and patted her exuberantly.

I glanced back to see Bethany getting up and pulling on her coat, while Jack said a few more laugh-inducing things. Then she walked towards the washroom.

I made a beeline for my friend, who was already looking lonesome. "Hey, so you were talking with her . . . ?" Delivering the open-ended line that had started off these discussions through the ages, nodding and smiling.

"Yeah. She's beautiful and intelligent and will be out of my life in seconds," Jack said, blinking frantically. "What else is new?"

I started to ask if he got her number, but stopped. It was too stark a move for Jack; it left his amorous intentions too naked. "She's going home early. And alone." I thought about the dangers of a woman walking alone and then it hit me. "Offer to walk her home."

"What?"

"It's dangerous to walk alone at night. You have to at least offer," I insisted, just as Bethany arrived back to say goodbye. I offered a hand and said *nicetameetcha* and made myself scarce.

Mark and the drummer were talking animatedly. I approached them, pointed out that she was leaving. I couldn't bear to look back to see if it was with Jack.

"Ah-ha," Mark said, lifting his hand in farewell. "It appears she is leaving with Mr. Jack." There was a funny smile on his face as he said it. I noticed that the drummer was watching Mark's face just as intently as Mark was watching them. "Well, Jack's a good egg. And Bethany's a sweet kid. She came out of a four-year relationship almost a year ago," he explained to me, and my hopes rose a notch. "I think she could use some male companionship."

I liked the way he said that. It wasn't sleazy, it wasn't coy; it was just the way you could talk frankly about friends.

"C'mon," Nick said. "Help me pack this shit in the van."

I had left a message on Ken's machine:

"Hey man. Give me a call when you're out of the poky." I figured a bit of light humour was in order, but not too boisterous, so I toned down the Vegas showman the long beep usually inspired in me.

I didn't get a call back until Wednesday. I was getting ready to leave for class.

"Hi. I'm out."

"Ken! Oh man, how are you?"

"Bleeeaaaaah," he said in a singsongy way.

"Fuck." A thousand different prison-related jokes danced before my eyes, ripe for the saying, any of which could have been too close to the truth. "Fuck."

"Yeah."

"Well, I mean, is that it? You're not really going to court for a joint, are you?"

There was silence on his end. When I was about to jabber on, he said, "Yeah. A funny little routine called the Controlled Drugs and Substances Act means I may be inside for six months. Pretty awful, eh?"

Now it was my turn to say nothing. It was more than awful. I imagined him now, holding the phone as if it were a dumbbell, staring into the floor and bent by misery.

We didn't say too much more that day. Ken was tired, despite having slept most of the last forty-eight hours. "I keep waking up and checking to see if my door is locked."

A bedroom door latch ain't gonna keep them out, I thought but didn't say. And of course he knew that, knew it better than I.

"Have you got this one?" Mary said, holding up a clipping with the headline SUPERHEROES FIGHT FOR WOMEN'S RIGHTS.

"Yeah, that's in the 'friendly' section near the back."

I was flipping through the scrapbook that Cassandra had put together. "So is this definitive?"

"No, not really," said Cassandra, wiping off a corner of Jessica's mouth with a wet thumb. Jessica's face squinched when she did it. "Mary says that people have told her about papers all over the country covering it — mostly as a joke story, but covering it all the same."

"Huh!" I started putting away the sandwich stuff. "Anyone for another?" I offered, swinging the mayonnaise jar temptingly.

"A porn mag in Britain called *Knave* printed our e-mail address, the fuckers," said Mary. "I don't know what they said but they sure got a few twits excited."

"Dear Superheroine," I said in me best cockney accent. "Oim a lonely cab driver in London, and oi want yuir boots all over me body. Oi have been bad and oi need to be brought to justice."

Mary was spreading the e-mail printouts on the kitchen table. I went and locked the kitchen door — Jack and Phil were out, but there was no point tempting fate. I don't know how I'd explain this mini-battleroom atmosphere.

"Are they here?" said Cassandra. "The porn ones?"

"I didn't print 'em out. They're still on the system, though. I just printed out the ones I thought you might want to reply to."

There was one from Mexico who expressed his solidarity in sterile English.

There was one from a little girl (for Miss Place) and from her younger brother (for Fly Boy) wanting to know how old we were and how they could get superpowers. This made us laugh nervously — such a basic question, yet one which we had absolutely no clue about ourselves.

There were a few from university newspapers, in the States and Canada, that had dozens of questions and subquestions in neat, numbered lists.

"Damn, this is exciting!" said Cassandra. She looked around at us for confirmation. "And oh, Mary, we didn't even tell you about our friend's band!" She gave details. "It's so amazing to think that we're inspiring people . . . that we're becoming these *symbols*. That it's *working*."

I saw, for a brief second, the wildness of it. I raised my eyebrows at Mary. She shrugged and nodded, then looked back at her papers.

"There's a lot of misinformation and rumours about the details of your lives," said Mary.

"Good," I said.

Cassandra looked at me.

"There's always going to be stuff like that," I explained. "Let it lie. In the articles I've read there's misinformation galore. About the size of Superheroes for Social Justice, about the things we've done and possible theories on how we've done it. Why try to correct it when it's so interesting? We can't even explain everything if we wanted to. There should be conflicting information about legendary things. Myths aren't fact-checked."

"Let mystery prevail," said Cassandra, in a dreamy way.

"That's our PR strategy, right there," I said, and Mary sighed. "Let Mystery Prevail."

"Well, it means less work for me," Mary said. "And it's safer. So what

I can do is thank them for their interest and put them on the press release list."

Cassandra picked Jessica up and sat her in her lap. "How'd the *Varsity* thing go?"

A sliver of a smile wedged its way onto Mary's face. She cleared her throat. "Well, it went . . . well. She got what she wanted for the story." Mary stared out the window. "We're meeting again."

"For follow-up questions?" Cassandra said.

"Uh . . . no."

I knew what was going on before Cassandra, for once. "For ooogabooga?"

Mary showed her teeth in a nervous smile.

Cassandra slapped her forehead. "Oh no! Not another baby dyke falling to Patricia's Vagina Dentata!"

"I know, I know," said Mary. "She's a wolf. I know when I'm being seduced."

I looked at Jessica for guidance. "Tell Mary she shouldn't mix business with pleasure, Jessica." Jessica turned her oval eyes on Mary.

"Just make sure you keep your mouth shut. No pillow talk. Remember, this could all be some elaborate way to pump you for information. She's entirely capable of that." Cassandra clenched her teeth. "Patricia," she hissed to the skies.

"OK," Mary said, as meek as I've seen her.

"What? You'd sanction this unholy joining?" I said to Cassandra, but really to Mary.

Mary started gathering all her papers up. She looked up, her eyes shining. "She says she's going tree-planting this summer."

"She goes tree-planting every summer," said Cassandra with a dark smile. "It's to keep her lovers at arm's length."

Mary looked at her.

"Trust me," said Cassandra. "She's a heartbreaker. Leave your feelings at home."

I watched Cassandra very carefully as she said this. There was nothing in her face that helped me divine her own feelings about Pat. I supposed she had her reasons for not telling Mary of their affair. If she had, I figured that Mary would discount everything she said about Patricia as jealousy. In Mary's place, that's what I would have done.

"So," I said. "If we're well and done with that, I'd like to bring an item of business to the table." I thumped the table for emphasis. "Ken and the injustice of hemp prohibition."

Jessica leaned over and thumped the table, too.

Mary smirked a bit. "Hemp prohibition?"

"Hemp prohibition," confirmed Cassandra. (OK, I admit it, we had planned this tag-teaming in advance.) "In the 1930s Dow Chemical patented a chemical-based process to turn tree pulp into paper. Wanting to get rid of their biggest competitor — hemp-based paper — they formed an alliance with their biggest customer: the newspaper empire of Hearst. So there was a propaganda campaign to get rid of hemp. They deliberately renamed it marijuana so that it sounded foreign and strange, and were able to criminalize it on the basis that it was an immoral, corrupting drug."

I had heard all this before — usually far less succinctly, from some stoned friend — but it looked like it was news to Mary. And then Cassandra took it another step.

"I was reading this book on the Poll Tax — you know how it was beaten in Britain, right?"

"I remember the picture of the guy with the brick," I offered. I didn't think there would be Pot Riots, though. Kind of a contradiction in terms.

"Anyway," Cassandra said. "The original Tory name for the tax was the Community Charge. But activists kept calling it the Poll Tax, which was the name of a similarly hated tax that was beaten during thirteen something-something. So eventually, it was universally known as the Poll Tax — even in the newspapers — which was a significant victory."

"A significant semantic sally," I quipped.

"Yeah," said Mary. She seemed a little distracted.

"All of this is premature, though," Cassandra said. "In a nutshell: our friend has been arrested for the possession of a single joint. We feel this arrest is neither politically nor ethically justified and are going to take action. You don't have to help out with this mission, if you don't want to. You can take a hiatus from the Superheroes for Social Justice." Her face was calm.

I cocked my finger like it was a piece. "Our retirement package includes a small apartment in either pine or oak."

Mary smiled, raising her sensible shoes. "Can't you fit me for something in concrete?"

"Seriously, though," Cassandra said, twist-pinching me. "I know you got into this for other issues. No hard feelings."

"No hard feelings. You'll *hardly* feel anything." Laying my hands out mobster-style. This got a punch my bone felt. I gave her a wounded-puppy look and got a shut-the-fuck-up look back.

"OK," Mary said. "This is my perspective — I'm not a big yay-drugs person. When people make this their issue, they're usually not up front about their hedonistic motivations."

I was quiet. I had had the same feeling, almost exactly. I wanted to see if she came to the same conclusion I did. She was staring at the sheets on the table, then continued.

"I guess I can't blame people for having a personal interest in the thing they're fighting for. Or I'd have to call every gay involved in politics a selfish cruiser. Not that some white boy who figgers out wearing a Rasta hat and talking politics gets him laid has anything in common with a life-long dyke activist." She gave us both sharp looks, as if to make sure that that's not what we thought she meant.

"But I think that it's crazy that people can choose to poison their bodies with alcohol and nicotine but not pot. It's hypocritical. Plus, pot fucks you up less, physically — so I've heard." Mary looked at us. "I've never done it."

Virgin Mary, I thought tenderly.

"So OK, I've convinced myself. I'll do it."

Cassandra smiled and lifted a fist. I announced that I was going to celebrate by voiding my bladder.

I left the kitchen and shut the door. I paused, just to make sure I couldn't hear what they were saying through the door — I'd never had occasion for stealth in the apartment before, so I didn't know how sound-proof the doors were. I felt a little guilty for sneaking around two of my best friends. But they never knew everything about me, anyway.

Just as I was making my way to the washroom, Jack slipped out of it with a guilty look on *his* face.

"Thought you guys were busy in the kitchen," he mumbled, trying to get past me into his room.

I realized what it was. "Oh, no, never too busy to hear about what went on after the show, Jack-me-boy." I put an arm out and gave him the sharkiest grin I had. "Well?"

There was a smile on his face, his eyes pleaded with me. "C'mon, Ryan, I can't talk about what happened or didn't happen. You know it's impossible."

We had discussed this on a previous occasion: how it was impossible for a guy to talk about any romantic action, even in the most clinical of terms, without being a Pig. A woman, unfairly, could lavishly and elaborately detail her conquests without sleaziness.

"Well, tell me about the future, Jack. Are you seeing her again?"

"Yep!" He pushed against my arm and I let it fall. I followed him into the room, ignoring him as he tried to close the door on me.

The first thing he did was close his writing journal.

"Love poetry, Jack?" I guessed, and by his pitiful smile, guessed correctly. "Oh, Jack . . ." I flumped down on his bed.

"What are you guys doing in the kitchen, anyway?" he asked, clicking his mechanical pencil out and then pushing the lead in again.

"Secret stuff," I said. Click click click, he said. I noticed a new tattered poster on the wall, a kid's big eye visible. "No, we just needed the table for a project. Whered'ya get that?" I said, pointing to the tatter.

"Piece of a huge mural. Can't really tell what it was. Talking about paintings, Bethany has this great series of paintings based on the superhero thing — you know it, the people in the city pretending to be superheroes and doing political stuff?"

I nodded, stifling my urge to protest "pretending."

"Well, she's done pictures of them. Ms. Place and The Fly."

My stifling powers slipped. "Fly*boy.*"

"Right. Well, they're actually *good.* I was so happy she was *good,* Ryan! I didn't even have to stretch the truth." His eyes were shining.

"Your eyes are shining," I said. "Stop that. When did you see these allegedly good paintings?"

Click click click.

"So you went up to her place? What did she say, Jack? *Come on up and I'll show you my etchings?* You disgust me. You artist types," I said, rising from the bed and wearing a look of haughty disgust. "You artists and your slack moral codes and bohemian lifestyles." I reached for the doorknob but thought better of it, using the cuffs of my sleeve to germlessly turn it instead. "I'll leave you to your lunatic fantasies."

"I wanna make supper soon!" he called after me.

"God forbid you deny yourself anything!" I shouted. "Indulge every base appetite you have, you cad!"

Vitalized with glee, I re-entered the kitchen with a huge grin. They looked at me, Cassandra with *what?* eyebrows.

"Oh, just listening to Jack's sordid tales of his latest fling. 'One poem and her pants hit the floor,' he claimed."

Mary looked disgusted, but Cassandra crossed her arms and said, "Jack's not like that. You fucking lie."

"Of course I lie," I said. "It's what I do."

chapter sixteen

Val wasn't there, and I was worried. I had got there dead on time, but it took another ten minutes for the meeting to start as the stragglers descended into the basement and found seats. Mark was one of them, and he took the milk crate beside mine.

"Hey Ryan," he said. I heyed back.

"You facilitating this meeting, Mark?" said a guy with short blond hair.

"Nope."

A guy leaning against the wall said softly, "I am. We'll start in five minutes, OK?" There was no disagreement. I had time to reflect that this was the second time in two months that I had found myself in Who's Emma's anarchist bowels, although it was less crowded than it had been for the FUCK LOVE performance.

Someone dressed in a tie and freshly pressed trousers carefully descended the stairs and, after saying hello to the facilitator, sat cross-legged on the dingy orange carpet. I gave Mark a look to see what he thought of this jewel amid the rubbish, but he was more affected by the next person who came down.

"Ah fuck," he muttered under his breath.

A few guys called out "James!" and he headed for them. "Wussup?" he said, grinning and slapping skin. He squeezed into the narrow space between his friends and some girls that had obviously been left as a comfort zone. With exaggerated care, he removed his jester hat, trying not to shake the bells.

"Ten to one he works his band into the discussion somehow," Mark said to me under his breath.

The soft-spoken guy looked up from his clipboard. He had dark eyes and looked like he could have been Filipino or Thai. "OK, this is the first meeting of the End Hemp Prohibition action node. This meeting was called in response to the arrest of local artist Ken Matthews for possession of one joint. It's pretty rare to be convicted for such a small amount, but whether he is sentenced or not is beside the point — his life has already been considerably disrupted for doing something that millions of Canadians do every day: consuming a benign drug for recreational purposes."

His delivery was fluid and polished. There was nodding all around, not that that was surprising. Val came in with her backpack and sat down. I beamed at her, and she gave me a surprised smile back.

"While I know Ken only slightly, the whole community can benefit if we build up grassroots resistance. Mr. Patterson here," he indicated the man with the tie, "has flown in from Vancouver to offer his considerable experience."

"I got off the plane half an hour ago, so you'll have to forgive me if I'm a little scattered," Patterson said, and then proceeded to deliver a perfectly prepared meal of soundbites. "First of all, I'm the proprietor of Hemp Canada, a business that recently won the legal right to sell hemp-related paraphernalia again after being shut down by the authorities over a year ago. We did it through a concentrated blitz of protests and media coverage which swayed public opinion to the point where they had no choice but to do what they did. We aim to do the same thing here, except with the right to consume hemp."

Most people looked impressed. Val was staring at him intensely. Mark shifted his boots as if they were too tight.

The facilitator started up again, without missing a beat. "What we'd like to start with is a go-around," he made a circle in the air with his pen, "and find if anyone has any suggestions as to how we can best help Ken. James Heron and I have already discussed a benefit show. The money will go towards defraying the legal costs."

"Yes, my band, The Krazy Kats, will be performing along with a number of other fine local acts," James said, playing with his jester's hat. "If you'd like to play, talk to me."

Mark raised his hand sharply. The facilitator, who looked as if he was considering continuing, paused, then acknowledged him.

"While it all sounds *awfully* entertaining," Mark said, his voice level, "what I would like to know is whether there will be a videotape of the event for Ken to watch in his prison cell?"

This brought a round of laughter (someone muttered *satellite feed*), which didn't soften Mark's expression any. I was a little surprised at his vehemence, but he had a good point.

The facilitator smiled tightly and said, "Look, it's only one thing we're doing."

"Yet it's the very first thing you mention."

"Well, we're looking for other possible routes —"

"Here's a route," interrupted Mark, "a direct one. Let's get Ken out of the country."

"How's that going to help the hundreds of political prisoners already in jail for hemp possession?"

"By showing that we won't put up with it," Mark said. "We won't put up with our friends being put in jail when they haven't hurt anyone."

The facilitator held up his hand. "OK, let's keep going around. Does anyone else have any suggestions?"

There was a pause before a girl with bright red hair and a nose ring said, "Posters. Like, on poles and stuff."

The facilitator nodded and wrote it down on his clipboard. "Good. That's fully legal," he said, looking at Mark.

Val, from the stairs behind him, leaned over and offered him a marker. "Here — your pen seems to have run out of ink. Oh, unless you were just *pretending* to write it down . . ."

The facilitator took the marker, and silently wrote on his clipboard.

"Fucking bullshit," someone muttered.

"While you're doing that," Val said. "I'll just read this out. I was in contact with the Superheroes for Social Justice via e-mail about this very issue, and they said that they think a grassroots group would be great, but they want us to keep in mind that regardless of the court's decision, Ken's not going to jail. 'Ken Matthews isn't doing time' is their final statement."

This, I was pleased to see, sent a ripple of excitement through the group. "Yay SSJ!" said the girl with the red hair. The acronym sounded neat. I decided I kinda liked being famous.

"Look, that's fine for him, but what about the people who don't have vigilante friends?" the facilitator said, losing all of his soft-spokenness. "This kind of thing will take years to do properly. We're just laying the groundwork here."

"Not with Ken you're not," said Mark, and strode out of the meeting. A bunch of people went with him, mostly punk kids, and I took up the rear. There were a few uncertain people left, hippie-types, and the facilitator made an effort to go on. I would have liked to stay to see what they were planning, but I was worried I'd lose face.

"You know that clipboard guy is planning to open a Hemp Canada franchise outlet in Toronto, right?" said Val. She was seething, a clump of people around her. "Patronizing, scene-hijacking capitalist!"

I didn't know what to think. Obviously, those two had their questionable motivations, but I thought their legal approach would complement our direct approach. They seemed a little too comfortable with losing the first couple of rounds, mind you, and Ken wasn't going to be martyred for some elaborate multitiered legal scheme.

The proprietor of Hemp Canada climbed the stairs, alone, with a sheepish smile on his face. "Well, he botched that, didn't he."

"You should pick your business partners more carefully," said Val.

He looked a little sad, and said as he left, "I hope you're not putting all your faith in superheroes rescuing you."

The door shut and she muttered, "Hope he's not putting all his faith in lawyers rescuing him." We laughed and Val frowned. "Fuck, why didn't I think of that a second earlier?"

Mark suddenly slammed out the door, yelled the line, then returned, blue tuft wagging.

"Just as he got in the taxi," he reported happily.

The omnipresent Mrs. Grachie failed us. We had planned to go see George Bush get his honorary degree from the University of Toronto, but Mrs. Grachie surprised us with her own selfish demands — some nonsense about a goddaughter's wedding.

Jessica was busy making a Tinkertoy pipeline right across the apartment. I was reading the homework I had told Cass I had to catch up on — the reason why I didn't mind looking after Jess. While I wanted to see the Gulf War president catch a SCUD up the ass, I knew Cassandra wanted it worse. She knew the organizers of the secret protest — not well enough to know exactly what they had planned, but well enough to know it was gonna be good.

"What are you doing, Jess?" I called.

She came out from the bathroom and stared at me.

"What are you doing, hey?" I said with a smile.

"Playing," she said.

"Can I play?"

She thought for a second. "OK," she said finally. Then she disappeared.

There was something about her thoughtfulness that endeared her to me. I had to watch it, though, because I didn't want to become a father by default. Not that Cass had ever mentioned it, but our romance was progressing so quickly that it was hard not to look ahead.

I went back to the book for nearly four words when the phone rang. I leaned over for it with a grin, glad to blame the world for conspiring against my homework getting done.

"Ryan!"

"Cass!"

"You wouldn't believe how well it went," she said with the perfunctory eagerness of pay-phoners.

"How well?"

"Well, first, the school had this bizarre formal setup — you'd think the bastard was getting knighted or something."

U of T graduation ceremonies were notoriously pretentious, and I would have liked to skip mine. But my mom was a stickler for those things. *Of course*, an unwelcome voice said, *she may not be around by then.*

"By the time the actual presentation came, I was itching to do something. So when they pulled out the scroll —"

"Let me guess — it vanished into thin air?"

Cassandra laughed. "Apparently you mistake me for a rank amateur. No, using the tried-and-true magician's trick of misdirection, I disappeared part of the flag-stand first — and as the crowd watched the American flag crash into and topple over the Canadian one, I sent that nasty little scroll elsewhere."

"Took the Canadian flag down with it, eh? Nicely symbolic," I interjected. Jess came into the room and started building an extension on the Tinkertoy joint near my foot.

"Yeah — half the crowd was laughing hysterically, and half was looking embarrassed for Georgie. The scroll-giver seemed a little flustered, naturally, having no more scroll to give. He kept looking under the stage. But that wasn't the best part."

Jess had built the extension so that it reached my hand. Now she scrambled up beside me and made me close my fist around the green stick. "OK," she said, then retreated into the bathroom again. "Where are you now?" I asked.

"Near Robarts. Anyway, right at that point — and keep in mind that I had no idea what they were up to — the Devil pushes through the main entrance and strides up to the front. He's got two minor demons with him, one with this bright red podium, and they put that right beside the real one. No one said a word to them."

"Holy!" I said.

"Yeah! Well, unholy, actually. I recognized the guy then, he was this huge guy with this black beard that I had met at an OPIRG party. Anyway, in costume he was terrifying. He took the mike and put it on his podium and tapped it with his pitchfork to make sure it was on."

"They didn't pull the plug?"

"No! They were completely dumbfounded. George was still standing there, still waiting for the scroll from the real guy. And Satan starts to congratulate Bush . . . for cleverly hiring a PR firm to generate animosity towards a puppet leader he himself had helped install when he was the CIA director, how maybe it didn't get him another term as he had intended but that the war was still a wonderful romp — it damned the soul of many an American bomber and sent hundreds of thousands of innocents to their deaths. In fact, Satan said, because of gratuitous damage to the infrastructure in Iraq, many innocents were dying every day, causing a delicious feast of torment for the underworld."

"Delicious?" I said, still holding the Tinkertoy.

"Yeah! Oh, it was so campy and fun. Really well thought-out. Then he said that on behalf of all Hell's denizens, he was proud to bestow upon Bush a Doctorate in Evilology."

I laughed. "Man, that's great!"

"Then it burst into flame! The scroll Satan was holding, I mean. I guess they had it rigged. That's when the secret service guy came up and whisked Bush away. There was only one bodyguard."

"I guess they don't take Canadians very seriously, if he had only one bodyguard."

"Yeah — I got the feeling that he didn't really know if Satan was part of the ceremony or not. And the demons were really funny, sticking their tongues out and capering about through the whole thing."

"OK, you're making me jealous. Did anyone tape it?"

"No, but there were about four people taking pictures."

Jess walked back into the room and started making another extension a few feet away.

"How's it going with Jess?"

"It's . . . good. We're just playing with Tinkertoys."

Jessica finished what she was doing and came to the phone. I said goodbye and passed it to her.

I let go of my Tinkertoy when I stood up. Jess didn't seem to mind. "Playing," she said to the phone.

I looked at the extension she had built — it ended in her floppy box of crayons.

"OK," said Jess.

I followed the main pipeline to the bathroom and saw she had built it so that it angled up and through the small hole in the screen window. I looked out, at the sky and the clouds.

I went by to visit Ken at his place. His roommate let me in and I climbed up the jumble of staircases that led to his room, catching glimpses of tattered punk rock flyers and duty rosters and strange collages.

I got to the last few steps and could hear his laugh already. I smiled.

"Hello!"

Ken was there with two of his friends, Gillian and Kurt. My friends too, but very close to Ken. Their bond seemed to come partially from being very sad from time to time, and helping each other out. I wondered what it was like for them in the same way I wondered about the frogs who sleep in the mud underneath a frozen pond for the whole wintertime.

"What's s'damn funny?" I demanded, taking a chair.

"Oh, Ken's just telling us his prison stories. They're terrible," said Gillian, laughing.

"Just *awful*," said Kurt with a smile.

"Tell 'em again, tell 'em again," I pleaded.

"First of all, I get strip-searched in a parking garage. Then, because of it being federal jurisdiction, I get shipped off to the Don Jail, the worst jail in the city." He laughed. "Oh, I didn't tell you guys this," he said to Gillian and Kurt. "But when I was first being brought in, the cops were fucking laughing at me and stuff, talking about how I was going to get raped." He laughed again, pulling his knees up and rocking back and forward on the bed.

"But the best part was how they were saying, 'Oh, we're going to party with this joint after work, man, thanks a lot.'" Kurt and Gillian burst out laughing at his dumbguy accent.

"Wow, they've still got that grade six mentality," said Gillian. "How do they keep their minds so fresh?"

"It's wonderful, isn't it?" I said, shocked and angry and jaded and apathetic.

"Did they play 'Monkey in the Middle' with it? Na-na, na-na-na," Kurt said.

Ken laughed and reached out as if trying to catch the joint way above his head. Then he continued. "Then I got put in this totally metallic cell and it was fucking freezing in there, and they had taken away my shoes."

"You had socks, right?" I said.

"Yeah, but they had big holes in the bottom. You know when the tips of your feet get so cold that it feels like there are balls in them?"

"Whaaat?" said Kurt.

I knew what he was talking about, so I nodded.

"Well, Ryan, my feet were like that after about half an hour and I was there for *three hours.*"

"Did you get fingerprinted?" I asked. I had been thinking about that a lot because I couldn't remember if *I* had ever been. I knew they couldn't catch me — I could just fly away — but I was worried I had left prints on the billboard that would let them trace me.

"Yep. The ink they use is just horrible, it takes three solution washes to get off, and it didn't even come off my fingers." He sniffed his fingers. "The smell is gone, finally. That's another thing! So many stories . . ." He addressed us all again. "So they put me back in the metal box and I've got this black shit all over my hands, so I start drawing with it."

"Didn't they confiscate your fingers?" Kurt asked.

"No, they totally didn't know I was doing it. I ended up doing a whole comic on the floor. It might still be there right now."

Gillian giggled. "Some guy who's just killed his wife is looking at it saying 'Why is the triangle talking? Triangles can't talk. That makes me angry!'"

"That's neat," I said. "So no one can ever do the *Definitive Baby Sneaky 5000* because one of them will be lost forever in the belly of the beast."

"So did you get fucked, at least?" asked Kurt.

"Nope," chuckled Ken. "No such luck. The one thing society promises you . . . But who knows what the future holds." He looked at me. "There might be a lot of jail editions of my comics."

"Oh no," said Gillian. "There's —"

"Though my little angels might come rescue me, my supersonic angels," he said wistfully. "I like to think about that. She's supposed to be able to make things disappear," he said with a wave of his hand. "I always wonder where the things go to . . ."

Once again, I was baffled by Ken's insight. He came at things from diagonals, incising when you least expected it. "Maybe she'll make me disappear," he said, his eyes wide with the possibility. "I'll end up in a land where the honey tastes like soap . . . but honey-flavoured soap is as plentiful as sand."

"Or sand is so rare that people kill each other just to hold a grain of it for a second," said Gillian.

"And cops drink fingerprinting ink, or else they die of thirst," I offered.

We spent a while creating this world in Ken's belfry. It was good he didn't ask me about whether I believed in his angels, because he considered me his most stable and linear friend. It was true and it always made me sad, because when I was with him I liked to pretend I could see into his worlds when all I was doing was listening closely and recreating sterile likenesses in my own mechanical brain. But it was fun all the same.

And as his stable friend, it would be up to me to tell him that I didn't believe that they had "superpowers" (I would make the fingersigns for the quotes), that they had pulled off some neat pranks but it was all fraudulent. I wanted Ken to be unworried, but I couldn't even say I believed in them without being so out of character that I'd risk freaking him out.

"So did you hear about the End Hemp Prohibition meeting?" I said. "Everyone wants a piece of you, it seems." I gave him a rundown of the events, down to Mark yelling at the guy's taxi. Gillian looked mad, a rare thing for her. "Vultures," she said.

"I've read interviews with the Hemp Canada guy," Kurt said. "He seems on top of things. He wears the suit to make the movement appear more respectable — to show that there's more diversity to it than Rasta hats and patchy kids."

Gillian said, "It's a good idea, but I imagine the people that were there thought he was just a rich bastard."

Ken got up and opened a window, saying, "I ran into Damien at a couple of hemp rallies, and I just got a weird feeling from him. He was always trying to sell grow kits and that kind of thing. So when he called me about the meeting I just told him that I wasn't up to it. He gave me a fake sympathetic thing and said something about how it was my responsibility to do it blah blah blah . . ."

"What a fucker," Gillian said.

"But I like the benefit idea," said Ken. "That's really nice."

"Mark seemed to think it was a publicity thing for what's-his-name — James," I said.

Ken shrugged. "Not really . . . Mark just hates James. But all my friends are going to be there, playing music and dancing. It's like a party that I don't have to clean up after," he said, wiggling his bum in a little dance. "Whenever people suggest I skip bail, I just say — I can't, I'd miss the par-tay."

"Is that the only reason?" I asked. Rescuing him before he went back into custody would make things less dramatic, but easier.

"Well, it would mean my mom would lose ten grand," he said, still dancing. "She had to mortgage the house." He put on a tape labelled Guitar Army, and cheesemetal issued forth from the speakers. "These guys are great," he said with his eyes closed, using his long fingers to wail away on an air guitar.

He stopped. "I might get let off. My lawyer says I will."

"Lawyers never lie," said Gillian dispiritedly.

Kurt looked glum too. Then he said, "Well, you've got those friends in Memphis . . ." Ken had gone to art school for a year there on scholarship, before I knew him well.

"Yeah! Nicole, Sam Wastrel, Christian . . . I never should have left," Ken said. "You jerks should have come down instead. It may be a little rednecky, but you don't get busted for one joint."

He thought for a moment. "I don't really want to leave. I *really* don't want to go back to that fucking place," Ken said, a frown on his face. "But it'll be OK."

"Gotta go," Kurt said. "It's almost six."

Ken saw him as far as the top of the stairs, talking quietly.

I looked at Gillian, who was lounging on the bed. "Do you think he could . . . get through six months of jail?"

She shook her head and looked down at the comforter. She traced a pattern with her finger. "No. He's putting up a cheerful front with us . . . but, no."

I shook the limply hanging imaginings from my head and asked her about pleasanter things. "So how did the reading go? I'm sorry I wasn't able to come."

Gillian was busy replacing Guitar Army with a tape labelled Picastro. "It went fine, I suppose. I was so distracted with the jail thing that I just read some stuff I had done before, instead of rewriting and rewriting that night." She got the stereo configured, all the switches aligned, and a child's voice came on. "It was great. I just have to make sure Ken gets arrested every time I do a reading."

Later that night, I talked to Mom. I had been calling her on Sunday nights, but she called to say that she had plans to go to a play with "the girls." Her voice on the message was matter-of-fact, a routine rescheduling.

"Hi there, Mom," I said when she answered.

"Oh hi, honey," she said. "I thought you were your father for a second." It was something she said often, so often I thought it must have been a surprise each time she realized that her boy was a man.

"Nope. So how are things?" Meaning, in order: 1) cancer, 2) the rest.

After the requisite niceties, Mom always got to the point. "Bad, I'm afraid. They couldn't do anything for me." She sighed, and it mixed in with the static of the mobile phone. "Sid took it pretty hard. He's drinking a little too much," she said, and I was surprised she would voice that.

"Yeah," I said, more to comfort than to agree.

"But I've been keeping away from the smokes, and there's still one more test they're going to run before — But how are things with you?"

Before what? Before it kills her? *Before they remove the breast*, I guessed. I wondered if she couldn't say that to me, or if she couldn't say it at all.

"Um . . . well, a friend of mine got arrested for having a joint. He might go to jail, and he's not the kind of guy to be able to live in that place," I said. I wouldn't normally have told her that, but it was a pretty big part of my life.

"Oh, that's horrible."

"Yeah. Exactly. Don't tell Dad, though. He already thinks I'm living the life of a criminal."

"He doesn't think that!"

I paused, and something that had occurred to me a lot came to the surface. "I *do* find that I am hanging around a lot of unstable types. I have a lot in common with them, despite being different, because I'm so . . . functional."

"How do you mean?" she asked.

"Like going to school and having a job." I thought about how that must seem odd to her, to lament my normality. "I'm glad I'm stable, though."

"So am I. What about Cassandra? She didn't seem delicate at all." She continued, as if to make sure that she didn't offend me: "That is, she seemed to have a lot of self-confidence going for her."

"Oh yeah. It's going great with her."

"I'm glad. I'm so happy we got to meet her and Jess. I really felt a lot better. How did your exam go?"

"It went. It was fine."

She must have heard the dip in my voice. "But?"

"I'm really sick of school, is all."

Mom sounded disappointed. She was really big on school. "Well," she said firmly, "you're almost through, now."

"Yeah."

"I better go, the battery on the phone is pretty weak," she said. The static had gotten progressively louder.

"Fine," I said, always ready to end an expensive long-distance call. "If you want to get rid of me, I understand."

She made the obligatory noises to the contrary, and we said goodbye.

chapter seventeen

I decided I liked Joe. We were well into our second pitcher at a place near work I had never been before called The Iron Unicorn. There was a little angry representation of it, too, just outside the door. Half its horn was broken off.

"It's just a case of following your interests," Joe said. We had been talking careers, how his flowered and mine had promising buds. "You needn't be worried about money. If a person is focused, they become an expert almost by accident."

I nodded sagely and drained my beer. We were sitting at a table by the window, the dusty panes made cheerful by the sun. "I have two friends — one's in law school and one's in med school. Or applying to it. Neither of them are especially interested in it, they're just there for the money." Actually, I wasn't positive that was the case with Albert, the pre-lawyer. He was really into taking advocacy cases, he said, but he was studying corporate law — so I assumed he was going to be an advocate for Coke or Benetton.

Joe shook his head and smiled. When he was quiet, he looked like he belonged there in the pub, with his rolled-up blue shirtsleeves and his thinning hair. A beer in his beefy hand looked natural — but then he'd hold that hand out as he explained his perspective on pedagogy in endless, cohesive assertions, and your first reaction was *Is someone throwing their voice?*

But I had become accustomed to that. After working for him for the last few months, I had found only one thing wrong with him — he was smarter than most people, but was saddled with an utterly average appearance. This made his intelligence unnerving and his appearance inappropriate.

"Did you ever have another —" I balked at the word *obsession* and my drink-addled tongue floundered for a synonym "— equally powerful interest?" I finished, finally.

"Nothing as powerful as insects. No . . ." His eyes went

distant for a moment, and I imagined *childhood, adolescence, young adulthood* flashing through his mind like one might thumb through a paperback. "I've had other interests, of course, but nothing that was nearly as satisfying, nearly as *compelling*." He looked right at me, and our eyes locked. "It's the same compulsion that most people get to overturn a rotted log. They know that they'll be uncovering a city of bugs, and they don't know why they do it, but they do it anyway."

"Do you think that people do it for the power?" It was poorly phrased, and I once again wondered about the wisdom of mixing conversation with drink.

"I don't think that's the main reason," he stated. "Otherwise they'd kill the insects. The usual drill is this: they consider the matter, then work a toe under the log and flip it." He used his hand to demonstrate this. "Then they stare at it in horrified fascination and finally go away. They'd probably even put the log back, but they think it'd cause more harm than good."

All of this sounded very likely to me, so much so I wondered idly if Joe had ever set up candid cameras in remote wooded areas. "So it's curiosity, then?"

"I know it's a fine distinction to make, but I feel that people are compelled to discover rather than just be curious. Curious implies a casual, pedestrian interest, while the person that overcomes their revulsion and apathy to the point where they'd flip a log over is clearly more strongly motivated."

"True," I admitted, watching the waitress burst out of the back room. She stubbed out her cigarette at the bar and picked up some menus.

I checked my watch. It was nearly six-thirty, and we'd been here an hour. I had told Cassandra I'd call her, but hadn't specified a time. We had plans to make plans.

"You guys want menus?" the waitress said.

"Yes," said Joe, leaning back to give her space to place it on the table. She placed it with, I felt, sarcastic care. He flipped it open and scanned the contents with calm speed. By the time I was able to read anything beyond the gravy stains, he had closed his menu and folded his hands. I glanced up and he was looking off into space, composing.

"I suppose my fascination is a compulsive one. I wouldn't say it's an obsession because it moves forward, from one area of study into the next, rather than being caught in the amber of fixation," Joe said.

I nodded, thinking: *I suppose I should get something. I guess we're going to be here for a while.*

"But I had a few rough starts with my career. You mentioned your dissatisfaction with your entomology class — I, too, discovered that the rote classification and biological specification bored and even dismayed me. I spent two long, unfruitful years in the employ of a European company before I realized that I wasn't a watch-maker, I was a watch-seller."

I looked up, half-decided on a Unicorn Burger, and absorbed what he had said. I was flattered he considered the two experiences we had to be alike despite the large differences. I didn't know, however, where the hell watches came into it.

"That is," he continued with a small smile at my confused look, "I enjoyed talking about insects a lot more than I liked taking them apart. Rather than look inside insects, I started to look around them — their lives, their habits, and eventually even the stories surrounding them."

I nodded, and when the waitress reappeared to take his order it suddenly occurred to me that his comment about watches and watchmaking was a deliberate non sequitur — it was intended to stick out and poke you in the eye. It was a very deft linguistic trick.

In light of this realization, I ordered the Unicorn Burger without making a little joke about not having had unicorn meat in a while.

"When did you develop your speaking skills?" I asked, when she'd left.

"You know, it's just been the last ten years or so that I've been a confident speaker," Joe said, and this made me feel better. Perhaps this, too, was intentional. "I started out writing books for children. I realized then that this was what was right for me, that something about writing insect stories for children satisfied a whole range of needs for me — not just intellectual, but psychological and even . . . spiritual." Joe looked out the window, and the light was waning now. "I don't know why, really, although I have theories. None of them fully explains it, though."

I never thought I'd see the inarticulate side of Joe, but here it was. But unlike most people, he was silent and brief on this subject by choice, rather than out of necessity. He could, no doubt, delineate his theories at length, but he realized that they all fell short of truth.

I caught myself — I was thinking of him a little flatteringly. Who's to say that he didn't have other reasons for being close-mouthed about his motivations? It was a little like assuming the silent man was silent because he had reached a higher understanding, and words were meaningless ciphers; you had to be sure that he wasn't just a dolt with a profound look, first.

But Joe hadn't a profound look, and if he was a dolt, he was the best fake I knew. But I liked assuming the best about him; he seemed to do the same for me, interpreting my slow production as extra thoroughness.

Right on cue, Joe said, "I've been very pleased with your work. It was a bit of a thrill to meet, by chance as it were, a young person with a developed focus so closely aligned with my own." The waitress arrived and clinked our plates down. Joe lifted the bun and removed his tomatoes, then continued. "And I was a bit wary at first, because I've been disappointed in the past. But you have a combination of diligence and mental keenness that I really value."

I smiled, keeping myself from being swept away by the pleasure of the compliment by thinking of the "disappointments." Joe took a bite of his hamburger, and chewed, ruminating. "I think what most impressed me was your cross-referencing of that Thai myth." He started on another bite, and before he finished he spoke (wonderfully!) through his burger, almost more to himself: "That's the kind of innovative thinking you get from people who haven't been locked up in the ivory tower all their lives."

I started eating, not really tasting it in my amazement. I wished the teachers who'd been giving me Bs all my life could hear this. I wished everyone could hear this. Unfortunately, our only audience was the waitress, who stared at the racing cars on the TV as her cigarette ash tempted gravity.

What the hell could I say? That he was a mentor to me? A bit of a hero? I couldn't say that, it was silly. And it wasn't even wholly true, just mostly. But I felt like I should say something, as long as it was entirely sincere, so before he started up again I blurted, "You're the best boss I've ever had, I mean . . . no one ever appreciated me before."

He nodded and smiled a thin-lipped smile, the only one he had. It was a little ugly, and he seemed to know it, and consequently used it sparingly. He reached across the table, and for one jolting moment I thought he was reaching for my hand. He picked up the salt shaker and I slowly relaxed, thanking every god in my cosmology that I had been paralyzed.

Why had I nearly recoiled?

Cass was right — my homophobia was pretty bad. Or fear of intimacy. Or something.

Or was it something about Joe?

He salted the tomato he had removed earlier, a healthy-looking specimen for a bar burger condiment, and ate it. "I don't know why you were drawn to this subject, and your conscious reasons, no offence meant, don't interest me that much. They only tell half the story. For instance, this Flyboy — why would he have chosen to claim to turn into an insect when he could have said he could just disappear? For onlookers, that's what they would see. It would make him less vulnerable."

I nervously picked at my fries. Why hadn't I thought of that?

"I think I would find that he was someone not too different from you and I, someone fascinated by the insect world," he said, and I gave a non-committal nod, the yes-go-on nod that can even be interpreted as no-but-go-on-and-finish. "At least in his early development. But he took a turn somewhere along the way," he said, holding up his fork to make the point. "He became obsessive and delusional. And turned to a life of crime."

I raised an eyebrow. This sounded provocatively facile. "You been reading true-crime fiction, Joe?"

"No? Not that simple? Well, this is what my friend the sergeant believes. Or says he believes. But there's nothing to prove that they're truly delusional, just that they portray themselves as such."

This sounded more like Joe. "Well, I've heard they have an e-mail address," I said. "You could try to get in touch with him there." Flyboy, however, would not respond. The idea of corresponding as Flyboy with Joe was a harrowing, rather than amusing, idea.

He nodded and shrugged, which seemed to indicate that it was just bar talk. But it wasn't that at all.

"This is what I wanted to talk to you about. I've been commissioned to aid in the outstanding warrant for these two faux-superheroes."

"Commissioned?" I asked. "By who?"

"By the police," he said casually, sucking a bit of something out of a tooth. "They want me to try to trace them via Flyboy's psychological profile."

I looked at him, crushed and hysterical by the absurd coincidence. Yet, given our "focus," was it surprising? It wasn't just a case of following your interests. Your interests could decide to follow you.

"I realize it's kind of a hokey idea, and it's just because Carleton has a bit of extra cash to throw around. His department's budget will shrink next year if he doesn't spend it. Harry Carleton's an old friend of mine, the guy who gave me the photos I showed you."

I made a show of not remembering, then remembering. Then I

memorized the name Harry Carleton. I pictured the University of Carleton covered with fur, and that did it. Hairy Carleton.

"It's not really his jurisdiction, but he's taken an interest in the case. I get the feeling he admires them. We usually end up talking about it when we get together, and I had mentioned how much I feel freed up with such a competent research assistant, and he made a generous offer. So I'm asking you if you'll be able to work full time in the summer. I'd be able to start paying you eighteen dollars an hour."

Immediately my mind crunched the numbers. It would mean that I would be able to pay off a huge chunk of my student loan. But there were one or two complications.

"Well," I said. "Can you give me a day or two to think about it?"

"Of course. I'd probably have you working on the book and the Flyboy project simultaneously. We'd start with a media analysis and move on from there . . . yes, I'd really like your younger perspective. They're supposedly between the ages of twenty and twenty-seven."

He reached under the table and laid his daytimer out on top. He flipped to a date two weeks hence and I could see "2:30 — Carleton" scrawled in his now familiar block capitals. "I just need to know before I meet up with him next, so take your time thinking about it."

I'd need the time to weigh the fifty thousand variables involved. But I was already thinking: *Hey, we already have a media scrapbook done! That'll mean a day or two of quality dog-fucking.* Then I imagined how funny the phrase *quality dog-fucking* would sound when I told Cassandra, how she'd laugh and how there were few sounds I coveted more than Cassandra's laugh. I looked at Joe with a strange, full feeling of complicated gratitude.

He handed his credit card to the waitress.

Later that night, I was waiting for the 9:45 p.m. bus to London in the bus station, thinking that there were many worse places to wait. For one thing, the place was clean, high-ceilinged and well lit. It was bright, night and day, and this gave it a hyperfamiliarity — it looked *identical* each time you entered it. I had the feeling, occasionally, that no time had passed since I had been there last, like I had always been there.

I usually talked on the phone, too, because I sometimes — well, often — missed the bus I was aiming for and had to wait for the next one. This time it was Joe's fault, rather than my optimistic guesstimate, since we spent an extra fifteen minutes outside the Iron Unicorn discussing his upcoming speaking engagement at the University of Toronto.

"Hi there, Lady Fair," I rhymed into the receiver.

Cassandra laughed. "Who's this?" she asked. "L.L. Cool J? I told you not to call me here. My man will get jealous."

"Your man ain't sheeit," I said. "He's probably hanging out at some fuckin' bus station, slangin'."

"So you missed the early one, eh?"

I seated myself on the edge of a chair — the phone cord was just a little short, an inconvenience I regularly cursed. "Yeah. But guess what? Joe's offered me full time for the summer! At eighteen an hour! And guess what I'm doing?"

"Uhhh . . ." Cassandra said. "You'll be reading stories and *not* having to write anything about them? I'm just trying to think of an easier job than the one you already have. It's hard."

"Well, it *is* skilled, professional research," I said proudly. "And hey! You should have heard him today, talking about how good I was at it and everything?"

"Reeeeally. No argument from you, I suppose."

Someone made a call at the next booth, and I turned down my volume somewhat. "Nope. There was this Thai story I cross-referenced, right, and he was saying how 'marvellous' it was — and he said it when his *mouth was full*."

"So?"

"He never talks with his mouth full. But he was so amazed by my work that he violated politeness. He's very — mannerly, I guess."

"He's pretty psychotically controlled, eh?"

Suspicions washed around my mind, black waves. "He's not," I said.

Cassandra was silent.

"Guess again. About my job. There's a new subject we'll be studying, related to insects."

"Tell me already."

"Flyboy," I said, quickly looking around. There was no one within earshot.

"What?"

"Yep. His buddy is a cop, head of some department, who's hired him to do a media analysis of this alleged superhero. So Joe thinks my 'younger perspective' will help out. Wild, eh?"

"Weird." She was silent for a second, then continued. "Do you think it's a good idea?"

"Why not?" I said. "I mean, they're looking at it as if Flyboy's delusional, or pretending to be for media exposure. And I know when they're meeting, Joe and — Hairy Carleton."

"So you can check up on it. See how much they know."

"Exactamundo," I said, quite pleased by the neatness of it all. Then I realized why it all sounded so familiar. "Through a scanner darkly," I blurted.

"What? The book? By . . ."

"Phil K. Dick. Where the narc is so deep undercover he's assigned to spy on himself. Wow," I said. "My life is mirroring that of a paranoid science-fiction novel. Wait till I tell Jack."

"He'll be jealous. His life is mirroring some cheesy romance, at the moment," Cassandra said. "What's my life mirroring?"

"Your life, sweetheart," I said, "deftly side-steps any genre classifications. A person would have to be an idiot to try to make you into a character."

"Save the silver tongue for my honeycrack, honey," she said fondly. "Where did you go?"

"Unicorn something? I don't remember. A smoky, greasy pub. Reminded me of first year. Iron Unicorn. Hey, tell me something. In all your experience with watching people eat, have you ever noticed someone taking off a topping . . ."

"Yeah . . ."

" . . . and then eating it at the end?" I finished.

"Did Joe do that?" she asked.

"Yep."

"People can be weird about their food," Cassandra said, warming to the subject. "There was this one cat who would come in and use about half a salt-shaker with each meal. We started calling him the Cow, not 'cause he was fat but because what he really needed was a salt lick. And if he finished one shaker he'd go on to the next — no embarrassment at all. The Cow."

"I keep wondering about that tomato," I pondered. "Did he decide not to eat it, then change his mind? It doesn't seem like Joe."

"You're not listening to me, asshole!" chided Cass. "What, do I have to cross-reference my waitressing myths before you take them seriously?"

"I was listening," I said.

"And you're lucky I grew up with two university professors as parents," Cassandra said, "telling me how fraudulent higher education is. Otherwise you'd be giving me a complex, calling me at my decent working-class job about your bourgeois paper-shuffling."

"Does that bug you?"

"When you ignore me? Of course it does!"

"No, I mean about the working class versus university thing," I said, uneasily clarifying it further.

"I'd turn into my parents if I went to university," Cassandra said. "No, waitressing is better than most jobs. I feel like I've chosen it, rather than it being the only thing I can do. I mean, I could have been a rock star, but I turned that down." Her voice was quiet and matter-of-fact. "I coulda been a contenda," she said, and I chuckled, a relieved sound. "I'd rather be at Sok than at an office job. I did that for a summer, and it was all poorly veiled flirting and dress-up shit."

"Plus, Sok's a great place to pick up hunks," I attempted.

"You're telling me? Four last week, hon."

I'm probably not the best person to tell this story. I feel like any time I describe the stuff we do as superheroes that I'm bragging. I think that another person telling the Flyboy and Ms. Place story would do it properly — that is, build up tension here, suspense there, and roll inexorably towards the momentous climax of The Rescue. This chapter might even be called that. But I can't really do it, even if it'd be more exciting or whatever. It wasn't that simple.

What happened was this. When I got back from London, Ken's court date had been moved up. Because of the "vigilante threats," the newspapers said. Not that everyone was against us — the weekly paper *Now* did a feature on the case that made us look embarrassingly good, and a bunch of papers had op-ed pieces that discussed the hemp prohibition issue in a balanced way. Talk radio had a field day, and Cass eventually gave up on trying to tape it all. So this minor case, that probably would have been dismissed, was now a huge media circus. One that society would be watching carefully — one that was now an example of something much bigger than a lad and his reefer — one in which Ken was probably gonna be convicted and sent away for the maximum.

And it was our fucking fault. We were the big talkers, even though after our "Ken Matthews will not do time" statement we were silent — Cass didn't want it to become about us, and had Mary politely turn away any interview requests. I couldn't see Ken because he was in "protective custody." Cassandra was worried, but also thrilled. "They're taking us seriously," she said, amazed. "Do you think they actually believe we are what we say we are? With real powers?"

We didn't know the answer to that until all the action went down.

Valerie answered the door herself.

"Oh, good!" Val exclaimed with pleasure. "Jack said you might be coming." She threw open her door and waved Cassandra and me in, introducing herself to Jessica. "I'm Valerie," she said formally, with a handshake.

"My name is Jessica and Sailor Moon."

We laughed a little at that. Val was trying not to adore Jessica, but her glasses couldn't hide her magnetized eyes. "Everyone else is in the rec room," she said finally, leading us down once we had added our shoes to the pile.

"Are your roommates here?" asked Cassandra.

"Nope. Yuf is at shiatsu and Pauline's out at her ma's." We passed by a kitchen with well-stocked open shelves and a chore wheel. "So Jack told you about the *Superhero* special on right before the *X-Files*, right?"

"Yeah, the Flyboy and Ms. Place thing, right?" I said.

"You guys haven't heard anything new about Ken, have you?" Cassandra asked.

"No — nothing on the news and nothing from him," Valerie said, leading us through the laundry room and under its laden clothesline vines. "'Scuse the mess," Val said airily. "I don't expect him to get in touch with us," she said. "And for all we know, he's drawing cartoons in the sands of Honolulu by now."

We nodded, knowing better.

We emerged into the rec room, furnished with cast-off couches (Bethany and Jack sat on one and Mark was sprawled out on another) and the finest in neon beer signs.

"Pretty wicked signs," I said, after the hellos had been said. Mark scrambled up and did something to the cord of one of them, and the neon pulsed like a strobe.

"They came with the house," Val said modestly.

I sat down beside Jack. I thought about winking at him or pinching him or doing something to celebrate his casual couch-sharing with Bethany, but couldn't think of any way to do it without being overt. I contented myself with a small smile and a thought about how far away our bachelor bitterness seemed.

"What?" Cassandra said, smiling a little herself.

Avoiding her eyes, I looked over at Mark. His eyes were narrowed back at me. It would have been unnerving, but his feet were tucked behind his knees in such a wussy way that it just made my smile larger. "What?!" he demanded.

Val walked in with two bowls of chips. "Snackies!" I said with the same small smile. I glanced back at Mark. He was still watching me. "Nothing!" I said.

Val ignored us to concentrate on the VCR. "I wanna tape this," she said. I glanced at the readout: 7:58 p.m. I was a little nervous about the broadcast. We had no idea how it would portray us, or if it would be immediately obvious to the others that it was *us* on the screen. I took Cassandra's hand and found it a little sweaty.

Val snapped on the TV and adjusted the sound, then went to sit with Mark, who didn't move fast enough and squawked as Val bounced on his legs. She had a look of malicious glee on her face that I'd never seen, and I realized as she settled down to watch just how excited she was about the show.

It started with a pan across a blue, cloud-filled sky, then 3-D comic lettering ("S-U-P-E-R-H-E-R-O-E-S") slammed onto the screen with rapid-fire metallic sound effects, then the word "or" without much fanfare, and then "Terrorists?" hissed onto the screen in dripping red spray paint.

Mark shouted laughter.

A familiar newscaster got on the air and started an intro, giving the details of the case. He was careful to use words like "claim" and "alleged" when describing our powers, and got the date wrong on the *Sun* box mission, but other than that, he got most of the details right.

"One of the most notable features of the Superheroes for Social Justice is their expert handling of the media. While refusing to be interviewed, they regularly issue press releases to draw attention to, and explain the political agenda behind, their crimes."

The screen filled with a picture of the fax release issued after Take Back the Night, with certain high-lighted sections read aloud in a female voice.

"Making full use of cyberspace for their anonymous communications, a web site and an internet discussion group have already sprung up."

"*Two* discussion groups," Val corrected distractedly. "alt.fan.msplace and alt.fan.flyboy. Not that anyone posts to .flyboy . . ."

I shot a slit-eyed glance over at Cass without moving my head. Her eyes were wide with innocence. But it wasn't really a surprise. Hell, I *was* Flyboy and I was more interested in Ms. Place.

Then Bethany said, "His costume's cooler, though."

I squeezed Cassandra's hand gloatingly, a long and satisfying one.

"Ah, he stole it from the *Sandman* comic book," said Mark.

"Good superheroes borrow, great superheroes steal," said Jack.

"He doesn't wear a hat," Bethany retorted. "It's more of a doughboy look."

Val said *pffft*. "I guess if you like military themes."

Bethany stuck her tongue out at Val. It was all on that level.

I had hoped there would have been more interviews with people, about what they thought about us and our motivations and stuff. But it was a rush job, I guess, since the rescue had happened the day before.

I was beginning to wonder if they had any footage of the rescue at all when it came on. It was a little spooky, because it was utterly silent and the people were so small.

The camera was fixed, some distance away, on the front of the court-house. We had sent out an extremely brief and direct communiqué an hour before, and the media had shown up, clustered around the stairs in a mass. The doors opened and Ken was led out, his handcuffed, gawky tallness looking strawlike between his two escorts. He was led down the stairs.

At the same time, a licence-plateless Oldsmobile pulled up, and some cameras in the mass swivelled as if powerless to resist.

Cassandra's costume lit up the drab silent world and she took the lead through the split in the media crowd. I followed behind, like death or a dog.

Ken raised his cuffed hands to wave at us, his happiness visible more in his animation than his face, and he suddenly found his hands free. The cops lost their weapons, uniforms and underclothes, and I had an idle wish that they had added sound effects. The silence was eerie.

"Stop motion," guessed Jack, but his mouth was agape.

Ken ran for the car and jumped into the backseat. The naked cops, small black dots appearing immediately over their genitalia, moved towards us. Ms. Place walked, queenlike, past me and towards the car.

"Go, Flyboy, stop those streaking cops!" cheered Bethany.

"What's he gonna do, buzz up their nose?" said Val.

The cops came and grabbed Flyboy, then one of them tried to go after Ms. Place. But Flyboy grabbed his hair and by the time he had extricated himself, Ms. Place had shut the door. The cops stood there, with Flyboy in their nude-but-firm grasp, one moment. The next moment they stood there with an overcoat and a mask.

Obviously, the escaping fly couldn't be seen, but the sudden movement of the cops, as they looked at the empty coat and the unsupported mask fall to the ground, made it clear what had happened.

A few seconds later, the car (driven by Ken) peeled out.

"Wow," said Mark.

There were a few seconds of footage showing the press-cop mayhem aftermath, during which one of the nude cops put on the overcoat. This seemed unreasonably funny to us.

"What happened to Flyboy?" said Jack, eventually.

"Maybe he's in the backseat," I said in what I hoped was an unsure voice.

Cassandra said *squeeze, squeeze, squeeze.*

chapter eighteen

We walked on the black-pebbled tracks, Cassandra, Ken and I. Cassandra was the one who noticed the small enclave in the trees, two ratty lawn chairs and some trash.

"I bet that's for hoboes," I said. "It's close enough to the train yard that the train would be going slow enough for them to hop on."

Cassandra stopped. "Should we do that? Maybe it'd be safer."

"Running beside a train?" I said dubiously. "It doesn't seem safe. Especially when the ground's so muddy."

Cassandra looked at Ken. "What do you think?"

"I liked the idea of getting on when it's stopped," said Ken. "The other seems like a recipe for disaster. Muddy disaster."

"Muddy, bloody disaster," I rhymed.

"Yeeee!" Ken said with a shudder, and we walked on.

It was barely dawn. We had started out from Toronto at 3 a.m., and had parked the car on a London side street at 5:30. But we had no idea when the train would be leaving, and all I knew about trainhopping was what I had retained from a book I had read two years ago. Which turned out to be quite a lot, actually.

"Sounds like they're making up the trains," I said in reference to the giant clanging sounds.

Ken laughed, in high spirits. "I ain't riding on no made-up, imaginary train."

"They've got a pretty noisy imagination," Cassandra commented. She was wearing a cap backwards, her hair tightly under wraps. I had pulled out an old jean jacket for myself. We looked like rockers, not too out of step with our surroundings. Ken's normally white-blond hair was now black as pitch, and nearly as manageable.

We were approaching the sign. The scale of everything was so big out here — the poles, the warnings, the distances between roads. The sign said that we were entering the Canadian Pacific Intermodal Train Yard, and that trespassers yadda yadda yadda.

"This is what we want," I said. "Intermodals are freight trains," I said as we passed the sign. The tracks were flanked by trees, and the track curved out of visibility about half a kilometre ahead of us. I kept an eye fixed on the visibility point, watching for people or movement. I didn't know what I'd do if I saw anyone, except hide in the bush.

Cassandra and Ken were talking about Jessica and her drawings of Sailor Moon. "She really likes your drawings, Ken. She draws Baby Sneaky all the time. You've got a real talent for inspiring people that way, I think. Ryan talks about it, too."

I nodded.

"Well, it's not exactly in the same class as your talents," Ken said. "Like, if I could make my drawings come to life, *that* would be talent."

I had hoped we had exhausted this subject on the way down. He hadn't had much time on the day of the rescue to talk about it — he had spent much of it trying to figure out why we had impersonated the superheroes. But after having two days in hiding to wonder about it, he was full of questions.

I didn't mind answering questions, that wasn't it — it's just that I was a bit embarrassed and ashamed that I had never told him. But he never intimated any annoyance at this — and for some reason that just made it *worse.*

From the backseat came these questions:

"What do the colours of your costumes mean?" Nothing.

"What happens after it disappears?" Dunno.

"Are there other people with powers?" Not sure.

"How did you first find out about your powers?"

I answered this last one, because I knew Cassandra didn't really want to answer it and because I didn't want him to think that we were the most secretive people on Earth, even if we were.

"Well, I did something wrong. Something bad. When I was a kid. It was Boxing Day, and my mom had sent me to the guest room to punish me. She couldn't send me to my room because all my Christmas toys were there. It smelled like adults in there, and baby powder, and the bed had this big satiny pink bedspread. As I stared at it in five-year-old disgust, I noticed a fly had landed on it."

I was driving, so I turned my head to the back to make sure Ken was still awake — I had his rapt attention. I also had Cassandra's, and I said, "Haven't I told you this?" She shook her head.

I looked back at the road and the white flashes of highway lines. "So I whacked the bed, meanly, and the fly lifted off and buzzed under the door and to freedom. He could go anywhere he wanted, any time. I felt this really intense envy. I got all tingly, and then I was a fly. My first thought was 'How did the bed get so big?'"

"Then what?"

"Then I realized what I was. And I wanted to be a boy, wanted badly to be a boy again, and then I was. Naked, which added to my feeling of having done a bad thing."

"Huh," said Ken. "Envy's a funny little emotion. But it doesn't usually give you magical powers."

I was thinking about the tingling that accompanied the first time — and only the first time — while Cassandra complained about not having heard that story until now.

"You fight the forces of evil with someone, and you think you know them, you know?" she said to Ken with a pained expression as we walked along the tracks.

"I know," Ken commiserated with a smirk. "How could he have kept that from you? What a monster."

I just kept my eye on the visibility point. After a few minutes, I saw the edge of movement. It was the back, luckily, so we wouldn't have to approach facing the engine. We kept walking, silently now. The car stopped at one point and started going the other way. We stepped up our speed.

But there was nothing to hurry for — it stopped and stayed still until we got to it. By this time we could see most of the train, but no workers. One of the cars was painted with an American flag motif, so I knew this was heading the right way. Or I hoped.

We kept walking until I found what I was looking for — a car that looked like a beer can set on its side. I pointed to a hole in the side with a ladder leading up to it, and Ken nodded. Then I led us into the brush beside the tracks.

"This is perfect," said Cassandra, once we got settled. The brush was this long, four-foot-high grass that you could just disappear into. Nothing but planes would be able to spot us. We just squashed down the dry grass until there was a secret camp for the three of us. I opened up my knapsack and handed out buns (flattened) and fruit.

"So you can read the names, right?" Cassandra said, referring to the list of American friends and crashpads that she had given him. We thought it would be good for him to stay away from his known friends and contacts, at least for a while.

"Yep," Ken said, chewing away at a bun. "You sure have a lot of friends, Cassandra."

I wondered if he was thinking about all the people he was leaving.

"Travel friends. They don't miss me as much as your friends are going to miss you."

"Just till the heat's off," I said again, even though it sounded hollower every time I said it. We didn't really know when he would be able to come back — six months? a year? — all we knew was that he was too hot now to drive over the border. His face was on the news, looking like a joke or a staged photo with him holding the little criminal sign.

"Detroit will be fun," said Ken, leaning back and looking at the sky. "It's so grotty and oily."

"In Detroit," Cassandra started, and I could tell by the tilt of her head and the little smile on her face that this was one of her Travel Stories. I tuned my ears to her voice. "In Detroit we had to get some serious repairs. Good place for it, we figured, it being the Motor City and all. So when Linda took the van in — she always did the car stuff — Erin and I go to this wig store. This was when doing chick stuff was still OK, and Linda was more easygoing. She'd roll her eyes and whatever, but she wouldn't get nasty.

"So we were in the wig store — there was this really ugly one that Erin wanted for on-stage, she was seriously considering it, taking forever — and I was bursting I had to pee so bad. So I get out of there and see this diner. First of all, the place had a revolving door, this heavy grime-and-iron thing that made me seriously wonder — when did this place, this skinny little place, ever do so much business that they needed a revolving door?

"As I said, it was a skinny little place with the tattered red counter stools and a big black girl reading an electronics textbook. I ask her for the washroom, and she thumbed back behind her. I go past her, not into another room exactly, but it's where the cooking was done and the stuff on the shelves, it's packed so much that there's hardly any room to walk.

"Then it opens up a bit and there's these three old folks at a folding table playing *cards*. One of them says 'Gin rummy,' and the other one asks me if I want the washroom. I nod and *she* thumbs behind her. I go down these stairs and they're really strange — I forget what was strange about them. But they seemed to have been built at two different times, like maybe for an addition or after a fire — they didn't fit. Anyway, halfway down the stairs there's this door, this black door with strips to reinforce it and a spyglass sticking out of the centre of it.

"I look out of it — despite the screams of my bladder — and it's a normal judas hole, giving me a view of the alley. I keep on down the stairs and end up at the washroom. As I'm peeing, I wondered if that was like the prototype of the judas hole, and if this place used to be a speakeasy or something and people entered through there. The place was *old.* I could hear it in the pipes when I flushed, I could see it in the archaic design of the toilet seat."

Ken and I waited, quietly, in case there was anything else.

"So I was telling this to Ed — friend of mine, back in Vancouver — and he said that that's why he loved America. Every so often you'd come across a place like that, and it was like finding a broken diamond ring in the dust."

"Wow," I said. "That's a super story."

"It's almost like I'll be travelling back into the past," Ken said, leaning over and brushing the grass aside to get a view of his chuffing time-machine-to-be. "To a place where history hasn't been erased by the forces of real estate." Then he laughed. "Where elves and fairies enjoy the pleasures of urban living."

"Where crack, a kind of candy enjoyed by inner-city youths, is plentiful and delicious," I said. I unfortunately reverted to my small-town biases of big Yankee cities, despite Cassandra's story. It seemed to tell more about her than about Detroit — her ability to find beauty in the least likely places. Once she had told me she liked the way my brow furrowed and how my hands looked when I was writing.

I looked at her, trying to keep the adoring cast from my eyes. She was wearing floppy overalls and was looking at the palms of her hands, where the grass had left an imprint. There was no way we could be caught here, and even if anyone (perhaps a watchman on stilts) was to peek over and see this cross-legged lotus they wouldn't do anything but return her lazy smile.

Hours passed. I tried to get some sleep. Ken drew in his book, chuckling occasionally and showing Cassandra. The sun was creeping up in the sky and gradually depriving us of shade. It was, I realized in the half haze, very hobo.

"*Très* hobo," I said out loud.

"What?"

"This whole thing" — waving my hand around our camp. "Waiting for the iron horse and all."

Ken nodded. "I had a friend who did this a lot. A few decades ago. He said there were places in every yard where there were books buried, in plastic bags and stuff. For other hoboes to read."

"Still?" I said. Ken shrugged.

"Maybe over by those chairs we saw. We should check on our way out," Cassandra said. After a second she said, "You know, Ken, I never thanked you for cheering me up on that night you had the party. You were talking about the book project, do you remember?"

"Yeah. On the roof, you mean?"

"Yeah. I was really depressed by the *Sun* illustration of me, and hearing you be so flippant about not getting the deal was really inspiring. It was just your attitude."

"Oh! That's so nice to hear!" he said, happy. Then his face screwed up. "That illustration was *awful.* Val showed me it. Boy, was she mad."

"Well, at the time I was just so crushed by it. But then after that night we went box hunting."

"Oh right! Amazing!"

"I just wanted to tell you. 'Cause I couldn't before, obviously."

"Yeah. Huh!" he said, with this amazed look on his face.

"Talking about the *Sun* . . . did you see the cover the day after the rescue?"

Cass and I nodded. There was nothing to say that hadn't already been said.

"Man, I got so sick of the interviews. And you know what bugged me?" Ken asked. "It was the constant single-joint theory crap. Who cares if it was just one joint?!" He held his hands up to the sky.

"It just made things . . . more symbolic, I guess. Highlighted the absurdity of it," Cass said, chewing on a blade of grass.

"Yeah, yeah. I know. But I was still tempted to say to that *Now* guy, after he started up with the 'postmodern hero' crapola, 'Well, it was one joint *that* night, but I've had more. I've had so much I've sold dope to people before. I sold to my younger cousins.'" He looked at us with mischief in his eyes. "You guys saved a dealer, a scummy degenerate who sells dope to minors. Some heroes."

"The press would have had a field day with that," Cass said, "but they didn't do their research. They didn't even bring up the mailbox thing. I was surprised."

"But they usually played it off like it was a prank, like we unbolted and carried all the boxes away. We wouldn't have done that to a mailbox by accident. So it probably didn't make any sense to them, and they decided to just leave it out," I guessed.

The train was ready by 10 a.m. The sun was high in the sky but not hot, a perfect bright spring day. I was jealous that Ken was going to get to go trainhopping, but then I saw how tired his face was and that moment passed. The train hadn't moved for a while and we waited, tensely, as the conductor walked by us on his way to the head of the train.

Ken had a backpack with a foam roll attached. He looked at us.

"Take care," Cassandra said. Ken hugged her and took the water bottle she handed him.

I was at a loss for words. "I . . ." Ken hugged me, and my nose tingled something fierce. "People will love you wherever you go, man."

"Goodbye, my sweet angels," he said with his slow wave. "Don't get caught."

He ran for the can car and scrambled up the ladder. He squeezed into the cubbyhole and was obscured by darkness. I looked away, down the length of the train, to see if it had reacted to the parasitic invader. Nope.

"Hey look!" laughed Cassandra. I looked at the cubbyhole and saw Ken waggling a beer bottle — I guess there had been a previous occupant. That was a good omen.

There were no further communications.

Cassandra and I moved closer in the grass and did something illegal. Then the train moved away, and took our friend with it.

May 16th finally arrived. I had circled it on my calendar, but in a move that was half intentional mystery, half paranoia, didn't write anything on it. Several times during the week I had gone through the same thought process: *Why'd I circle that day? What's going on? Why didn't I write any— oh,* that's *why.*

I just went into work, as normal. Stuck my head in and said hello to Joe. Went to the common room and got the coffee brewing.

"So you're the one who steals my mug," said a thin, casually dressed woman in the doorway. I had the I'm 50 and I Don't Give a Damn mug in my hand, which I chose on the merit of its size. I relinquished it with a charming smile. It was a mission day, and mission days always made me smiley. Not happy exactly, but charmed by the tininess of everyday life.

"I didn't know that these were *people*'s mugs," I said. "I thought they were *common* mugs. Common room — common mugs."

"Most are. Just not this one. So are you Mr. Crawford's assistant?"

"Yeah. What do you do?"

"I'm the secretary for the anthropology department. I've been off on vacation until this week."

"So you're the person who makes the second pot!"

"And you're the person who makes the first."

The coffee was ready. I poured her a cup, and then eagerly helped myself. "This is the first job I've had where the coffee was free. Even the café I worked at charged the employees."

"No!"

"Yeah."

She put in too much whitener — that stuff tasted like dried paint to me — and asked how I found Joe.

"I think he's a brilliant man," I said, tossing my spoon in the sink, "and a great boss."

"I'm glad to hear that."

There was just enough hesitancy in her voice to make me doubt it. Slightly annoyed, I nodded goodbye and went to the office.

I'd been gearing up for this all week — I had enough work done so that I was covered. I just had to kill about a half hour or so. I was pretty stoked about today, even more than usual on mission days, because I had such a big part in it — and I was flying solo.

Don't get the idea that I didn't like doing missions with Cassandra — it's just that I was usually just along for the ride, in one sense. She did all the planning, and I just followed directions. That was fine, because I didn't have a sidekick complex.

But this time, I had to do all the planning. I had presumed she would do it, but she had shrugged her shoulders and said I knew better what I would be doing. At first I thought she didn't think it was important enough, but she just knew that it made more sense for me to plan it. So I did — figured out the nuts-and-bolts logistics, and planned for contingencies — and now I was ready for some action.

A little earlier than I had projected, Joe stopped by the door. "OK, I'm off — see you later today."

I nodded and smiled, and as he left the doorway I casually called out, "You got the file, right?"

He reappeared in the doorway. I got up and walked up to him. "File?" he said.

"Yeah, the one on Flyboy. Today's the day you're meeting with Harry Carleton, right?"

Joe nodded briefly. "Eventually."

"I finished the clipping collection last night. I put the file on your shelf. Didn't you see it?" *You weren't supposed to*, I thought craftily to myself, *and judging by the blank look in your eyes you didn't.*

"Wonderful," Joe said, but not looking overjoyed. I was a bit surprised — it was a tremendous amount of work. Or would have been, if Cassandra hadn't already done it.

Joe turned around and headed back to his office. I shut the door, quietly, and locked it. I ran over and crawled under my desk. Then I bugged out.

I shot out of my collar and flew low across the carpeted terrain of my office, and dipped to fly under the door. I caught a glimpse of Joe as he entered his office, leaving the keys hanging there in the knob. I was in his office, or rather on the cusp of his office, having landed on the door frame to wait for him to find the file. He set his briefcase on the desk and I made my move.

Just as he was placing the file in the briefcase, I was approaching from behind, and as he was slowly (to my fly-speed) closing it I coasted into it. The twin click of the locks sealed me in the darkness.

Before I could get all smug, the contents of the briefcase shifted ninety degrees. There was a tinking sound that sounded like glass.

We were moving along. The only thing that worried me was that Joe would check my door. He was usually in a hurry, though, so I hoped he would just leave the building.

His footsteps stopped. My little fly heart was capable of frightening speeds. I waited for a knock.

Then there were quick steps — sounded like he was running. No, they were stairs. I started to relax again, and then I heard the deep click of the door to the outside.

I couldn't tell by the sounds of his footfalls if we were outside or not. I started to worry about the whole briefcase plan. I had decided on the briefcase route (rather than the shoulder route, for instance) because it was the stealthiest. Now I was beginning to worry that it was *too* stealthy.

I could hear voices fine from in here (I had tried it out with Phil's briefcase at home) but I couldn't recognize many sounds at all. I was blind and — I was anxiously realizing — I was utterly trapped. I heard a bang and couldn't place it. Then I heard the roar of what was obviously the car starting up, and I figured out it was the door closing. I felt a little more confident — if I couldn't directly identify things, I could figure them out by their sequential context.

It was in this way that I identified the scary chunky grind of the parking brake (after the motor stopped and before the door slammed shut). I could tell we had stopped at a corner because I also heard the honking of cars nearby. Then I heard a bell, and I realized we were passing a school at recess.

Of course, I had no idea where we were. I had hoped Joe might be a regular at the Iron Unicorn, because that place was nice and quiet. But we drove for a while longer than it took to get there, so I assumed he had another place in mind.

The sounds of a bunch of kids echoed suddenly, and I heard the sound of an outside door clicking. We were inside, I figured, somewhere where there was a bunch of kids. Maybe it was a mall with a pub or restaurant.

There was a man's voice, greeting him by name and bidding him to follow. I guess they had reservations in some swanky place. I was a bit hungry myself. *Maybe I should have just asked to come along,* I thought, *and I could have found out what the cops knew about us and got a free lunch besides.*

Then another door closed and I couldn't figure that out. A separate dining room? A washroom? The briefcase shifted suddenly again, and then *thup, thup.* He opened it up and I looked out.

To see not a smiling waiter, or a hard-eyed investigator, but silent, rapt children. We were in a classroom.

After a file was extracted, the briefcase became dark again, but not before I caught a glimpse of an unfamiliar glass jar. I sat in there, stunned, trying to figure out what was going on. I didn't have a contingency plan for Joe lying.

But maybe he wasn't lying. Maybe this was scheduled for before the meeting — he left earlier than I had thought, after all.

The class erupted in laughter. Joe continued with his familiar routine and something occurred to me. Joe might have changed the meeting time with the cop but decided that he wanted me to have it done on the same day anyway. That was why he wasn't all that concerned with having my clippings. I was a bit disappointed in him — I hadn't figured he'd play those head games, especially considering that I was pretending to work overtime to finish it up.

I spent the next half hour trying not to fall asleep. I couldn't tell if I was just tired, or whether I was suffocating from the lack of air. But I mean, how much could my little fleck of a body need? I was also resisting the crumbs and fragments of food that I could smell left over from Joe's past lunches — aged to insectile perfection. But I stayed put, half listening to Joe amuse the class and half thinking about how I could deal with this when we were back in the office, without letting on how I knew.

At the end of the hour, the class was dismissed for lunch.

I braced myself for when Joe would pick up the briefcase and everything would shift around again. Eventually, the hubbub lessened, like water going down a drain, and stopped completely with the click of a door. Joe had forgotten his briefcase.

It was strange, because I'd never known him to forget anything before, and certainly not something as important as this. I was pretty sure he'd remember pretty quickly and come back — the files for Hairy Carleton were in here, after all.

There was a rush of sound and a second later the briefcase was grabbed — I hoped by Joe — and then set down again. What was going on? The door clicked closed on the hallway noise.

Then I heard his voice, echoey.

"What are you doing here?" he said.

How does he know I'm here? I thought, and then I heard a girl's timid voice say something about cleaning.

He opened up the briefcase and left it open. My eyes adjusted without the human pause, and I saw a small girl with a long grey eraser held loosely in her hand. I figured her for grade two, maybe, with unhappy eyes.

He glanced quickly at the closed door and seemed to make a decision. Joe took the jar out of the briefcase, his ham hand covering it completely. He sat down behind the teacher's desk and told her to pull up a chair.

She did, setting the eraser on the desk with a small puff of dust.

"Now, I noticed that you seemed to be frightened of spiders. When I mentioned them you made a sour face." Joe's face was a study in calm. His voice was the same folksy one he used for his children speeches and nowhere else. He removed a small black tape recorder from the briefcase, placed it on the desk and started it recording.

Her face was penitent. "Bugs are scary," she explained.

"No," Joe said softly, entreatingly, "they are not. They are God's creatures, and you should love them. Now I'm going to help you get over your fear, so you won't be scared any more. Would you like that?"

She nodded, her body relaxing as she unfolded her arms. She was ready to learn.

Joe showed her the contents of the glass jar. Inside, a dozen spiders scraped mindlessly against the transparent wall. My heartbeat increased to that frightening-bursting level. *Aw Joe*, was all I could think, looking at his pale blue eyes.

The girl was squirming with terror, making a low keening noise from her tight-drawn mouth.

Joe unscrewed the top and left it on. He put his hand down the front of his pants.

"I want you to remove the top of the jar," Joe said, masturbating.

Her keening increased in pitch, but she didn't move, just writhed in her chair.

I couldn't stop him. I couldn't change. I flew to the edge of the briefcase and hopped around. If I turned back to human now, I'd have to confront Joe naked, and reveal my identity.

I saw another option.

As I flew to the closet I heard Joe say, "Remove the top of the jar."

I heard her say *no*.

There was a cloying disappointment in Joe's voice. "You are a *bad* girl. A *very* bad girl."

I flew under the door and transformed. I felt shoes under my feet, and fell backwards onto some woollen jackets. Then I pounded on the door, pounded my fury into the flimsy wood. I stopped and heard the clicking of the briefcase. I switched back and flew into the room.

The girl was standing by the chair, looking dazed. Joe finished putting on his jacket and opened the door, giving her a dark look as he left.

I flew after him. The girl, in quick movements, screwed the cap back on the bottle. As I flashed by I could see tear tracks, but also a strange twist to her mouth.

I caught up to Joe, bashed against his shoulder. I flew again and again into his unfeeling body, pointlessly, the rubber band of my mind snapped but something spinning regardless.

chapter nineteen

I told her what had happened.

I told her what had happened and now I just sat there, in my office, holding onto the armrests of my chair and staring at the closed door across the hall.

I talked to Joe in my mind. I asked him why.

After I got back and put on my clothes I called Cassandra. *Come here,* was all I told her. When she showed up I told her all. All of it. And then she left, her eyes blank and her lips white. She knew where his office was. She had visited before. Joe had liked her.

I talked to Joe, calmly, rationally, in my mind. Paranoia had leaked over everything. *There was no Hairy Carleton, was there, Joe? How did you find out we were superheroes? Did you tap my phone? Do you like fear? Did you live with fear?*

In my mind, I questioned Joe. I asked him about complimenting me with his mouth full. I had the leisure to, while Cassandra went in to clean up. I despised myself at that point.

What is she doing?

But that I knew the answer to. And I would receive confirmation very soon.

I left with Cassandra. I shouldn't have done that, I should have stayed and pretended that I thought Joe was late or whatever, but I couldn't handle sitting alone in my office for four hours looking at the books and photocopies as blankly as if they were chunks of granite.

We walked silently for a few blocks. It was an unfairly beautiful day. Every breath of air was a mouthful of warm life and it was hurting me, as spicy food hurts when you're sick.

"Was it quick?"

"No," Cassandra said, "but he didn't seem to feel much."

I looked at her. Her neutrality had given way to a deep misery. "I wish I could get angry again," she said. "I wish I could burn away everything else in my mind with a final burst of anger."

I nodded.

"I think I'm a monster. Evil. I feel like that guy in *La Femme Nikita* who's called in to dissolve the body, who uses the bathtub and an acid solution. Not as messy. No blood on my hands," she said.

I hardened myself. "Any in the office?"

"No. No, I was sharp as a razor in there. I was careful and methodical in *there.* I had no mercy or hesitation in *there.*" She was crying now, not sobbing but just leaking. "It's just now that it's over that I — "

"I was . . . paralyzed in there, Cassandra." I held her hand, not knowing what else to do.

"There was nothing for you to do. Other than call me."

"I couldn't have done it if I had had to do something," I said, not near crying, but there was a widening void pulling at my heart. "And it wasn't fear. I was — I don't have your resolve. I think we had to do it and that it should have been done, but I couldn't do it." My cheeks were burning now but I felt better that it had been said. I felt less dizzy, more grounded.

She squeezed my hand, brushed my knuckle against her lips. She took a moment to look at my ring. The sticker with Sailor Moon standing proudly was a little bit the worse for wear.

We stopped at my corner. She still had a long way to go to get home. I gave her a big long hug.

She crossed the road and we went off at ninety-degree angles. I walked the last bit in amazement, looking at all the familiar gardens and houses lit up by the season. I felt like I did when I came home from an all-night drunk, frazzled and exhausted and a little like an intruder. But my mind was starting to slowly chug to life, sorting through the details of the day and designating tasks.

I stopped at the tree outside the place I had lived for two years. There was a hive of honeybees in a crook where two branches met, and I could hear a slight buzzing. I stood there, swaying, looking at the windows to see if I could see any activity. I walked up to the porch and into the house.

No one was around when I went up to my room, which was just as well. I didn't feel like talking, and there was nothing I could tell them anyhow. I shut my door and picked up the phone.

The first message was from Mary. She wanted to know what I'd found out about Hairy Carleton but I skipped on midway. I was afraid she would say something funny.

The second was my father. He started by clearing his throat, and I could tell a few words in that he was drunk.

"Ryan, I don't know if this is the right way to tell you. But I have to do it sometime. Your mother passed away last night. It was an accident. She had too much to drink, and — coughed up some liquid when she was sleeping. It choked her. I — Just give me a call when you get this, OK? Call me right away."

I hung up the phone. Nothing. I picked up the phone again and dialled Cassandra.

"I knew you wouldn't be home," I said. "I just got word that my mother died. I can't face — any of this. Could you cover for me? Say that Joe and I left today for some fieldwork in a remote part of Africa. Be vague. I'll be back when I get my head straight," I said, ashamed at using the cliché. "I'm so fucking fucked right now, Cassandra. It feels like no matter how much we do, bad stuff still keeps happening. I love you but I can't be around any of this now."

I hung up and felt my face. It was dry. Painfully dry. I feared what would happen when the dam broke. I looked over at the window, pulling it up to air out the crypt smell. I could see the tree from here, and the just-visible indications of motion around the hive. I realized then that I didn't need to pack anything. I didn't really even have to leave, just change rooms.

I looked at the hive and let the desperation in me have a focus. Imagine a life with a beautiful clarity. With an easy-to-understand goal and where all the important things could be said in dance.

Imagine being a bee.

I wanted it so badly. And then I was it. My clothes had fallen away. The buzz filled my new ears and I floated lazily. A buzz deeper than the fly — a speed less frenetic. I floated out the window and sailed through the slips of warm air towards the honeycomb.

On days when it was not so busy, I would make a detour from the pollen places and into the house.

"Well, I'm sure he'll call if he's in any trouble," said Jack. He and Phil were talking over a noon breakfast. I had been up for hours and had a moment of righteous bee scorn. *Lazy humans . . .*

"Cassandra seems to be OK with it, she doesn't seem worried," Phil said. "It's only been — what? Two weeks?"

"I saw her Saturday, out on the street. With her little girl. She didn't seem worried, just distracted," Jack said, finishing his cereal with a spoon clinking that made my antennae sting. My bee self was a lot more sensitive and responsive to stimuli than either my fly or human self.

"Well, don't you find everyone gets a little distracted when you talk, Jack? That people nod off once in a while?" said Phil, putting away the milk.

"Oh — sorry? You were saying something?" said Jack. "I find my brain has trouble distinguishing your monotone from the hum of the refrigerator."

There was a moment of silence. "We need Ryan here. To fill in these comedic lapses," Phil said.

I decided to leave. I didn't want to hear this.

They'll forget about me soon enough, I thought as I buzzed towards the exit. On the fridge door was a new postcard, so I doubled back to get a look at it. I looped slowly and landed on the counter.

Jack said, "Do you think we should eat his food?"

Phil shrugged. "Does he have anything good?"

It was a collage, involving Detroit bus transfers and drawings of trains, done in the inimitable Ken style. He was OK! I was so happy I jumped up and did the "lots of pollen" dance and immediately felt a little foolish. It was the same silly tendency that makes a person say "Rad!" or "Wicked!" automatically because all his friends say it.

"There's a bee in here," said Phil ominously, and I didn't even look back.

If I was to write a letter, it would go something like this:

Hi Mom,

I've been working in the hive for the past three weeks. It's the best job I've ever had. No one orders me around, and there's been a variety of things to do. When I got here, I was doing cleaning for a while — throwing dead bees out and such. It wasn't much fun (they give off the death pheromone which smells really nasty) but it was only for a few days. Then I was nursing, which was weird at first being a guy (in human form) but I got to like it. What else was I gonna do with those leaky glands, anyway?

I was thinking about you a lot during that time, partly because of all the death stuff, but also because I remembered you said I wouldn't let you breast-feed me when I was young. I'm sorry for that Mom. It must have hurt your feelings to have me act like that and I know I was a baby but I wish I hadn't been such a brat. Now I'm crying.

I thought the jobs were a neat introduction to the hive, like the Death and Birth cycle, but I suppose it's not meant to be anything profound. After the glands dried up I was a builder, and that's helpful too, because you really get to know your way around the hive. The wax glands are great — it's fun having a cement spray gun inside your abdomen!

For a couple days after that you're a receiver, which sucks. The work is fine — you just put pollen away — but the attitude of the field bees is snooty and ignorant. It's like how the jetfighters treat the privates. I almost got into a fight with one really jerky one. But it's all patched up now.

There's like one day of guard duty — which is totally useless in my opinion, because who wants to invade a hive? — and then it's field duty.

Now I'll be a field bee, foraging at flowers for the rest of my stay. Which is amazing because I love it — just flying around, picking up pollen, and bringing it back. It's simple yet satisfying. People respect you, although I always make sure I'm friendly to the receivers — they end up working with you as field bees, anyway. Not that the other bees have a long memory, but still . . .

So I really enjoy it, plus I've got an ace in the hole — I know the outlying area really well, and where the gardens are, from my human days. No one else will go as far as me, because they're scared they'll get lost. I remember the first time I showed the distance to the other bees — it's a waggley little dance we do — and they kept expecting me to stop, because I had to waggle for at least twice as long as usual. Only two or three were brave enough to go, but we brought back a huge amount of totally fresh pollen. They introduced me to the queen for that.

Anyway, I'm telling you all this because you might be in a position to be reincarnated. If so, I suggest you become a bee. I didn't think about the afterlife, really, until you died. Then I figured that it's no weirder than I am.

Also, I apologize for not going to your funeral. It was during the nursing period, and if I'd left, my young ones would have died. I can't have any more deaths on my conscience. I couldn't face it and I knew you'd understand. I hope Dad does.

So once again, be a bee! And come to my hive. I know all the guards, so don't worry about that.

Love, Ryan.

It was near the end of the day and I was tired and happy, and I didn't even notice her until I was almost inside the hive.

"I know you're in there," Cassandra said. I stopped on the surface of the hive and just watched her.

"Jessica kept giving me these drawings, when I got morose and mopy. I couldn't tell they were beehives until she drew little bees around them."

She stopped and looked around. Her eyes were tired. "I feel so stupid. I've been watching this tree for the last ten minutes, looking for a fly in a honeycomb. A fly would show up pretty obviously, you'd think."

Cassandra was wearing a flower-patterned dress and her hair was down. It was a cloudy day and I hoped it wouldn't rain and soak her.

"It's no fun being a superhero by myself, Ryan. I don't have . . . I took the ring from your room and wore it but it didn't help. Mary called me the other day and I just wanted to talk about you. She kept talking business but eventually I just said I wasn't up to it."

I watched as she took off the two plastic rings. "Mary doesn't think you're coming back," she said.

She put the rings in a knothole. "I . . . hung up on her when she said that. I think you are."

She looked back at the hive with a little of the old Cassandra. "You fucking better be."

I flew into the kitchen again. I wanted to see if I could push the postcard off the fridge and see what Ken had written on the other side. It had occurred to me that it might be bad news. At the time I told myself that I just wanted to make sure that it was good news, which would close the issue — any worries I had as to making Ken's situation worse by interfering could be dismissed. Truthfully, though, I was pretty sure that it was good news, because it was such an energetic collage. I wanted to know what Ken was up to. I was curious about the human world I had left behind, but I didn't want to admit that to myself yet.

Phil and Melissa were sitting at the table, their hands touching under the table. This was a rare sighting — I had only occasionally seen the two of them show public affection. Not that this was public, exactly. I landed on the counter, enjoying the feel of the wood grain under my feet — I loved the hyper-sensuality of being a bee — and watched. Maybe I would even see them smooch!

" . . . It was just very strange, I mean, why would he come back three times?" she was saying.

Phil shrugged. "Did he even pretend to have a reason?"

"No . . ." she said, then looked up quickly. "Have you heard from Ryan?"

"No . . . I thought he'd send a postcard or something."

"Nothing?"

Phil shook his head. "That rat bastard."

"Well, he's in Africa or whatever, right? Maybe there's no postcards or mail system or anything," Melissa said.

It was weird listening in. It felt a little like I was attending my funeral. But it was more jovial, because they didn't know I was gone for good.

"I went to visit Cassandra at work. She hasn't heard from him, either. She doesn't seem worried. But the feeling I got from her was that she thought he might be gone for a long time."

"What about the rent and stuff?" said Melissa.

"I know! I didn't get anything solid out of her, though. We talked about him for a little while." Phil laughed. "I kept calling him a jerk and insulting his manhood as usual, but she seemed bothered by it. I tried to stop."

Melissa smiled. "You *tried?*"

Phil gave a short laugh. "It was hard."

I wished I could talk with Phil. Bees were good companions, but they weren't good at banter. Communication was really limited, to be quite honest. But there was this tremendous feeling of goodwill and camaraderie with most of the bees that made it feel like you didn't have to talk. The hive was kind of a monastery, full of tiny yellow-jacketed monks sworn to silence and filled with the joy of a common goal. I missed talking, though, even if it made things more complicated.

Phil got up and filled the kettle. "Do you want some tea?"

I realized they weren't going anywhere. I had known this, or at least suspected this, from the beginning. I pretended I was just waiting for them to leave so I could take a crack at pushing the postcard off, but I really wanted to spend some time listening to them. When I left I anticipated "having" to come back to the kitchen, although if I wanted to, I could likely push off the postcard and find out what I wanted to know before they could take action.

I was considering waiting around to see if they used honey in their tea — it would have been a neat crossing of worlds — but I had already spent too much time. I would have to work quickly to collect the amount of pollen I felt was my responsibility.

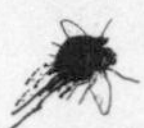

I missed my friends, and I missed Cassandra more. After her visit (which had left me cold, at the time) I would idly hope when I was returning with a load of pollen that she would be there, under the hive and staring up.

These idle hopes turned into longings, and I found that instead of proudly dropping off my load or reporting a new motherlode, I would be depressed that the figure I had seen from a distance was just an anonymous human passing on the sidewalk.

I hadn't been able to think of Cassandra for the first few weeks. It just sent me into an anxious spiral, I would start thinking thoughts like *Should she have, Couldn't we have, Why didn't I* . . . and because it happened practically simultaneously, or perhaps because all awful memories are linked together in some lateral way, I would think about my mom.

I found the longing helped pull me out of it. I started to think about Cassandra looking up at the hive, and I realized that I wanted to be with her. Eventually all the other anxieties and misery associated with her fell away like dead scales, and the new, slick skin of longing was left behind. I don't know why it worked like that.

Yes I do. I saw in her eyes a sadness that mirrored mine. Looking up at the hive.

One day I had a fantasy that she came back, this time with a tank of kerosene. She'd pour it over that hive and light it with the spark in her eye. My home would melt into its base elements and my comrades would die quickly and mercifully.

I wouldn't have a choice, then. A bee-phoenix from the flames, I would change back into my human form and collapse at her feet.

I enjoyed this fantasy for quite a while before I realized how horribly wrong it was. One — Cassandra, despite her world-crushing power, would no more burn a hive than she would slap her child. And two, no way could I revel in the destruction of the place that had taken me in and healed me.

Because I *felt* healed.

I felt like I could start eating solid foods again. Talking and thinking and even, maybe, acting. I thought it might be sometime soon, too, and I was right.

I didn't wake up until I was being carried down out of the comb. It was a cleaner bee that had me on his back. I tapped him with a leg, but he kept moving along. I tried to get free, but he really had me good. There was this huge stench of the death pheromone, which was strange.

I just waited until the worker brought me to a place close to the outside, then let me go and left. I started back to my compartment — I wasn't supposed to be out collecting for a while yet — and ran into another cleaner.

He grabbed me, too. *Christ, these new guys,* I thought, and waited until he got to the surface of the hive. Then he chucked me out.

This was really odd. I hovered there for a few minutes, trying to suss it out. Were the workers just crazy? Sometimes there were some mental defects in the larvae, and they were eaten when they were discovered. But two of them . . . and the smell of the death pheromone was still so strong! Even outside —

It was me, I realized.

I smelled of the death pheromone. There was a moment of shock when I felt like I was dead, hovering there in the air and feeling nothing under my feet. Bees didn't hover when they're dead, however, even though it was kind of automatic.

I entered the hive again, heading for my quarters. I was disconcerted but intrigued. From my bio class I remembered that one of the experiments with pheromones had involved the scientists smearing the death pheromone onto a live bee, and how the bee had been thrown out of the hive kicking and screaming. I thought at the time that it was the bee equivalent of being buried alive, and I was damned if I was gonna let it happen to me without a fuss.

I encountered a field bee that I recognized, but he just crawled over me as if I wasn't there, ghost-style. I tried the friendly antenna tap, but it was ignored. I decided to make my way to the queen, to see how she'd react — a kind of royal supplication.

It was a disorienting feeling, not just because the other bees were so ignorant, but because I realized that what I had taken as friendship with unspoken understandings and memories might have been nothing of the sort. Did they remember how I found that park flowerbed three weeks ago? Did they know who I was beyond someone they recognized the smell of?

I encountered another cleaner and he scooped me up just as handily as the last guy did. It was getting a little frustrating, since I was completely unable to break out of the hold — it was like a bee full nelson. He was moving a lot faster and surer than I had been, so the cautious headway I had made towards the queen was undone in a few seconds.

Once again I was hovering outside the hive. I decided to just go about my work and see what happened. I collected some pollen, a small, sweet load, and headed to the unloading docks.

The guard blocked me, knocking into me and nearly making me drop my load. He seemed to forget about me in a second or two, so I made a quick dive and deposited my pollen in the proper spot. He pushed me away, then kicked my pollen out of the hive — looking like he was taking care not to touch it too much.

Contaminated.

I looked at the hive with a bit of sadness. I had known something was going to happen — most of the bees that were around my age had died. My four weeks were up.

I hovered around for a little while longer, like a melancholy spirit, then headed towards the next plane of existence. I flew through the familiar halls of my house, passing Phil in a housecoat, and into my room. It was as messy as I had left it, with a small pile of mail slipped under the door.

I wanna be human! I thought, using the longing for Cassandra like rocket thrusters, and the transformation happened. My room seemed a little roomier, and I realized that my perfectly-normal-smelling armchair had disappeared. I stood still for a few seconds, trying out my knees, then walking slowly. My feet left a slight stain on the carpet and, over by the window, I looked at my body.

I was covered, in various thicknesses, with a yellow gel. It was as odourless as the green goop that accompanied my fly transformation. I picked up a towel, held it gingerly around me, and made a break for the bathroom.

No one saw me, luckily — I would have had to do some quick 'n' wild inventing if they had. As the yellow stuff melted off my body, I wondered if every insect had its own colour. That segued into wondering if I was able to turn into any insect — any animal — any*thing*. I turned off the water and got out, not able to think about that any more. I took a piss, enjoying the feel of my penis, and noticing how horny I was. *Did my testes keep the factory running while I was out?*

I put the non-gooky side of the towel around me and left, noticing the state of the sink before I did. *Those irresponsible slobs*, I thought, then felt a wave of guilt about the rent. I guessed that they'd been able to get it together for this month, if we were still here.

Back in my room I dressed and lay back on my bed, snatching up my phone and checking my answering machine. "You have . . . thirteen messages," the automated voice said, and I felt a thrill run through me. I had never come close to getting numbers in the teens before! This was one of the reasons I was back in the human world again — the contact with articulate humans who cared about me.

The first message was a hacking cough from my articulate and caring friend Phil.

The second was Cassandra. "Yeah, I came over when I got your message. You were gone. Give me a call when you get this." I had a sudden worry that most of the messages would be Cassandra and she would be getting more and more desperate. I didn't want her to be desperate. Angry, OK, but not desperate.

There were two messages from Dad, about the funeral. They were strained and confused, and hard to take. One was from Lisa, and it was accusatory. This was easier to take.

One was from Val, saying that she had heard from the brownie eater, had I?

"I don't know if Val called," Cassandra said, "but she tells me the *package* arrived safe and sound." She said it with a grin in her voice, which was great to hear. "I know you'd like to know that. Hopefully that'll take some of the stress off your shoulders, which is a mixed metaphor but you know what I mean." She sighed and my stomach tightened up. "I keep thinking it's what I did. But I know you're not like that. I have to keep reminding myself, though. I get Jessica to say it to me, 'He's not like that.'" In the background I heard Jessica chime in, and Cassandra laugh. "Give me a call."

I got two computer calls from the library saying that my reserve book (*Favourite Folktales from Around the World*) had arrived. I got a call from Tom, to go see a movie that was probably out of the theatres by now, and a to-the-point one from Jack:

"We need the rent, rat-bastard." I guess they had given up after that. I decided to try to get out of the house and get the money before I officially "arrived."

The last one was from Mary. "I know you're out of town or something, Ryan, but there's a couple of interview requests from the *New York Times*. I don't know if they're for the same story, or research interns or what, but there's two people dying to talk to you. Cassandra doesn't feel like doing it. Normally it wouldn't be a big deal, but this is one of the biggest and best and they sound sympathetic. I've got some clippings to show you too. So call me ASAP, because I'm leaving soon. Trees to be planted, you know."

Mary's professionalism hit me like a Mack truck. I felt like a petulant rock star, dodging demands on my time for flakey reasons.

I got dressed and snuck out, whipping by the occupied kitchen like a ninja, willing myself invisible. I passed the tree and glanced at the hive — it looked tiny. I'd hit the bank and come right back.

Well, after I stuck my head in at Sok, I decided with a bounce in my step.

chapter twenty

I rang the bell, then stepped back. There was something in the time of day or the light that reminded me of the time that I was wearing my Flyboy costume for the first time.

It took longer for the door to make the clicking and shushing noises, though, and the landlady didn't open the door. It was Jessica.

She was smiling, and in retrospect it seemed like a triumphant smile. "Hello," she said, and stepped aside.

"Thanks, Jessica," I said. I presumed she remembered me, that it only *seemed* like a long time since I saw her last, but I still had to stifle *do you remember me?*

She led the way, saying in a normal kid's blare, "He's he-re!"

There was a pause, then I heard Cassandra saying, "Who's here?"

Jessica didn't deign to answer. Walking up the stairs, she asked me, "Were you a bee?"

"Yeah. It was peaceful."

"Do you get honey?"

"Yeah. All you want."

As I was going up the stairs I wondered if everything had changed between us. I wondered if I would know right away, or if things would seem normal.

I stopped at the top of the stairs and turned slowly. Not for the drama, but because I was weighed down by emotion. Cassandra was sitting on the couch with a book in her lap, looking at me. She had her feet on the banana crate and a bottle of beer resting on her thigh. My eyes bounced from the book (*Labyrinths*) to the beer back to her face.

By the time I completed the circuit she had a crooked grin. "Been drinking since the day you left, darlin'," she drawled.

"Hi," I said. "Sorry about being so — abrupt about it." I

was very careful to say what I meant. I had thought about it, and I wasn't sorry I left. I *was* sorry I had left her alone.

"OK," she said. "Do you want a beer or something?"

"Sure."

"They're still kept in the fridge," she said, nodding backwards.

I walked to the fridge. There was a picture of a hive, the yellow crayon shiny under the light.

"So Jessica's been drawing, I see."

I sat on the other end of the couch — not presumptuously close, nor as distant as the armchair — and looked at her. Her face was relaxed and rested. *It's her day off,* they had told me at Sok, *she's probably kicking back at home.*

"St. Anthony's successor, over there, kept giving me pictures of a beehive. Not that I'm asking where you were," Cassandra added quickly, raising a hand.

"I was working at the hive outside my house. The one you left the rings at." Saying it like that, I felt like it was as normal as saying, *I was fighting forest fires up north* or *I was packing salmon tins out east.*

"Oh," Cassandra said, closing her book and tossing it on the crate. "So you saw me, eh? That was my lowest point. Erase it from the tapes."

"I kept hoping you'd come back. After I got over all the — confusion — I started to really miss you."

My eyes focused on a small painting, maybe six inches square. It was mostly black with a few traces of white, and after a few seconds of looking at it I could see a figure with stumps for arms, teeth clenched in pain or anger. "Joe?" I asked.

Cass swallowed her beer and looked at it. "Therapy. Chalk it up to my hippie parents. Art cures all."

The phone rang. Cassandra paused, and then went to answer it. I watched Jessica, who was playing with Tinkertoys. I slipped off the couch and crawled over to play.

"Pretty good, pretty good. Guess who showed up?"

Jessica pushed a pile of Tinkertoys in my direction. I wondered who it was on the phone and distractedly picked up a stick and a knob of wood.

"Nope. Beeboy himself. And Jessica was right." Well, there was only one person it could be — Mary. I kind of wanted to talk to her but didn't feel like totally breaking up Cassandra's and my talk. I looked at her, but her eyes were floating in phone middlespace.

I put knobs on both ends of the green stick and made like it was a mini-barbell. "Hey Jessica," I said, and pretended to pump iron. She gave me a small "keep trying" smile that made me understand just how very lame I was.

"Well, do you want to talk to him?" Cassandra said, and then held out the receiver towards me. I jumped up, almost kicking over Jessica's structure, and took the phone.

"Hi Mary!"

"Just don't tell me you're changing your name to Beeboy," she said in a monotone.

"I'm not," I said, smiling in spite of myself.

"Good. 'Cause there's product recognition to consider. We'd have to recast the action figure moulds."

"Of course."

"Oh, and you know I'm gonna kick your ass, right? I'm leaving for tree-planting but I've scheduled it in. 5:30: Fix Ryan's Caboose."

"That sounds fair," I said.

"We'll talk more about this when Cassandra's not in the room," Mary said.

"Exactly," I said.

We signed off and hung up. It was nice to talk to someone who I didn't feel as responsible to as Cassandra.

Cassandra was holding her beer with two hands and staring at me.

"Mary said that she'll make time in her busy schedule to kick my ass."

Cassandra smirked.

I paused, then looked at her and said as plainly as I could, "Couldn't you just do that and be done with it?"

"I'm not mad at you," Cassandra said. "Just a little indifferent. It's the same thing all over again. The same lesson that I've learned again and again."

I waited silently, fingering a Tinkertoy.

"That in the final reckoning, you're alone."

I dropped my eyes. It wasn't shame that I felt, only a sadness at the truth of this. I looked up. "It wasn't the thing with Joe so much. It was that and my mom at the same time. I didn't — snap — because of you."

Cassandra looked off into middlespace, again. "Yeah. But it took a while to convince myself of it. Because we had decided that we would do something about that fucker, but it was me who decided what that something was. Even though — it was obvious what I would do."

I nodded. "Well, I couldn't *tell* you to do that, either, even if it was the . . . thing to do." I didn't know if it was the *right* thing, or the *only* thing, but it was the thing that happened.

"I went back to the school," Cassandra said, twisting the beer bottle in her hand. "I talked to the girl. She thought it was her fault, that she had done something wrong."

She stopped.

Then, "She was so confused."

Then, "We did the right thing."

I started to feel like she wasn't sad because of me at all, that it was the situation, and my guilt had translated her face wrongly.

She told me that she had got the list of schools he'd been at and faxed them. Saying that Joe was a known pedophile and that any children that had been left alone with him should be counselled.

"Not that counselling does much," she said.

I just nodded sombrely at points and offered the occasional question: *Did you fax it out on Superheroes for Social Justice letterhead? How did you get it out of his office? No* and *His office was unlocked.*

"What time is it?" I said suddenly.

"Almost four."

"I should get to the bank," I said. "I haven't paid last month's rent."

When I stood up, Cassandra was coming up to me, looking at me with sad, sad eyes. "I'm really sorry about your mom, Ryan." She pursed her lips. "I . . . she was a wonderful person."

She hugged me, and it was exhausting somehow to have her squeeze me, to feel her breathing against me. When she let go I felt energy run into me like fresh water. An emotional sponge, that's me.

I touched her shoulder and looked at her chin. It wasn't trembling, thank god. There was only room for one fragile soul in this relationship, and it wasn't her. "Yeah. Talk about it later."

I went out into the mild July day.

I waited in line at the bank. Previous to my bee days, I would have been extremely impatient, but now there was something soothing to the ritual, the orderly control. I thought about being a bank teller for a while, since my job as insect folklorist was probably permanently on hold. I realized, however, that the tellers had to deal with impatient humans rather than sublimely mindless bees — what I really wanted was a job *standing in line-ups.*

I was thinking about ways to profit from that (working out a Bureaucracy Navigation Rep service I could pitch to students at my university) when my turn came up. I almost regretfully left the line-up.

The teller looked at me blankly. He even kind of resembled the worker bees that'd receive the pollen from the field bees! I handed him the slip and account book.

"Do you find this job has a soothing regularity?" I asked when he came back with the money.

He shrugged and tapped out a rhythmless beat on the thin plastiwood. "I suppose. Mostly it's just boring." He gave me a quick tight-smile/eyebrow-raised combo and turned his head to look at the next person in line.

I wouldn't let go, though. "But isn't there a certain primal tranquillity in it all?"

He laughed, a little harshly, I thought. "Not for me there ain't." Then, reflective, "Though the line does look a little like ants, sometimes. Endless."

I went away, a little dazzled by my success. As I left the building I marvelled at him seeing the insect comparison when I had not brought it up — there *was* an inherent connection.

Then I started thinking about ants. They had a collective behaviour similar to bees, but with many exciting differences. For instance —

I realized what I was gearing up for, and I stopped myself. I forced myself to think of other things, trying not to think about how much fun it would be to scramble into an anthill and hoist something ten times my weight onto my back.

Jack was out on the porch, enjoying some lemonade with a book. I managed to sit down beside him before he looked up.

"Who do I give *this* to?" I asked, holding up a sweaty handful of bills still inside my bankbook.

Jack, almost successful at keeping a smile off his face, turned back to his book. "What's that for?"

"Rent. For whoever covered my rent. There's an extra *two dollars*, too."

"Oh, I recognize you!" he said. "You're the guy who used to live in Georgie's room! I'm afraid we had all your stuff sent off to Goodwill. They wouldn't take it, and we had to ship it off to the dump. Then *they* said they weren't equipped to dispose of toxic —"

"Funny how Georgie's got all the same stuff as me. I've already been up there, Jack-o."

"Phil! Phil!" he yelled, in a wavering shrill voice. "We've had an intruder." Then to me: "Phil fronted your part."

Phil appeared in the doorway, saw me and slammed the door shut, audibly locking it. "Leave the money with the doorman," he called.

I just waited for the silliness to abate.

Phil came out, and snatched the bills and book from my hand. He leafed through my bank book. "Just as I thought," Phil said. "The bastard is loaded." He showed the balance to Jack but was met with indifference. "I'm keeping the armchair," he said, challenge in his voice.

Jack said, "So, tell us about Africa, Unca Ryan."

Phil sat down and stared out into the street.

"There were pythons and lions and cursed diamonds and shifting sands," I started, my hands lifted as if I was shaping the stories in the air. Then I dropped them. "No, I'm sad to say, these are all lies."

"As usual," said Phil, and sounded happy about it.

"We went to a conference in Cairo but it was all in this airtight hotel. I couldn't leave because I hadn't had my shots. So I didn't see anything."

"Oh man," said Jack, horrified, and Phil laughed.

"There was four hours between getting the word we were going and actually leaving. Registration and flight times and stuff like that. So I forgot a few details. Sorry."

Phil went *pfft*.

It was quiet for a moment, then I said: "I missed my mom's funeral, too."

Phil leaned forward.

"Cancer?" Jack asked.

"More or less," I said. She wouldn't have been drinking if she wasn't trying to forget about it.

Phil said nothing.

"Did anyone pay my phone bill?"

They shook their heads. "They wait sixty days before they do anything," said Phil, showing he had considered it.

I got up. Stretching, I said, "I had thir*teen* messages waiting for me. That's gotta be a record. I should flake out more often."

"So . . . was the conference interesting? What were you doing?" Jack asked.

"There were a few interesting seminars, but mostly it was procedural meetings on policy and crap like that. I was running around on errands for Joe, mostly. For really stupid stuff, too. He was jockeying for a position on the foundation's board, so I got involved with these idiotic political fights." I put some anger in my voice.

Phil said, "What was the food like?"

I gave the so-so hand.

"So did Joe get the position?" asked Jack.

"I don't know. I quit and took an early plane out of there. There's still a week left for the conference."

"You quit?" said Phil. "Just because of how he acted? Everyone hates their boss."

"I know, but everyone doesn't have to work as closely with them. He really revolted me, by the end. I couldn't believe what a bad judge of character I was."

That was especially true. It was best, when constructing a lie, to make it as close to the truth as possible, so I had decided to paint Joe in these nasty colours. In the event that I brought up Joe in the future (and with it, my visible distaste) I could express my genuine feelings without raising suspicion.

"You never can know everything about a person," Jack said.

I nodded. So true. It was a little depressing, thinking about that, because it was true about me, too.

Jack rattled the ice in his empty glass and drained the runoff. "No one would know about Phil's insecticidal tendencies, for instance, if it hadn't been for the sign in your room."

"Now even the mosquitoes won't go drinking with me," said Phil despondently.

His mention of mosquitoes made me drift off again. I wondered what it was like to drink blood from irate, slap-happy humans? The thought was slightly nauseating and thrilling at the same time.

"Oh, Ken's having a great time! He's in Maine, we got a postcard from him," said Jack, and I tried to fake surprise. Jack rushed on to give me the details, punctuated by Phil's interjections and suppositions.

I soaked it up, one the finest perks of human society — friendship — just as another part of my brain considered the possibilities of non-human society.

I was going through next year's academic syllabus like it was a pulp potboiler. The grey newsprint didn't, for once, mirror my lack of interest in its blocky timetables and drab class descriptions. Although as carefully drained of intrigue as always, this year's syllabus actually excited me.

Next year I wouldn't study the biology of insects — I'd study their *societies.* Like no one ever had in the history of science.

All these years I had been hoping for a reason, a cure. Well, fuck the reason, and doublefuck the cure. This was better. My eyes burned, I had been staring at the tiny print so intently.

I took a moment to close the book and massage my eyes. And question my sanity. *Had I gone bughouse?* I asked myself. My first reaction was: *Who cares? I'm not hurting anyone.*

I imagined myself explaining it to my father. That brought a twinge of guilt — because I hadn't contacted him or Lisa in the few days I'd been "back" — but it subsided. I planned to just go visit them. When the topic of the future came up, the conversation would go something like this:

Me: So I'm not working for him anymore, but I am gonna continue along that route of study.

Dad: Insects again, Ryan? Remember, some things are interesting at first glance, but they're not something you want to actually *study.*

Me: I *know,* Dad, but it's like this. Imagine one of the great painters going into chemistry, and learning about how to create paint, how it's mixed and stored and sold . . . that's basically what I did. I knew it was interesting to me, but I wasn't focused enough to know exactly what aspect of it was interesting.

Dad: But you do now?

Me: Yeah! It's the society of insects, how they interact and communicate, how it differs and corresponds to human culture. I got this ant farm, kind of as a joke, from Phil for my birthday. I ended up spending hours and hours in front of it — drawing maps, watching how they would overcome obstacles I introduced — basically coming up with a total analysis of the ant.

Dad: Huh!

Me: Yeah, and I found myself thinking about it when I was just walking around, puzzling out some weird thing they did. I was talking about it with Jack — we were just out on the porch, drinking beer — and I was like, "Fu— Damn, this is it! This is what I want to do!"

Dad: Talk about it? Teach?

Me: Maybe, maybe. What Joe did was really important, and I figure I could do that for everyone, not only kids. Be a liaison of sorts between the two worlds.

Dad: [lightly] A bug ambassador?

Me: Exactly. Like do you know about the bee's death pheromone?

. . . and I would go on to describe the harrowing adventures of the luckless bee who found himself hurled out of the hive and left to die.

Mom had always wanted a doctor in the family, and I knew I'd have no problem riding this idea to a PhD.

I had the two plastic rings in my hand, and I was shaking them like dice.

We were on a huge expanse of grass on the commons at York University. Mary, eager beaver that she was, was taking a summer course there and Cassandra and I had decided to come (all the way) up to the suburban campus. I was glad we had, because *damn* if it wasn't the wickedest day. And this was the place to lounge. People all over the expanse were proving it so, their two- or three-person clumps of slackitude ("loafs," we dubbed them) smiling lazily at the moving saps around them.

I was fully laid out, my head on my backpack and one hand dice-shaking and the other laced up with Cassandra's. She was leaning back on the heels of her hands and keeping an eye out for Mary.

I knew she was there when her shadow covered my face. "Oh I wonder who that is, blocking my sun," I said.

"It is She-Who-Brings-the-Darkness," said Mary, sitting down on the grass and pulling open her bag. "And-Cookies!"

Yays all around. The cookies were thin, sugary, only slightly burnt and had nuts. I complimented her.

"She's gotcha baking already?" Cassandra said once her cookies were securely in hand.

Mary grinned a little, maybe sheepishly. "I always bake." She looked at us both and said, "OK, I've got a favour to ask you guys. My uncle thinks I'm going tree-planting alone."

"When in reality you're riding Patricia — that is, riding with Patricia, to the Northern Lights," Cassandra said, with a lewd grin that you had to love.

"Right, and I know you don't approve, but I was hoping—"

"Whatd'ya mean?" Cassandra said, leaning forward in a cross-legged position of concern. "I don't disapprove. I had a bad experience with her but it doesn't mean — "

Mary's face showed guarded relief. "Oh, good. I mean, I really think — I — "

"I know, I know," Cassandra said. "You're really diggin' it. That's why I didn't say anything beyond my initial warning."

Mary nodded and brushed away her bangs in a bashful way I hardly ever saw. I was stunned myself — I had just presumed they had compared notes, shared insights, *discussed at length* the subject of Pat. Didn't all women gossip? I gazed up into the sky and reflected on my stupidity and congratulated myself on not having revealed it once again through some presumptuous remark.

"What I was trying to say was I want you guys to take care of the car while I'm gone."

Cassandra and I looked at each other. *Does she mean we can use it?* I asked her by means of my nonexistent telepathy.

Mary picked up on it. "So if you want to go smashing evil in other cities, for instance, you can — as long as the car ends up with a believable amount of klicks on the odometer. And no bullet holes."

"Sounds great," I said, my eyes closed. "One of my most pleasant fantasies while working at the hive was driving down the desert highway, backlit by the raging inferno of a cigarette factory."

"All right!" said Cassandra.

I didn't open my eyes, but the next thing I felt was a kiss pulling at my dry lips, and the cheek tickle of a hair strand.

I remembered what I was shaking in my hand, and I sat up. I opened up my hand and there were our two pink rings. Cassandra smiled when she saw them, and Mary winced.

"Pick one. The stickers must have come off with the rain or whatever, so I put new stickers on them."

"Oh, good!" Mary said. "I was always afraid that reporters would get ahold of that creepy Sailor Moon connection."

Cassandra was laughing. She slipped hers on and showed it off to Mary. It was a price tag that read $1.49. "That's the last time anyone calls me a two-dollar whore," she said.

Mary looked at me with an annoyed smile. "I don't get it."

"Nothing to get," I said innocently. "I didn't have any good stickers, is all. I think these have an absurdist charm." I looked at mine, which was a sticker I had peeled off a banana I ate last night. I sniffed it stagily, and said "Mmmm . . . banana-y." I shot Cassandra a sly look, to remind her the time she outraged Hawaiians.

"Yeah, I left you the banana one," Cassandra said with a smirk. "What with the sexual fetish you have for them . . ."

I almost died. I seriously thought my heart was gonna smash right out of my chest.

"What?!" said Mary. "Bananas?" Her face was painted in three colours of joy. "Ryan Slint — Banana Pervert?"

"How — could — you?" I managed to stutter, staring at Cassandra's mild look. I couldn't bear to look at Mary, but I could tell that she was getting up. "Have you never heard of *discretion*?"

Cassandra shrugged.

I ran my hands through my hair, disgraced.

When I looked up again, Mary was doing a little dance. A little dance to my depravity. "I mean, a melon I could see, Ryan, but a banana?! It's so — well, it has to be said — so *phallic*." Her eyes bugged out when she said this.

Cassandra laughed away, merrily.

Mary sat down and I thought it had subsided when she leaned forward and said in a British accent, "So you loike a 'nana up your bum?"

I looked into her eyes (which had continued to dance) and appealed to the God in her. "I just like the smell, is all." Then, to be honest, I added, "And the texture," with a bit of lustiness.

This sent them off into Laughland again and when they looked up I was rapturously smelling the sticker, so they went back for another visit. I was responsible for it though, so I felt better.

"So when would we have the car for?" I said, hoping to innocuously move to a non-banana topic. I was successful, because Mary gave me dates (which I promptly forgot) and then mentioned that she could probably get us some info on the locations of the cigarette factories, a detail that hadn't been a part of my vivid fantasy.

"You're awesome," I emoted, and she casually acknowledged her awesomeness with a nod.

"I'm getting pretty handy with the info-gathering skills — from the net, e-mail contacts, a bunch of places." She turned into a radio announcer: "'I've developed a whole new skill set — that's important in today's job market. That's why I recommend aiding vigilante superheroes as a career move to *all* my friends.'"

"Do you think you could start finding information on Mumia Abu-Jamal?" Cassandra asked quietly.

"That wouldn't be the world's highest profile death-row prisoner?" I inquired. "The former Black Panther information minister who shot a cop?" Jack's back issues of *Socialist Worker* had come in handy, and I almost came off as totally in the know. Almost.

"Who was *framed* for killing a cop," said Cassandra.

"Why don't you wait till I get back for that one," said Mary. "It would have a *lot* of repercussions. And we could do it really well. Video release."

"*Yeah!*" said Cassandra, and I drank in her look of pleasure.

We took a moment to visualize this.

"Oh! And we could visit *the package,*" I said, "which I understand has made its inanimate way to Maine." We talked about this for a while, wondering what the heck Ken was doing in Maine, and coming up with some amusing suppositions involving lobsters.

"Did I tell you guys I'm going for my PhD?" I asked casually. I plied their doubts and amazement with the heady brew of my Interest, distilled through my lifetime to its current purity. Cassandra glowed, and Mary even ran out of objections.

"I'll be like Indiana Jones," I said. "Bespectacled professor by day, but having fantastic adventures from time to time. And of course, with a bevy of beautiful students who futilely attempt to seduce me."

"And all of them very understanding about the penis-shaped-fruit obsession, right?" Mary said.

"Well, they'd have to be," I said.

We must have stayed there till six, and what did we talk about the most? Not our bright and splendid futures, full of many-plumed explosions and shapeshifting and wit. Again and again I was pummelled with the banana thing.

Fucking bananas.